Head Coach

By Lia Riley

HELLIONS HOCKEY ROMANCES
Mister Hockey
Head Coach
Virgin Territory

BRIGHTWATER SERIES
Last First Kiss
Right Wrong Guy
Best Worst Mistake

EVERLAND, GEORGIA SERIES
It Happened on Love Street
The Corner of Forever and Always

OFF THE MAP SERIES
Upside Down
Sideswiped
Inside Out

ANTHOLOGIES
Snowbound at Christmas

Head Coach

A HELLIONS HOCKEY ROMANCE

LIA RILEY

AVON

An Imprint of HarperCollinsPublishers

HEAD COACH. Copyright © 2017 by Lia Riley.

VIRGIN TERRITORY. Copyright © 2018 by Lia Riley.

Excerpt from PUCK AND PREJUDICE © 2025 by Lia Riley. All rights reserved. Printed in the United States of America. No part of this book may be used or reproduced in any manner whatsoever without written permission except in the case of brief quotations embodied in critical articles and reviews. For information, address HarperCollins Publishers, 195 Broadway, New York, NY 10007.

HarperCollins books may be purchased for educational, business, or sales promotional use. For information, please email the Special Markets Department at SPsales@harpercollins.com.

Originally published separately as *Head Coach* and *Virgin Territory* in the United States by Avon Impulse in 2017 and 2018.

Interior text design by Diahann Sturge-Campbell

Library of Congress Cataloging-in-Publication Data has been applied for.

ISBN 978-0-06-338344-9

24 25 26 27 28 LBC 5 4 3 2 1

To Chanel, Jen, and A. J. . . . thank you for being a friend. Your hearts are true. You're all pals and confidants. P.S. Who wants to bet Jen doesn't get this reference?

Chapter One

STUCK IN A RUT?

*T*he billboard's tacky font splashed across the image of a blonde woman dressed in a corset, high-waist underpants, and garter belt. Neve Angel scowled through her windshield at the rest of the tagline.

SHIMMY INTO A WHOLE NEW YOU!
BEGINNER BURLESQUE CLASSES
AT THE TWIRLING TASSELS

"Humph." Neve tucked an escaped strand of hair back into her bun. Ms. Blondie could pop an egg in her perfect pout and suck it. Since quitting figure skating at the age of eighteen, Neve had developed an allergy to glitz and glamour, favoring low-key personal grooming.

Fake lashes were out.

Foundation contouring? Negative.

Waxing? Please. She wasn't a masochist.

These days the word *pragmatic* carried far more value for

her than *pretty*, thanks very much. Flicking on the radio, she relaxed her shoulders as a familiar guitar riff filled her '78 wood-paneled Jeep Wagoneer. She had an unabashed love for classic cars and classic rock, and Tom Cochrane was a guy who knew his stuff. Life *was* a highway, except forget the part about driving it "all night long."

Or driving anywhere for that matter. Satan would ice-skate through hell before this insane gridlock budged.

A silver Prius inched forward until it practically dry-humped her bumper.

Meep! The driver leaned on a wimpy-sounding horn.

Honking under these conditions was a ballsy move, akin to sitting in the last row of an airplane and standing when the cabin crew disarmed the doors—a good way to tempt ordinary citizens to commit murder.

The driver beeped again.

"Use your eyes. There's nowhere for me to go!" Neve glanced to the rearview mirror and gazed at the distinctive red cursive on the Prius's license plate.

A California driver. *Surprise, surprise.* She'd bet the loose change in the bottom of her purse that this chick was a Bay Area transplant, relocating her traffic problems to Denver along with skyrocketing home prices. The whole West was getting Californicated, from Nevada to Montana, Texas to Colorado.

The horn beeped a third time. She fisted her insulated travel mug and then took a careful sip. Madam Prius better thank her astrological chart that Neve had hot coffee within arm's reach because otherwise things could get ugly.

A minute passed.

Two.

Blessed silence reigned.

After blowing up her bangs, she pulled an everything bagel from the flimsy paper bag on the dashboard, cramming it into her mouth. In a parallel universe, Alter-Neve woke with ample time to prepare a nutritious breakfast, perhaps an acai bowl topped by sliced bananas and kiwi fruit or Greek yogurt and granola, Instagram-worthy concoctions bursting with enough omegas and fiber to make any Prius driver water their home herb garden with organic tears.

But in this world, Einstein Bros. and a dark roast had to do the job.

She brushed stray poppy seeds and flecks of dried garlic off her charcoal pants with a muffled sigh. Charcoal, i.e., dark gray . . . *not* black. Her somber closet palette might be as cheerful as a funeral home, but it never required expending mental energy at seven a.m. trying to coordinate funky colors or mix and match patterns.

From her roadside perch, the burlesque model appeared amused, as if she knew Neve ate the same humdrum breakfast day in, day out and dressed in the same humdrum wardrobe. Or that while she might have an impressive LinkedIn profile, that didn't translate to a social life worth posting over.

Neve poked out her tongue at the model's image. This low-maintenance duckling had grown up to be . . . if not a preening swan, a confident duck.

She had a good—scratch that, great—career as a sports columnist for the *Denver Age* covering the hockey beat, and her life was too consumed by deadlines to bother with extra fuss. Work was the priority, and as for her biological clock . . . well, it could keep right on ticking. She had another baby to grow, her side hustle, a podcast—*Sports Heaven*—that kept climbing iTunes rankings; she had even been featured in their New and Noteworthy section last month.

Rut-shmut. By any measure, Neve was doing great in her career and living her best life. Except her smirk faded as she glanced to the console clock. She'd risk missing the puck drop if traffic didn't improve soon.

Hopefully, the Hellions would get a much-needed win tonight. After their recent back-to-back championships, it appeared the team's days in the sun had fallen into one serious shadow. The roster had been shaken ever since the unexpected retirement of captain Jed West last summer. This season had started as a big disappointment for Denver fans, and worse, whispers of NHL labor disputes were gaining traction. For the past few weeks, trusted sources had even uttered the dreaded term *lockout*—a word that kept her up at night restless and fretting.

Fingers—and toes—crossed that the powers that be would navigate through the negotiations and get the league back on track. During the 04–05 lockout, the whole season was canceled—the worst possible outcome. Stadiums sat empty. Fans grumbled. Refs and arena workers forwent paychecks.

She shuddered, mentally elbowing away the terrible idea. Hopefully this time around, cooler heads would prevail.

And as for the Hellions, there was another place where cooler heads needed to prevail. Maybe if their goalie would practice a little Zen meditation and quit getting players sent to the penalty box every damn ga—

Meep! Meeeeeeeeep! Madam Prius hit the horn as if she'd face-planted on the steering wheel and died.

Tension migrated from Neve's neck, making the slow climb

to her temples. The first throbs of a headache emerged. Between lockout worries and this racket, she might spontaneously combust. To release steam, she rolled down the window and flipped the Prius the bird before grabbing her phone off the passenger seat.

Ignoring the new—and so far unlistened-to—mindfulness podcast her friend Margot had recommended, she clicked on Byways, the popular navigation app that relied on community-sourced traffic updates to create the fastest routes. It needed to get her moving before she found herself arrested for disorderly conduct.

She plugged in the Hellions stadium address and an avatar of a pitchfork blinked from a quarter mile ahead. Her tummy performed a flawless triple-axel jump.

Rovhal30.

She took a deep breath and issued herself a stern reminder. There had never been any official confirmation that Rovhal30 was even male, but in her mind, he was six feet of strapping sexiness, lounging behind the wheel of a black Subaru Outback—a ginger-haired Ewan McGregor doppelgänger. Not *Trainspotting* Ewan either. Not even *Moulin Rouge!* Ewan. No . . . straight-up Obi-Wan Kenobi *Attack of the Clones* Ewan, with the shaggy hair and delicious beard.

One thing was for certain, the pitchfork avatar meant that Rovhal30 was a Hellions hockey fan.

Or a devil worshipper who lives in his mom's basement handfeeding his pet bull pythons.

The pitchfork didn't budge. Rovhal30 was stuck in this traffic too. She sucked in her lower lip, debating: To message or not to message? That was the question.

No point glancing to Burlesque Blondie for advice. The model would just shimmy her tassels in a "you go, guuuurl" affirmation.

Eenie, meanie, miny . . . *ugh*. Fine. She was doing this.

> **NEVERL8:** Fancy seeing you here

She hit Send before she could second-guess her actions. Here was hoping that her tone came across more cheerful than creepy.

> **ROVHAL30:** *(typing)*

It always took Rovhal30 time to type back, credible evidence that he was a sixty-plus grandmother learning to operate her first smartphone, but why ruin the fantasy?

Neve drummed her thumbs on the steering wheel. She didn't bother with online dating. The idea of some random dude swiping left on her profile while taking his morning dump left a lot to be desired. But this meant that her one meaningful online relationship was with a fellow commuter on a traffic app—someone who *felt* male and *might* be attractive.

The ugly truth was that she hadn't gotten laid since the first Obama administration, even though her "office" was a locker room populated by sweaty men who rivaled Olympic gods. Every time someone heard about her job as a sports reporter, they'd gush, "Oh my God! Do you ever get to interview the players in their towels? Is it amazing?"

For the record, she had at one time or another glimpsed most of the Hellions team sans towels. As for the endless question "Is it amazing?" try asking the Louvre gallery attendant who guarded the *Mona Lisa* if they ever got used to the portrait's iconic smile.

Sure, the players were sexy with their cut bods and muscular buns, but a glimpse of wang didn't exactly send her heart racing. She was there in a professional capacity, not to be a pervert.

> **ROVHAL30:** Hello there

The Byways app made it impossible to text another driver unless the car was at a complete stop. Sadly, she too often found herself in this situation at the same time of day. A month ago, Rovhal30 had posted a community traffic update about a brush fire in the median. She'd asked a clarifying question and they'd struck up an odd friendship ever since.

> **ROVHAL30:** I've been saving a joke for you

Neve ordered the flutter in her stomach to stand down. "He probably looks like a cross between Homer Simpson and Steve Buscemi," she muttered.

But still, he'd saved a joke for her . . . which meant he thought of her. At least a little.

> **NEVERL8:** Lay it on me

Perfectly casual response—*excellent.* For all Rovhal30 knew, she was a Byways floozy, texting with dozens of users on a regular basis.

> **ROVHAL30:** What kind of computer sings?

NEVERL8: I give up

ROVHAL30: A Dell

She snickered. Good one.

NEVERL8: Actual LOLZ

ROVHAL30: LOLZ?

NEVERL8: Uh . . . like laugh out loud?

ROVHAL30: Why the Z?

NEVERL8: It's nonstandard spelling of the suffix "s" . . . i.e. just for fun.

ROVHAL30: Remind me what i.e. means again?

NEVERL8: Latin for "id est"' which translates roughly to "in other words." I like it. Use it all the time.

She attached the nerdy-face emoji for good measure and hit Send.

Pause. No response.

She chewed the inside of her cheek and waited. Still nothing.

Gah. Had she driven him away with an obscure-grammar geek out? She rocked her head back against the seat and groaned—she sucked at this. Her gaze connected with Burlesque Blondie. Fine, not only was she stuck in a rut, she won all the awards for awkward internet flirting.

It could be time to accept her spinster status, drive to the shelter, and finally choose a kitten for that cat tower that she'd bought last summer at a garage sale.

Traffic crawled forward, Rovhal30's pitchfork avatar ticked away on the upcoming off-ramp, her own exit. She gave a slow exhale and clicked out of the app.

A journalist's first obligation was to tell the truth. Hers was that she was undersexed and overworked. She wasn't living her best life. She didn't even *have* a life, too busy to even be a crazy cat lady. Her rut had masqueraded as a comfortable routine for too long. It was high time to climb out and put herself into the world. Find her inner sex kitten and make it purr.

Faster than the speed of second guesses, she snapped a photo of the phone number for the Twirling Tassels, shifted out of first gear, and hit the gas.

Chapter Two

*T*hey were going to lose.

Tor Gunnar grabbed the Tic Tac container from his pocket, thumbed open the flip lid, and popped a mint into his mouth. The five-two scoreboard told a dismal tale, one that had become increasingly familiar since the start of the season. The San Francisco Renegades, the long-standing archrivals to the Denver Hellions, were wiping the ice with them.

No heroic comeback was in the cards for tonight. Not with the way his team was disintegrating out there. Already fans were leaving their seats to get a jump start on traffic.

Third period. Five minutes left. The mint turned to dust between his molars.

The Renegades might have plunged the proverbial knife into the heart of the Hellions' morale, but now they twisted the blade, antagonizing his guys, looking for ways to draw blood—both metaphorical and actual—as they settled old scores. The goalie, Donnelly, hulked in front of his net as the offense bore down. His goalie was territorial, an enraged bear protecting a cub from rogue wolves. Renegade winger Ryker Fury didn't even have the puck in possession yet had invaded the space, a clear taunt.

"Come on," Tor muttered. It was plain enough to see what was going down. Fury was out there looking to provoke a reaction. Donnelly's hotheaded temper was legendary. As much as Gunnar had tried to find new ways to cool his ass, if someone messed with him, the kid messed back. Every damn time.

"Don't do it. Don't take the bait." Tor crossed his arms. Donnelly had what it took to be a star. Someday he might be a legend—if he could learn to control his fucking temper. Even with today's score, the kid had made unbelievable saves.

Fury shouted something.

Donnelly dropped his gloves in response.

Tor hid his inner wince behind a stoic mask.

Someday Donnelly might be a superstar goalie, but today sure as shit wasn't that day.

Fury was big—strong and mean—but Donnelly had the devil in him. His fists flew fast and hard. It wasn't long until Fury was on the ice and Donnelly towered on top.

"Get him off, get him off," Tor roared at the team.

But it was too late. Ref made the call.

Match penalty.

Now he was down a player. Andrew Kelly, the Renegade coach, signaled who he wanted out. The Hellions' star forward, Petrov, skated toward the penalty box, head down, shoulders slumped. Donnelly trailed after.

"Nate," Tor snapped. The second-string goalie was going in.

"On it, Coach." Nathan Reed checked his laces and headed out.

Donnelly didn't even glance in Reed's direction as he passed; his cheeks were flushed over his ginger beard and he breathed hard.

"Happy?" Tor growled.

"You didn't hear what that bastard said." Donnelly ripped off his mask and hurled it at the plexiglass. "Fury talked a bunch of—"

"I don't give a rat's hairless pink ass if he insulted your mama, your little sister, or your mama *and* your sister. Your job is to keep your head. Did that happen tonight?"

Donnelly stared at the floor with a sullen expression.

"I just asked you a question." Tor dropped his voice to a subzero whisper. "If you have the slightest sense of self-preservation, you're going to give me an answer."

A muscle twitched beneath Donnelly's left eye. "Lost my head."

"You're making it a habit."

"Look." He covered his face with his hand. "I'm trying not to, Coach. I'm—"

"Sucking air in my vicinity," Tor snapped. "Just get outta here and let me watch us lose in peace."

Donnelly hesitated. "I am sorry, Coach."

"So am I. I don't know what it's going to take to get through to you." Tor turned his attention back to the play. And as soon as the game was over, he got called to the owner's box to receive even worse news.

Now here he was, thirty minutes later, glaring at the Hellions' locker room door while straightening his tie. Everyone on the other side would have questions, and he couldn't provide a single answer. The league negotiations had crapped out. A lockout was now in effect over salary caps, the cherry to the night's shit sundae.

Swallowing back a frustrated sigh, Tor banged open the locker room door and strode inside. All conversation muted as he marched to the center of the room and stopped short of the pitchfork emblazoned on the floor. No need to invite further bad luck by standing on top of the team logo. He drew his gaze up to his favorite Gretzky quote stenciled along the curved wall before taking in the expectant men on the benches.

These players were a unique breed. Many had left home at a young age to chase a seemingly impossible dream. Some had traveled overseas to build resumes. Most, at some point, had lived far from parents, friends, and the comforts of home, forging new friendships with those who had made similar sacrifices.

It was these bonds, a brotherhood strengthened through sacrifice and physical and mental hardship, that sustained a player through tough times both on and off the ice. One of the reasons he'd insisted on the new locker room being shaped as an oval and not a square was so everyone could always see each other, no one relegated to a corner. And his commitment to keeping the focus on team over individuals had worked, at least until this season.

He pressed two fingers to his temple. He'd kill for another Jed West on the team, a natural leader with the rare combination of poise and skill.

The press corps stuffed into the room's perimeter, holding their collective breath.

Waiting.

Waiting.

The silent question was almost audible. *Will Tor Gunnar go rogue?*

The powers that be had made one thing crystal clear. With the lockout in effect, NHL staff were instructed to cut off contact with players. Violating the terms was to risk bringing down hell, everything from fines to forfeiture of future draft picks. Simply walking in here took steel balls, especially with the jackals from the press prowling the room's perimeter.

But these guys were family. *His* family. And he'd be damned if he let them go without some sort of send-off. He wanted them to know he was here. That he cared no matter what . . . win or lose, rain or shine, good times and bad. This game was bigger than a paycheck, bigger than a contract.

They were brothers-in-arms.

Take Munro and Nicholson on the right, defensemen with matching navy blue Mohawks. Once fierce rivals, they had even gotten into a fistfight their first year, but were now next-door neighbors in Cherry Creek. There was Petrov, the center who'd finished the game stuck in the penalty box, engaged to wingman Ericksen's twin sister.

Tor turned to face Patrick "Patch" Donnelly, hunched in front of an end locker. Even though the kid would be the death of him, he lived and breathed the sport as if it was more than a game, something vital to his existence. Patch glowered back, elbows propped on his knees, hands clasped, a picture of forced calm, his eyes as bright and menacing as a caged tiger's.

He'd demonstrated that same feral intensity at Boston College when Tor had personally recruited him after hearing rumors of a prodigy player who'd almost joined the seminary to become a priest. A walking contradiction who had a broken nose and reputation for brawling, and yet had majored in theology and was conversant in Catholic conciliar traditions— everything from Nicaea to Vatican II.

One of the journalists coughed in his fist and Tor refocused, remembering his greater audience. He'd deal with Donnelly's anger issues later. He'd come in here to exploit an elephant-sized loophole. As head coach, he might not be allowed to talk, but not all communication was verbal. Who knew what his team would get up to during the ongoing negotiations? Some might head overseas for pickup work. Others might turn to liquor and ladies. All of them better double down at the gym, remain in peak fitness, ready to hit the ice at first word.

He shot his goalie one final glance. Here was to hoping that Patch didn't retreat to a monastery on an island in the middle of the North Atlantic. He seemed the type to pull a Luke Skywalker and vanish into thin air.

Tor raked a hand through his hair and turned away with a terse nod. He'd made his point without crossing a line. Sure, the suits would be pissed, but as the door slammed, he allowed a grimly satisfied smile.

They better believe that he'd go into this lockout on his own terms.

The press poured out, hot on his heels. And—no surprise—there *she* was, front and center, jaw jutting as their gazes locked, tenacious as a goddamn bulldog even though she was as tiny as a Chihuahua.

Neve Angel.

No other reporter in this city got under his skin the same way. As much as he wanted to ignore the electric jolt that shocked him every time she was close, he had to admit he was a sucker for the pain.

He'd be tempted to find her snarky columns amusing if she wasn't so hell-bent on making him the butt of every goddamn joke. How he was too serious in his mannerisms. No nitpick was too small or too petty. She even took him to task over his fucking tie collection, and started a now-popular meme about the fact that he never changed his stoic facial expressions, no matter if the Hellions lost a game or won the championships.

Their fractious relationship made for popular YouTube fodder. She'd slip in a sly question at postgame press conferences, seemingly innocent but designed to slip under his collar and rankle. He never got the sense she was intimidated by his frosty temperament.

He could make a six-foot defenseman weep without raising his voice, but this hellcat? She'd just cock one of those defiant brows and smirk.

While not delicately pretty, she possessed an elusive allure, like starlight on water, a sort of face that a man could lose hours studying and still never grasp all its secrets.

"Care to comment on the lockout, Coach?" Todd from the AP called.

Jesus, pull it together. Tor refocused and took off walking. "This is between the players and people way above my pay grade."

"What does this mean for your losing streak?"

"How are you going to handle the Donnelly situation?"

"What are your plans to ride this out?"

"Do you think the contracts are unfair?"

But he meant it. He wasn't saying shit.

They began dropping off. Only one person kept pace.

"Coach Gunnar." Neve's voice was as brisk as her trot. "Coach Gunnar!"

"Not today, Angel. I'm not in the mood." He wasn't going to let her track him like a damn deer all the way out to his car. And she wasn't going to back off. Time to execute plan B.

"Coach!"

"Let me be clear." He paused in front of the men's room. "It's been a long night. I gotta drain the tank, so unless you're volunteering to hold it for me, we'll have to leave things here."

He veered into the john without a backward look. Because if he did, he'd be forced to reckon with those unnerving eyes, the ones that always saw too much.

At least Neve Angel hadn't sniffed out the day's other breaking story . . .

Join Maddy Kline and Daniel Cox as
they embark on a shared life . . .

The invite had arrived in the mail this morning. Maddy had mailed the damn invitation to his office, probably a silent reminder to the day she'd walked out, saying "It's your job or me. Choose."

And he did.

Maddy had moved on and it was all water under the bridge by this point. But her upcoming marriage shone a spotlight on the fact that he was still stuck. Work was his whole identity. He didn't know who he was if he wasn't "Coach."

But with this lockout in effect, he might be forced to find out.

Chapter Three

I'll hold it for him all right," Neve snarled at her fellow reporters. "And then I'll tie that man's dick into a bow."

And if his insinuation about her hand being anywhere in the vicinity of his Big Lebowski left her mouth dry, it was just a reminder that she needed to drink more water.

Hydration was important.

"What do we do? Draw straws for who goes in after him?" Bill from ESPN reached into his pocket as if to pull out a handful.

Everyone wore identical, terrified "not I" expressions. Tor Gunnar was a force of nature and no one had enough bravery—or stupidity—to bug him during a piss. They could find a urinal cake shoved down their throat for their trouble.

Neve noted the group mired in indecision and turned for the exit with a one-shouldered shrug. While they all clucked like nervous hens, she'd swoop in like a hawk and snatch the scoop.

"Didn't expect *you* to give up so fast, Angel," someone shouted.

She didn't reply, hoping they'd laugh off her finger bomb. Because maybe . . . just maybe . . . her hunch on the coach was right on the money. There was the old adage "Keep your friends close and enemies closer." It totally applied when it came to her hate-tionship with Tor Gunnar.

She didn't break into a run until she had pushed out the exit into the crisp night air. The door snicked shut and she dug in, arms pumping, messenger bag knocking against her hip.

Thank God she'd been setting the treadmill to eight-minute miles at the gym.

She skidded around the corner and straight into a good news/bad news moment.

The good news was that her instincts were right. Tor Gunnar wasn't the type to be treed like a cougar by a pack of bloodhounds. He was far too wily. The men's bathroom window screen lay on the pavement, right where he'd kicked it out with one of those big lace-up leather boots he wore, the ones that went well with that tailored suit that matched his dark blue eyes. In the streetlight, they shone a rich twilight blue, a color that made smart girls stupid.

The bad news was that she gaped at him from an uncomfortably close vantage point. They stood chest to chest, or boobs to ribs to be exact. She'd smacked right into him, but it wasn't like running into a wall. No. There was nothing wall-like going on here. This was all man, flesh and blood, even if he was as immovable as mortared brick.

"Well, well, well." She forced her body to lock up, stiffening her muscles so as not to betray the slightest tremble, even as a hot wind blew through her ladyparts, clearing away the dust and cobwebs. "Fancy meeting you here. That was some game tonight. You getting your goalie enrolled in an anger-management class or what?"

Muscles bunched in Tor Gunnar's jaw, ones that never

seemed to appear unless she was around. The rest of the press pool called it his "Angel anger muscles." She wasn't one to toot her own horn, but when it came to pissing off this man, she possessed a remarkable gift.

"You never quit, do you?" His tone was flat, but he didn't protest or ask what she was doing there. He gave her that credit. As much as he rubbed her the wrong way, she respected him as a worthy adversary.

"I aim to live my life so that my tombstone can say *Nevertheless, she persisted.*"

That earned a snort. She'd take that as her in.

"Anyway, look on the bright side. The lockout news was even worse than the final score, am I right?"

He didn't take the bait. Nor did she expect him to. He was far too disciplined to drop a useful quote so easily, at least not right away. She'd have to play him like a conductor, work him up until he sang like a pissed-off canary.

"My source in the commissioner's office says that there's a chance this could drag on for the rest of the season. But then maybe it's a blessing."

Those twilight eyes darkened to midnight black. Most people would shrink at the warning.

Good thing she wasn't most people.

"A blessing?" He leaned in, his voice a lethal whisper.

Something shifted in the air between them, a magnetic force that sucked air from her lungs.

Her shrug was a study in nonchalance even as a shiver shuddered down her spine. "It would be such a shame for the Hellions to have an epic flop after enjoying back-to-back years on top. But there's no way your team is even going to qualify for the playoffs. Lends credence to the idea that the real credit for the Hellions' success was Jed West."

"Bullshit." His carved features were schooled in careful impassivity. "My team's still finding their feet with the new lineup. If the knuckleheads on the Board of Governors pulled their heads out of their deskbound asses for two seconds, they'd see . . ." He froze, realizing what he had done. Two lines etched his high forehead. Two more between his arrogant brows. Cracks in the stony veneer.

"Mmm-hmm. Knuckleheads . . . and deskbound asses— now, there's a turn of phrase." Neve licked her lips in slow triumph. "I'm afraid their rebuttal won't be nearly as flowery."

Shadows haunted his high cheekbones, the angles sharp and unforgiving, inherited from whatever Viking ancestor also bestowed that thick blond hair. It didn't take much imagination to picture Tor Gunnar's doppelgänger plundering hapless Scandinavian villages during the Dark Ages. He looked warlike even when standing still and breathing.

And yet . . .

And yet.

She didn't step back in retreat. He couldn't take a full step forward either, not when she was still squished against him. The only feature not absolutely brutal in his face was his wide mouth, the bold, sensual lips that hovered close to hers as he bent and whispered in a rasp, "What the fuck do you want?" His breath held a trace of wintergreen.

She was ready to dish back a serving of sass, except no plucky banter came out. Only a moan, one that hitched raggedly on the end note and carried a heavy dose of breathlessness.

Her brain stuttered, unable to get back in gear. What was

she doing, standing here dazed and confused, thinking less about getting a scoop and more on what it would be like if *he* scooped *her* up? Hauled her against the brick wall behind them? Tore open her shirt and sucked her nipples through the thin cotton of her bra with those big mean lips?

His gaze lasered on hers in stunned surprise, as if he'd been granted security clearance to review her most confidential fantasies. A hum buzzed through her stomach. No gentle fluttering of butterflies, but a hive of bees, and it wasn't clear if they were about to sting or make sweet, sweet honey.

Somewhere a door slammed and voices filled the night. The press pool rounded the corner. The best and brightest had finally pieced together what she had deduced two minutes earlier.

Tor was making a getaway.

Her face heated; thank God it was night. She moved back, but her gestures were awkward, clumsy even. Restless energy coursed through her. In the distance a siren wailed.

"Shit," Tor muttered.

Her colleagues gaped, their eyes still adjusting to the darkness.

"What's going on?" Todd's nose had gone red from the biting November wind. He'd invited Neve out for drinks once. When she'd turned him down, he'd inquired if she was a lesbian, as if that was the only plausible explanation.

"Nothing." Tor strode toward his car.

"Didn't look like nothing a second ago," Todd kept pushing. "What gives? You two have a thing?"

"Yeah. Right." His laugh was dismissive. "Sorry, not into cold fish. If I got off on a dick freeze, I'd fuck a penguin." With that he shot off without so much as a backward glance.

Neve didn't flinch. Later she was going to be proud of that fact. Instead she pursed her mouth into what might appear to be mild amusement. She could nail this look better than those double salchows from her figure-skating days. No, she didn't give a single sign that Coach's words sliced through her softest, most sensitive pieces.

Cold fish. Cold fish? Cold fish! Hell no, she was a red-hot barracuda of revenge.

His Porsche roared to life, mirroring the blood accelerating through her veins. She watched him tear from the parking lot with steely-eyed resolve. Freedom of speech was all well and good, but Mr. Fuck-a-Penguin had issued serious fighting words.

This meant war.

Language could be wielded like a weapon; she knew that better than anyone, and with the lockout in place, she was going to have to get more creative with her story ideas. Readers, and her pain-in-the-butt editor—Scott Moore—loved top-five lists. She mentally rubbed her hands together as she selected the perfect clickbait title to pitch:

TOP FIVE WORST COACHES IN THE NHL

Guess who'd just earned himself a primo spot?

Chapter Four

Tor stalked into his foyer and kicked the front door closed behind him. He bypassed the couch and flat-screen in favor of the kitchen, where he opened the liquor cabinet and removed a dusty bottle of Johnnie Walker Blue Label. He didn't drink much, but when the urge struck then he didn't mess around.

The new leopard gecko that his daughter, Olive, had suckered him into buying sat on a log under its aquarium heat lamp. He checked its water. His ten-year-old daughter hadn't been able to decide on a suitable name before her mother had picked her up and so it was stuck nameless until her return.

"What was I supposed to say?" he asked the lizard.

The gecko stared back, eyes wide, body unmoving.

"I'm telling you, buddy, Neve Angel drives me to drink."

He picked up the bottle, ready to pour half the contents down his throat if it meant softening the hard-on busting through his pants. This bad news day was made all the worse by the fact that his traitor cock had been standing at attention ever since his parking lot encounter with Neve.

"I envy you, you know," he muttered to the gecko. "Happily alone. Minding your own business. Good life."

He poured a hefty double shot into the tumbler, no ice, and

took it to his master-bedroom bathroom, shooting back the amber-colored bourbon in a single gut-searing gulp before shedding his work clothes.

No need for a tie for a while.

He ripped it off his neck and tossed it onto the stone floor. Once naked, he stepped into the shower and turned on the spray without waiting for the temperature to adjust. The chill before the hot water would douse the throb in his balls.

A quick glance at his shaft showed the thought for what it was—a whole lot of wishful thinking. He gripped himself hard at the root, hissing more from the sensation shooting to the pit of his gut than the now-hot water needling his bare chest. He eschewed lubing with the body wash perched on the ledge, stroking himself the old-fashioned way. He kept his rhythm methodical, *up and down, down and up, up and down, down and twist over the head.* His other hand braced on the granite tile.

But try as he might to make this a run-of-the-mill jack-off, his mind unlocked a back door and forbidden thoughts slipped through, ones where Neve watched him, her dark eyes riveted on his cock as she devoured every inch.

His fingers on the wall curled into his palm at the idea, making a fist, and before he pounded it against the stone in a half-hearted, frustrated punch, he paused to imagine what it would be like to slide his hand down and cup the back of her head, to press her to his groin, urge her to take everything he had to give. Her wavy dark hair always looked so lush, so shiny. Yeah. He'd grab a great greedy fistful as her tight little mouth took him straight to heaven.

He rocked his hips harder. How long had it been since any-one had touched him?

Not since Maddy left.

A pathetic fact when so many puck bunnies would be willing to spend a night with a championship coach. He registered on a basic level that he was good-looking. At forty, there was no sign of middle-aged paunch. He kept his body lean with a shit ton of running. But random hookups had never been his thing. Not even in his twenties. He was a feast-or-famine kind of guy, either in a serious long-term relationship or alone.

And more often than not . . . the latter.

He increased his rhythm, frowning at the sound of friction, the rasp of skin against skin. Hard for a guy to lie to himself when he was working over his dick. Neve Angel had lodged under his skin with all the ease of a barbed cactus. God, that woman was a pain in the ass. Always quick to call out a question that he had hoped would pass unasked, and with that small pouting smile that communicated one thing: *Gotcha*.

Heat licked up his neck. He needed to come, to purge his body of the poison, the unwanted attraction toward his small, sleek nemesis. But his body revolted. Unwilling to grant him the victory of an easy release.

Instead, desire pressed like a weight to the pit of his belly, increasing in pressure bit by bit until a shudder ran through his quads, the muscles tightening and bunching in small, involuntary contractions that sent microbursts of heat up his hamstrings and a targeted blast of heat to his sac. He removed the hand propping his weight against the tile, slid it down, his rough palm caressing the thin, ruddy skin encasing his balls, and expelled a ragged "Fuck."

The spray peppered his chest in tiny licks. As beads of water trickled over his sensitive, flat nipples, the tip of his cock held a gleam that had nothing to do with the shower. He pressed the flat of his thumb down hard over his head, barking out a frustrated moan.

"Come on," he ordered himself, his cock.

All in good time, Bossy. He imagined Neve's annoyed tone with such pitch-perfect clarity that the orgasm took him by surprise.

His cock jerked in his hand, the deep, aching muscles clenching even after he came with a roar that might have made his elderly neighbors dial 911, thinking he'd just been murdered.

He leaned his forehead against the tiles, splaying both hands for balance. But his neighbors wouldn't be more wrong. Because he was more alive than he'd been in recent memory. His nerves tingled. His body was primed, ready to take on the whole damn world.

A frown tugged at his lips. As awesome as he felt, this wasn't good. What the fuck had he been thinking? This was a dangerous road. He better turn around and get his ass back to safer ground.

After flicking off the shower, he stepped out and reached for a towel, not the plushy soft one either. No, he grabbed the scratchy thin gray one that he'd had since his college days and for some reason never trashed. He scraped it over his damp body until his skin was red. He couldn't be getting his rocks off to Neve Angel. She was the enemy who baited him every chance she got. She'd even written a piece on his divorce for a lifestyle mag. Probably earned a pretty fucking penny and took a vacation on his personal misery. She was just another jackal who feasted on the remains of other people's lives.

If this was what happened when he stopped thinking about work, then he was in for a world of trouble. He tied the towel around his hips and stalked back to the kitchen, empty tumbler clutched in one fist. There was only one thing to do with this secret attraction—numb it with more whisky. Time to give himself one hell of a hangover, one that ruined him so much that he'd never be able to equate Neve Angel with sexy times again.

A WEEK LATER, and there was still no deal to end the lockout doldrums. Neve shuffled into the Twirling Tassels and eyed the line of folding chairs with a growing sense of trepidation. There was a world of difference between having a big idea and executing it.

"Yeah. So. Maybe this isn't such a good idea," she murmured to the two women a step behind her: her little sister, Breezy, and their friend Margot, who looked effortlessly sexy in high-cut black dancer pants and a midriff-baring royal blue tank top that revealed toned abs still bronzed from her summer trip to Baja.

"Well, for starters you should have worn heels," Margot hissed, pointing to her own Louboutins for emphasis. "The welcome letter specified that—"

"She doesn't own heels." Breezy sighed.

In contrast to Margot's eagerness, her sister's face was tight with unease, the same way it was whenever she was called on to do something athletic. But she still rocked a pair of ruffled hot pants that showed off her every curve.

Neve's heart sank into the soles of her Converse. Breezy's beehive and cat's eye makeup gave her a smoky Adele appearance, while Margot looked like the classic girl next door, albeit one who'd shimmy down the apple tree outside her bedroom window to get jiggy in the neighborhood park. But in her gray yoga pants and UC Boulder college T-shirt, Neve felt about as sexy as a mushroom.

This was a big mistake. Huge. She was a confident duck, not a sexy swan, and leaving her rut didn't mean climbing Striptease Mountain. Her jaw clenched. There was one person to blame for this serious overreach.

Tor Gunnar with his cold-fish, penguin-fucking comments.

As if on cue, bump-and-grind jazz music began to play and the other students took their positions straddling the chairs.

She adjusted her bun, stomach queasy. If the Hellions' coach hadn't acted like the idea of being attracted to her was a joke, she'd have never pulled up the burlesque studio's number that she'd photographed while stuck in traffic. And she'd have never been irritated enough to go out for emergency drinks with Margot and Breezy at their favorite bar.

And she certainly wouldn't have knocked back three Jack and Diet Cokes before revealing Tor's smart-ass comments.

After Margot and Breezy had wrapped up their gasps and "Oh, honey, no! What is he talking about? What a jerk!" comments, she'd sheepishly confessed her half-baked burlesque idea with every expectation that they'd laugh her under the table.

Instead, Margot had slammed her hand down on the table so hard that one of the empty glasses went flying halfway toward the pool tables. "Yes," she shouted. "Yes! Yes! Yes!" She banged her hand as if in the throes of pleasure. "You need to do this. Take back the power, hold up your head, and be the badass woman not afraid to shake her booty. Heck, all of us should get more bow-chicka-wow-wow. It's good for the soul."

"Speak for yourselves," Breezy had sniffed, even while her

eyes danced. "If I have any more bow-chicka then I'm not going to be able to sit down for a week."

"No one likes a humble bragger," Margot had scolded with mock severity. "Although you can't keep secrets about Jed West's bedroom prowess all to yourself. Throw us a bone ... er." She'd waggled her eyebrows. "Like does he talk dirty? Huh? Huh?"

"I'm not telling you that!" Breezy looked as if she'd stuck her face in a plate of ketchup. "It's private." She'd fallen hard for Jed West, captain of the Hellions, over the summer after he'd showed up for a literacy event at her library. One thing led to another and the rest is history. After concerns due to symptoms arising from a nasty concussion, he retired from the sport and took a position coaching college hockey for Denver University. Breezy had moved into his condo and cue the cheesy happy-ever-after music.

In her desire to save Breezy from more embarrassment, Neve had declared they would sign up right there. Now she wished she'd demanded her sister give Margot the gossip.

"Bonjour, bonjour." A svelte fortysomething woman bustled into the room in a black bodysuit and fishnets. "I am Madam Monique and you are 'ere for ze beginner 'eel class, *non*?" She had a French accent to boot. Striking a pose, hands on her hips, she surveyed the class.

There were ten women in total, all dressed in fashionable dance wear and ready to flaunt their moneymakers. Neve caught her own dumpy reflection in the studio mirror. She looked as if she'd gotten lost on the way to FBI boot camp training.

"*Alors*, where are your 'eels?" Madam Monique cast a finger to Neve like a Renaissance painting of an Old Testament god.

"Uh . . . I don't have any," Neve mumbled.

Someone in the back row tittered.

Her cheeks went from warm to scalding. It was like being back in middle school again.

"But zis is a 'eel class." Madam Monique seemed honestly confused.

That made two of them. Her mouth dried. Why had she signed up again? In trying to mentally one-up Tor Gunnar, she was only serving to humiliate herself.

"That's what I told her," Margot sang out.

"Stop being the teacher's pet." Breezy giggled.

"Next class, 'ave the 'eels and an outfit that makes you feel fabulous, okay?" Madam Monique refocused on the rest of the class. "Zee dances you master in zis class will change your life. You will 'ave power. Sex appeal. Radiate charm and confidence. Men will see you coming and ooooh . . . notice you going."

One girl raised her hand. "When do we get to wear the pasties?"

"What's a pastie?" Breezy murmured.

"No clue," Neve shot back. "But I think it's making me hungry."

That set Margot to giggling, and the problem with Margot's giggle was that it was contagious, a hiccupping snort that made the listener helpless against joining in.

Neve wheezed and Madam Monique froze. "Ah. *Bien*. Our first volunteer," she purred, crooking her finger to beckon Neve forward. Her grin was like a cat who'd eaten the cream. "*Mais oui*, a most excellent idea."

Neve drew forward with as much enthusiasm as a prisoner approaching the guillotine.

"Remove your shirt."

"Come again?" Neve asked. All she had on was a sports bra, one that used to be white until it got mixed up with Breezy's red sweater in the wash a few years ago when they were roommates. Now, not only was it old and stretched out, it was also the same hue as a slice of baloney.

"*Oui.* Your shirt," Madam Monique declared imperiously. "Strip."

An hour later Neve hurtled into the studio parking lot.

"To the Watering Hole, stat," she muttered to Breezy and Margot when they emerged a moment later.

"You were a good sport . . . trying on those pasties for the class demonstration," Breezy said. "But yes, after that drinks are in order. I'm going to message Jed and let him know our plans. He wanted to meet up and hear all about the class."

Neve groaned. Madame Monique had made her try on the nipple adhesive coverings and do a shimmy in front of everyone.

"Did you mean to get your arm stuck in the bra strap like that?" Margot asked, a little too innocently.

"That's it, not only are you buying the first round, you're also the designated driver," Neve growled, shoving her Jeep Wagoneer keys at Margot. "Ugh, that was an hour of my life that I can never get back." She crawled into the Wagoneer's backseat, letting Breezy and Margot take the front. "I think my tassels are twirled out."

"No way. It was your bright idea to sign us up for the whole month," Breezy said sternly. "I coughed up the money and it's nonrefundable."

"*Blech.* Isn't Jed your sugar daddy? Come on. You can't be

hurting for cash," Neve snapped, giving herself over to her black mood.

"Neve Frances Angel." Breezy whirled. "I'm giving you a pass for that comment. But it's the only one. Jed is my *boyfriend*. He isn't Mister Hockey or a punch line to your jokes."

"Okay, okay. I'm sorry," Neve muttered even as envy flared, a toxic brand of jealousy that she hated harboring anywhere in the vicinity of Breezy. Anyone could see that her sister was gaga for Jed, and not only that, the feeling was mutual. When she walked into a room, it was like she was the only person who existed for him.

No one had ever looked at Neve in that way. And before Jed, no one had ever looked at Breezy like that either, not even her old fiancé. But now she'd won the relationship golden ticket and was skipping off like she had an all-access pass to Willy Wonka's Chocolate Factory while Neve stayed stuck behind the gate.

"How do I get to the Watering Hole from this side of the city?" Margot asked. She had been raised in Portland and had come to Denver to attend yoga teacher training a few years ago. She still got turned around on city streets.

"I think I know but let me double check Byways in case it can get us there faster." Neve pulled up the route, and let the monotone voice call out the directions.

She idly watched the app screen as Margot drove through the city streets. Better than remembering Madame Monique's disapproving "tut-tut" as she ordered Neve to loosen up and "try and 'ave fun."

Neve's heart paid a surprise visit to her throat. Then there it was . . . the red-pitchfork avatar appeared on the screen.

Rovhal30 was out on the town tonight, and if the GPS signal was anything to be believed, he was currently in the parking lot at the Watering Hole.

Holy crap.

And here it was, ladies and gentlemen, the moment of truth. Her fantasy was about to become—for better or worse—a reality.

Chapter Five

"What the hell happened?" Tor barked into his phone in lieu of a greeting, pacing the back corner of the bar parking lot. The text message had come in as he was walking inside.

> **INGER:** I had a fall at the climbing gym. In the hospital. Okay. Mostly.

Typical Inger. To describe his sister as understated was an understatement in and of itself. She was like the Black Knight in *Monty Python and the Holy Grail*—she could be limbless and still chirping about how it was merely a flesh wound.

"X-rays came back twenty minutes ago. They're telling me that my femur suffered a hairline fracture." She blew out a frustrated breath. "And my kneecap is pretty much shattered. There were some other things, but I forget. Doc thinks I can kiss my spring climbing trip to Yosemite goodbye. I'd be mad, but I'm hopped up on so much Vicodin that I don't even know my own name. Who are you again?"

He didn't smile. Nothing about the situation was remotely funny. "Do you need me to get on a plane?" Inger lived in Minneapolis with her boyfriend and two corgis. They saw each other infrequently, but stayed in touch via short weekly calls.

"Nah, I'll live. At my age though, I should use a harness. That's a weird word, right, *harness*?" Her normally crisp voice slurred. *"Climbing harnesssssss."*

"Inger. Focus," he snapped. "I'm serious." His sister wasn't a rambler. She was a corporate attorney with a reputation for precision speech. She must be pretty messed up. "I can come, just say the word. Is Jason looking after you? Making sure you are getting pain meds? Staying hydrated?"

"So protective, little brother." There was a smile in her voice, but the tightness underneath made it clear that she was in a lot of pain. "He's being a big help. But this means I have to bail on being your plus-one to Maddy's wedding. I'm getting transferred to a rehab facility for a week or two."

"Don't give me a second thought, just focus on getting better. I'll be fine. Maddy and I are on good terms. Olive will miss you though." He hoped his tone was convincing. He didn't want to be a selfish asshole. His sister had sustained a serious injury, one that required a lengthy recuperation. He'd put in a call to a clinic he knew in the cities and get her squared away with some kick-ass PT. And she was right, her boyfriend would look after her. Jason worked from home for a tech firm and was devoted to her.

But now Tor would have to endure his ex-wife's wedding alone. It wasn't that he longed to have Maddy back. Not at all. They'd gotten married for plenty of the wrong reasons and too few of the right. But still.

The fact that she'd been the one to walk out had left a hurt that went deep. These days the pain was so familiar as to be a part of him, like the twinges in his lower back, old injuries from his days playing for the University of Minnesota.

She'd made him choose between work and love. But when it came down to it, he loved to work. He didn't just do his job, he *was* his job—and when she'd rejected that part of him, it'd felt like she'd rejected all of him. If she'd really understood him, she'd have respected that he didn't coach for glory or a paycheck . . . He did it because it was what he was meant to do. And yeah, the grueling NHL schedule demanded that sometimes he'd miss an event or a birthday, but he'd do his damndest to make it up. He'd established a FaceTime date with his daughter every night he was on the road. But his efforts were never enough. Maddy had crafted a narrative wherein she played second string to hockey and eventually he gave up and gave in to her story, becoming less emotionally involved.

Until she was gone.

He wasn't proud. But that's how it happened.

Inger called it "growing apart." He didn't know what to call it except a failure.

And he hated failing.

He bit down on the toothpick in the corner of his mouth, snapping the thin wood in two before spitting the shards onto the parking-lot asphalt. He'd given up smoking cold turkey when Olive was born. Toothpicks still took the edge off.

Two guys stumbled out of the Watering Hole front door doing a bad rap impression of Eminem's "Lose Yourself."

"What's going on over there?" Inger asked, her words slurry, sleepy.

"Don't worry about it. I'm getting a drink with Jed."

"Ooooh, *Jed West* Jed?" She perked. Woman always did

when hearing that name. "How's he doing in post-Hellions life?"

"Good." Great actually. The asshole was happier than he'd ever been, coaching on the college level and in love. Tor wanted to be happy for his friend, and he was, most of the time, when he wasn't cursing him as a son of a bitch for his good luck.

He'd found a woman who loved him for who he was. No apologies.

"Wow, thanks for the newsy gossip," Inger teased. "Hey." She yawned. "I should get some sleep. Jason will be back soon and the nurses wake me up every two hours on their rounds."

"Go. I'll check back in tomorrow."

"Love you, Twinkle Toes," she said sleepily.

"You too." And he did, even if he could never bring himself to say it. When he looked for the right way to express feelings, the words formed a logjam in his throat. He knew he could be dismissed as an asshole, but that was bullshit. He just didn't wear his heart on his sleeve.

The way he'd grown up, it was far safer to hide it behind a fortress of bone and ice.

His phone buzzed. He checked his texts. Nothing. He frowned. That was weird. Then he noticed his Byways app had a message. He clicked it open and a stupid grin tugged the corner of his mouth.

> **NEVERL8:** Hey! Not to sound like a stalker, but are you at the Watering Hole by any chance? I'm on my way and spotted your avatar. Maybe we could meet up and curse Prius drivers in person?

He lowered the phone and stared at the brick wall of the popular neighborhood bar. *Shit*. He wasn't prepared. He'd been chatting with this woman online for a month, the sassy one who used an avatar of angel wings. It didn't mean much, just idle conversation when stuck in gridlock. And yet . . .

His stomach muscles tightened. And yet it *had* meant a lot. He'd found himself looking forward to the short encounters. He wasn't a guy who made easy small talk. He wasn't given to flirting. He knew he was too serious and should smile more.

A Jeep Wagoneer tore into the parking lot and hit the curb. Music blared from the windows, some bubblegum pop song that made his teeth hurt from all the sugary sweetness.

"Damn it," he muttered. The racket from that tin can was making it hard to calm down. He dragged a hand through his hair and released a frustrated breath.

His contact with NeverL8 was such a small part of his day, and yet it felt . . . fuck it . . . pure. A moment where he wasn't the coach. Or Daddy. Or the ex. He was just a guy in traffic who could share a joke. It had always been a talent of his, remembering punch lines. Guess it was the one good quality Dad ever gave him.

Nils Gunnar was the man of the party. The self-proclaimed King of St. Paul. He had a joke for every occasion and a booming laugh heard down the block. The problem was that the jokes ran out the minute he got back home.

It took effort to put those memories on lockdown, but Tor tried his best.

Instead he scanned the busy road, bustling with Saturday-night traffic, and waited to meet his mystery friend. What would she be driving?

"Tor? Oh my God, it *is* you!" Breezy Angel ran across the

parking lot, the smile on her face bigger than her tiny black shorts. "Jed didn't mention you were here too!"

"Surprise, surprise." Tor gave a tense smile. His buddy hadn't mentioned that he was including his new live-in girlfriend in on their beer plans, but what the hell, it was impossible not to like Breezy.

"Are you coming inside with us?" she asked. "Because oh my God! We have got to tell you all about this class we just went to."

"And if you're lucky we will perform our newly learned chair routine." The leggy brunette piped up from beside her, propping a hand on her narrow waist and giving him an appreciative once-over.

"My best friend Margot," Breezy said by way of introduction. "And of course you know my little big sister . . . Neve."

And there she was, small and dark, hanging a few steps back in the shadows. If Breezy was all curves and Margot was legs for days, Neve was self-contained and sleeker than a black cat. She had the sort of direct gaze that dared others to try to pet her, but he knew if he ever attempted it she'd unsheathe her claws.

"I'm staying out here," he muttered. "Waiting to meet . . . a friend." *Of sorts.*

"Oh okay, yeah, sure." Breezy turned to Margot with a shrug and they both disappeared into the bar.

Neve loitered, studying his face. "I'm not used to seeing you out of a suit," she said after a beat. "You look different in jeans."

There were a hell of a lot of things going on inside that sentence, and he hated how much curiosity he had over every unspoken word.

"What are you doing, Angel?" he asked dryly, tapping a

hand against his denim-encased thigh. "Still trying to get me on the record for the lockout?"

"Meh, resist all you want. It's just a matter of time." She fluffed her bangs and swung her gaze to some undefinable point in the distance. What was that, a smirk?

"What's so funny?" he pushed.

"Life," she answered cryptically. "Except I think the joke's on me."

"Any time you want to speak in plain sentences, I'm all ears."

"Cool. Until then, why don't you keep waiting for your big mystery date, Rovhal30?"

The name hit him like a stick to the face, snapping everything into place. He shoved a hand into his pocket to resist slapping his forehead.

The wings.

The pun on her name.

Christ, could he be more of a fucking idiot?

But as he met her glare, he realized that was exactly what he was.

"*You're* NeverL8?"

Chapter Six

Was the man really so miserly that he couldn't spare a single glance in her direction? Neve leaned back in the booth and studied Tor's profile. If she wasn't so annoyed with his determination to ignore her, she'd have deemed his tenacity rather sexy.

She wrapped her fingers around her thumb and squeezed for good measure. So sue her, she'd modified a noun with the adjective *sexy* in relation to Tor Gunnar. And God help her, she wasn't even tipsy. In fact, she hadn't been able to swallow more than half a mouthful of her margarita ever since Margot plonked it down fifteen minutes ago. And it was top-shelf Patron Silver, for crying out loud.

Now Margot was back at the bar flirting with a dreadlocked bartender, his tight white T-shirt molded to his defined pecs, the color popping the deep bronze of his skin. Meanwhile, Jed and Breezy cuddled across the booth, cooing and whispering between kisses while studiously ignoring the curious glances from onlookers. Neve glanced at her watch. The lovebirds had exactly one more minute before she stepped in and made a citizen's arrest for the crime of PDA.

"Disgusting, isn't it?"

"Stop the presses." She glanced to Tor with a start. "Are you speaking mouth words to me?"

His glacial expression had the curious effect of heating her down to the tips of her toes. "As you don't have my ex-captain's tongue shoved halfway down your throat . . . then yeah. I suppose I am."

Neve raised her brows. "You know, those might be the most words you've ever voluntarily spoken to me."

He arched one of his own blond brows right back. "Hope you enjoyed the experience."

"I'm willing to be generous in my Yelp review." A small smile tugged her lips. "Let's go with a three out of five."

"Three?"

His unexpected smile drew her in. And it shouldn't. Tor was good-looking, but so were most guys in her line of work. After all, she spent her days in the company of professional athletes.

So what was it about this particular man that quickened her pulse?

But while her mind might stage a freak-out, her face never would. "What's the problem?" She kept her features a mirror to his own, one of cool, calculated amusement. "That's better than fifty percent."

He paused.

They might be enemies, but together they won at awkward pauses.

"I should have known," he said at last.

She was physically incapable of allowing this man to make a vague statement without pushback. "Explain."

"I should have known you were NeverL8. Your name was right there, not to mention those avatar angel wings."

"Can't say you earned a Scooby snack for your sleuthing skills, Shaggy." She winked.

His surprised bark of laughter hit her belly like a shot, swirling through her veins with intoxicating force. She'd heard his laugh before of course, in the locker room over the years, always while talking to one of his guys. But never at *her*. She liked it, she realized, crossing her arms tight across her chest. A lot.

Too much.

"Excuse me. I have to pay a visit to the little girls' room," she announced, almost tipping her untouched drink in her hurry to stand. Had someone turned up the heat? The room felt overwarm and too damn crowded. Breathing space. What she needed was breathing space.

Better yet, thinking space.

Pushing through the crowd, she thought Tor called out her name, but she didn't want to check only to discover that it had been wishful thinking.

She stormed ahead, chin down, arms swinging. Wishful thinking had bitten her in the butt enough in the past hour. The delicious Ewan McGregor fantasy of her Byways dreams had turned out to be a nightmare—worse, a guy who hated her guts.

A guy she hated right back, of course.

This was all a lot to take in. Too much to process.

She was a simple girl. Maybe her life had been stuck in a rut, but so what? Ruts provided protection from the elements, gave shelter—a cozy hiding place. If she stayed in a rut, she would never have to do anything uncomfortable, like put herself out there.

No bathroom line, thank God. She pushed into the single-stall unisex space, the door banging a cinder-block wall riddled by graffiti art and old concert posters. After turning the lock, she marched to the sink, flicked on the tap, and splashed cold water onto her face.

One of the benefits of never wearing makeup was having no mascara to ruin. She splashed and splashed again, her nerves going off like a Fourth of July fireworks show.

"You are experiencing a normal physiological reaction," she reassured the panicked expression staring back in the mirror while registering the fact that her face wasn't the only thing wet. "It's time to take Breezy's advice and invest in a battery-operated boyfriend."

She had always felt silly when perusing sex toys online, as if she was an imposter with no business owning clitoris-fluttering rings or body-warming lube. On the rare occasion when she'd attempted to explore the thousands of ways to get off in the world, she would always end up back at eighteen years old, hearing the words of a rival coach after she failed to qualify for the national figure-skating championships.

"Neve Angel?" She'd overheard him scoffing to one of his skaters while she curled behind a row of folding chairs, bawling her eyes out. He'd glanced in her direction with a sneer, as if sensing her presence. "With that jaw and those bushy brows?" he'd said a little louder. "That skinny little bitch isn't prime-time, and the judges instinctively sensed it tonight. Trust me, she's no threat. She's nothing at all."

After they had walked away, she'd scrubbed her mouth clean of lipstick with the back of her hand. Hard.

She'd said goodbye to the world of glitz and glamour, hung up her skates, and never looked back. Her sister had often complimented her looks, and seemed like she meant it, but when Neve was alone with the bathroom mirror, all she could ever think was *that jaw . . . those bushy brows . . . skinny little bitch.* Finally, Neve had avoided her reflection altogether. Instead, she put her head down and worked.

Forget flirting.

Forget fun.

She'd doubled down on being serious. And if she wasn't sexy enough to tempt men like Tor Gunnar, welp, so be it. She was used to it. It's just how she rolled.

Sometimes people mentioned her "bold brows" or "strong features" as if they were good things. And she didn't want to be a self-loathing woman nitpicking her faults. The last thing she wanted to do was admit that in a perfect world she'd love to possess the pixie face and effortless grace of Audrey Hepburn in *Funny Face.*

Because this wasn't a perfect world.

Far from it.

Smoothing her hair, she straightened, sucking in her abs and squaring her shoulders. She *would* go buy that cat. Eventually she'd figure out a way to ignore the hole in her heart, the one that ached to be filled even more than the lonely place between her legs.

And that was saying a lot.

"Enough." She dabbed the mysterious moisture collecting in the corners of her eyes.

Forget burlesque classes and trying to be sexy. She'd construct a roof on her rut and call it a home. After all, this was the twenty-first century. She could take care of her own business one self-administered orgasm at a time.

She had enough time on her hands with the stupid lockout in effect.

Sniffing twice, she turned to the door. Now that she had a plan, all she needed to do was survive this stupid night and that stupidly sexy man, who had managed to ruin the one bit of stupid harmless flirtation she had in her life. *Bye, bye, Byways.*

Good thing she'd turned in her "Top Five Worst Coaches in the NHL" piece for next week's paper. Petty, yes, but satisfying.

After drying her hands, she stepped into the small hallway and right into Tor Gunnar's chest.

"We have to stop meeting like this," he said wryly.

"Did you follow me?" She pushed off him, aghast. Was her face splotchy?

Just when she'd thought her situation couldn't get worse, leave it to fate to say, "Hold my beer."

"You left your purse on the table." He extended her purse with a stiff arm. "I thought you might want it."

"What?" She didn't have the first clue what thoughts marched through this man's mind.

"I should be asking you that. Were you crying?"

"No. Of course not." She snatched the purse and shoved it under her arm. "It's awesome to hang out with a guy who hates your guts. Super relaxing."

"Hates your . . . what?" he spluttered, glowering at her. "What makes you think I hate you?"

Great. This guy was Mr. Literal. Now she'd get some big speech about how technically he didn't hate her, only disregarded her, and somehow that was even more awful.

She straightened to her whole impressive five feet and a half. "Don't you?"

"Neve." He took a step forward, filling the whole alcove, the clean citrus scent on his skin permeating the air. Her entire world shrank like a deflating helium balloon and the only thing she could do was try to focus, her gaze fixed on the third button of his blue shirt, the one that fastened in the center of his chest. The same chest that was currently heaving as if he'd just completed a record sprint.

Okay, then. He wasn't unaffected by her proximity either.

Sweat misted the valley between her breasts. The soft, worn cotton of her bra was too rough against the sensitive peaks.

She shifted, clenching her thighs together. "Tor, listen—"

"If I hated you, then why would I want to kiss you so damn bad?"

Her heart gave up beating. She wasn't going to survive the heat melting his frosty gaze.

"Kiss me?" Her mouth formed the words, but she wasn't sure if she managed to squeak the question out loud until the corner of his mouth crooked.

"That an invitation?" Wry amusement entered his tone.

And there went the bones in her legs—poof, gone.

The only choice left was to fling her arms out and grip his broad, strong shoulders.

"If you want it to be." Her voice sounded like that of a stranger, a gal who danced burlesque in heels and applied bold lipstick, who could lounge in comfy sweats but also rock a pair of sexy, butt-molding skinny jeans when the fancy struck.

A woman not afraid to reach out and take a little pleasure.

And so . . . just like that . . . she did.

IT TOOK TOR's brain a second to register that he was kissing Neve Angel.

He was *kissing* Neve Angel.

No. Scratch that.

He was kissing the shit out of Neve Angel like a mother-fucking boss.

While his mind blanked, his body got busy. Mentally, he was still processing that her lips tasted cool, tart, and sweet like pink lemonade, while one of his hands dipped around her waist and hauled her against him, and the other found the bathroom door handle and turned. They tumbled inside.

And the real surprise wasn't even that he devoured the glorious heaven that was Neve Angel's mouth. It was that she kissed *him* back. Her tongue stroked his with such sweet fire that his body ignited.

He couldn't decide where to touch first, so like a greedy bastard he tried to get everywhere at once. Her hair was even softer than it looked, but thick and wavy. He coiled his fingers in deep, tugging to turn her head back, intensifying the kiss. She was a thunderclap on a sunny day, a four-leaf clover in a sidewalk crack, hitting every green light the whole drive home. Wholly unexpected. Better than anything he'd ever imagined.

And he'd imagined, all right. Even as he'd tried to push the thoughts away, the fantasies had reeled him back time and time again.

"Neve." Was the word a question or a prayer? All he knew was it tasted right, like taking a sip of good wine and letting the complex flavors linger on the tongue.

"No more talking," she ordered. Their lips crushed back together, teeth knocking. He skimmed his fingers to where her shirt rode up. When he grazed that sliver of bare, smooth skin, it was like everything in his life made sense, every bit of bad luck or stroke of good fortune had a single purpose—to bring him here. Right here . . . to this moment in a dive-bar bathroom, where he got to explore a perfect landscape of silky skin.

Neve commenced her own explorations, but like with everything else, she was direct—cut right to the chase. He sucked in a rasping breath as she skimmed the bulge in his jeans, pressing her palm flat, the pressure cording the muscles in his neck.

"So much for foreplay," he choked.

She might have snapped "Screw foreplay," but it was drowned out by a loud bang from outside.

"Yo! Did someone fall in and drown?" A deep, drunken voice slurred. "Open up. I've got to take a leak."

And just like that the spell broke. Neve leapt back and her hand flew to cover her mouth, wiping her lips as if removing evidence of his kisses.

He watched her wordlessly as she threw open the door and dove into the noisy bar. How fucking stupid to think that there was anything magic about a frantic hookup in a dingy bar bathroom. This wasn't a happy accident but one giant mistake, which for a moment felt so damn right.

Chapter Seven

"What the hell, were you two fuckin' or what?"

"Such a lovely command you have of the English language." Neve grimaced at the frat boy's sour beer breath as he blocked her path from the bathroom, leering from beneath the brim of his white hat. "I'll go with 'or what,' thanks."

"I better not be slipping in no sticky shit." The white hat's wet mouth twisted in a lecherous smirk as he tried focusing over her shoulder. His eyes widened as he noticed who stood behind her. "Hold up . . . Coach? Tor Gunnar, dude. Holy shit, no way, you're a legend."

The dude-bro frat boy pushed past her, literally shoving her out of the way and extending a hand. "Those were some legit plays that last game, man. The lockout blows. Guess you deserve getting a little stinky pinky—"

What fresh hell was this? Neve's throat slammed shut and she bolted out of the back hall into the throng in the bar. It was like playing the world's worst game of Would You Rather. Would you rather maul your nemesis in the Watering Hole bathroom or hear a frat boy use the words *stinky pinky* in reference to your own vagina?

Two sets of curious eyes watched her approach the table.

Breezy and Jed had called a halftime in their round of tonsil hockey. Neve heaved an inward groan. Guess she was supposed to be the entertainment.

"Where's Margot?" she asked, as if she'd merely gone to the bathroom and never in ten million years compiled research about the size and shape of Tor Gunnar's dick.

But if there was one person in the world who was impossible to fool, it was a sister.

"Margot's made a new friend, as per usual." Breezy gestured toward the bar, where Margot sat on the counter, legs swinging and still whispering to the cute bartender. "But what's up?" Her gaze narrowed. "Your cheeks are red."

"Hey."

Neve stiffened as Tor slid into the seat beside her. She refused to glance over and instead focused on his hand, the one that had just roamed the wilds of her body like Davy Crockett. It sported fresh scrapes on the knuckles, the middle one split.

"Hey! You're bleeding, man," Jed said, passing him a napkin. "What were you doing?"

Tor grabbed a napkin and pressed it to his hand as Neve's heart skipped a beat. From the corner of her eye she saw the frat boy from the hallway storming to the exit with one eye swollen shut.

"He defended my honor," she broke in wryly, still unable to believe it.

Had Tor really done that? Punched the white-hat asshole?

Breezy and Jed paused before bursting out laughing.

"Good one." Her sister's shoulders shook. "You deadpan better than anyone. For a second I almost believed you."

Breezy didn't mean her amusement to come across as

mean. Neve abstractly knew she laughed out of disbelief that Tor would ever be called upon to be her heroic knight in shining armor.

But to a sour, hurting part deep in her soul, it sounded mocking.

The gorgeous head coach of a professional hockey team body checking a drunken frat boy on my behalf? Yeah. Right. Dream on.

"Got my hand jammed in a door while trying to get some air." Tor drained his glass without further explanation.

Such an obvious lie. Confusion swept through her as her brain grappled for any logic. Tor Gunnar *had* punched that jerk. Did he really fight for her? The notion shouldn't be sexy. Violence was never the answer. But—*gah*—there was something so undeniably delicious about a straight-laced man turning into an utter caveman.

But then again, look at the facts. He wasn't giving her a pent-up look full of secret "I shed blood for you" passion. In fact, he stared past her shoulder as if she wasn't even there, like what had happened in that bathroom meant nothing.

As if he'd already forgotten it.

A wave of insecurity swept away any arousal.

"We got a game this weekend, playing Michigan State. Want to come offer some advice?" Jed asked him after a beat.

Neve appreciated her sister's boyfriend's low tolerance for conversational silences. Let him fill the air space and keep the attention off her. And Tor's knuckles.

"Can't. I'm going to a wedding." He made it sound like he was getting a root canal.

"Shouldn't that be a happy occasion?" Margot plonked down, jumping in mid-conversation as usual.

"It's for my ex-wife," Tor said crisply. "I'm sure *she* is looking forward to it."

Neve's mouth dried. He was going to watch his ex-wife marry another man. Eeesh. That *was* on par with getting a root canal. Without novocaine.

"Ouch, that's no bueno." Margot wrinkled her nose. "Hope you've lined up a hot date as a matter of pride."

"I'm flying solo," Tor grunted.

"Are you crazy?" Margot was never one to beat around a bush. "No, no, no! You can't do that. That's a rookie move. Think over your options. Who can you ask? *Someone* has to volunteer as tribute."

"My sister did. Then she fell rock climbing. Unfortunately, her rehabilitation doesn't gel with that timetable." Tor's frosty rebuttal settled over the table like another ice age, freezing them into another awkward silence. Even Margot appeared to be quelled.

"The air-hockey table has opened up." Jed pointed, once again saving the day.

"I'm in," Neve announced, eager for the distraction, just as Tor muttered, "Sounds good."

"Ooh, competition! I like it!" Margot rubbed her hands together. "Let's play battle of the sexes! First round Breezy and Neve versus Tor and Jed."

"Hey now, this isn't going to be fair." Neve hoped her sarcastic drawl hid the fact her nipples could cut glass.

"It's going to be awkward when we school you boys in front of the whole bar," Breezy crowed.

"You're that good, huh?" Tor said patronizingly.

"Not me." Breezy held up her hands and shook her head. *"Her."*

"I've been hearing for a while that Neve here has mad air-hockey skills." Jed fed a dollar into a machine, nodding to a trio of college girls who snapped his picture before rushing off in a fit of giggles.

Breezy didn't even bat an eye.

"Doesn't that ever bother you?" Neve whispered.

"Nah, why should it? I mean, he *is* gorgeous. Let 'em look." She winked. "I'm the one going home with him at the end of the night."

Neve's laugh felt hollow. Her sister was confident in her love. So optimistic in his devotion that trust came as easily to her as breathing. No doubt or hesitation. Could love really be like that?

The puck went whizzing by her defenses into the goal.

"Hellions one, Angels zero." Tor smirked. He was back to his usual self, no trace of the passionate man from minutes ago. All cool confidence. Handsome and untouchable. His Scandinavian features were as severe and inscrutable as a Norse god's.

"It's like that, is it?" She dropped her chin and pushed up her sleeves. "That point was a gift."

He rolled his eyes. "That a fact?"

"Stick it on Wikipedia and let it be known."

"All right, trash talkers. Let's sweeten the pot," Margot said, ripping the hair elastic off her wrist and tying her long brown hair up into a ponytail.

"What are we talking about here, a wager?" Jed drawled. "Because I could call in a whole lot of favors."

Breezy blew him a kiss.

Before Neve could say anything that included the words *gag* and *me*, Tor broke in. "The winners get to call in a favor from the losers. One deed."

A few minutes ago she'd played tonsil hockey with this guy. And he hadn't treated her like a cold fish but a triple-layered chocolate-fudge cake. Then he'd ignored her. Now he wanted a favor if she lost? No way.

But at the exact same time, an idea dropped on her head with the force of a cartoon anvil . . . If she won, she could force him to agree to an exclusive no-holds-barred, in-depth profile. Forget the measly top-five article. She'd grill him hard. Figure out what made him tick. Ask nosy questions to her heart's content.

If he wanted to mess with her, she'd mess back.

"Deal," Neve shot back. "As long as it's not illegal."

Jed groaned. "Where's the fun in that?"

"Enough, you." Breezy giggled as if this was some sort of private joke.

Double ew. Neve was happy to let them have their mystery. Some things she just really, really didn't want to know, like what her sister got up to in the boudoir. "Enough chitchat." She set her striker on the table. "Got to be in it to win it."

Because she'd win. Probably. The problem was . . . Breezy sucked at air hockey. She loved her sister, but as she blocked one of Jed's blank shots and pulled back quickly to guard the goal, Neve had to concede the obvious. They were outmatched.

From the sly look in Jed's eyes, it seemed as if he knew exactly what favor he wanted to collect from her sister. And from the erratic, clumsy way Breezy kept trying to score, there was a real and pressing danger that her own teammate might be throwing the game to be in her boyfriend's debt.

But Tor wasn't flirting. Or smiling. He played like a man possessed. She'd never seen him on the ice, at least not in person. There was a chance she'd *once* dredged up some old footage from his Gopher days on YouTube while devouring an entire pint of Cherry Garcia.

But that fact was never to be spoken about, or acknowledged.

She doubled down on the offense, scoring a point, but then Breezy bumped her elbow as she tried to play defense. They were back to being tied for the game point.

"This is it, ladies and gentleman," Margot drawled in a deep, announcer-type voice. "The moment of truth." And she wasn't just hamming it up for her own amusement. A small crowd had gathered, recording the game on their phones. She'd bet five bucks that the majority of these women were focused on capturing shots of Jed West, although to give Coach his credit, he wasn't without his own cadre of female admirers.

"Come on," she snapped to her sister. "Let's get it together."

Her potshot fooled Jed as she tricked him with a fake out by intentionally aiming her shot not into their goal but off the table in front of him, sending the puck back, where she could quickly attack with a rebound.

But Tor, damn it, he was too much of a coach, cataloguing her plays and reviewing her weaknesses. He was ready for the pump fake and stopped it short. Then he struck his mallet hard, sending the puck bouncing off a side wall.

Neve saw it coming. She knew she could stop it. But he played with such a strange intensity that her own curiosity was sparked. If she was in Tor Gunnar's debt, what favor would he request? Her mind screamed *No!* but her body was . . . curious.

And his puck slipped into her goal.

"Oh darn!" Breezy squealed, sounding less than dismayed.

Neve lifted her gaze straight to Tor's. Her cheeks heated.

He stared back, a flicker of confusion crossing his face. It had been subtle, but he knew she'd just thrown the game.

But he didn't know why.

And that made two of them. Damn it. She tucked a lock of hair behind her ear and glanced away. She'd just thrown away one heck of a professional coup. And for what?

He'd likely humiliate her in some way. What would it be . . . ? Stroll down Sixteenth Avenue dressed in a tutu? Go to a karaoke bar and sing "Don't Stop Believing"?

"Good game," Margot said as they filed back into their booth. "Now the winners get to call in the debt. This should be interesting."

"That's one word for it," Jed said.

"Stop," Breezy pleaded in a giddy tone that made it clear they had about two more minutes before she asked to close the tab and run home.

"Inquiring minds want to know." Neve addressed her comment to Tor, even as she studied her drink. "What's it going to be? I know my pride is about to take a beating so let's get the suspense over with." Her stomach felt so tense that there was no way she'd risk a sip at this point. The last thing she needed to do was choke at the table.

Or get more mouth to mouth from the coach.

"I thought it over and you all are right. I can't go to my ex's wedding alone." Tor's tone was pure confident arrogance, even as he drummed his index finger on the table.

Neve's body didn't have time to release a flood of adrenaline before she was hit with the second part of his statement.

"Since you lost, Neve, you'll go with me. Two days in Telluride. Ever been?"

"I-I had friends go there for music festivals while I was at college, but I always stayed behind to do summer school," she managed to stammer, trying to comprehend the magnitude of what he just said.

"Then it's a date. I'll send you the details."

"A . . . date," Neve repeated blankly.

He nodded once, a dare in his eyes.

Whisky. Tango. Foxtrot. Her stomach did its best impersonation of an amusement-park log ride and splashed down to her toes.

Because no matter how much she wanted to pretend, she couldn't fake that the kiss in the bathroom hadn't felt oh, so real. He might be setting her up for a fall, but she couldn't quite stop herself from tiptoeing to the edge.

She needed to keep her head in the game. Look for the opportunity. After all, for better or worse, she'd be alone, more or less, for a weekend with Tor Gunnar, the biggest enigma in NHL coaching, and she'd figure out what made him tick at last—by hook or crook.

She couldn't wait to tell Scott about the trip. This was just the kind of opportunity that would cause her editor to freak out.

When life handed her lemons, she made delicious lemonade.

Two deep lines materialized between his brows—at least he had the good sense to look concerned.

"Game on," she said blithely, picking up her drink and giving him a toast. "After all, I've never been over to Telluride. It will be an . . . adventure." Perfect. She'd swashbuckled through his little dare with expert precision. All the points to her.

You don't scare me, Tor Gunnar.

She took a long swallow of the margarita, the frozen slush sluicing over her front teeth and creating one heck of a brain freeze. Try as she might, she couldn't hold back a wince, because all her tough talk sat on a throne of lies. Tor Gunnar might not scare her, but the unfathomable expression in his eyes sure as heck did.

He had an agenda. She needed to figure out what it was for her own sanity.

Chapter Eight

*T*or sat, disoriented. The clock beside his bed read three in the morning. Looked like he'd fallen asleep after all. The way he'd tossed and turned after the bar, he'd figured it would be another one of those restless nights where he watched the sun rise.

The phone ring registered in his sleep-drunk brain.

"Shit." He sprang into action. His first thought was Olive. But the number on the screen was unfamiliar. One of the guys?

"Hello?" he said, frowning.

"It's stupid to call, but I can't sleep. I need to know why. Why'd you do it?"

The familiar woman's voice jolted him like a triple-shot espresso. "Neve?"

"Do you enjoy messing with me, is that it?" Her tone was strained. "Because I've been going over tonight's events with a fine-tooth comb and nothing adds up. I mean, you went and ate my face after informing my colleagues that I was a cold fish. Then you rearranged that dumbass frat boy's face after he insulted me. And *then* the coup de grace . . . an invite to a weekend away in Telluride? For your wife's wedding?"

"She is my ex-wife," he bit back. "Very much *ex*."

"Still . . . color me confused, Coach."

"What's so hard to understand?" He kicked off the comforter and eased back against his headboard. A shaft of moonlight shone on the end of the bed; if he reached out he'd be able to touch it. "Who knows? Maybe I'm interested in getting to know you more."

"Good story. Except does the phrase 'fuck a penguin' ring a bell?"

Shit. He'd said that. And the stupid cold fish comment. Both were knee-jerk reactions designed to deflect attention from the truth . . . that he couldn't get enough of this maddening woman. He'd acted like a middle school doofus, teasing the girl he crushed on.

He wasn't proud.

"All I can guess is that you must enjoy torturing your enemies."

"Was kissing me torture?" His cock stirred in his boxer briefs at the memory.

"Don't fuck around, Gunnar."

"Nice mouth you've got."

She made a choking sound. "Pot meet kettle."

"I'll be honest. I *am* interested, all right? I think you know that though. I think you've always known. And what's more . . . I think you might be curious too."

Silence dragged. For a second he wondered if she'd hung up. Maybe he was reading this all wrong.

"Well . . . this is an unexpected direction."

"I'm full of surprises." He raked a hand through his hair. The darkness made him honest. "But here's more truth. I'm glad you agreed to come to the wedding. I'm glad you said yes."

"It can't be an easy event." She cleared her throat. "I mean, you loved your ex, right?"

"Once upon a time. But it wasn't a fairy tale. We've been co-parents for years and it's Olive who wants me there."

"Your daughter."

"She's ten." Not many things made him smile on demand, but Olive always did. "And I don't want you worrying about logistics. We'll have separate rooms. I've already called the hotel. I'm not looking to take advantage of you."

"I see," she replied, sounding a little confused. He didn't blame her. Nor was he being entirely truthful.

Their chemistry was undeniable. Hell yes he wanted to take advantage. He wanted to take her every which way and twice on Sunday.

"What's the game plan? We drive down this weekend?"

"Yeah." He cleared his throat. "It'll take seven hours. The valley is an out-of-the-way pain in the ass to get to. But believe me, the San Juan Mountains are something to see."

"I'm Colorado-born and -raised and have never spent much time in the ski towns. It was too expensive for my family when I was a kid, and now my winters are too busy for vacations."

He sighed, smile fading. "Mine too."

"What have you been doing since the lockout?"

"Watching tapes." His mouth flattened. "Reviewing plays. Climbing the walls. You?"

"Yesterday I wrote yet another lockout think piece, *blech*. Then I tried learning to knit off YouTube. I'm making a pot holder . . . I think. Or a lap blanket for a guinea pig."

"Pot holder." He tried and failed to picture her in the kitchen, being domestic. "You cook?"

"No. Ew. I barely toast bread." She gave a short self-deprecating laugh. "But circle back to the lockout for a second. Are there any rumors floating around about negotiations— please say we're close to a deal?"

He stiffened. "No." The easiness from a moment ago disappeared, the question a reminder that she wasn't NeverL8, a woman he'd flirted harmlessly with online. This was Neve Angel and any slip of the tongue could have real and lasting career consequences. He couldn't forget she was a journalist, and he was playing with fire.

"I'm not fishing," she said testily. "I didn't call you at three in the morning to try and trick you out of insider NHL information, if that's what you're thinking."

"I wasn't." He massaged an ache spreading across his forehead. "I'm not."

"You're a good kisser, but a terrible liar, Tor Gunnar. But it doesn't matter because whatever game you're playing, I'm going to win." And that was when she did hang up.

Tor groaned and dropped his phone off the side of the bed before bracing his face in his hands. How were they going to spend the entire weekend together and not commit murder?

And out of all the women in the entire fucking world, why was she the one who made him come alive?

Since his divorce, he'd been frozen. He didn't miss feeling that he was always disappointing someone, that he was never enough. Maddy used to cry in the shower, where she thought he couldn't hear. But each and every time he'd go stand by the door, put his hand on the knob, and tell himself to open it, to go inside and see what was eating at her.

But he'd been too chicken shit.

At work he'd always had a game plan and the right answer.

Coaching made sense. He was good at it in a way he'd never been as a spouse.

Yeah, he might have been a better husband than his pop. He didn't yell or get drunk, and he'd hack off his arm before raising it against a woman. But that didn't mean he knew the first thing about how to be a significant other, as that disastrous phone call just confirmed.

He knew how to be a father. He knew how to be a friend. He knew how to be a coach. But he was clueless how to prevent himself from driving a lover away, giving them no chance but to end things on their own. His reticence wasn't about a fear of commitment. He wanted someone to nestle beside in the darkest nights, to know what they ate for breakfast, how they took their coffee, to give and receive love.

He rolled over in his empty bed and flung an arm across his forehead. But it had always been easier to push women away, so he didn't know what the hell to do about this strange pull toward Neve.

Or if he could do better this time and not screw everything up.

"NEED HELP?" THE shop assistant chirped.

Talk about a loaded question. Because yes, Neve needed help. Lots of help on multiple levels. But she'd rather freeze her tongue to a flagpole before admitting as much. "No." She issued one of her tight "back away slowly" smiles. "I'm fine."

"Are you looking for any particular occasion?" This redheaded assistant wasn't giving up easily.

"A wedding." Her curt tone disinvited further questions but the girl still seemed undeterred. Neve tucked her chin and walked self-consciously toward a little black dress on a center rack. That could work. Timeless elegance. A little Audrey Hepburn. And after all, black was her color.

"Aw, love a wedding!" The woman sounded like she meant it too. "Who is the happy couple? Friend? Sister? Brother?"

"The ex-wife to my date," she answered crisply, leaving out the part where she was also going to commit espionage and root out her archenemy's secrets and win whatever secret game he played.

"Ohhhhhh." The assistant's eyes rounded just a bit. "This is a challenge. You have to look gooood."

Neve stiffened. "What do you mean?"

"Your date is taking you to his ex-wife's wedding. Wow. That means he's showing you off."

Neve pressed a hand to her chest. "Me?"

Her confusion was met with a sage nod. "You're a statement. The evidence he's got a chance at his own happy ending. And you need a dress that's going to make a splash."

"Yeah, about that." Neve's shoulders curled in as she took in the assistant's tiger-print heels. "I'm not really a statement kind of a gal."

"Let's see." The woman gave her a critical appraisal. "I know just the thing. Follow me."

Neve trailed after, too flustered to argue. Tor wasn't bringing her to show her off or out of interest. He probably wanted to make a fool out of her.

"Yes, this. This is perfect." The assistant pulled out a short, intricate scalloped-lace dress in a rich greenish-blue hue.

"But . . . it's so feminine." Neve was scared to even touch it. The color was beautiful, vibrant and lush but classy. If she wore a dress like that she'd be noticed, not as a tough-as-nails reporter but as a sexy woman.

And that thought terrified her.

But another powerful thought took root. She'd like to see Tor try not to be tempted by her in this dress.

"With your dark hair and those eyes, and that mouth. Dear lord, your poor date. It's just not fair. He won't be able to take his eyes off you." The assistant swung the dress beneath Neve's chin and tittered.

Neve stared at herself in the mirror, taking in the unforced compliments and imagining herself wearing it. Misgivings waged a final last stand. "This isn't my usual style."

"It should be," the assistant responded firmly. "You have such bold, classic features. You can pull it off."

There was no doubt the color suited her. Neve would never have thought in a million years to pick something so bright.

"And remember, you want to keep the makeup simple. With your complexion, that shouldn't be a problem. You have lashes to die for . . . Are they natural? And can we talk about your eyebrows? Because yes. So much yes."

"You mean bushy." She hated to give voice to her deeply private insecurities. It was so much easier to march around life pretending to be ultra-confident. But what the hell, sometimes honesty was the best policy.

"Those brows are fierce. We're talking *Vogue* eyebrows; people pay good money trying to get them. I'm not kidding. There are Facebook ads for eyebrow wigs on my timeline at least once a week. Wear the dress, let your hair down and do loose finger curls, and then treat yourself to a really killer shade of lipstick."

"Lipstick?"

"Oh, honey." The assistant's wince didn't hurt as much when she rolled her head to one side and gave a kind smile. "I'm going to hit you with some real talk. You're getting this dress aaaand a few lacy things in our undergarment area. Then I want you to head across the street to that shop over there." She pointed out the window at a makeup boutique. "Ask for Sally. She's a friend of mine Tell her that Kendall sent you and she's to hook you up with Inner Diva."

"Inner what?"

"Trust me, it's a lipstick that is bright red with a blue undertone. Perfect for your alabaster skin."

"I think you mean *pasty*."

"Hun, no, no, no. Stop this all right now. This is a No Negative Self-Talk Zone. You've got to be unapologetically your own gorgeous self," she chided.

What a unique idea.

"Remember that you are perfect in every imperfection. Now come take a look at these garter belts."

The muscles in her throat constricted. "Garter belts?" Well, then. It looked as if she was well and truly crawling out of her rut. If she took away her limits, there was no telling how far she could go.

At least one thing was certain: she'd go into this weekend guns blazing.

Tor Gunnar better hang on to his hat.

Chapter Nine

*L*ife could be one fickle bitch. For months Tor had dreaded attending Maddy's wedding, but ever since Neve agreed to be his plus-one, the days had crept by at the pace of a narcoleptic snail. No cure existed for this level of restless agitation, except work. With the lockout showing no signs of letting up, he resorted to taking long, punishing runs along the High Line Canal, but even that lung-busting exercise brought limited relief. Same went for the trips to the racquetball court. His sanity—and body—were taking one hell of a beating.

Speaking of beating—best to ignore the fact that his morning shower routine now included a mandatory jack-off session . . . with a certain dark-eyed sports journalist serving as muse during the grand finale.

But the day had finally arrived. In seven hours, he'd be pulling into Telluride Valley with Neve Angel sitting shotgun.

His head rocked back as he swallowed a groan. This was how Superman must feel when staring down a pile of kryptonite. When it came to trying to squelch his attraction for that woman, he was fucking powerless.

He mulled over the upcoming day's game plan while finishing packing. Not much space would separate them inside his

Porsche—a foot at best. And she'd smell damn good. Fresh-cut grapefruit sprinkled with a pinch of sugar. During those stolen moments back at the Watering Hole last week, he'd breathed in her shampoo's crisp citrus zest. The memory of that scent still clung to him, tangy and addictive. He had to be strong, ready to brace for that sweet assault and the "getting to know you" small talk that rubbed his mind like sandpaper.

Strange how this woman had orbited in his sphere for years, and yet he hardly knew anything about her apart from the byline.

Hockey. The idea shot into his head with lightning-bolt force. *Of course. Yes. Jesus.* It was so obvious. They'd discuss hockey. Neve Angel loved her job. That much was never in doubt. And they shared a love for the game. Their strong work ethic could serve as common ground, except—he frowned—that whole part where her life's work apparently relied on her being a thorn in his side.

Scratch any idea about discussing work and steer to neutral ground. Back to the drawing board. Music made for a good Switzerland, and he owned a shit ton of music. If she was a Springsteen fan, they'd be in business. He owned every track The Boss had ever laid down.

He could crank *Nebraska* or *The River* and hope for the best. Not the wiliest strategy ever devised, but it might cloak the fact he was uncertain on his positioning and plays.

Striding into his walk-in closet, he selected two dress shirts off the hangers, the light blue and a darker navy one. After folding and packing both, he shut the lid to his suitcase. Fuck it, no point stewing. Besides, the drive into the mountains was just the beginning of the adventure. On Sunday afternoon, they'd have to make the return journey, and then there was the matter of the hours between . . . and the two nights in the same hotel.

Although not the same room. He'd share a double-bed suite with his daughter, Olive, while Neve was safely sequestered down the hall. Out of reach. Out of trouble.

He rolled his shoulders and cracked his neck. Separate rooms. Safe. Yes, good. It wasn't like they were going to get naked.

The image of naked Neve appeared unbidden in his mind's eye. Her small body, lithe and sleek, shining like pale moonlight while a feline smile curled the corners of her mouth. It didn't take much brainpower to imagine all the things that might make her purr.

The air in his lungs went as shallow as the water in a kiddie pool. Getting a deep breath was nothing but an exercise in wishful thinking. Rocked by a wave of dizziness, he snapped the suitcase locks shut and braced his hands on top of the lid, taking a moment to regroup.

Note to self: do not picture Neve Angel naked unless wishing to invite a full-scale panic attack.

This lust-filled distraction was unfamiliar territory. He wasn't a guy who lost his shit over a woman. He'd seen this kind of thing happen to other guys but had never gone there in real life. Not even with Maddy.

If he was going to survive the weekend with his sanity intact, he'd need to start using the head located on top of his neck, not just his buddy south of the border.

Although—he chewed his lower lip, pondering—as a purely hypothetical exercise, would the idea of stripping Neve down to her smile send her running for the nearest mountain? He glanced at himself. He wore his usual outfit: polished brown loafers, khakis, navy sweater, and a sport jacket. No woman had seen him naked in a long time—years—but all was in working order.

"Working order?" He spat out the thought. "Jesus Christ, Gunnar." He grabbed his suitcase and stormed out to his garage. He was head coach for a two-time-champion professional hockey team and had no game. What a joke. The world should be his oyster, and here he was, acting allergic to shellfish.

He needed to nut up and calm down. After throwing the suitcase into the Porsche trunk, he climbed behind the wheel and turned on Byways to navigate. Neve had texted him her address this morning without any accompanying "Looking forward to the weekend!" Or even a generic smiley face. Not one single message expressing interest or excitement for the journey ahead.

An auspicious start.

He started the engine and backed out. Sweating about their upcoming proximity was pointless. He'd made his bed, and Neve wouldn't be lying in it, clothed or otherwise. He had forced her into an awkward situation by insisting she serve as his date to his ex's wedding. Not exactly the kind of romantic gesture that made a woman swoon. But there was no going back. No way out of the next forty-eight hours but through.

He idled at a red light. A dead leaf swirled through the air and skimmed across the gleaming black hood. A shadow of doubt darkened his mood. This weekend was only happening due to an impulsive game of air hockey. It wasn't like she *wanted* to come.

But then . . . he'd never forced Neve to take an oath signed in blood and notarized by the devil. She'd lost a friendly bet, and if she didn't want to come, she could have refused. So seeing as she *was* open to coming along for the ride . . . maybe she felt the same spark. Or at least a curious flicker.

Or maybe this was her chance to torment him in some fresh new way. Suspicion gripped him once more.

The ugly truth was that either option was just as likely as the other. He wanted to play with fire, and she was a book of matches. No telling what might burn down between them.

When he reached her town house, she was already waiting outside on the curb, perched on her suitcase beneath a bare oak. Head bent, her face was shielded by an inky curtain of hair. When she raised her head, he sucked in a sharp breath. Here was a face that was impossible to judge at first glance. For too many, a quick glance at Neve might not afford much reward. But for those who made an effort, the payoff was huge.

Her looks weren't easy, nothing fragile or cute on offer. Each of her features was as strong as a shot of whisky, not unlike the woman herself. Truth be told, part of what intoxicated him about her was that intangible air of toughness.

He wasn't a soft, easy man. And she didn't look like she'd break at the first sign of trouble.

"Hey!" She stood, cheeks pink from the crisp air.

"Hello," he said after clearing his throat, trying like hell not to focus on the way the autumn sun reflected off her hair. Instead, he got out and went for her bag; more useful and a hell of a lot easier than making continued eye contact.

"Hey, it's cool. I can get that." She reached for the bag handle.

"I know," he said, not releasing his grip. "But there is this new thing that I'm trying."

She frowned a little, cocking her head. "Which is . . . ?"

"Trying to be nicer," he muttered in a gruff undertone.

That seemed to give her food for thought. "To me or in general?"

Sassy thing. "You, but got to say, Angel, you don't make it easy."

She stared boldly as he picked up the suitcase, refusing to blink first. Her hair was different this morning, down and soft around her face. And her white puffy jacket enhanced her dark hair and red lips—making for an arresting combination of Snow White and Lisbeth Salander from *The Girl with the Dragon Tattoo.*

"You're wearing lipstick," he observed, opening up the passenger door for her.

"So?" Her hand flew up as if to hide the evidence.

She was jumpy as a grasshopper in June. "Simmer down. So nothing." He frowned. What had he said wrong now? "I'm just making a simple observation."

"Yeah right." The faintest trace of a snort.

By the time he'd walked around the front of the car, climbed inside, and jammed his key into the ignition, nervous anticipation filled him to the brim. He had to play this exactly right or he was going to slosh shit over the side and make a mess of everything. "I said something wrong." He waited a second. "What was it?"

"Nothing." She waved one hand before plucking some invisible string from her denim-clad knee, a moment of vulnerability flickering across her face. "At least not technically. I just . . . Gah. It's stupid. But please don't tease me about makeup."

Her surprise admission momentarily stunned him into silence. "I'm not following your train of thought."

"Forget about it," she said, mouth mashing into a hard line. "That's not what I'm asking."

Okay. He didn't speak woman, but something was definitely off. "I wasn't teasing you, Neve." He spoke her name with intention, wanting her to hear him. "Wear lipstick. Or don't. What do I care? You look good either way. But I'm allowed to notice you. Making an observation doesn't necessarily make me an asshole."

She huffed a sigh. "You're right."

She's shy.

The realization caught him by surprise. It was like peeking through a brick wall, and inside was a strange and beautiful garden.

"Hey. Listen up. I've got a proposal." He turned and met her gaze straight on, elbow propped on the console. "What if we declare a truce for the weekend?"

Out of any of the millions of combinations of words he could have uttered, he appeared to have found the ones able to render her speechless. "Truce?" she repeated at last.

"Just until we get back and then you can return to your regularly scheduled loathing."

"I don't loathe you . . ." Her mouth slid into a half grin. "At least not all the time."

"Hey, I get it." He shrugged and started the car, the six-cylinder engine purring like a jungle cat. "For what it's worth, Rovhal means *asshole* in Swedish. I'm third generation. My grandparents were farmers outside Älmhult."

"Sorry, I'm not up to speed on Scandinavian geography."

"In the south, not far from Denmark. Home of the first IKEA store."

"For real?" That got her attention. "What a claim to fame."

"There's a museum."

"What's there?" She grinned. "Displays of flat packs with unfathomable names? Shrines to cheap Swedish meatballs?"

His brow creased. "I never went. My father wasn't one for nostalgia . . . at least not until the end of his life."

"Ah," she said lightly, as if sensing they skated over conversational thin ice. "Well, at least that solves the mystery of Rovhal. I'd wondered." She reached out a hand and when he shook it her palm was warm, her fingers soft, even as her shake was firm. "Nice to officially meet you, Rovhal. Since all is being revealed, mind clueing me in on what the thirty stands for?"

"My lucky number." He didn't release her hand as he made his confession. "That's how old I was when I had my daughter. She's the best thing that's ever happened to me."

"What a . . . lovely thing to say." She blinked in surprise, as if seeing him for the first time. "All right, then. To a truce." Neve glanced to their interlocking fingers and then back up. "At least for the next two days. Telluride or bust."

"Thank you for coming with me," he said quietly. "I . . . didn't want to go alone."

Silence fell. "I won't tell anyone," she said at last, slowly withdrawing her hand. "Or the fact that unlike your alter ego suggests, you aren't a totally awful person. Who knows, I might have just made the discovery of the century. Tor Gunnar might be a good guy."

"I like that level of optimism, Angel."

"Thanks, Coach." But her snort didn't appear unkind. Her gaze was cautious, but also curious.

As if she wondered about him, as much as he wondered about her.

He made good time getting out of the city despite the morning traffic. It didn't take long until he had them cruising southwest on US 285. But it soon became obvious that despite their agreement to a cessation in hostilities, the drive wasn't going to be full of warm fuzzies. Any of his initial strained questions were met with monosyllabic answers.

Time for plan B. Operation Saved by Springsteen. He cranked up the stereo and focused on "Born to Run." But despite the music, an unsettled quiet took root and spread. His heart beat in time to the melody. His shoulders tensed.

He was trying his best and didn't know how to steer them back on track. Neve had hunched in on herself, shoulders stooped. Didn't so much as glance his direction, or even straight ahead. Her hand splayed on the passenger-side window as if she wished she was anywhere else. This was it. His worst nightmare. They drove past deep, dramatic canyons and up along the winding road lined with ghostly aspen. He could barely register the scenery. Hard to focus on anything when his heart was going as cold as the surrounding alpine tundra.

Time to reconcile the truth. Wanting something didn't make it happen. This was a terrible idea, the trip a bust before it even began. As much as it would have sucked to attend Maddy's wedding solo, it was going to suck a magnitude of an order worse to bring along an unwilling guest.

"My ears popped." Neve spoke for the first time in an hour as they crested Monarch Pass. The highest point of the drive.

"Not surprised." He cleared his throat, his voice rough with pent-up tension. "We're at 11,312 feet."

His sharp answer got her attention. She turned to face him dead-on. "How do you know that so precisely?"

He forced a tight smile and pointed at the road sign. "I can read."

MONARCH PASS: 11,312 FEET. CONTINENTAL DIVIDE.

"Oh." She put her hands on her cheeks and rubbed slow circles under both eyes. "Sorry. I'm a little out of it."

"Is the altitude bothering you? We'll start dropping now all the way into Gunnison, but Telluride still sits at close to nine thousand." He slowed, dropping into third with a slight frown. He'd been so in his head that he hadn't stopped to study her. Now that he did, she didn't look all that good. She was always pale, but her coloring seemed off, almost gray.

She made a sound that might be a grunt of "Don't worry about it" but could also be a soft moan.

Shit. Something *was* wrong.

He pulled into the empty parking lot for a scenic mountain tram—closed for the winter—and yanked the hand brake. "What's up? You're not feeling okay, are you?" Once they got to Telluride, he could take her to the clinic and get her a prescription written for an oxygen concentrator. Most Colorado ski towns had rental companies as altitude sickness was so common for visitors.

"I'm not too hot." She mashed her lips. "It's cold out but mind if I open the window? At least for a moment. See if that helps settle my stomach?"

"You're carsick?" Everything fell into place. The strained silence. Her rigid posture. "Why didn't you say anything? I would have pulled over." He'd been torturing her for hours without the first clue what was wrong. He'd been so fixated by his worst fears that he hadn't considered the most reasonable solution. Relief and frustration hit him in equal measure.

"It always happens. Since I was a kid. Breezy used to call me Nauseous Neve whenever we had to drive more than a half hour. I didn't want to make a big deal about it to you. I dosed with some motion sickness meds before leaving. They are making me woozy but otherwise that's about it."

His chest thawed. "Is that why you haven't been talking."

"Yup." Her laugh was queasy. "What's your excuse?"

He thought it over and decided to go with honesty. "Social awkwardness."

She grimaced or smiled. Hard to tell under the conditions.

He felt like the biggest dumbshit. She had been sick on his watch and he'd had his head implanted straight up his ass. The urge to fix the situation took over. He'd do better, starting now. "I've got more water in the back."

He went to the trunk, opened a small cooler and grabbed her a bottle, plus the sandwiches that he'd made last night when insomnia made sleep impossible. He grabbed an armload of supplies and got back inside the Porsche.

She stared at the sandwich after he handed one over.

"What is this?" The cellophane baggie crackled between her fingers.

"Nothing fancy. Just plain turkey and cheese." He hesitated. "You aren't a vegetarian, are you?"

"No . . . I just . . ." She blinked. "You made me a sandwich?"

"Is that bad?" Why was she looking at him as if he'd just sprouted horns? All he'd done was take some sourdough bread, slap down turkey and Kraft, smear a little mayo.

She glanced to the sandwich and then back up at him.

"It's . . . unexpectedly cute. Tor Gunnar made me a turkey sandwich."

"Cute?" He didn't know what she was so impressed by, but not going to lie, he liked the fact he'd scored a win. "Got to say, I'm not used to hearing those words directed at me, especially from you."

"Trust me, I'm not used to thinking them." She fiddled with her seat belt, studying the panoramic mountain scenery, and sighed. "This place really is out-of-control beautiful. I need to get out more."

Tor was undeterred by her attempt to deflect and change the subject. "I thought you weren't talking to me because you had second thoughts."

"Look." She glanced over with an uncertain expression. "Let's promise each other one thing, okay? In addition to a truce."

"I'm all ears," he said gruffly.

"There is enough crap in the world without us shoveling more on the pile, don't you think?" The wind blowing in through the cracked-open windows was cold. There was already a few inches of snow dusting the ground even though it had been a drier autumn.

Her coloring improved and she managed a few bites of the sandwich. "You going to answer?" she asked, covering a hand over her mouth, half-filled with food. "Or sit and stare?"

It was damn hard to give words to his truth, to let down his guard and speak from the heart. That he liked this feeling he got watching her eat his simple food. It was nice to feel like he was taking care of her in some small way. "You're right. I'm just glad that you feel better. No crap."

"Good. And can we discuss the magical Tor-turkey-sandwich carsick cure?" Her face softened into a rueful smile. "You could infomercial this. It's amazing how much better I feel. No offense, but I wouldn't have thought this would work in a million years."

"Sometimes magic happens in unlikely places." And from the startled glance she cast him, he knew they were talking about more than unusual home remedies.

THE ADELINE WAS a redbrick boutique hotel nestled in the heart of Telluride's picturesquely historic downtown. Neve took a moment to soak in the updated but undeniably Old West vibe—John Wayne meets modern-day luxury. It was a hundred-year-old brothel given a fashionable new life.

"Let's get our rooms. Let you rest for a bit," Tor said as they walked into the lobby, a cozy and inviting space with pressed-tin ceilings and stuffed leather sofas.

Since Monarch Pass he'd been gravely solicitous, ensuring the windows were cracked and making frequent stops at various scenic pullouts. He might have a hard outer shell, but she couldn't help but wonder what softness hid behind that tough exterior. Just because he wasn't loquacious didn't mean he didn't communicate. As the hours passed she'd found herself becoming more attuned to the little things, the nuanced expressions on his face when he glanced her way or when a certain song came on. His little quirks and gestures that showed he enjoyed her presence.

Or at least didn't actively dislike it.

It was strange, and disorienting, drawing closer to this standoffish man, breathing in the same air, inhaling the faint cedar and pine undernotes from his aftershave, wondering if maybe she didn't know him at all.

He'd Mr. Darcy–dissed her in the stadium parking lot, but maybe she was Elizabeth Bennet–ing him with all her preju- dice. There was so much toxic masculinity in the world that sometimes it was hard to remember that good guys existed.

"Daddy! Daddy! You're here!" A cry cut through the lobby chatter as a wiry girl with braces sprinted across the room and leapt into his arms. She was in that ephemeral stage between child and teen, but one glance at her ice-blue eyes and blond hair made it obvious whose child she was.

Tor's face transformed into an expression Neve had never seen. Complete happiness.

"Hey, baby girl," he said, then spun his daughter around twice and planted a quick kiss on her forehead. "You beat us. I didn't think you were arriving until dinner."

She giggled, adjusting her braid. "I rode up in Aunt Amber's minivan. She said that I can sleep with Lane and Paige. Can I, please? They have connecting rooms with a door to Aunt Amber."

"Your cousins?" He frowned with mock severity. "You sure you won't just be awake talking all night? Remember the last time they came over to my house?"

She was the picture of innocence. "What? It was fine."

"There was that incident with the marshmallows. And the microwave. And the—"

"Pleeeeeeease, pleeeeeeeeasee. We'll be good this time." Olive broke off from her begging to take stock of Neve stand- ing beside him.

"Oh. Hi." Her smile broadened. "You're Neve? He said you had bangs. I like them."

"Uh, yeah," she responded, thrown off balance by the same blue eyes that haunted her dreams in a smaller, perky face.

Of course, Tor must have told his daughter she was coming, but she had been so wrapped up in what this trip meant for her that she hadn't fully thought through what it would be like for *him*. The fact that this crowd was made up of people from his life, and he was giving her a backstage pass into what made him tick. For all his mistrust of the press, that was a big gesture.

The evidence was mounting that Tor had no sinister agenda. And the biggest scoop of a story might be that he liked her.

A feeling vibrated through her chest like thunder.

He might like her a lot.

Olive wrapped her arm around Tor's waist and leaned into him, assessing her with an appraising look Neve knew all too well. "Daddy told me all about you."

"Did he, now?" Neve was used to hearing Tor Gunnar called Coach, of course, and less savory things—mostly insults muttered under her own breath—but to hear his daughter speak of him with such bright affection gave her pause.

When he glanced down at his daughter, there was nothing reserved in his face. He looked like any amused father who was slightly skeptical about what his precocious child might say next.

"I *will* be good." Olive shot her father a quick mischievous look. "He made me promise to go easy on you."

"Is that a fact?" Neve placed a hand on one hip. She had limited experience dealing with children and didn't want to make a misstep.

"I ask a lot of questions."

"Me too, as long as it's a day ending in *y*," Neve answered. At least they had something in common. "I look forward to your interrogations."

"Sounds good." Olive laughed, turning back to Tor and batting her lashes. "But, Daddy, seriously, can I share a hotel room with my cousins? I've never done it and I am bigger and I will be good. Please, please, please? I'm dying to. Dying, I say."

"Let's go have a word with your aunt. I'll be right back." He gave Neve a curt nod. "If you'll excuse us a moment."

"By all means." Neve gaped as Tor walked over to a gorgeous blonde who was drinking a glass of wine by the roaring fire. While it was fascinating to glean insight into Tor's life, she was also going to smack into his past. A past that was striding into the lobby in a pair of impossibly elegant heeled winter boots and with a delicate heart-shaped face framed by lustrous blond hair that would make Rapunzel weep.

Neve remembered her face from the article she'd written on his divorce, one of her first at the *Age*.

Maddy gave Tor a stiff embrace, air-kissing both of his cheeks. Neve chewed the inside of her lower lip. He'd been married to an air-kisser?

The beautiful woman spoke with animation, twin lines of concern creasing her high, smooth forehead, and as if on some unspoken cue, they both spun and stared in her direction. Neve tried not to grimace. She was so busted, she couldn't even pretend to be inspecting the large Thanksgiving-themed cornucopia on the mantel.

It was obvious she'd been taking in every word.

"Neve?" Impossibly marvelous Maddy took off like an elegant rocket, speeding in her direction. "Hello," she said in a breathy, sleepy voice, as if she'd just woken up from a delicious nap. "Wonderful to meet you. I'm Maddy, Tor's . . . well . . . the bride. Look, there has been just a teensy, tiny mix-up. The hotel is overbooked and when I saw Tor had reserved the extra room, I assumed it was a mistake. My great-aunt Agnes has settled into what was evidently supposed to be your room and she's ninety-one and . . ." She threw up her hands in a frazzled gesture. "For Pete's sakes. You know what they say about assuming . . ."

"No! N-No, it's fine. You must have a million and one things to think about. Don't give me a second thought," Neve stammered. "Let's leave Aunt Agnes right where she is."

Brave words as her stomach lurched.

She and Tor Gunnar were going to be sharing a hotel room alone for an entire weekend. And she had a suitcase packed with very new and very, very tiny French lingerie.

Chapter Ten

$\mathcal{N}$ice bed, emphasis on the singular," Neve deadpanned, dropping her suitcase onto the hardwood floor with a dull thud. The impact echoed the crash of his heart against his rib cage.

The room was a blend of rustic and modern. The stuffed chair by the window looked like an inviting place to curl up with a book, while the framed photographs of wildflowers gave the room a touch of feminine whimsy. But there was no denying the space was dominated by the pine-framed king-sized bed.

Perfect for sprawling like a starfish and taking a long winter's nap.

Or trying to medal in the Sexual World Championships.

His mouth filled with invisible sand, going drier than the Sahara. It was impossible to look anywhere else. Was Neve really going to crawl up onto that giant mattress, her body next to his? He blazed so hot it was a wonder he didn't turn to flame. He set his own bag by the dresser, half expecting to see smoke rippling off the back of his hand.

The light-canceling drapes were long and dark, and he flung them open, needing head space.

"Wow. There's a sight," Neve whispered.

Above them rose the soaring mountains that framed the valley's box canyon, snow blanketing the rust-colored peaks, aspen forests devoid of leaves, gleaming like bone. A frozen waterfall hung suspended off a cliff. Maybe, just maybe, an avalanche would trigger right now and extinguish this mad hope.

"Another mistake. There were supposed to be two beds," he said stiffly before she could accuse him of masterminding a hookup. It had been a while, but he'd never press his advantage.

"I'm not great at math but . . ."

"Shit." His mouth dried at her teasing tone and he spun around, defensively raking a hand through his hair. "I feel like I brought you into a mess. First the shared room, now . . . this . . ." He waved his hand at the thick mattress that looked capable of handling the urgent thrusts of even the longest dry spell.

She didn't look over. Frown lines bracketed her mouth as she reached out and touched the comforter as if it were dangerous. "Well, I'll tell you what. After that drive, we need a drink and a nap."

"I never nap."

"Neither do I." She shrugged off his glare. "But you just drove seven hours. And I spent six of them feeling fifty shades of warmed-over death. So I don't want to stress over Bedgate. I do want to pop open that minibar, treat myself to a stiff drink, and pass out until I wake up feeling vaguely human."

"A plan that I can get behind. Two highballs coming right up." He leapt into action and opened the fridge, peering inside. "Vodka. Check. Ginger ale. Check. We can pretend it's a Moscow Mule."

"It could be a Moscow Donkey Surprise and I'd be perfectly content."

"You're on." It was exactly what he needed, a task. There were two tumblers on the desk. "I'll show you a trick I learned on the road. Hold on a second." After scooping them up, he went into the hallway, filled them with ice cubes from the closest machine, and came back in. Neve sat on the edge of the bed, legs dangling, feet not quite touching the ground.

Her smallness intrigued him. It would be so easy to toss her against those goose-down-stuffed pillows, open her up, and let her ankles dig into his shoulders while he drove in hard.

The easiest and hardest thing in the world.

The image of her perfect breasts arching up to meet his hungry mouth redirected a wave of blood to his cock. Before she could notice his hard-on, he strode into the bathroom, seeking out two smaller drinking glasses to finish the task at hand. *Focus.*

"You've got me all curious with this fancy-schmancy prep," Neve announced as he came back.

"Nothing but the best for you."

She mashed her lips, gaze riveted to his face. "Who are you and what happened to Tor Gunnar?"

"What do you mean?"

"If I looked up *charming* in the dictionary right now, your face might be staring back. I'm getting a glimmer of Rovhal30 with the daily jokes. Which were corny as a Kansas farmer, by the way." A beat. "And I meant that as a compliment."

He dropped his chin and poured the ginger ale into the vodka, trying not to fizz everywhere. Even though he had a hundred reasons not to smile, she gave him one.

When he placed the smaller glasses on top of the large tumblers, Neve gasped.

"Poor man's cocktail shaker," he confirmed. "Necessity is

the mother of invention. And I'm on the road enough that I had to get creative."

"You must miss it, right?" she asked as he mixed their drinks. "Your job? The games? The players? That road? The last two weeks must have felt strange. To put so much buildup and preparation in for a season, get started, and . . . poof."

"I miss it every second of every day," he admitted, but didn't let on the whole truth. He loved his job. He made no apologics for the fact that his work was his life. His passion. But whereas the lockout should be an exercise in torture, it hadn't been as bad as he'd expected. He'd had a distraction. *Her.* "Try this." He cleared his throat and passed her the glass.

"Yup. This'll do nicely—delicious," she said after a small sip, kicking off her snow boots to reveal a pair of brightly colored socks.

Socks that were . . .

"Yeah baby, feast your eyes." She noticed his gawking and smirked. "Rainbow-shitting unicorns."

"On your feet," he deadpanned.

"Socks are one of my weaknesses." She clicked her heels. "These happen to be my favorite pair."

He took a long swallow of his own drink, shoulders dropping. "I don't know what to say about that."

She stared down at her feet, turning them left and right. "We are all allowed to have a vice. Quirky socks are mine."

They cheers'd to that.

"What's your guilty pleasure?" she asked in a mock-conspiratorial tone.

"Dark-haired journalists who bust my balls."

"Hah, I wouldn't quit your day job for stand-up comedy just yet," Neve said after a short silence. After another sip, she set her glass on the nightstand, drew back the comforter, and burrowed underneath. "Oy. What a day."

He tensed. "What are you doing?"

"What's it look like I'm doing? It's nap o'clock. You're . . . uh, well . . . welcome to join the party if you don't mind dimming the light."

Tor crossed the room and tugged the blinds back shut. The world disappeared and he was alone in an alternate universe comprised solely of a big bed and Neve Angel.

Chapter Eleven

A cool lick of air brushed Neve's cheek as she stirred awake. The floor creaked and creaked again as if someone stealthily tiptoed across the old floorboards. But it couldn't be Tor because he was here. Right here. A shiver ran up her spine before she slit one eye open. Her goose bumps were caused less from unease and more from something warm and molten.

Cheese and rice, how long had she been getting her cuddle on with Tor Gunnar? He was sprawled on his back, his face more relaxed than she'd ever seen in waking. In sleep, her own hand had found its way to his chest and currently rested over his heart, her head nestled in the crook of his shoulder. His blond spikes were mussed on top. And there was the matter of the tiny mole dotting the left side of his bottom lip.

She'd never noticed that mark, had never trusted herself to stare long enough to register all the little details in his face. To do so would be like staring straight into the sun. Even now, if she closed her eyes, this image, his face in repose, was probably seared on her retinas for all time.

"I'm not drooling, am I?" he rumbled. Not opening an eye.

"No. No." She moved to draw back her hand and crawl to safer territory on her side of the giant bed. At the very least she should apologize for being all over him like a human barnacle.

Instead, he took her wrist and stopped her retreat, then slid his hand down until their fingers laced.

They were quiet, in bed and holding hands as if it were the most natural thing in the world, as if beyond the drawn curtains a world didn't exist that was black-and-white, where he wasn't a head coach and she wasn't the tough-as-nails reporter.

"You're an octopus when you sleep," he murmured. "An octopus genetically mutated with a honey badger."

"It's a bad habit." Her nose wrinkled in embarrassment. "Breezy used to hate sharing a bed with me when we were younger. It's annoying."

"Not to me." His Adam's apple rose in a heavy bob.

She lay on her hip, her thigh casually slung over his waist. The evidence of just how much he didn't mind her unexpected cuddling bored into her inner thigh.

His body went rigid as if he registered the hard-on at the exact same moment that she did.

"Neve." He cleared his throat. "I don't want to make this weird."

"Too late." She dared wriggle a fraction closer. "Don't tell anyone but . . . I think we're mutually weird."

"Speak for yourself." He squeezed her hand and finally opened one eye. His pupil was large and dilated in the room's shadows. "You talk in your sleep."

"Sometimes." Her cheeks heated. "I didn't say anything terrible, did I?"

"My name."

Shit a brick. She could never remember her dreams. Hopefully, she didn't tack on anything dirty.

"But then you said, 'Hold the pickles.' So I don't know how to take that."

"Pickles?" Her mouth twitched. "Maybe you were making me another sandwich."

A chuckle rumbled deep in the back of his throat. "Flattering."

"Hey, it was a pretty darn good sandwich."

He opened his other eye, and the force of his stare was seismic. Something shook her deep inside, setting off a core chain reaction that left her flushed and aching.

He mashed his lips before speaking. "I've been meaning to clear the air. I shouldn't have kissed you in the bathroom the other day at the Watering Hole."

She blinked as his words registered, her stomach flipping over. Her free hand slid to the edge of the comforter as the urge swept through her to duck and take cover. Here she was, so lost in this helpless wanting, her sensitive underbelly on full display. And he was about to let her down, remind her that she didn't tempt him, that she never could—

"Because I've been thinking about that kiss for a hell of a long time and it might have deserved a more upscale location."

She swiped her top lip with the tip of her tongue. "Well, you didn't hear it from me, but kissing burns six calories a minute. And I didn't get any exercise on the car ride."

His gaze darkened, tracing the shape of her mouth with such intense heat that it was a surprise her skin didn't respond with a sizzling hiss. "The thing is, see, my thoughts never ended with just one kiss. I kept going. Tasting you . . . everywhere."

Her nipples strained against her bra, volunteering as trib-

ute. "All right, Mr. Big Talk. Are you going to show me or am
I going to have to go home and lie in my diary?"

"That all depends," he rumbled.

"On?" She was afraid to move, to breathe, to jinx the magic.

"Whether you want me to."

Her core clenched.

"I want my mouth on every inch of that gorgeous body. But
if I do that, I'm taking my time, doing it right until you scream
my name. But I won't lift a finger unless you beg."

"A finger?" She pretended to think it over, like the scrap of
lace masquerading as panties beneath her jeans hadn't melted
into a puddle. "If I'm going to be brought to my knees, I'll expect more than one finger, just FYI."

For a guy who had a reputation for being so cool, he had a
heck of a smolder. "I can see about that." She didn't see him
move, yet he was closer. "Go on." Closer still. His sexy-as-sin
smile left her salivating. "Ask nicely."

"No." She leaned in and bit the corner of his lower lip.
"Nothing about this is going to be nice."

When they came together, it was like there'd never been
any distance to close, like they'd never done anything else
in their lives. Her mouth felt as if it had been made just for
him. His lips fit against hers perfectly. When he coaxed, she
opened and his tongue slid against hers, the heat of the kiss
surging to the tips of her toes. She put her whole body into
the answer. Her arms wrapped around his neck, his muscles bunching and cording beneath her fingers. He grabbed
her hips and rolled her on top. The hard length of his cock
drilled into her lower belly as he grabbed her ass and pressed
her down hard.

This wasn't soft.

This wasn't romantic.

It was clawing. Savage. And fucking amazing.

His fingers worked their way up to the waist of her jeans and, dipping under, he paused.

"This is interesting." His light snap of her panties' elastic waistband made her gasp.

"And very tiny," she teased.

His swallow was audible.

His hands migrated to her front, and with a quick button pop and zipper grind, her jeans came down. She kicked them off her ankles.

"Sit up. I want to see you." His voice was deeper and rougher than she'd ever heard.

"Has anyone ever said that you are bossy?"

"Mostly you. I think you like it though." He brushed his thumb along the seam of her pussy, encased in the pale pink silk, scorching her with his possessive gaze. "Not going to lie, it seems as if you like it. A lot."

She was so wet that the material skimmed over her, his touch the lightest whisper of pressure against her clit. Her hands balled into fists and her head rocked back.

"Good?"

"Not bad," she gasped.

"Still sassy." He eased one finger inside her underwear, and inside her.

Good lord, she could hear it, the soft sucking sound of her own arousal. Her muscles tensed in expectation.

"You wanted more than a finger, right?" He joined it with another. That was good. Perfect, really. Enough that she felt full without being too stretched. His eyes glittered.

"Yes," she gasped.

"Fuck, Neve." He trembled. She felt it right there, at the core of herself, at the center of everything. He crooked the fingers up in a come-hither gesture and her body bowed.

"Take off your shirt," he crooned.

She raised her brows, even as her hips began to rock as if of their own volition. "You first."

"Now who's bossy?"

"The way I see it, two can play at this game."

"Fair enough." He had to pull his hand free. She hadn't thought it through, because that was the last thing she wanted.

He raised those fingers that had just been buried inside her to his mouth and slid them inside. "You taste better than I imagined," he rumbled. "And believe me. I imagined."

It was so sexy and filthy that she almost came from his words alone.

But then he unbuttoned his shirt and she forgot everything. How to breathe. Her own name. Sliding her hands down, she parted his shirt to reveal a smooth chest, a light dusting of hair framing each nipple. His chest was broad and his abs weren't individually defined but flat and lean.

She circled his navel. Here it was—definitive proof he was a man, not a god. But good lord, he was beautifully made. She bent and licked the center of his chest, savoring the muscle with the flat of her tongue.

He frowned like thunder, a faint sheen of sweat at his temples. "Keep that up and you'll be in trouble."

"Good." She licked again. "I like your version of trouble."

It wasn't clear who undressed who. Clothes came off in short order. It wasn't until she went to slip out of her pale underwear that he stopped her. "No. Not those. Those I need to enjoy a little while longer. Then I'm going to rip them off with my teeth."

She clenched her inner muscles and dropped her gaze to his boxer briefs, the erection straining the black cotton. "I can't say the feeling is mutual." She wanted him bare, Tor Gunnar in the flesh, and for her pleasure. A tug of the waistband and she had him exposed in all his glorious thick inches.

He was rock hard.

She did that to him.

He sucked in so sharply that his lower ribs stood in sharp relief. In her time working in the Hellions locker room, she'd seen many specimens of the perfect male form, in all their hard, chiseled, athletic glory.

But Tor, he managed to exude brute strength and arrogant confidence just by breathing. And yet stripped down, there was a whisper of vulnerability. Not embarrassment, just a sense that he was offering himself up, exposing more than just his body. He was the definition of a closed book and now here he was, cracking the cover and giving her a peek at who he was beneath.

She wasn't sure what to make of it, but was certain of one fact: good God, he was perfect. Cut and long. He was rock hard and it was all for her. She didn't feel like an ugly duckling. She didn't even feel like a beautiful swan. The predatory hunger in his wolfish gaze made her feel like a sex kitten, ready to purr, to arch, to drag her claws down his back and mark her territory.

"I love you looking at me like that," he murmured in a low, intense voice.

"Then you're going to adore me after I do this." She moved

to lick his shaft but he pushed down on her shoulders, halting her mouth, mere inches away from her desired target.

"Damn it. No," he rasped, even as his eyes were glazed and eager. His chest—sheeted in sweat—rose and fell in uneven breaths.

"You don't want me to?"

"Not yet." His headshake was short but definite. "I want to take my time with *you*. You touch me the way I am right now and it's going to be over too soon. Not going to lie, it's been a while for me."

"Same." She gave a frustrated laugh. "Look at us, arguing over oral."

A flicker of provocative mischief crossed his face as he reached down and lifted her chin, drawing her away. "There is one solution. A win-win."

She gave his gorgeous cock a longing glance. "I'm all ears." A bead of precum gleamed from the tip, refracting light like a diamond.

"How are you at multitasking?"

"I'm a woman." She furrowed her brow, unsure where he was going with this. "It's sort of our specialty."

"Then how about flipping over. I want to lick your sweet pussy while my cock's halfway down your throat."

Whoa.

Of all the things that could happen when Tor's ice-cold veneer melted, this was more than she'd dared hoped to discover.

He didn't treat her like something fragile or delicate. Far from it. He seemed to know exactly what she wanted—to use and be used in return.

Her thighs pressed together on instinct, the slick caress of her panties almost too much sensation against her mound.

"Go on." He nudged her, his gaze more wicked by the moment. "I promise I'll make it worth your while. You're going to come while I fuck that pretty face."

He knew what he was doing. Oh, this man knew exactly what sort of effect his dominance had on her. She wanted him to take her in every position he could think of. But she paused halfway through her pivot, trying to process what was about to happen.

Intensity and hesitation warred within.

"Neve." His voice seemed to ache with the same need gripping her, squeezing at her center, throbbing through her thighs.

"I . . . I feel sort of shy?" She was acutely aware of just how small her underwear was and the fabric was more or less see-through given her wetness.

"You just tore off my pants."

"Hey. I'm allowed these feelings."

"Right now you're only allowed to be one thing." She felt the force of his gaze like a tantalizing caress.

"Illuminate me." Her voice was faint.

"Hungry for my cock."

Blue stars exploded on the edge of her vision.

That was it. He won all the dirty talk forever. She couldn't beat his mastery, but needed to regain some power. Some foothold here in the bedroom. He wanted to be dominant, that was fine. She was here for it.

But if she was going down, she'd bring him to his knees.

Crawling up, she spread her legs over his face, her knees pressing into his broad shoulders.

She expected him to slide her panties to the side and feast. That was what she'd mentally prepared for. Instead, he stared, stroking the ledge of her panties leg elastic until she was almost begging him for relief. Then slowly, oh, so slowly, he slid a finger under the thin, soaking fabric and hissed a breath.

"Good lord." It sounded like he had to force the words out. "Do you always get this wet?"

Her ears turned pink. The room was so quiet that she could actually hear herself as he stroked her.

"You smell incredible," he growled. "And I already know you taste even better." And then he was there, driving his tongue straight into the center of her slick, tight pussy.

Her mouth opened in a silent scream, and she let her lips close around his shaft. He tasted like clean, warm skin with a faint trace of salt. She circled her tongue around his smooth head and the tangy flavor intensified, as did the shuddering in his muscles.

She'd never done this, never worked over a guy's shaft while he brought her the same pleasure. She gripped his hard thighs, back arching, as the connection thrummed between them. When she took him down all the way to his root and held him there, pressed against the back of her throat, she relaxed the muscles so she could accommodate his last impressive inch while grinding down on his hungry mouth. True to his word, he fell on her like a starving man and she twisted and turned her hips, grinding over his face with so much greed that she'd be embarrassed if she wasn't so needy.

He groaned and she felt the sensations all the way to her core.

Her heart thundered and then he was there, nipping at her clit, setting a slow, fluttering pace that was gentle and yet increased in pleasure. She bobbed her head, gripping him at the base. He was big enough that it took all her focus to ease him down her throat, and yet she couldn't concentrate. She braced her hands on the mattress, her fingers digging into the sheets.

The sound that came out of her was so bare, so exposed and needy. It was a cry of near want. A mewl. She'd never believed she was able to make such a helpless sound. He hooked three fingers inside her. Crooking his fingers, he pressed hard. She didn't just see stars but the origins of the entire universe and the forever blackness that preceded everything. And she made that sound again and again.

She was coming. The force of it slammed her head down on him, and she felt his legs tense as his cock throbbed. He was there too. And she'd brought him to that point.

He lunged his tongue down straight into her contracting pussy and that decided it. She'd never swallowed. Never wanted to with another guy. But her brain must be blown because she reached down, skimmed his sac with the bottom of her finger, and he lost himself.

"Fuck," he groaned. "Fuck. Holy fucking shit."

She took it all, loving every second. Shudders racked them. Their bewildered cries vibrated into their most secret skin. All she knew for certain was that she had one hell of an unfolding crisis on her hands. Because while Tor Gunnar might be infuriating, he was also completely irresistible.

Chapter Twelve

Sorry there, Mr. Pie, I want cake," Neve rambled in a husky voice.

Tor choked down a laugh. Good one. She'd woken him a half hour ago with more sleep talking, most of it unintelligible gibberish, but some lines were pure gold:

Into the dungeon!

Is it shank *or* shark? *Never mind, he had it coming.*

Gray dawn light seeped beneath the curtains. He hadn't moved a single muscle, unwilling to break the strange spell spun around the bed, even to taste her soft lips. This moment was good—better than good. The mattress a perfect balance between soft and hard, her naked body spooning into his. When was the last time he'd felt this relaxed in his own skin, this peaceful—

"You have to die," she announced drowsily, eyes still closed. "But it's okay because it's funny."

Christ. She was something else. His brow wrinkled in amusement as he smoothed a strand of damp hair over her flushed cheek. Maybe not peaceful, but one thing was for certain—being in the company of Neve Angel was anything but dull.

Memories from the night before engulfed him like a rising river, leaving him tossed about and breathless. The lithe weight of her body settling over his torso. The shy way she initially ground into his mouth, tentative at first but more confident and insistent as the need set in. Never had he experienced anything close to the wild urgency that had taken hold. It wasn't as if he'd spent the past twenty years as a meat-and-potatoes missionary man, but he'd never been that uninhibited. The idea of loosening up was as foreign as another language. It was hard to take down walls that he'd built during his childhood.

For the first thirteen years of his life, he'd watched his father systematically abuse his mother. There'd been the time when he was seven and jumped in front of his mom, facing down his drunken father with a scream of rage. *Stop hurting her!* Dad didn't listen. That time he hurt Tor too, took him into the garage and beat welts into his ass with jumper cables. Afterward, his mom made him put his hand on the family Bible and promise to never speak up when his dad drank again, to stay quiet and never *ever* air their family's dirty laundry in public. Not to relatives. Not to teachers. The worst thing a person could do was share their business. And then she got cancer and his old man quit drinking and took up religion, never losing an opportunity to praise his dead wife as the best woman he'd ever known.

Tor frowned darkly. He couldn't find a way to forgive or forget. Dad had ruined his mother's life as a lousy husband. A waterfall of crocodile tears couldn't bring her back. In college the next year, on a hockey scholarship, Tor had declared a major in psychology. He'd never felt easy with other people, and yet, it seemed smart to get a better understanding of the way they ticked. What motivated them. What enraged them. Their hopes. Their dreams.

And he was damn good at the subject, at least when it came to his specialty—sports psychology. But when it came to women, all bets were off. He didn't understand them. But he also knew why. He was afraid to get close to them. He'd lived through his parents' devastated marriage and then his own. He'd learned his lessons from childhood well, too well—suck it up, don't cry, don't feel—and despite every wish to the contrary, had never been able to fully drop his guard. Even with Maddy. Instead, he put his head down, toiled like a caveman hunting water buffalo. And it worked. He had professional success. No one could fault him as a good provider.

But it hadn't been enough. Apparently the old saying was true and money couldn't buy happiness.

Thump.

The noise came from the bathroom.

"Enchilada," Neve mumbled.

The Adeline was an old hotel. It could have been a pipe—hot water kicking on in another room.

Just as he began to turn, ready to wake Neve up with that certain ear-sucking trick that drove her wild last night—*Slam!* The bathroom door banged shut.

He jerked. "What the hell?" He swung his legs out from under the blanket. Feet pounding the floor, he grabbed a towel and slung it around his bare waist. "Olive, honey? Is that you?"

Silence answered.

He walked around the corner. No one was there. He opened the bathroom door and flicked on the light. His own reflection stared back. A bite mark on his chest.

No one was there.

Goose bumps broke out across the base of his neck as he turned to check the windows. All were closed.

"Mmm, what's going on?"

Tor turned around as Neve rubbed two fists, grinding the sleep from her eyes.

"Nothing," he said quickly. Not wanting to look like a Ghostbuster. "Nothing at all. Just checking the weather." He opened the curtains. The peaks were shrouded in iron gray clouds. A few sullen flakes swirled past the window, hit the small balcony, and disappeared. "Might snow later."

"I'm not that big of a cold-weather fan." Her gaze focused on his chest. "I prefer it warmer. Hot even."

It was cute how she checked him out. Her cheeks were a little flushed and her hair looked freshly fucked. They hadn't gone that far and yet . . . he had the unsettling sensation of seeing her more exposed than she'd been last night, writhing and falling apart over his hungry mouth.

"Have I grown horns?" She patted the top of her head in a self-conscious gesture.

"No." He picked up his dead cell phone and plugged it into the charger.

"That's it?" she asked with mock incredulity. "That's the sum total of your reaction? And here I gave you a perfect setup for a *horny* joke. Most guys would have gone for it."

"I'm not most guys."

She nodded. "Ain't that the truth." But she didn't sound like she poked fun. No, she sounded as confused as he felt. "Tor," she said, right as he said, "Neve."

"Ladies first."

"Last night . . ." She hiked the sheets against her chest, hiding the swell of her breasts. "I—look—do we need to talk about what happened last night?"

"You don't sound like you want to?" He was expecting a conversation, to make a game plan to set some ground rules. Neve was the bravest, strongest woman he knew. She faced down his bullshit and called him on it every time. And here she was, wiggling into her lace bra and tiny panties and sliding past him as if she hadn't swallowed him balls deep. As if they were strangers.

"I don't know what to think, let alone what to say. Honestly, I'd rather get up, take a shower, and go for a run."

The room was haunted all right, by all the things going unsaid. He had two choices. Start rebuilding his walls or build a bridge to Neve.

"Want company or is this a solo mission?"

She gave him a double take. "Are you asking to share my shower?"

"The forecast is for a lighter-than-normal snowfall in the Rockies this winter. I figured I'd be proactive with water conservation."

"Is that a fact?"

"Hey. No pressure. But if you're on the fence, I'm an excellent back washer." He kept his tone light even against the weight of her assessing stare. He was putting himself so far out there that the branch he was clinging to might crack and fall at any second.

"Okay," she relented and it was all he could do not to exhale. "But I like a hot shower."

"I like anything that involves steam and you being naked," he said gravely.

She did a double take again and burst out laughing. "I never knew you were funny. I like it."

"I'm being serious." He winked. "Come on, Angel. I'll scrub your back and then you can scrub mine."

The tub was an old claw-foot. They were already barely dressed, so it was short work to drop his towel and step into the warm spray once it hit the proper temperature.

"Fancy meeting you here," Neve said, tilting her head back, eyes closing as the water streamed through her dark hair. He took the opportunity to look his fill. Her areolas were small, the size of a quarter, and pale pink, like the inside of a conch shell. They rose up, puffing out from the smooth mound of each breast, as if little invitations. His mouth watered but he forced self-control, even as his cock heated, rising proud and resistant.

Her hips were narrow, the bones in each one sharp and hard. But her stomach was soft, the faintest hint of a belly, and it fascinated him. He wanted to drop to his knees and kiss her there, then travel lower, settle between her open thighs, and lick her past the point of sanity.

"I know you're staring." She wiped her eyes and glanced down.

"I want you." He spoke plainly, the need for her, to possess her, to make her his if only for a few stolen moments, left him without the ability to tease, flirt, and banter. "But I'll have to go to the store and grab condoms if we're going to go further."

"Did you fail Eagle Scouts?" Her gaze shot to his face. "I thought, like, every guy kept one in his wallet."

"I don't do the whole hookup thing," he admitted. "I haven't been with a woman in a long time."

"*Long* sounds different depending on the person. I knew a guy who considered it a drought if he went longer than two weeks. And I can tell you right now that my dry spell is years. Literally years."

"Same. Seven to be exact."

That got her attention. "Seven years?"

"Since my divorce. I . . . haven't been with another woman like that. Or at all."

"Same. Not the part about being with another woman. I mean seven years. That's where I'm at."

Now it was his turn to be surprised. "But you're so . . . sexy."

"I could say the same for you." She reached out and rested a hand over his heart. "But I am on the pill, have been since sixteen. If you're serious about this whole dry-spell thing, we could, you know . . ."

"You're sure?"

"Let me process." She pressed her hands over her eyes. "I'm considering having sex with Tor Gunnar. It's a lot to take in."

"I hear he's a great lay. And did I mention the charm?"

She dropped her arms to her sides. "If I have one nemesis in this world, it would be you, Mr. Fuck-a-Penguin. But maybe the altitude's getting to me. Because the idea of you inside me is . . ." She broke off, searching for the precise word.

"Nice?"

She made a face. "Puppies are nice. So is chocolate milk. Sex with you would be the reverse of nice." She peered up, nibbling the corner of her lower lip. "Bad in the best of ways."

"We're doing this. You want it?"

"I think . . . yes. I am amenable to having your penis inserted into my vagina."

"Inserted?"

"Injected? Implanted."

Nothing about her jokingly clinical tone should make

him hard, and yet . . . his cock twitched. "Maybe leave the dirty talk to me, babe."

"So how do we start?" Neve's uncertain laugh echoed from the tiles. "It feels like I'm Cinderella getting an erotic offer to the ball."

"I recommend we do a little of this." He closed the distance, then wrapped his arms around her hot, slippery body. His mouth found hers and there was nothing in this kiss but confidence.

For all he didn't know about women—particularly the woman in his arms—he knew he wanted this. And maybe once he was inside her, everything would make sense.

Even though he held her tight, making sure she was completely kissed, her head tilted back as his tongue boldly explored hers. She remained curious. Her hands exploratory and restless. She roamed his lats, grabbing and squeezing as if trying to root out softness. A wild hope flared that maybe he'd finally found a woman he could open up to and risk exposing his secret sensitive underbelly. A woman who was fearless. Who wouldn't run from his demons. Who wouldn't flinch or back down if she saw him for who he was.

"Hurry," she pleaded. "I need—"

"I know exactly what you need," he growled. And the thing was, he did.

He hadn't touched a woman in years. And yet . . . he knew how Neve was going to want him. Not slow and gentle this first time. He flipped her around. "Stick out that sweet ass for me, Angel."

Her gasp was audible but she obliged. He bent and licked and bit the side of her neck until she rocked against him.

Sliding down a hand over her trembling belly, he cupped her pussy, held it in a firm grasp. "This is mine."

She leaned back, her hands pushing off the tile. "If you can earn it."

"Challenge accepted." He wasn't going to pop in a finger or two and rub until it was wet enough for his dick. This was a focused, deliberate campaign. He wasn't going to stop until she'd fallen apart, her smart talk replaced by begging. And that would only be the beginning. He put his dominant hand over her clit, already beginning to swell like a hot pearl. With his left, he slipped a finger inside, just the tip, caressing her inner lips with slow, gentle pumps.

"Do you like it better when I fuck you with two fingers or three?" he murmured in her ear.

"The more the merrier . . ." she panted.

"Greedy." He obliged and she arched, the crease in her ass sliding over his cock, working his shaft in a tight clench.

His fingers were soon covered in her natural lube. He got the best reaction when keeping the pressure right on the rough patch a few inches into her pussy. When he pressed the top of her pubic bone with the heel of his hand, it became more exposed.

"Oh God, oh my God," she groaned. Shudders rolled through her with growing intensity.

He switched over from the light pressure on her clit, drawing back the hood and giving a few quick taps as he pressed harder to her G-spot.

Her head fell back and he leaned in over one shoulder and kissed her hard, let her scream into his mouth, holding up her weight as she collapsed against him. The force of her orgasm broke over his fingers, milking them in waves.

Her lips parted, her eyes glazed. "I've never come that hard in my life."

"That's going to be a short-lived record." He spun her around, grabbed one of her legs, and propped it on the edge of the tub.

If he wasn't in her in another second, he'd lose his damn mind.

"Look down," he ordered. "I want you to watch me take you. There's going to be no doubt who's making you feel so good."

"Tor . . ."

"That's right." He pressed the head of his cock against her. "When you're screaming again, it's going to be my name."

"Okay."

"Promise?"

"Pinky promise. I'll watch. I'll scream. But . . . will you?" Her eyes dared him.

It was a tight fit. She was still clenched from her recent orgasm and he wasn't a small guy. He took his time, rocking his hips in short micropulses.

And she was a woman of her word. What he didn't expect was how watching her slowly become undone would slay him.

"You're so beautiful," he said.

Her eyes shone. "You're the first person to make me believe it."

He tilted up her chin—what he had to say was important and she needed to hear that truth to the marrow of her bones. "This confirms my long-held suspicion." His tone was grave. "The world is mostly made up of idiots." He leaned in and kissed the tip of her nose. "But all the better for me."

He began to move, dissolving into her skin, his hands memorizing the topography of her body as if to mark the path—he was lost. Lost in her. In this slow, sucking grind. The slap of their bellies wasn't subtle. It was the bass note to the song they were writing. Her soft cries, the chorus.

It was hard to keep the rhythm steady. The control he had cared about was gone. He wasn't going to dominate her. The idea was a joke. Because the truth was he could never possess her without losing a part of himself. And he was willing to make the devil's bargain.

His finger dug into the underside of her thigh. He gripped her roughly, trying to keep them balanced while getting them both where they needed to go.

His whole world was wet heat. The shower spray. Neve's pussy. His stomach flexed as the need bore down. He'd never forgotten how good it felt to be in a woman. Maybe that was why he'd resisted for so long. It was his punishment for failing in his marriage.

But Neve already knew he wasn't perfect. Hell. She'd seen him surly and snappish. Cold and calculating. And for some unfathomable reason, she was still here. Maybe she'd hate him again tomorrow. But he sure as hell wasn't ever going to let her regret today.

And close as he was—his sac heavy and tight—he wasn't coming without her. He stepped back. Nearly groaning when his cock slipped free. Before she could ask him a word, he flicked off the shower.

"Come here," he ordered, stepping out of the tub. He grabbed a large plush bath towel, threw it open, and sat on the floor. "Get on top."

She looked at him, sex dazed and pleasure drunk. When she crawled onto him, draping her thighs on either side of his, he fastened his lips to her throat as she slid down, enveloping him. "Ride me rough, Angel."

Her sex clenched as her eyes glittered. No tears this time. Just hot determination.

Tor rubbed slow circles into her perfect ass as she worked her body, using him while giving everything he ever needed.

He cupped her breasts, rolling and tugging her nipples. Steam filled the room from the hot shower, the condensation comingling with their sex. His lower back arched, tilting his pelvis so she could grind her tender flesh right where she needed. A tremor rippled through her, invisible to the outside but stroking his shaft.

He leaned up and sucked her tit, lavishing it with his tongue and gentle nips. He felt her groan in his core, at his goddamn center. He was primed as fuck but wasn't giving an inch until her surrender. Hunger built. Release taunted. Blood roared through his ears. Her teeth closed down on her lower lip as if biting back a scream.

He gripped her hips, white-knuckled. Her ass bounced on his thighs.

"I need," she gasped. "I need . . . I need . . ." She shook her head as if to clear it. "I just *need.*"

"I know, Angel." He breathed as hard as she did. "I know."

Her gaze never left his. An undefinable sense of rightness bore down. They were at the edge of a precipice.

When her pussy spasmed, he muffled a groan. She thrashed, bucking, riding him harder than cowboys in the spaghetti Westerns he'd watch as a child. Her thighs convulsed. His abs tightened.

This need for her was a drug. Heady and obsessive. Intoxicating.

She was close. So close. A strand in his threadbare self-control snapped.

"Come," he ordered. His tone hard with the command. "Come for me."

Her hands flew up and dug into his hair.

He quickened the roll of his hips. "Let go. I've got you."

Her whole body jerked. With a throaty gasp, she froze into place, the stillness deceptive because inside she was clenching, her orgasm rolling over his cock from root to tip in an undulating, silken wave.

And then he was there too. Pleasure exploded from him in thick, hot pulses. On and on it went, wringing him dry, demanding nothing less than complete surrender. How many times had they warred with each other? And at last they'd found a battle they could both win.

She fell against him, utterly sated.

He didn't ask her how it was, because he already knew. That was just the single most goddamn explosive sexual event west of the Mississippi. He rubbed slow circles into her back and time turned abstract. At last he nudged her. "Hey."

"Hi." She looked over at him with a sleepy smile.

"How about I draw you a bath, get you cleaned up?" He smoothed back her hair.

She gave a dazed nod.

He moved into action and it didn't take long until the claw-foot tub brimmed with hot water and lemongrass-scented bubbles. After picking her up and cradling her in his arms, he lowered her into the tub. She let out a soft hiss as the warm water enveloped her body.

"I feel like I don't have a bone in my body." Her eyes remained closed.

He picked up a washcloth and dipped it into the bath, soaking it. Moving it over her body, he cleaned her with gentle caresses. No words were spoken. It wasn't that he didn't know what to say but that words simply didn't matter. All that did was this simple act of caring. With every touch, he worshipped her body and what had just transpired.

"I need to be honest about something," he murmured.

Her eyelids cracked. "You've got my attention."

"When I invited you to come to Telluride, deep down, I wanted this to happen." He took a deep breath. "I wanted us to happen. I know it's risky for you. For me. But I wanted a weekend. Just one to remember."

A frown tugged her pretty mouth. "You've never been straight with me about something." She sat up, bubbles clinging to her breasts, covering her nipples. "The night the lockout was announced. Why did you say all those terrible things in the parking lot?"

The pain in her eyes twisted his gut.

"Because the world doesn't get to know the secrets of my heart." He reached out to take her hand and give it a gentle squeeze. "But that night was a mistake. I panicked and lashed out. When I saw the other reporters, I didn't want them to think something was going on. That wouldn't be good for either of us."

"Not going to lie. It sucked. But you're right about one thing. There's a lot of risk here. I cover your team. I can't exactly *be* with you and pretend to be fair and balanced."

He pushed back a lock of hair from her cheek. "You could cover football. The NFL has a lot going for it."

"That better be a joke."

"I see, you prefer ice sports. What about curling?" He tickled behind her ear. "That's cool."

"You have some sort of a death wish, huh, wise guy?"

He sucked the lobe of her ear just long enough to make her gasp. "Just wanted to see that pretty smile again."

But her answering grin didn't reach all the way to her eyes. "My kind of job doesn't just spring into being. I had to bust my ass to get where I am. Sports journalism isn't a field rolling out the red carpet for a woman. Being here, with you, having, you know . . . *sex*? That's complicated. I'm not saying I didn't enjoy it. I'm not saying that."

"Why did you come? I know it wasn't for the bet, at least not alone. You could have found an excuse."

"I'm curious. I guess I—"

A phone rang in the other room.

Chapter Thirteen

What the heck does Scott Miller want? Neve glanced at her phone. Her pain-in-the-butt editor had called three times in as many minutes, disrupting her bath. She took a deep breath. *Look on the bright side.* While annoying, maybe this call was the adult version of getting saved by the bell. She'd had her fantasy fun—time to get a taste of reality.

She stared at the screen, debating whether or not to hit Answer. Hard to switch gears when she'd just spent the past twelve hours getting up close and personal with the head coach's baby maker. Right now he was in the bathroom brushing his teeth. She could hear the scrub of bristles against his enamel. A spit. The sound of the faucet turning on as he rinsed his mouth.

She flicked off the screen and ran her fingers through her hair.

How was this happening?

She understood the concept of hate fucking. After all, love and hate were opposites, so a certain magnetic attraction made sense given the right circumstances. And Tor was sexy. It was an objective fact. Like the sky was blue. Or sucking hard candies was pretty much drinking flavored spit.

What she had done with Tor could be called many different things.

Passionate.

Tender.

Sweet.

IntensemindblowingcanIlockthehotelroomdoorandspendthenexttwodaysdoingitanddoingitanddoingitwell?

But it wasn't hate sex. It wasn't quick and dirty in some broom closet in the bowels of the stadium. She'd gone on vacation with him. There could be no slinking away into the shadows thinking, *Good lord, that was incredible, and not only can it never happen again, no one can know.*

Who knew what Scott was calling about, but she'd call him back downstairs, outside, before they went on the valley run.

Speaking of a run, she slipped on her tennis shoes, lacing them up as Tor came out of the bathroom.

His running pants clung to his hard muscles like a second skin. His quads rose, thick and defined, while his hips were tapered. Abs flat. The merest suggestion of a bulge, if someone wanted to get their perv on.

Which, God help her, she did.

"Like what you see?" He gave her a wry look.

"I . . . just had something in my eye. Dust." She rubbed her lids in an unconvincing pantomime. She wasn't going to be winning acting awards for her "lady doth protest too much" routine.

"Dust. Is that what they are calling getting hot under the collar?"

"Hot under the collar? I think my granny Dee uses that expression."

"Your granny Dee sounds like she has a way with words."

She grinned. "My granny is also ninety."

His mouth twitched. "I've been meaning to ask. How old are you?"

"I thought that question is off-limits once a lady passes the age of twenty-nine."

Something like relief settled over his features. "So you are over thirty."

"Fine," she huffed. "I *am* thirty. Turned June 2nd. Gemini." She threw out her hands in a ta-da gesture.

"I'm forty."

"Congratulations?" She raised her brows. "Given the circumstances, it's fair to say we are both of a certain age. Like in cavemen times, at thirty I'd be ready to call it a life after having sixteen kids and once eating a handful of berries, so have some perspective. It's not like I'm fourteen and you're twenty-four. Speaking of which, the year I was fourteen, that was a good time. The iPhone came out. The craziest news was that Britney Spears shaved her head."

"Simpler days."

"No doubt." She bent into a deep leg stretch, preparing for the upcoming run. "I'm more grizzled and the world harsher. And you sure as heck aren't going to be able to do much to corrupt me and/or my delicate virtue at this point."

He inclined his head. "Bet I *can* kick your ass in a sprint."

"Oh, you didn't go there."

He made a show of glancing around. "Pretty damn sure I just did."

And while what had happened with him in the bed, in the tub and, God help her, on the bathroom floor over the past few hours gripped her in uncertainty, on this point there would be no doubt: Tor Gunnar would eat her dust. She'd outrun her confusion and hopefully, at the end she'd arrive at clarity.

When they walked out of the room, an Adeline staff member moved to the side, pushing a room service cart down the hall. He gave a friendly smile before glancing at the room number.

"Room 309, huh? How'd you sleep?" He said the room number like it meant something.

Neve furrowed her brow as her stomach muscles tensed. How loud had they just been? Good lord, had the people around them complained? If so, she was ready to get a shovel and bury herself inside the nearest snowdrift. "I'm not sure," she said hesitantly as the guy was clearly expecting an answer and not making idle chitchat.

"That's good. Lots of the maids won't even clean in there. They have to draw straws."

"Why?" Tor asked in his usual no-nonsense tone. Even casually dressed for a run he had a way of looking in charge, aloof and cool—a master of the universe. Nothing like the guy who fell apart against her last night, a helpless look in his normally ice-blue eyes. Her mouth dried as she remembered his raw growl as he came undone in her mouth.

If she didn't have a stubble burn on her inner thighs, she'd almost be inclined to believe it was all a dream. The sexiest dream she'd ever had, but impossible to conceive.

"They didn't tell you at check-in?" The staffer seemed honestly surprised. "It's often specifically requested by guests, as a test."

"Test of what?" Tor asked, clearly inching toward impatience. His jaw was beginning to tighten and his gaze narrowed.

"The dueling ghosts can predict your love. Adeline Rose and Big Jim Cartwright."

She and Tor exchanged quick glances.

"I'm sorry, can you please elaborate on this?" she asked. "I can't say I'm familiar with dueling ghosts or love predictions."

"There's a plaque about it downstairs next to the front desk, but they say they only make an appearance if a couple is the real deal, so congrats! Now I've got to deliver these eggs to the bride before they get cold. There's going to be a wedding tonight." He whistled as he wheeled the breakfast cart away up the hall.

"I was bound and determined to get coffee before anything else, but I sort of think we have to go see this plaque." She peered closer. "You look pale. What gives? Did you see Slimer floating around last night? Or maybe a giant Stay Puft marshmallow man wandering by the window?"

"No . . . but . . ." He shook his head as if to clear it. "Never mind."

"Are you sure?" A chill stole down her spine. "For real, you're starting to scare me a little."

"Let's go take a look at the plaque." His tone was impassive. "Then we run."

Down in the lobby, right near the check-in desk, was a silver plaque beside a turn-of-the-century black-and-white wedding photo where neither half of the stern-faced couple appeared remotely happy.

"Why are people always so serious-looking in these old-timey photos?" she murmured.

"They had to hold still for so long. Forcing a smile might have been too hard."

She pointed at the plaque and began reciting the text. "'Adeline Rose and Big Jim were a famous bank-robbing duo known for their passionate arguments and even more passionate makeups. After a bank heist in Grand Junction, they came to Telluride to hole up at Adeline's sister's brothel. But for reasons no one is entirely clear on, the feisty couple got into an argument in their room. The result was a duel in the street out in front of the brothel. They walked ten paces and each turned to fire. Neither aimed to miss.' And get a load of this last part." Neve nudged Tor. "'But the two deadly lovebirds seemed to have found peace in the afterlife. Couples in love often find ghostly signs from the duo and take it as a sign of good luck.' I guess that's one way to spin a sketchy situation. Kudos to the Adeline's marketing team."

"You aren't armed and dangerous, are you?" Tor murmured in her ear, his breath heating her skin.

"If anyone is packing a big weapon here, it's you." She turned and glanced between his legs with an arch look.

His laugh was short and gruff. "Your sexual-innuendo game is as strong as your sarcasm."

She smirked. "And here I didn't even know that I possessed this rare talent until spending time in your orbit."

His frank gaze went wolfish. "I can't stop wondering what other rare talents you possess."

She had the grace to blush even as heat sparked between her legs. "I suppose you got a taste last night?"

"And here I am hungry for more."

"You make me sound like your personal smorgasbord."

"Must be the Swede in me," he deadpanned before adding,

"But look. Today we're in Telluride together and on a truce. I'd like to spend time hanging out. And maybe with Olive."

"Your daughter." Before she could let the full impact of his invitation sink in, her stupid phone rang. Again. Scott. "Ugh, I'm sorry. This is my boss. I have to take this. He is being relentless."

"He's being a bastard. But I get it. Work's important. Go ahead and do what you need to do." He paused before turning away. "Oh, and try to resist checking me out while I walk over here to stretch."

That sense of humor, where had he been hiding it?

She flicked on her phone, walked across the street, and leaned against a streetlight. "Scott. You're persistent. I was about to call you back."

"Tell me more, Angel," he snapped. Typical. Her boss always cut right to the chase. Not unlike the man doing calf stretches next to the building across the street. Or at least his old version.

"I don't know what you are talking about."

"Don't play coy. I'm looking here at the last article you sent, and in the email you mentioned you were taking a weekend trip out of the city. To go to Telluride. With Tor Gunnar. What's the deal?"

"Well, it is just . . . I lost this bet and I sort of kind of ended up with him here at this wedding in Telluride."

"Bullshit."

"No bulls. I speak the truth."

No one had a laugh like Scott—a cross between a braying donkey and a hyena.

She'd hear that laugh after the punch line to off-color jokes in the newsroom. Usually referencing women.

Hey, Neve. Why do women make better soldiers? Because they can bleed for a week and not die.

She'd try to eye roll it off. After all, he was happily married. He had a kid up at the University of Wyoming and a grown daughter in Boise. He didn't have groping hands or a wandering, lecherous gaze.

It wasn't like she had some big case to take to Human Resources. What was she going to say? His jokes made her feel annoyed and uncomfortable? That he made her dream job far less dreamy? That he'd been bemused to come into the editor role and find her covering the hockey beat? Once he'd caught wind about her being a former figure skater, it was all over. She'd had to prove she wasn't a girly girl.

What irony—not feminine enough for figure skating but too girly for sports journalism. She wished at this point in history that things like sexism and gender inequality never reared their ugly heads, but the truth was there was a great deal of work still to be done.

When it came to her field, there was an undeniable gender imbalance across print, broadcast, and online platforms in sports journalism. Men—especially white men—dominated, while female reporters were left getting nitpicked on the internet about their outfits or bodies rather than respected for their sports punditry.

Sexism sucked and provided yet another reason—besides her lack of a life—to keep her social media interactions to a minimum. If she rocked a good hair day, someone would comment, speculating which player was her current hookup. If she pulled her hair back into a bun or ponytail and looked too severe, she was dismissed as "manly." There was literally no winning. Her boss didn't do too much to add to the culture of toxic masculinity, but he sure as heck didn't do a lot to diminish it.

So she managed.

After all, she'd had experience. Heck, she should add "dealing with the male gaze" under her LinkedIn skill sets.

Finally Scott's laughter dwindled. "So what's the deal? You working undercover on a big story?"

"He knows that I'm a journalist, Scott. More like I'm here as his guest."

"So he invited you?"

"Yes, don't sound so surprised."

"You two aren't an item, right? Because you—"

"No! No. Nothing like that." Those words could be a career killer. How many hockey reporters had ended their careers by getting involved with players or coaches?

Lots.

"Whatever you say. I don't know what you're up to but I want a story from this, on my desk, first thing Monday. Something juicy."

Yesterday morning she would have given him a thumbs-up and gone in guns blazing. But shifts had happened. Earth-shattering, tectonic fractures.

"I'm not sure that is going to happen."

"What do you mean?" Scott's tone cooled.

"I mean that I don't think I want to be on the record this weekend."

"Sorry." His laugh this time wasn't amused. "Who is Sports editor?"

"Let's not play rhetorical twenty questions. It diminishes both of us."

"Here's what I know. Numbers are down here at the paper.

Print is sucking. Digital subscriptions aren't where they need to be. You know what that means?"

"I'm sure you are about to tell me."

"Heads are on the chopping block. And your smart-mouthed head could be added to the pile."

"Is this a threat?" She bristled. "I mean, come on, Scott, we've worked together for a couple years now. You are better than this two-bit 'Mafia gangster meets medieval executioner' routine."

"You think I'm kidding. I'm not. What I'm saying isn't an if. It's a when."

Neve's stomach bottomed out. What she wanted to do was tell her boss to take the bacon cheeseburger that was probably sitting on his desk and cram it down his throat and choke. Not die. She wasn't a monster. But definitely see the light and have a fright. She poured her heart and soul into her career and had always been a team player. Now he wanted to threaten her over reluctance to do some sort of profile on Tor?

But if she refused too hard, he'd get suspicious and he wasn't a subtle guy. The last thing she needed was for it to get around that she'd gone off with Tor for the weekend and send chins wagging. Was she trying to sleep her way into better stories?

God. Men never had to deal with this bullshit.

But she also had a mortgage on her townhome. Her Wagoneer didn't have a payment, but it was old and it wouldn't take long before something big broke down. She couldn't up and move to chase a new job or she'd leave her family. And she didn't want to do that. Denver was home. It was where she belonged.

She had to stick it out, and by hook or by crook she'd do it.

"What's it going to be?" he said.

"Fine." She couldn't risk her job. Not in this current economic climate. She'd have to find a way to sell the idea to Tor. At the very least she'd be up-front about her intentions; she owed him that much.

"Good girl," he said approvingly, then stuck something crunchy into his mouth and chewed away her last nerve.

Good girl.

Like she was an obedient dog. *Sit. Shake. Roll over. Woof. Woof. Woof.* She nearly growled.

"Don't be sulky. I also come bearing good news. Your article on the top-five worst coaches is going great. In the top-five article views and third in most emailed. Nice work."

Oh shit. Her "I come in peace" sales pitch to Tor just took a nosedive. He was never going to believe her when she'd put out that snarky hit piece.

She'd let her petty show and now it had come back to bite her in the butt cheek.

"This is going to be great. You've had a public feud with Gunnar. Now you're down there one-on-one. Pardon my *le Francois* but my instincts are fucking phenomenal. With the lockout in place, we have to keep the masses entertained. This . . . Tor and Neve's Excellent Adventure? It's the gold standard in entertainment."

"Glad to amuse you." She swiveled her head. Tor paced up and down in front of a Western-themed saloon next to the Adeline.

"Don't take this the wrong way, but I never pictured you as Tor Gunnar's type."

"Two things. We're just friends. Well. Sort of for now. And second . . . ouch. Who talks like that?"

"Hey, don't getting sulky on me when I'm just yankin' your

chain. But take one look at the guy. He looks like he stepped out of the pages of a Norwegian ad. Looks ready to milk a reindeer or some shit."

"Sweden," she bit off. "His heritage is Swedish."

"You're no fun."

"That goes both ways." She wasn't trying to be cute. She was a hundred percent serious. "This has been real, but it hasn't been real fun. Listen. I got to go."

"Good luck. I look forward to all the juicy details."

She hung up. "I didn't realize the *Age* had become a tabloid," she snarled under her breath. Shoving the phone into her pocket, she crossed the street. Tension radiated from her muscles. This energy was only going to be expended one way.

Her sex clenched when she met Tor's watchful gaze. Okay, technically there was another way she could expend this tension, but running would leave her with a clearer head. Her boss's words rang in her head. What did a Norse god want with a woman like Neve when he could have anyone?

Ugh. Insecurity was an insidious asshole.

"Think you can keep up, old man?" she called with a wink, feigning an ease she in no way felt.

He took her measure. "Cocky much?"

"Not cocky if it's true. I'm fast."

"You talk more trash than Johnny in 'The Devil Went Down to Georgia.'"

"I guess that makes you the devil." She should tell him about the profile right now. Just blurt it out and be done with it.

"Want to make another wager?"

"Let's do it. I'm feeling lucky." She bit back her tongue to keep from teasing, *And win or lose, I'll probably still get lucky.*

"We get to the river. One mile. Slowest buys the other coffee."

"Sounds good. I look forward to forgoing my usual dark roast. That coffee shop on the corner looks delightful. I'm in the mood for a double-shot mocha. Extra whipped cream. I won't be a cheap date."

"All right. Let's put up or shut up." He gave an "after you" gesture. "Ladies first."

"Why, thank you, good sir."

He grinned and the sun broke through the steely clouds. Yes. She'd ask him about doing the profile. But after the run.

Chapter Fourteen

Tor had planned to let her win until halfway through their race. That was when he realized there was no "letting"—he didn't have a prayer. They flew past aspens, their spindly branches bare and ghost white. He pumped his arms, his heavy breaths fogging the wintry air, while she skipped along like frigging Bambi in the meadow for the first time. She looked up and smile lines creased the corners of her eyes.

"Hanging in there? I can dial back the pace if it's too much."

"Fine," he gasped. "I'm fine."

"You sure? Because there's no harm in stopping. It's beautiful, isn't it? We could pull over. Let you rest and catch your breath."

"Angel," he snapped. "You'll be the death of me."

"Stay away from any bright lights." She wiggled her hips, jogging in place. "I really want to win that coffee. I forgot my wallet."

"What's your average-pace mile?"

"Seven thirty." She didn't even pause before answering.

Jesus. "That's fast."

She heaved her shoulders in a told-you-so shrug. "I tried warning you."

"You run marathons?"

"Not yet but I'd like to start. You?"

"No."

"Sorry, can you repeat that? It's a little hard to hear you through the panting."

He tried to snort but it came out a wet gasp. "Pace yourself. We're almost at the end. That was a three-quarter-mile mark."

"You're slowing."

He was. By a lot. "Just saving something for the finish."

"Admit defeat. You can't catch me." Her legs pumped faster. "TTFN! See you on the flip side."

He pushed hard, but he couldn't catch her. Once the realization sank in, his frustration was replaced by admiration, and a little ogling of her Lycra-clad ass. He slowed, sucking in greedy gulps of air.

Here was a woman who could kick his ass into next week, and he'd keep coming back for more.

She blew past the mile marker and turned, throwing her arms up like Rocky on the steps of the Philadelphia Museum of Art. Her victory whoop rose into the crisp air, cut off by a thrashing from the undergrowth lining the river.

"Neve!" Tor shouted, lunging forward as a male moose emerged. "Don't move."

A few weeks ago, while lifting at the gym, one of the televisions had showed a feature on dangerous animals. Near the top of the list was the moose, right after the grizzly bear.

Neve's muffled swearing was audible, but the animal blocked any view of her face. The moose stood in the middle of the trail, head raised, ears alert. It was still technically autumn. Had mating season ended? The animal could be merely on the lookout for breakfast or succumbing to raging hormones.

One second went by. Two. Three.

No movement. They were having a moose-off.

"Um . . . Tor?"

The bull grunted at Neve's hesitant call. Its powerful hooves churned gravel on the trail. Deep nostrils flared.

Big Boy didn't look happy. Tor cracked his neck and went into game mode. Shut out panic. Shut out the snow beginning to fall in thicker, heavier flakes. Ignored the physiological sensations currently amping his body, the shortness of breath, tingling limbs, racing heart. He'd coach Neve out of this situation.

"Tor, I'm freaking out. Nature is great and all, but this is too much."

"Listen, Babe. I want you to take a breath. Don't move." He surveyed the surrounding area. "Do everything I say and you'll be okay."

The moose stamped again. More huffing. Big Boy clocked in at almost seven feet. If he trampled Neve, she'd be in serious trouble—life-threatening trouble.

She whimpered. The moose tossed his shaggy head.

A plan took shape. "Behind you, on the left, is a wooden fence. It's not tall. From there is a forested slope down to the river. On my command, you're going to run as fast as you can, get over that fence and behind a tree."

That way if the moose charged, there would be not one but two barriers to keep her safe while he figured out a distraction.

"You can do this."

"Thanks for the confidence vote, but I don't think I can. My legs are jelly. I might pass out."

"You can and you will. Remember how you whipped my ass in that race?"

No response.

"Neve." That was an order. "Stay with me."

"I just nodded. You just couldn't see it because there's a giant moose blocking the view."

She still had spunk. That counted for something.

He raked fingers through his hair, his hand not quite steady. "Do what I say. I'll take care of the rest. Nothing bad will happen to you. Trust me."

She sniffled. "I do."

The moose kicked out a back leg again. Its long black tongue came out to lick its nose and mouth.

"These things are vegetarian, right?" she asked.

The two bristle-haired ears flattened, the thick hair along the back rising in hackles. Tor didn't need Animal Planet to inform him that this was a clear sign of agitation being replaced by aggression. The moose had two choices, flight or fight. Big Boy appeared to be leaning toward the latter.

"Go," Tor barked sharply. "Go now. Head down, ass in gear."

Neve took off like a shot. He could hear her shoes crunching up the trail.

The moose whirled its big head and Tor picked up a rock, threw it away from the river, away from Neve.

"Hey, you. Pick on someone your own size." Okay, not his finest line, but it didn't matter. The moose didn't speak English. But it did appear to understand a loud, deep voice.

He'd gotten its attention. Neve jumped the fence as the moose turned to face him. No huff this time. This sound was more of a . . . growl.

Shit. Moose growled? There was a fun fact he'd never needed to discover.

As for his lame "pick on someone your own size" comment,

the moose rose a foot above him. Not only did the hairy bastard growl, it looked smug about the size difference.

The only choice was to channel the biggest badass he could think of. An image of Samuel L. Jackson from *Snakes on a Plane* came to mind. Good 'nuff.

The moose lunged, as if in a charge. Somewhere from behind the shrubby willows, Neve screamed.

The moose pulled up short. Lifted its great shaggy head and sniffed the air.

A fake out. Well played.

It cocked its head, turning its gaze to him. From end to end, the spread of the animal's antlers must be at least equal to his own height of six-two.

Christ, what did one do with a moose charge? Was it like a grizzly attack, where you were supposed to fall over and play dead? Or was it more of a black-bear situation, where you should fight back?

The moose stamped, the massive slabs of muscles in its chest flexing. Tor frowned. Fuck playing dead. If he fell to the ground and got run over, he'd look like roadkill. Nothing for it but to override his urge for flight and flip the switch to fight mode. Throwing his arms up over his head, Tor faked his own lunge. Arms extended above his head to give the impression that he was larger than he was, he bared his teeth and gave his best snarl.

No reaction.

Shit.

If the moose did charge, those powerful legs were going to hurt. But he had no intention of letting that happen. Tor had a rep for making big gambles that played out. Maneuvers where his players would achieve the impossible, leave fans delighted and opposing teams scratching their heads.

But he'd never physically put himself on the line.

This moose wasn't going to back down without a good reason. He knew a fake out when he saw one.

Time to mean business.

Tor ripped off his running top, grabbed both sleeves, and raised it above his head, whipping it wildly. He ran forward screaming. This time he wasn't going to stop. It would be him or the moose. There could only be one. And he knew who would win.

Fifty feet. Forty feet. Thirty feet. The moose held its ground, eyes growing wide.

Tor yelled again. Fifteen feet. Ten feet.

At five feet, the moose veered and ran for the hills. Literally.

Tor bent over, bracing his hands on his knees.

"What the heck were you thinking?" Neve emerged from the woods. "Are you insane? No, don't bother answering. I already know. Yes. Yes, you are. Crazy as they come. You just chased down a frigging moose!"

"I didn't want it to hurt you."

"I've never been so scared, and also turned on." She reached out and touched his abs. "Why did you take your shirt off?"

"I figured it might make me look bigger if I waved it around."

She grabbed him at the elbows. "You. Are. Crazy."

"Come on." He arched a brow. "You aren't a little a-moosed?"

She shook her head even as an unwilling smile tugged her lips. "Too soon."

"It appears I moose-spoke. I moose have thought you had a better sense of humor."

"Tor Gunnar. Head coach. Moose slayer. All-around punny guy."

"It's no joke, make no moose-take."

She groaned, burying her face in his chest.

He kissed the top of her head. "I can keep going."

"I beg you to quit. Seriously, let's get out of here before Bullwinkle on steroids decides to pay a repeat visit."

He slid on his shirt. "Good idea. Plus this snow doesn't look like it's letting up."

They only took a few steps before he noticed she ambled stiffly, like someone trying to repress pain.

"You hurt yourself." Not a question.

"Oh, it's nothing. I just turned my ankle fleeing a giant woodland creature."

"Sprain?" His voice sharp.

"I'm sure it's nothing." But her tone was tight.

"Let's take a look at the nothing." After dropping into a crouch, he moved to roll up her leggings.

She sucked in a sharp breath. "Maybe don't touch. I'll get some ice on it back at the hotel."

"Jesus, you are in pain." It was clear she had swelling. Now standing, he held out his arms. "I'll carry you."

"What? All the way back to the hotel?"

"It's not far."

"A mile!"

"Well, how do I put this? You are little. Are you even five feet?"

She drew herself up to her full small height. "I'm bigger than a penguin, Mister."

He chuckled. "I'm just saying, I think I can manage."

She shifted her weight, hesitating, and winced. "Normally

I would rather crawl than ask for help, but my moose fear is overriding my pride."

He scooped her up and cradled her against him. A snowflake landed on the tip of her nose and he kissed it off.

"You've saved me twice before breakfast."

"I'm quite aware of this fact."

"You seem pleased."

"Very much so."

"Smug much?" she asked.

"Always."

They shared a quiet laugh.

"Thank you," she said quietly. "I'm not used to a guy having my back."

"I'd like to have you on your back."

"I'm being serious."

He dropped the teasing. "I know. Truth. I was scared. More than scared back there."

"I couldn't tell."

"If something had happened to you? I don't think I'd have forgiven myself."

"It wasn't your fault. At all. It wasn't even the moose's fault. It probably wanted to catch a quick bite before this snow and we upset its mojo. But . . . I was scared too. Watching you on that trail. I haven't felt like that before."

"I'm hazarding a guess that there've been times in our past you'd have paid good money to hire a moose to pay me a little visit."

She wrinkled her nose. "I'm going to plead the Fifth on that one."

"All right, confession time. Here's the deal. I never disliked *you*, Neve. I hated how you made me feel."

"And how was that?" she murmured.

"Like my heart was trying to climb out of my chest."

"Sounds uncomfortable."

"Very. But I think it was trying to tell me something."

She tapped a finger against her lower lip. "Let me guess. Neve Angel is very lovely and you should pull your head out of your ass and make sweet, sweet love to her?"

"Something like that, yeah."

"Well, if we're baring it all. Here's my secret. I always found you attractive. I mean I have two eyes. But I think it was safer to be a pain in your ass than, you know . . . ogle your ass."

"Why?"

"In my job, I can't fall for a player. Or a coach. Or pretty much anyone affiliated with sports. It makes things murky."

"Are you saying you feel . . . murky?" This was getting dangerously close to a talk about feelings—and strangely he didn't have a single desire to run away screaming.

"I'm like nineteenth-century-London murky. Or a dark and stormy night. Murkier than a twilight walk in a forest filled with vampires and wolves."

"Don't forget the moose." He cocked his head. "Is *moose* a plural . . . It's not *meese*, right?"

"Fine. You are a-moosing."

"Murky and punny. We're quite a pair."

The wind picked up, sliding cool fingers around his neck, down his shirt, and across his chest. He hugged Neve closer, her warmth comingling with his own body heat.

Let the storms do their worst. He'd found shelter, and in the most surprising place.

Chapter Fifteen

*N*eve smoothed her hands over her dress. It really was gorgeous. The color did her pasty skin all kinds of favors, and the pop of red lipstick brightened her eyes. She'd feel like a million bucks if not for two things: her ankle was a mottled mess of purple, indigo, and gray, and all she'd brought for shoes were her sneakers and a pair of spiky heels that she'd impulsively purchased on her dress-shopping trip.

Those options were both out, and Telluride wasn't a big town. Stores closed early. By the time she'd realized her mistake, there was nowhere to try to nab anything else. So she'd have to go to Maddy's wedding wearing not only this amazing dress, but also her scuffed New Balances.

Hot.

No way to cut this. She'd look ridiculous. But maybe she deserved the penance because she was being so chickenhearted. She had yet to ask Tor about helping her with the profile. He'd been in such a good mood all day and avoidance was easier. They'd gotten coffee and spent the afternoon in bed, her leg iced and elevated, watching tiny cooking shows on her iPad— one of her guilty addictions.

Here he was, Tor Gunnar being the corny Rovhal30 from Byways. Sure, he could still be uptight and surly, just like he could be adorkably fun loving and full of moose puns. Just like she could be all work but in his arms wanted to do nothing but play . . . and play dirty at that.

They were both dichotomies. And maybe that was absolutely fine.

Better than fine even.

Except there was a pesky *but* to all this . . .

She had a decent sixth sense about people and knew as surely as she knew her outfit was a disaster that he was going to close down on her if she got professional. The question was, how hard and for how long? Followed by the even bigger question, was it for the best?

Because this weekend wasn't real life. Real life hovered elsewhere, around the corner, at the end of town. And it would come soon enough. Monday morning. Denver. Her job. His job. They would go back to worlds that repelled them like two opposing magnets.

There was a knock on the hotel room door. She gave herself one last fuss in the mirror and stepped out to open it.

Tor's daughter glared at her.

"Hi." She smiled, unsure why she was getting a death stare.

"Is my father here?"

Maybe the daughter had second thoughts. It made sense. After all, her mom was an hour away from getting married. The idea of her dad shacking up in a hotel couldn't sit that easily.

"Honey?" Tor came around the corner, doing up his tie.

Neve sucked in a breath. Good lord, could that man wear a suit or what? If she was going to be brutally honest, his clothes were one of her favorite parts about Hellions game days. The sight of Tor Gunnar in an Italian-cut jacket and expertly knotted tie sent her pulse racing faster than any player in pads and a jersey.

"Nice shoes," Olive muttered, taking her full measure. "Dad, can I talk to you a second. Alone?"

"Yeah, sure, uh . . ." He glanced to Neve, puzzlement grooving the space between his brows. "Do you mind?"

"No, no, of course not. I'm all ready to go. I'll just head down into the lobby and wait." She forced a smile that she didn't feel.

She might have empathy for the girl, but that didn't mean her words didn't hold a sting. Gathering her jacket and purse, she gave an awkward wave before bolting for the elevator, or hobble-bolting. Whichever way, it wasn't a good look.

Down in the lobby, well-dressed people paraded, many of them no doubt guests for the wedding. It was to be held in a fancy restaurant up on the mountain. They had to ride the town gondola to get there. She'd be able to shamble around; the ibuprofen and ice and elevation had made the pain bearable. But her plan should really just focus on hiding her sneakered feet under a table and calling it good.

Snow came down harder out the window.

"Ski season is right around the corner," the bellman said, walking over to join her, rubbing his hands. "I can't wait."

"No offense, but I've never been a huge fan of snow."

"Really? Then you picked a bad weekend to come up to the mountains."

"Why's that?"

"You fly in or drive?" he asked without taking his eyes off the flurries.

"Drive. I live in Denver."

"Big storm. We're missing most of it. Up north, it's dumping hard. You have snow tires?"

"I don't know. My . . . uh . . . date drove us here. I'm sure he's got everything dialed. He's pretty ana—detailed oriented."

The bellman nodded absently, clearly visualizing the fresh-powder turns to come. "Yeah. Drive safe."

"Ready?" Tor appeared. Olive stood beside him in a long navy blue coat, her pale blond hair hidden beneath a large white fake-fur hat.

"All set. Everything good?" She was fishing, but father and daughter shared identical frowns. Something was wrong.

"We should start walking to the gondola now so we aren't late. You sure you can—"

"I'm fine." She zipped up her coat. Tor's gaze frosted over. That fact cooled her more than the temperature outside.

Their walk to the gondola lift was silent. A group of people strolled past, laughing and talking animatedly. It was Saturday night after all. The restaurants and bars in the ski town had lines out the door, everyone jubilant that the weather had turned wintery.

At the gondola-loading building, there was another line. Tor greeted a few people with curt nods while Olive hugged a woman in a red coat.

Neve shoved her hands into her pockets, internally nodding. He must be uptight because his ex-wife was getting married. Of course it was awkward. She needed to get a grip.

The gondola filled up. There was room for one more and the woman in the red coat asked Olive if she wanted to come along.

"No thanks, I'll wait with my dad." Olive took his hand, refusing to glance at Neve.

They stood together for a few tense beats.

"Hey, Olive, did you hear how your dad was a big hero today?" Neve inwardly winced at her tone, clearly too chipper. The tween frowned accordingly.

"Yeah. You scared up a moose and almost got him trampled."

Ouch.

Looked like the kid had her mind made up to dislike Neve. But yesterday she'd been different.

Another gondola came around. This time they were the only ones there to ride.

"Want a wool blanket?" one of the lifties said.

Tor shook his head. Olive said, "No," right as Neve said, "Sure, thanks."

Once they'd gotten in, the liftie shut the door. They sat on the bench opposite. Neve smoothed the blanket over her lap. "Well, well, well. This is cozy."

No response.

Good lord, she was trying her best. It wasn't like she had a lot of experience talking to small people. Tor stared out the window into the darkening sky as the gondola lurched upward.

"My aunt said you should never take one of the blankets," Olive said. "She said people get up to who knows what in here, and—"

"Olive." Tor's growl was soft but effective.

"Ew. Good to know." Neve slid off the blanket with a grimace. "It doesn't sound very hygienic when you put it like that." She drummed her fingers on her thighs. Tor doubled down on the outside staring, but she called bullshit. It was dark enough now that all he could see was his own face reflected back.

"Hey. So can I clear the air? What's going on?" She forced a thin laugh. "I don't mean to sound paranoid, but I feel like I was caught streaking a graveyard or something. What's going on?"

Olive glanced to Tor. His jaw stiffened. Familiar muscles bunched and released. She knew them. They used to be her friends. The reminder that she could bug the heck out of him no matter how cool and calm he wanted to appear. But that was not what she was going for now.

"Tor . . ."

"I showed him the article you wrote," Olive said accusingly. "Some jerk from my school posted it on my Facebook page. 'Top Five Worst Coaches in the NHL' by Neve Angel. Ring a bell?"

Busted. "I can explain, or at least try to."

"You're Neve Angel, right?"

"That's enough," Tor said finally, relenting and turning around to join the conversation.

"I'm sorry," Neve said bluntly. "I was mad when I wrote it. You had just said . . . you know . . . some unkind things in the parking lot that day and I wanted payback. I promise that I didn't mean it."

"I know," he said simply.

That was unexpected. "You do?"

"I figured that part out right after Olive told me. I did the math, and after our conversation from this morning, I figured where you got the inspiration."

"I don't understand." Olive glanced between them.

"I have to admit, I'm with her," Neve said. "You haven't been speaking to me since we left the Adeline."

"You aren't even mad?" Olive looked disgusted. "She was a jerk to you."

"No," he told his daughter. "I decided that I'm not and here's why. Because I'm not always perfect either. And sometimes Neve and I, well, we've done unkind things to each other. And neither of us is proud of that fact."

Olive gave a dramatic groan. "Why are grown-ups so confusing?"

Neve shrugged. "When I was younger, I thought once you hit twenty, things made sense. I hate to let you in on a secret, but I'm thirty, and I still don't feel all that wise."

Olive crossed her arms, even as a ghost of a smile haunted her tight-pressed lips. "That sounds pretty terrifying."

"I know. But I do mean what I say. Your dad isn't a bad coach. He's amazing. And today, when I thought I was going to be trampled into a moose patty, he talked me through it. He saved me."

Tor put his arm around Olive. "I appreciate you wanting to defend me, sweetie, but I promise you, Neve is one of the good ones."

"For a jackal?"

Neve snorted. "Out of the mouths of babes."

"Guess the apple doesn't fall all that far from the tree." Tor planted a kiss on top of his daughter's head.

"You both have loyalty in common. And that's to be commended. But I do hope you'll forgive me, Olive, and we can move on."

"I need to think about it," she said gravely.

"That's all I can ask."

"And we're here," Tor said as the gondola came to a stop.

Stepping outside was like leaving a cocoon for a wind tunnel. This high on the mountain, the wind blew without mercy. They bustled toward Solitude, the restaurant hosting the event. As much as Neve was relieved to at least start to smooth things over with Olive, she couldn't help but be acutely aware of her shoe situation.

Maybe it was shallow, but for once, just a night, she wanted to feel like a beautiful swan.

And here she was, the duck in sneakers. As they got their coats checked, it seemed as if every woman in the world was wearing impossibly thin and elegant heels, teetering about like graceful gazelles.

They found seats and soon events were unfolding in the usual way. There was the wedding march. The bridesmaids. The bride.

Neve had never been to the wedding of an ex to her date and she didn't know what to make of it. Maddy wasn't competition. What she and Tor had was ancient history, water under the bridge. Maddy was getting married and Tor was holding *her* hand.

So why did she have this feeling inside her, slithering, cold, and venomous?

Look at Maddy's hair, so pretty. Yours would never do that.

She can pull off that dress. You'd look like an adolescent who hasn't hit puberty.

She is all style, composure, glitter, and gold. She is worthy of love and happiness. You only have to look at her to know.

You are nothing.

She hated that voice with a red-hot passion. Hated it for how it spoiled what should be a happy moment. Hated that it made her jealous and resentful of another woman, practically a stranger, who'd done nothing to deserve it. Hated that it diminished herself, left her bruised and hurting.

And yet the voice didn't care.

It kept pressing on all the places that hurt.

Not enough.

Not enough.

She squeezed Tor's hand. His answering grip felt like an anchor.

That voice could take a long jump off a short pier.

"I'm so happy I came here with you," she whispered. Her words were arrows unleashed, flinging straight and true into that Doubt Monster. *Take that, sucker.*

"Likewise."

And that was when she decided. Scott could screw himself. She wasn't going to push Tor for an interview just to appease her boss. No way. She was a good reporter. Her track record was solid and reputation sterling. He'd be crazy to let her go. There was no way.

And there was no way she was going to jeopardize the flicker of hope inside her, the one she saw reflected in Tor's gaze.

She leaned in and put her lips against his ear. "Do you feel sad at all, watching this ceremony?"

He paused a moment before leaning in and whispering, "No. Maddy's the mother of my child. I wish her all the happiness in the world."

Good answer. Good man.

He wasn't finished. "It makes me hopeful. I'd like to love again."

Heat radiated through her core.

"By the power vested in me by the state of Colorado, I now

declare you husband and wife." The officiate gave a theatrical pause. "You may kiss the bride."

The room burst into applause. Then everyone stood and began to file into the adjacent reception space. Even though it was ridiculous, it felt like everyone stared at her shoes. "Sorry your date is the big klutz."

"Not a chance." He wrapped his arm around her waist and drew her in tight. "Pretty sure mine is the one who is bold and beautiful, who has a sassy mouth and gives me a run for my money. Let them stare. You know how you got that ankle injury."

"Tripping over a piece of granite hiding in a patch of dry grass?"

"No. Not *literally*, Angel." He kissed the top of her hair. He'd been doing that all day, finding sneaky ways to kiss her with affection.

These kisses were getting seriously addictive. She craved them. The gentle sweetness. The shared affection. She'd never had this feeling before—this sense of belonging to someone.

"You went up against a moose," Tor said.

"Well, technically *you* did."

"We both did. You were amazing by the river. You kept your cool and damn it, girl, you can run."

She pretended to polish her knuckles on her chest. "Forrest Gump has nothing on me."

"That's a fact. He'd eat your dust."

They found their table in the back corner of the room. Well away from the wedding-party dais, and that was fine by them.

The candelabra on the table softly flickered and there were silver snowflakes strewn above the ceiling with fairy lights. She watched the dappled brightness cut across Tor's face, highlighting everything from his bold nose to his wide, sensual mouth, Scandinavian bone structure, and ash-blond hair. Every time she looked at him, it was a surprise, and not a little disorienting. Tor Gunnar wasn't her enemy anymore. He was her . . . lover. And more importantly, her friend. And when he returned her gaze, it wasn't with cool aloofness, or a slight sneer, but a smolder that took her breath away.

It had been a good call not to mention Scott Miller's request to him. She could take that fact to the bank and cash it. He'd let the worst-coach article slide without much drama, and accepted blame for his part in the lead-up . . . but . . . he *had* been a little hurt.

She smoothed her linen napkin over her lap. The strangest thing of all was realizing her power, not simply to hurt him but also to give happiness. It was like she was Peter Parker talking to Uncle Ben, being told that "with great power comes great responsibility."

But her superpower wasn't shooting spiderwebs from her wrists. It was melting this god of snow and ice and finding the man who'd been frozen for so long inside.

The dinner was tempting: roasted peppers stuffed with risotto, filet mignon, whipped potatoes, and roasted-root soup. Once the five-piece jazz band struck up the music for dancing, waitstaff appeared with trays covered in miniature molten lava cakes and flutes bubbling with pink champagne.

Dabbing the corner of his mouth, he leaned over. "You want to stay for dessert or be mine?" He stared at her mouth as if he wanted to devour it in slow, delicious licks, then let his gaze travel to other parts of her body with obvious hunger, an invitation to feast.

She'd always said there was nothing better than chocolate.

Looked like she might as well admit that there was a lot she'd gotten wrong in life.

"Can we go?" she whispered, her throat tight with anticipation.

"Sure. Olive's having a ball." He jutted a chin to where his daughter was skipping around the dance floor with her older cousins. "I already gave her permission to drive back to Denver in the morning with my former sister-in-law and her cousins. I've put in my appearance. Maddy already thanked me. The way I see it, it's time we have our own fun."

Her sex clenched with such force she almost moaned aloud. That would be embarrassing. She wouldn't even be able to blame the reaction on the untouched cake the waitress had just placed before her.

"What are we waiting for?" she asked, sliding back her chair.

"Nothing." He rose and extended her a hand. "We've waited long enough."

Chapter Sixteen

"How long does the gondola take to go from Solitude to Telluride village?" Neve asked the bearded liftie, her brown eyes wide with innocent curiosity.

"Thirteen minutes door to door," the liftie replied automatically, extending a wool wrap. "Blanket for the ride down?"

"We'll pass." Tor shook his head.

"Hah!" The guy's broad shoulders shook in laugher. "That's usually a locals-only secret. Never accept a gondola blanket."

They stepped inside and Tor turned as the doors shut. "Don't worry, I'm planning on keeping you warm for the ride down."

She grabbed his tie. "I was hoping you'd say that." Moaning, she opened her mouth, allowing him to sweep his tongue inside, tasting peppermint from the hard candy she'd popped on her way out the door, Merlot, and a flavor that could only be described as *Neve*.

In other words, heaven.

He brushed her cheek, then slid his fingers along her jaw and down her neck in a possessive caress. "I want to fuck you."

"What a coincidence, I was going to say the exact same thing." Her grin turned naughty. "But we don't have long."

"With you, that's never a problem."

"Let me guess. You have a thing for women in formal wear and tennis shoes."

"Get over here, Angel." He sat on the bench and pulled her on top. Sliding both hands up over her muscular inner thighs, he bunched her dress up around her hips. Fucking Christ. She was wearing see-through black panties connected by two flimsy pieces of string. It would take nothing but a flick of the wrist to have her bare, but if they were going for a quick-and-dirty fuck, he'd go all the way.

"Slide those to the side and spread yourself for me."

Her hand shook but she did as he commanded. Wind from the snowstorm rocked the gondola, setting the tempo for the slow rock of her hips.

"You're wet."

"It seems to be a side effect of the trip."

"Slide your fingers inside. I want you drenched."

"Not going to be a problem."

He tore his cock from his suit pants, the thick tip gleaming. She inched forward and he shook his head. "Not yet. Work your clit."

"I don't want to come first," she whimpered.

"You're not going to come until I say so."

Her head rocked forward. "Always so bossy."

"And you always fucking love it."

Her moan was one of assent.

He pumped his cock and gazed at her, eye to eye, the head mere inches from her heat. His erection pressed into the soft curls where her thighs joined her pelvis. The slow tickle on his sensitive cock heated his sac. His stomach muscles flexed.

"Now." He grabbed his shaft at the root and angled it up. "On me."

She braced one of her hands on his shoulder, easing herself down, slowing his thick length to stretch her slowly, drive her open, allow him to go deeper, and deeper, and—fuck—even deeper still.

When she was full of him, he grabbed the hand that had worked her pussy by the wrist, sucked her fingers in, lapping all her flavor. Her heat contracted around him on instinct.

"You fill me so good." Her moan was a delighted agony.

"Love it." His chest filled with rasping breaths. Fuck, he almost said the words. *The* words. It had to be the sex talking. No way could he say he loved her. It was the weekend talking. That and breaking the seal on his seven-year dry spell. The fact he liked her. That for as long as he had known her, he had liked her even if he wouldn't admit it.

Shit. For years he'd noticed her every time she walked into a room? He'd thought about her whenever she wasn't there?

Was it possible? His body temperature cranked. Was he in love with Neve Angel?

He grabbed her hips, hauling her against him, claiming her mouth, sucking her skin as if he could draw out the truth.

They were fully clothed except in their most intimate places. Fitting. They'd always guarded themselves around each other. Threw up armor. But there was no lie in the slick wet saturating his cock, slicking his sac. And none in the aching thickness of his cock.

She rode him with a grinding hunger. The wind screamed against the gondola windows, steaming from their heat and breath.

He grabbed her by the neck and took over the rhythm. She hung on, practically sobbing as he drove into her center, true and hard. He didn't even have to touch her clit. From the way she trembled, he could tell she was about to come from this and this alone.

Her velvet softness was tight, so tight, and yet she had just enough room to give him full access, bury himself to the hilt.

Her hips churned, her greedy body not yet satisfied. Needing everything. "Fuck, fuck, oh God, fuck."

He slowed until his lunges were brutally tender, gently punishing. Her flesh swelled, plumped up and primed. Ready to take every inch of his plunging cock.

"Neve. I want you. I've wanted you since the day I met you. Want to know why I haven't been with anyone in so long? Because I've only craved you."

She closed her eyes as he groaned her name again and fell quietly apart, lips parted, mouth drawn in ecstasy. He couldn't stop watching as his own orgasm bore down.

At the peak of the build she opened her eyes and looked right into his. "Tor."

She didn't say anything else, and didn't have to.

They were on the precipice of something big.

As they teetered they held each other close. Amazed. Awestricken and humbled. They might both be coming but he didn't have a fucking clue where they were going.

Chapter Seventeen

The next morning Neve watched the snow fall as Tor drove around the roundabout on the way out of Telluride's box canyon. Two elk bent near the shoulder, stoically chewing a few dried brown blades of grass. She hadn't managed to catch a wink last night and was jittery from sleeplessness and the triple-shot latte she'd guzzled before departing.

After the gondola lift, they'd gone back to their room and made love two more times, each more intense than the last. When it was finally over, she hadn't wanted the magical night to end so instead watched him sleep, feeling a little bit creepy but not all that sorry.

Not even the ghosts of feuding lovers dared haunt her peace.

So this was what it felt like to be cherished by a man. Her body was sore with it.

Praying the two Dramamine she'd popped with breakfast did the job, she flicked on her phone to text Scott the news that he'd have to learn to live with disappointment. Her job was to write assigned stories, but she was nothing if she didn't have integrity behind her. This trip was on her private time, in her private life.

She wasn't going to use it as material.

"You won't get clear reception again for another forty minutes," Tor said as they took a sharp turn. "Once we get down to the town of Ridgeway."

"Imagine living somewhere like this." Neve traced her fingers over the passenger window, regarding a log cabin up on the hillside. "Nestled away from the hustle and bustle of constant connection. Sounds peaceful."

He chuckled. "I'd give you a week until you'd be scaling the closest peak trying to get faster Wi-Fi."

"Guilty as charged." She joined in his laugh. "I like the fantasy, but I'm not sure life is worth living without HBO GO. The silence might send me stir-crazy."

"Can't have that." He flicked on the radio. It was an AM sports talk show, old-school but still considered classic. It only took a few words until she realized they were talking about the Hellions.

Tor turned it up.

"Hellions goalie Patch Donnelly found himself in hot water last night, charged with misdemeanor assault after an incident in Lower Denver. The victim, who has not been identified, was taken to the hospital and released. No official word yet on what prompted the incident, but eyewitnesses have stated there had been a fight over a woman. Not sure what impact this will have on Donnelly or his future with the Hellions. The local champs have had a rough time since ending last season on a high note and—"

"Do you have any bars on your phone?" Tor glanced over, jaw tense. "It's a long shot but . . . Shit. What the hell did Donnelly do this time?"

"Deep breaths. Patch has a notorious temper." She put her hand on his shoulder, but he didn't move, didn't look at her.

Just remained stiff and frozen as a block of ice. "Hey, remember last season, that time with the ref in the game against the Ducks? He left the penalty box to go after him. That was crazy town. I know you've tried to help him, but you can only lead a horse to water so much. You can't make him—"

"Be quiet a second, please. I'm sorry to cut you off, but I need to think," he muttered. "There's an explanation. I know it. This isn't like him."

"Of course it is. You have a hothead goalie who uses his big fists instead of his big-boy words."

"Patch isn't that simple to explain."

"Look, it's sweet you are going all Papa Bear for one of your players, but face it. He's a liability. Remember the article I wrote where—"

She must have picked up a bar because her phone started ringing. Surprise, surprise, it was Scott. Impeccable timing. And crap, she'd have to take it. If she ignored him he'd keep calling, getting more and more angry.

"Hey."

"Change of plans. Forget that puff-piece profile. You hear about this Donnelly situation? What a mess."

"A little."

"It's blowing up. I love it. He snapped the guy's arm like it was nothing but a twig. That's a big deal. Get a meaty quote from Tor Gunnar. You've got half an hour."

"Hey, wait."

"You mean 'Hey, great, Scott. Sounds good. Report back soon,'" he mimicked in a high voice before clicking off.

She glared at her screen. Talk about being out of the frying pan and into the fire.

But this time Scott had a point. This Donnelly story was in

the public interest and she was sitting in a sports car with the head coach of the Hellions.

"If you got a call in, I can make a call out. I'll pull over at the next lookout and try," he muttered. "You can take the opportunity to get some fresh air too. You took a Dramamine I grabbed for you, right?"

"I did." She paused, struck by his kindness despite the turmoil. She crossed her toes that he'd understand that she had no choice. She had to do this; it was her job. She had to ask.

"Hey, so that call was my boss. Scott Miller."

"Okay." Tor didn't take his eyes off the road. "What does my favorite person want?"

She bit her cheek at his sarcasm. "He's working on an article about Patch with quick turnaround. You're the coach, Tor. He needs a quote."

"No. No fucking way." Muscles worked in his jaw. The Angel anger muscles. "You're getting no comment on Donnelly."

"Tor, be reasonable. This is a story that the public is going to care about. They *should* care about it. Scott said your goalie broke someone's arm."

"I don't know the full story. Screw Scott."

"This isn't just about Scott. This is me too. You know this is my job. I understand that you have an insight about Patch. Maybe you see something different than a big angry dude that beats on people, I don't know. But neither will anyone else unless you say so."

"This is exactly what I hate about the press." He gave a disgusted-sounding snort. "They swoop in like vultures—like jackals—at the first sign of drama. There isn't even a full picture of the situation and already they are chewing on the meat, cracking into the bones."

"I admit that the media moves fast, and sometimes too fast for its own good. But I am the media too, Tor, and you have to accept that or else—"

"Or else what? Is it time to make a threat?"

"No!" She startled, taken aback that somehow they'd gotten here, to this familiar place of animosity, so quickly. "Not at all. Just that otherwise I go back to being your enemy. And I don't want that."

"I don't either." He was quiet a moment. "But tell me something, Angel. Scott Miller just called wanting a quote. How do you suppose he knew that we're together?"

Oh fudge.

"Aren't there bigger fish to fry right now?" Her blood froze in her veins.

"Answer the question." Permafrost coated his tone.

"I might have mentioned it." She sighed.

"I see."

The silence was excruciating. They had dropped down into a heavy cloud layer. The flurries had stopped but the wind was blowing drifts onto the side of the road over the asphalt.

"You need to slow down," she piped up. "You don't have snow tires and the conditions aren't safe."

"At any point did Scott Miller also ask you to do a story on me?"

Fog swirled by the windows, adding to the sense of claustrophobia. She could lie. Maybe she should lie. That would be better for everyone. But evading was easier. "Yes. But I decided that I don't want to mix my work with . . . you."

"Uh-huh. Nice sound bite. Except for that whole part where I happen to be your work." The Porsche wheels skidded on the next corner. Neve shrieked as the back of the car fishtailed, but with a muffled curse, Tor had the car back under expert control.

"Tor, please—"

The fog broke and she flew forward as he slammed on the brakes, just as she registered the scene.

A silver minivan had spun out, hit the side of the mountain. The front was crumpled in like an accordion, glass scattered across the road.

"Oh my God." Her hand flew over her mouth.

"Jesus Christ, that's Amber's van—my sister-in-law." He threw open the door. "Olive's in that car."

Neve was out of the car in a flash and ran after him. Pain shot through her ankle and she gritted her teeth, ignoring the fire spreading up her calf. It didn't matter. Nothing mattered but making sure the people in that van were going to be okay.

She looked into the front window and recognized the beautiful woman—Amber, Maddy's sister—behind the steering wheel. The airbag had deployed. She had a gash under one eye that bled, but otherwise she seemed okay, just dazed. Tor tried to tear open the side door, but it was jammed.

Neve pounded on the glass. "Are you okay?" she shouted at Amber.

The woman lolled her head to one side. "The girls? It's so quiet. Are the girls okay?"

Neve hit 911 and the dispatcher answered on the second ring. She gave their location and a brief description of the accident, unable to give an update on the girls in the back as the windows were tinted. Tor made a guttural sound, like a wild animal, as he hauled on the door. Muscles bulged in his neck. His knuckles were white. With a groan, the door gave way. But only a foot. He tried again. Nothing.

"Girls?" he shouted. "Olive."

Someone cried, "Help!"

Tor wedged his shoulder into the gap, but he was too big to fit.

But she wasn't.

"I can get through that," Neve said, tearing off her jacket. "Step back. The ambulance is on its way. Listen to me. They are going to be fine." She rested her hand on his tight jaw. "I promise."

"That's my baby girl in there."

She rested a hand on his cheek. "I've got her, I promise."

There were a lot of things that sucked about being five foot. Short jokes. The way clothes fit. The fact top shelves might as well be the summit of Everest. But when it came to crawling into a crashed van, there was a distinct advantage.

A girl curled into a ball in a middle seat, whimpering. "Are you okay?"

"Is the van going to blow up? I saw this movie one time where there was an accident. Gas leaked. There was a fire."

"Shhhhh," Neve crooned, placing a hand on the girl's arm. "Nothing is going to blow up. I promise. The police are coming. So is an ambulance. Everything is going to be just fine."

The two younger girls were in the back. One, Olive's cousin, was holding her shoulder. The knot in her clavicle made Neve's stomach churn. She'd clearly broken it. Olive was unconscious. Like Amber, she had a head wound. There was blood. A lot of blood.

She didn't want to unbuckle her or lay her down flat. First aid wasn't her specialty, but it looked like Olive had hit her head pretty hard. Blood smeared the back side window. There was a chance she'd hurt her neck and if they moved her it would make the injury worse.

"How is she?" Tor snapped at the door. "How are all of them?"

The sound of police cars rose from below the road. She couldn't tell Tor that Olive was unconscious. She had to distract him. "Get out into the road and be ready to greet the first responders. They will be here in a second. Any traffic coming needs to be routed."

"Neve."

"Do what you can, Tor. I'll do my part. I promise—you can trust me."

She was asking for a lot. For everything. Tor loved his daughter more than anyone in the world. Neve had to make sure she was going to be okay.

"Is Olive dead?" the girl next to her whimpered.

"No, of course not." Neve was aware that while Olive might not be responsive that didn't mean she couldn't hear them. She had to feign enough bravery for the little girl to believe she'd be okay. "There's a little blood. That's all."

"Lots."

"It's just because she cut her head. Heads are weird like that. They bleed a lot if they get injured. But that's perfectly normal." She took off her gray fleece top and crouched in front of Olive, pressing the material to her head to stanch the flow.

Olive moaned. A good sign.

"What happened?" she muttered.

"I think you guys spun out on some ice. Remember that big storm last night? It made the roads slippery."

"My head hurts," Olive moaned.

Thank goodness, she was speaking. And making sense.

"I'm not surprised," Neve said in a calm voice. "You gave it one heck of a whack."

"Am I going to die?"

The sirens were close. Tor was waving them in. Two paramedics jumped out.

"I'm going to tell you the truth. You'll have a headache. But you are going to get medicine that will make you feel better really soon."

"Can you . . . can you hold my hand?"

"Of course." Neve reached out.

The girl beside them started crying. "I'm scared."

"It's totally normal. You were just in a big, scary car accident. But I want you to look out the window. Do you see all those people? Police cars and two ambulances and a fire truck are outside. All those guys are helpers. They are here for one reason. To make you all okay."

"Girls?" Amber called from the front seat. "I'm sorry. I'm so sorry."

"Everyone is fine back here. They're a little shaken up. A lot scared. But they're going to be okay."

"I hate blood," Olive mumbled, her eyes flickering open.

"Me too." Neve gave her hand a squeeze. "But you are a brave girl. You are so strong. And you are going to sit here with me and take slow, deep breaths while your dad and these men save the day."

"I'm sorry that I said I hated you. I told my dad that. But I was mad."

Neve shook her head. "I promise, that doesn't matter. You love your father and I was kind of a jerk in that article, let's face it."

"Do you love him?"

"I . . . well . . ." Neve shook her head. "It's complicated, honey."

"My dad has never had a girlfriend. You are the first person he has ever brought around. Don't mess it up."

"I will do my best," she said.

"I like you," the girl said. "If you do love him, that would be okay with me."

There it was. The blessing from the daughter. Neve swallowed heavily. She didn't have it in her to explain that there probably wasn't going to be any relationship. That after these few strange minutes in the car, Olive would probably never see her again. Once they got back to Denver, there was every chance that she and Tor were going to be right back where they'd started. Head coach. Journalist. The divide between them was too great.

Firefighters ripped back the sliding door with a Jaws of Life wrench. Neve moved out, letting the paramedics have access.

Tor's hair stood wild. His shirt bottom hung untucked. His gaze was unfocused. "Is she . . . What . . . Did . . ."

"Olive's going to be fine." Neve took both his hands.

He glanced down. Blood streaked her fingers.

"That hers?"

Neve nodded. "She hit her head."

He kicked a piece of ice across the road. "Goddamn it."

"It's going to look worse than it is. She's talking. I saw her move her fingers and legs."

He heaved a ragged exhalation. "Her cousins?"

"One seems in shock. The other has a broken collarbone. Tell you what, why don't you ride with her in the ambulance? If you give me the keys to your car, I can follow along after."

He dug in his pockets and fished out the keys. "Thank you . . ." He hesitated, as if he wanted to say more, but just then they removed Olive on a stretcher.

"Go to her," Neve said. And she watched him climb up after his daughter into the ambulance. The other three were taken out on stretchers as well. She got the name of the hospital and walked back to the Porsche alone. Cars went by at a slow pace, everyone rubbernecking at the action.

When she got back into his car, behind the wheel, nerves set in. Her teeth clattered. Her hands shook. She'd been so frightened. But she knew her words were true. Olive was going to be okay. Maybe this was the payment the universe demanded—she and Tor couldn't work out, but the trade-off meant that a little girl got to keep her life.

She sniffed. Cedar. Pine. It smelled like him.

Two tears stole down her face. She glanced in the rearview and rubbed them away. She'd gotten out of her rut all right. In the past forty-eight hours, she had found not only her missing sex drive, but also a part of her heart that she hadn't realized was missing. A part that came in the form of a six-foot-tall, surly coach.

She wouldn't regret the experience. She wouldn't regret any of it. Putting the car into first, she steeled her jaw. No matter what happened, she'd always have the memory of these two perfect days.

Gaining a little speed, she got the car into second and then dropped it into third, huffing a frustrated breath. After all, there was no way in hell she'd be able to cover the hockey beat in Denver if she was having a relationship with the head coach. Zero. Zilch. The conflict of interest was simply too great. Today proved it.

Their relationship was hopeless, doomed from the start.

Chapter Eighteen

$\mathcal{T}$or felt like he owed the universe a favor. His little girl was going to be okay. She had a small concussion and a few bumps and bruises. Otherwise she was fine. Everyone else in the car had avoided serious injuries. A stroke of luck, the paramedics had said, seeing as there had been no guardrail on that particular stretch of road. If Amber had fishtailed left instead of right? He didn't want to think about the consequences too hard.

Maddy walked out to the lobby. "Hey, you." She plopped into the seat next to him. "What a day."

"Hell of a way to start a honeymoon," he said gruffly, then took a sip from his lukewarm coffee.

"A ticket to Tahiti can be replaced," she said. "Our little girl can't."

That was the best part of Maddy. She always said "our" daughter. Never "my." She valued him as Olive's father and never tried to demean him or diminish him in her eyes. For that, he'd been grateful and always did the same. They weren't right as a couple, but that didn't mean they couldn't be right as parents.

"Very true."

"Where's your date? From the wedding. The striking brunette."

"Neve."

She laughed, astonished. "I've read her column. Thought you two—"

"Couldn't stand each other?"

"Something like that, yeah."

"Guess we'd both been lying to ourselves. But it doesn't matter. I don't think it's going to work out. I asked her to take my car back to Denver. I'll stay here until they discharge Olive. They said another two days max. There's a few car rentals in town that do one-way service."

"What do you mean, it's not going to work out?"

He tried to ignore her probing look, but to no avail. "It's not like you and me. She loves hockey. She works as much as I do, more even."

Maddy arched a brow. "Whoa, defensive much? I just asked why."

"She's a reporter, covers the hockey beat. She can't be with me and do her job, not if me and the team are her job. It's a conflict. An impasse. What can I say? I played with fire inviting her to go away for the weekend, and it didn't do anything but burn us."

"There's no solution?"

"We're on opposing teams. We called a truce, but it's over now. My goalie got arrested last night. Posted bond. He's MIA. The lockout isn't letting up. She has to cover all of it. And I can't tell her to quit her job or go off and report on badminton or something."

"I didn't realize you ever backed down from a challenge," Maddy said lightly. "Or played to lose."

"Life isn't a game."

"Really? Because from where I sit it's rough, fast, exciting. Sometimes you get a throat punch. Sometimes you score." She glanced at her watch. "Anyway, I've got to go back in. I promised Olive I'd be there when the nurse gave her a bath."

He cleared his throat. "She's going to be glad to have you there for that job, and not me."

"You know, we might not have made a good marriage, but we're darn good co-parents." Her smile was small but genuine. "Amber and her girls told me what Neve did for Olive. How strong she was. How she kept her calm. She sounds like a good person, Tor. And I saw how you were looking at her."

"And how was that?"

Her sigh was soft. "Like you finally realized what true love is."

And with that she turned around and walked away.

His ex always did enjoy getting the last word—especially when she was right.

Chapter Nineteen

*N*eve hung up the phone in the *Age* lobby and stared at the massive modern-art piece hanging on the wall. It looked like a Rorschach test. Twenty minutes ago she might have been tempted to describe it as a tree branch dangling over a black hole. Now it was like a rising sun. A new day.

She'd barely hung on since getting back from her weekend with Tor. The Donnelly story was on lockdown. She'd been able to get a copy of the charges. Assault. He was out on bail and nowhere to be seen. The victim wasn't talking. The woman purported to be in the middle of it had disappeared.

All that lingered were rumors. Had Patch quit the team? Some suggested he'd decided to quit professional sports and return to his first ambition—joining the priesthood.

What a mental picture that made—a Catholic priest who broke arms with his bare hands. Neve didn't attend church but with that stage billing, she'd be curious.

Twenty minutes ago she'd sat in her gray cubicle at the *Age* dashing off an update on the lockout. There wasn't much to say about the negotiations. The thesaurus didn't have eight hundred words for *blah, blah, blah.*

That was when the phone rang. "Neve Angel, this is Tom Mc-Govern, senior vice president of Hellions Communications . . ."

Hugging her chest, she took the elevator back up to her office, walked to her desk, and stared at the computer.

There was only one person she wanted to share this news with.

She clicked up her email and typed *Tor.Gunnar@hellions.com* into the address box just as a commotion broke out up front. A few people made loud exclamations. Maybe it was someone's birthday. Usually free cake got people excited.

She looked up, but what she saw wasn't real. She knew that on a bone-deep level.

Maybe a disgruntled barista had spiked her dark roast with LSD as a joke. Because there was no way—no way—that Tor Gunnar was standing outside her cubicle holding so many roses that he looked like a damn bush.

She closed her eyes. Counted to three.

Still there.

"What are you doing?" she whispered.

"We need to talk," he replied. "And it's important. So I figured if I said it here, it would go in the papers."

Sure enough, curious reporters were drawing in, keeping their distance but within clear earshot.

"Speak of the devil. I was just trying to reach out to you."

"Guess I beat you to the punch. But here's the thing. I don't always have the right words, and it's not always that easy for me to express how I feel in a relationship, but I can't go another hour without you hearing this . . . I love you, Neve Angel."

She covered her mouth as the world tipped off its axis.

"Oh my God."

That shriek wasn't hers. An intern had whipped out her

phone, no doubt recording this for Facebook Live or something.

"That's right. Crazy in love." He turned around. "Are you jackals getting this? I am in love with Neve Angel. I have been for a long time, but I was too much of an idiot to know what was staring me in the face. I don't want to skulk around the edges. Or hide from rumors. I'm here on the up-and-up. Because dating a reporter might be unorthodox, but I'm ready to figure out a way to make it work. I work a dream job, but I'm a greedy man, and want my dream woman too."

Knock her over with a feather.

She rose to her feet, ignoring the slight tremble to her legs, but the moment her gaze locked on his warm blue eyes, she went still, as if a calm, tropical wave had washed over her.

"I guess we both have more in common than you can guess. Because I just so happen to be greedy too, and want *my* dream man, and *my* dream job." She looked around. "Where's Scott hiding?"

"Mmmph." Her boss stepped forward in a hideous purple tie that clashed with his yellow shirt, still swallowing the greasy-looking fast-food burger he was holding. He took a swig out of the sixteen-ounce soda he held in the other hand before snapping, "What?"

"I quit." Neve's simple sentence was met with an audible gasp from the other reporters.

"Neve, no." Tor stepped forward. "I didn't come to ask you to leave your job and—"

"I know that," she said with a wry smile. "You think I'd love you so much if you had? I am quitting for me. Because, Scott, let's face it, you kind of suck. You're a bully. Plus at least half your jokes would make the hair of anyone in Human Resources stand on end and frankly, I deserve better. So as of today I'm the head of public relations for the Denver Hellions, and I'm tendering my resignation here at the *Age* effective immediately." She glanced over to Tor. "I was just writing to tell you the news, but you scooped the story."

"Angel." A slow, devastating grin spread across his face, creasing the skin in the corners of his eyes and making her heart pound. "You telling me we're on the same team?"

"Looks like it." She arched a brow. "And my job is to make you look good."

He smirked. "Tall order."

"I think I can handle it." She didn't care that everyone was watching. All she cared about was getting Tor's mouth on her as soon as possible.

She jumped into his arms and he spun her around. The smell of roses washed over her and she knew that forever after, that scent would bring her back here, to this second. The velvet softness of his tongue. The feel of his arm clamping her lower back and hauling her to meet his hungry mouth. She wasn't all bushy eyebrows and a strong jaw. She wasn't a tough-as-nails reporter. She wasn't even the new kick-ass head of PR for an NHL team. She was just a girl, kissing the man she loved, a man who had just declared his love for her to the world.

"I love you," she said, pulling back.

"I already knew that." His brows rose. "I could tell."

She shook her head. "You really are insufferable, you know that?"

"And you love it." His gaze was hot on her face.

She hugged him close, pausing before the next kiss. "God help me, I do."

Epilogue

Four months later
Valentine's Day

𝒯he audience cheered before the curtains opened. Neve gripped the handle of her red-feathered fan. Her palms were so sweaty it was amazing it didn't clatter onto the floor. She nodded at the backstage tech and the music started. Michael Bublé. The curtains opened and there she was. In the spotlight. Wearing nothing but a top hat, garter belt, fishnet thigh highs, high-waist panties, and a corset. Her stilettos might as well be stilts.

This was recital night for the Twirling Tassels. The culmination of the weekly lessons. Each student performed a five-minute routine.

Four months ago, she'd been stuck in traffic. Stuck in a rut. Stuck in life, period. She'd been afraid of what it meant to blossom. To let loose. Be pretty *and* practical. She could be feminine and strong. Sexy and powerful. One word didn't negate the other. With the lockout over and games resuming this weekend, she'd now often be making that same commute beside her boyfriend—no, wait . . . Her gaze fell on the square blue sapphire ring winking from her finger. *Fiancé.* He'd proposed in bed before the show.

Their bed.

She'd moved in last weekend and never intended to leave.

I wish I could give you everything, he had whispered as he slid the platinum band onto her finger as they lay stomach to stomach. *But for now, I hope this is enough.*

She lowered her fan and peered out into the sea of expectant faces. It didn't take her long to find him. His bold features stood out in the crowd. He lifted his fingers to his mouth and let out a hog whistle, pride and liquid-hot possession showing from his eyes.

That's my girl, his gaze said.

She sashayed forward. She was doing this. Owning the moment. Embracing her power to be whoever the heck she wanted to be.

After blowing Tor Gunnar a kiss, she shook her shoulders in a shimmy, threw back her head, and began to dance.

Can't wait for more steamy hockey romance from Lia Riley?
Turn the page for a sneak peek of

PUCK AND PREJUDICE

in which pro hockey player Tuck Tyler accidentally travels
back in time to Regency England and finds himself falling
for a headstrong contemporary of Jane Austen . . .

Coming Winter 2025!

Chapter One

*T*ucker Tyler walked across the sticky floor carrying a second round of drinks for the table. The pub's best days were probably a few centuries ago, but that fact didn't seem to faze his companions, their voices rising from the dimly lit booth.

His younger sister, Tallula, gave a cursory nod as she reached for a pint and continued her argument. "Clearly, Jane Austen's impact is unparalleled. Her insights into social issues were ahead of her time, and her exploration of class and society remains as relevant today as it was then."

"Come off it!" Her friend Pip slumped back, her freckled features contorted. "The Brontë sisters were literary rebels. They gave us Mr. Rochester, the ultimate bad boy with a heart of gold, and Heathcliff, who defined the idea of having a situationship."

These two had been going in circles about dead writers for forty minutes. Tuck slid into his seat and absentmindedly checked his phone for the umpteenth time. Maybe something interesting would pop up. At this point, he'd settle for a weather update.

"You'd prefer misery and pining over wit, charm, and financial stability?" Tallula scoffed. "Who needs unhinged passion when you can have a comfortable marriage with a side of banter? Tuck . . . what would you choose: a person who was down for dirty, amazing sex, but keeps a spouse locked in their attic—"

"Or," Pip interjected, "a snobby rich boy who is embarrassed to be infatuated with you?"

"Uh?" Tuck froze, hoping he didn't look like a deer in headlights. "Neither?"

Both women groaned, exchanging eye rolls before resuming their debate.

Tallula, studying British Literature at the University of Bath, had already booked a short friend trip to the village of Hallow's Gate when Tucker had sprung his surprise visit. She'd insisted that he tag along. Tonight, they had all gone to celebrate Yule at the Ye Olde King's Head in the town square.

"What happened to the new king's head?" Tucker had mumbled when they parked out front. Pip, another student from Tallula's department, had responded with a half-hearted smile. So he'd wisely decided to sip his beer and zone out, only half listening to the marathon debate about which literary icon made the bigger impact: Jane Austen or the Brontë sisters. It didn't take long for his mind to wander again.

He drained his glass, wiping the foam off his mouth, and contemplated his own private dilemma. Who'd he pick for the goalie GOAT? Patrick Roy? Martin Brodeur? Dominik Hasek?

An hour later, Tallulah and her friend hadn't come up for air. He'd passed the time packing down battered fish with thick-cut, golden-brown potato chips, mushy peas, a giant bowl of sticky date pudding, and sending furtive texts to teammates.

Thousands of miles away, it was game day—the Austin Regals were up against the Denver Hellions—and he wasn't playing. Again. He should be eating his lucky pregame meal—a Texas toast turkey club, green apple, and a Coke. And wearing his prized underwear—the ones with cartoon kittens that his teammates both teased him for and secretly revered. Those boxers were a source of street cred in the locker room. After all, being a goalie came with a license for eccentricity. But no rituals ever prepared him for the team doc finding a lump in his armpit last spring or the diagnosis of Stage 1A Hodgkin's lymphoma. The good news? It looked to be easily curable. The bad news? Treatment and recovery meant he'd be sidelined for much—if not all—of the season.

"Hey." Tallula reached over and poked him. "We're boring you, huh?"

"No, it's all good." He swallowed back a jaw-cracking yawn. "But I don't have a lot to contribute."

"You'd rather tell us about how you hit a rubber puck really hard?"

He couldn't tell if Pip was joking or a pain in the ass. Maybe both.

"Come on, guys," Tallula pleaded, flashing a peace sign. "I'm positive there's some conversational sweet spot on the Venn diagram here."

Tuck shared a brief glance with Pip, and they both silently agreed to let their differences be like that one sock that always disappears in the laundry—mysterious and unresolved.

"Why don't you two stay here and bookworm to your hearts' content? I'll walk back to the B&B. We'll reconvene in the morning for crumpets or whatever counts for breakfast around here."

"Really?" Tallula furrowed her brow. "Pip and I can leave too. You do look tired."

"Nah. I'm fine." The lie rolled off easily. He'd been saying it enough.

"I know you'd choose hockey over South Hampshire any day of the week." Tallula squeezed his shoulders in a half hug. "But I *am* excited to play tourist together. You haven't gotten much of a chance to see the world beyond the rink. It's good out here. I promise."

"Sounds like a plan." He playfully yanked one of her braids.

She slid her hand across the table. It took him a second to realize she was passing him her car keys.

"No." His answer was firm. "I'll walk."

"You'd be doing me a favor," Tallula wheedled. "We need to drink more before we start on the romantic poets."

"At least we agree Percy Bysshe Shelley is the worst," Pip muttered into her glass.

"He took his second wife, Mary's, virginity on her mother's grave," Tallula explained like that cleared up everything. "Then that same Mary went and wrote *Frankenstein*."

How was he related to this walking Wikipedia?

"Anyway, I digress. Take the car." Tallula's tone was final. "Later, I'll text you and you can come back and get us."

"Okay, deal." He fisted the keys. "Be good. Don't talk to strangers."

"If anyone offers us a lolly, I'll kick 'em in the shins."

Tucker kept the smile plastered on his face until he walked out the door. Out in the small-town square, he jammed his hands into the pockets of his jeans, the rhythmic strike of his boots echoing against the cobblestones. Night mist hung low, full of woodsmoke and the earthy scent of decaying leaves—a far cry from Zamboni fumes and chlorinated ice. The brick row houses flanking on all four sides could be from a storybook, except he didn't believe in fairytales. Only the hard truth scraping against the back of his mind.

Shouldn't be here.

Shouldn't be here.

He made his way over to Tallula's Mini Cooper. It was as small and boxy as a toaster. He opened the door and frowned down at the passenger seat. Shit. Wrong side. Walking around, he made a mental note. *Stay on the left.*

Inside, his knees smashed against the steering wheel as he shoved the key in the ignition and he had to drop his jaw to his chest to fit. He snorted. This was a glorified go-cart. Reaching for the seat belt, he jumped as his elbow beeped the horn. Scratch that, this was a clown car.

Walking might have been easier. Even with the cold.

Shifting the stick to a low gear and releasing the clutch, he pulled into the empty laneway. Condensation clung to the windows, obscuring his view. With a reluctant twist, he cranked open a window, wincing at the sudden gust of December air. As he crossed a stone bridge over a narrow creek at the outskirts of Hallow's Gate, he reached for the radio dial. But a high-pitched cry drowned out the sound of water trickling over rocks.

A sheepdog bolted from a farmhouse on the hill, heading straight for the road. Hot on its tail chased a blond boy in red flannel pajamas and too-big rain boots. Tucker's stomach hollowed as he hit the brakes. Shit. Black ice. The dog and kid, illuminated by the headlights, froze in front of him, wide-eyed. Tires screamed in protest as he fought to stop. This wasn't going to work. Without a second thought, he violently cranked the wheel to the right, throwing him off the road like a rodeo cowboy on a wild bull. He bumped and bounced, completely out of control, plowing through the snow toward a frozen pond.

With a roll, the car hit the ice on the driver's side, and there was a heavy gunshot crack. A shock of cold water funneled through the open window, turning his insides to frozen slush. As his tongue recoiled, he fought to relax. Calm down. No big deal. This was just like the cold-water immersion therapy that PT staff made the team do to help muscle recovery after tough games. He just needed to breathe through it—slow and steady. With a quick motion, he got the seat belt off, and just in time. The car was sinking fast.

He pushed away the thought as he rattled the door. Stuck. Damn. He'd have to somehow squeeze through the window.

He'd been the Austin Regals' star goalie, able to run through box jumps, ladder drills, sprints, and cycling to keep his cardio fitness in top form. But just last week, he'd tried jogging and had to dial it to a walk after a measly quarter-mile. Fuck cancer.

He was paid to stay cool under pressure. Needed to imagine himself by a roaring fire, dry and warm, recounting the story to Tallula. He mentally rehearsed it, visualized it. With a determined crawl, he got halfway through the open window . . . then stuck.

You're better than this. Plow through.

He pushed, but his arms might as well be made of wet noodles. His strength leached out by the second.

Failure wasn't an option. Not after everything he'd survived. He bit his cheek, wrangling his focus. Each movement had to be controlled and efficient—no room for error or wasted effort.

His jackhammering heart filled his ears as he kicked free and started swimming for the surface. The top of his head cracked against a frozen ceiling. Unyielding. No way out. Everything was so cold, yet his lungs were fire, raw and burning. He punched violently again and again. His knuckles scraping a wall of ice. His nails tore, ripping and breaking. No exit. Shit! His lungs screamed for a single drop of air. Black water pressed on all sides. He couldn't resist the urge. Had to breathe. Needed release. As he reflexively gasped, the darkness rushed in. There was an odd sense of brightness, and emptiness, a sensation of wild spinning. And then . . . nothing.

Chapter Two

My Most Neglectful Offspring,

I set pen to paper to address the conspicuous silence that followed my previous letter. I can only surmise that your leisurely diversions have left scant moments for correspondence.

This past Monday, I had the pleasure to take an excursion through Kensington Gardens with Lavinia Throckmorton. Amidst this floral profusion, dear Lavinia unveiled a most astonishing revelation—her Augusta, at a mere eighteen years of age, has found herself betrothed. A marvel, considering you, my dear, have now completed nine and twenty orbits around the sun in solitary splendor.

In her usual delicate manner, Lavinia sought news of your well-being, and I conveyed that you were finding the rural air most invigorating. However, my dearest fugitive, you embarked upon your pastoral sojourn to visit your cousin with a promise to be gone for a fortnight. It's now been twice that time.

In your absence, your brother has undertaken the task

(again) of identifying several suitable men who, against all odds, remain unattached. I don't have to remind you that opportunities for a union are diminishing with each passing day. I eagerly await your prompt return.

> *With the deepest affection and a*
> *hint of maternal vexation,*
> *Your Loving Mother*

A hint? A hint! Lizzy dropped the letter to her lap with a snort. Hell's teeth. Her self-proclaimed Loving Mother was ready to paint the words "Please Marry My Daughter" on a bedsheet to hang out the front window of the family's Mayfair home. She knotted her hands into the picnic blanket she perched on to keep from shaking them at ducks paddling in the pond down the rise. The mallards were hunting watercress, minding their own business. Her mother could take a lesson. It was high time Horatia Dashwood developed a hobby. Archery, perhaps? Or the delicate art of watercolor? Possibly the solace of a well-chosen book, preferably a scandalous one? Anything to draw attention away from the subject of her daughter's matrimonial prospects, or rather, the lack thereof.

Last night, at another of Cousin Georgie's infamous dinner parties, Lizzy had been struck by a revelation during the fish course. A fact presented itself that was so painfully obvious she had inclined toward her friend Jane, seated on her left, and murmured, "It's a truth to be secretly acknowledged, that a single man in possession of a good fortune would be welcome to make any wise woman a widow."

Jane had choked on a bite of trout and caper, kicking her

under the table with the pointed toe of her shoe . . . a silent order to behave.

But where was the lie? While mourning wear wouldn't be her first choice—black was most certainly *not* her color—a quick review of the facts determined that the advantages of widowhood were many:

One: Financial independence. Widows could inherit property and income and then control their own affairs. No more begging her brother or mother for pocket money—or, worse, a future husband.

Two: Respectability. Widows might travel and socialize with less scrutiny and restrictions.

Three: Freedom. Widows made decisions about their households, finances, and social lives. They were not subject to the authority of a husband or any tedious marital obligations and had the power to remain forever single.

Of course, if one allowed emotion to get tangled up in it, the experience of widowhood could be tainted by grief, like her own mother after Father's sudden death ten years ago. But Mother, believing she needed a husband, had remarried, thus squandering any opportunity for independence. And if a man had less means, it would also put a widow at a disadvantage. That was why the only real solution was to marry someone with a decent income and then . . .

What? Wait for them to die?

She worried at her lower lip. Well, she certainly wasn't a murderess. Far from it. She couldn't even bring herself to kill spiders.

Could she ask her brother to confine his searching for men who were known to be sickly? That would be *quite* the conversation.

Nigel, please find me a wealthy husband, but could you be a dear and ensure he has consumption?

She settled back on her elbows, ignoring the tendrils of hair coming loose from the artless knot at the nape of her neck, and took a bite out of the apple she'd pinched from Cousin Georgie's cellar.

Involving Nigel was a terrible idea. He'd run straight to Mother and Lizzy would never hear the end of it.

She took another bite, frowning. The apple's flesh had a mealy texture, tasting more like a distant memory of the fruit, but chewing gave her something to do with the clenched feeling inside her—the one that wanted to break the rules which kept her as little better than a canary in an ornate cage. It was unjust that she was compelled to return to London and feign interest in dull men who couldn't engage in conversation beyond the topics of weather, hunting, or the evening's dinner menu. And that was if she was lucky. If not, she'd be stuck listening to thoughts on horse breeding or the worst of the worst, the gentleman's health and ailments, a gouty toe or watery bowels.

Talk about mental rot.

Here in Hallow's Gate, Georgie lived the life of a merry widow—a model of all that was possible. Her favorite cousin had an entire room in her house dedicated to scientific experiments and held female-only parties where women weren't encouraged to take dainty nibbles off their plates. No, they indulged with gusto. She had recently hosted a luncheon entirely composed of desserts! The table was piled high with trifles, jellies, macarons, cakes of all sizes, blancmange, syllabubs, and crème brûlée. They washed it all down with Irish whisky, Madeira, and rum until one of the ladies retrieved a violin and played a lively tune that sent them all into an un-restrained dance, devoid of any proper steps. They ended up collapsing against the walls or sprawling on the floor itself, laughter and panting echoing through the spinning room.

And in the nearby village, their friend Jane not only wrote books, but had even published one. *Sense and Sensibility*. It might have been officially printed with the nom de plume "By a Lady," to protect her privacy, yet still . . . she had done it. And even better, Jane gave the two main characters the same sur-name as Cousin Georgie, and by that extension, Lizzy herself. Dashwood.

Jane had recently even read the opening of one of Lizzy's own short stories, "The Enchanted Garden," whereby a cer-tain Lady Genevieve Devereux, a young woman of remark-able brains, arrived at an estate to spend the summer. She carried with her the weight of societal expectations from her family, who pressured her to make an advantageous match. One fateful evening, as Lady Genevieve strolled through the moonlit gardens, she stumbled upon a hidden gate that led to the enchanted garden. There, she discovered a sparkling fountain said to grant wishes. As Lady Genevieve pondered the nature of her wish, she encountered a mysterious man who was no lord or a gentleman of fortune, only a humble but strapping gardener . . .

Jane said her scribblings had "showed promise," and Lizzy tucked the compliment into a pocket of her heart. Promise . . . she would make good on that promise, if she didn't end up tucked away in some dusty house to keep a man's bed warm.

Which is what it felt like the world was conspiring to ensure happened.

With a frustrated shriek, she threw her apple core into the bulrushes and froze, cocking her head. There had been a strange sound. What was that? A duck? A dying duck?

A very big, very dying duck?

She scrambled onto her feet and gathered her skirts, straining to peer into the bulrushes as they waved on their tall green stalks, velvety brown seed pods bobbing cheerfully.

Her shoulder blades uncinched a fraction. Never mind. Maybe it had been the wind. Or some echo from the village. Or . . .

Blood drained to the tips of her toes.

There it came again.

It didn't sound like a duck. Unless that duck happened to be a groaning man.

"Hello?" She took a single tentative step forward, her throat drier than dust. "Is everything all right?" A perfectly ridiculous question. Whoever made the sound was in a murky pond. Of course they weren't all right. Far from it.

She suppressed a frown. Had a farmer drunk too many pints at Ye Olde King's Head? Or perhaps earlier, someone slipped down the hill, rolling into the water.

No point dithering. She shoved the letter into her bodice and strode forward. If she was in for a penny, might as well make it a pound.

She crept to the shore, swatting back an overzealous dragonfly as her slippers squelched in the mud, making it impossible to hide her approach. Gooseflesh prickled the back of her arms and she resisted the temptation to glance around as if someone might come and save her from this obligation. All was well. She'd handle this just fine. If anything dangerous was to emerge she'd . . . she'd . . . punch it in the nose. Georgie had been teaching her boxing. Or at least telling her she ought to learn.

Air whizzed between her teeth as Lizzy pushed her arms into the bulrushes and shoved them back. Glancing down, her gaze collided with a brutal-looking man glaring up with striking blue eyes, even brighter when contrasted to the blood smeared across his angular features.

"W-What happened?" She got the words out, just, wary but clear.

He pushed himself to a sitting position with obvious effort and dabbed the end of his nose, wincing. "I got hit in the face with a fucking apple."

The accent. That guitar-plucked twang. She'd heard it before in town, but not often.

American.

And gads, he was big. She'd wager once standing he'd rise a head taller than herself, and she was by no means a delicate violet.

Dozens of questions piled up. Why was his dark brown hair shorn to the nubs? His jacket was black, but why was the fabric so peculiar—too shiny—with strange metal teeth holding it together along a central seam? And his long-splayed legs were encased in a sturdy-looking cotton dyed a deep blue.

In turn, he gaped at her lavender walking dress, his expression shifting from coolly peeved to incredulous as he raked his gaze up, down, and back again. She'd never been an object of such single-minded focus before. The sensation made her oddly shy, but she fought back the urge to tame her wild hair, ignoring the fact her coif likely rivaled Medusa. Instead, she returned his stare, counting silently *one . . . two . . . three . . . four . . .*

Beneath the swarthy shadow of stubble peppering his jaw, a muscle twitched, breaking the stillness.

Lizzy blinked first. Unsure why her face was suddenly afire.

"Sir . . ." She paused, swallowing hard to steady her voice. "Are you sure that you're quite all ri—"

"What are you wearing?" he blurted.

Chapter Three

"What am *I* wearing? I beg your pardon, but I believe that's the pot calling the kettle black." The strange woman flashed her teeth. A pretty smile. Her lips weren't too full or too thin, but just right, like Goldilocks.

Tucker's head throbbed. A faint buzzing rang in his ears as if high-voltage power lines were nearby. What the hell happened?

The woman was talking a mile a minute, but he couldn't concentrate, not when a wave of dizziness knocked him on all fours. He vomited water that tasted like silt and algae.

"Good heavens." She gave a muffled shriek. "None of that please. Oh dear. I think I'm going to . . ." The woman spun away, hands on her hips, and gagged.

"Ma'am?" Tucker sat on his heels and swiped his mouth with the back of his hand as a few hard truths registered: it was daytime, warm instead of cold, he was soaking wet, and something was strange as hell about the surroundings. The old stone bridge was now wooden and while that farmhouse on the hill looked the same, the streetlights and road signs were gone. So was Tallula's car.

The woman turned back, her small nose scrunching like

she smelled something awful. "Are you finished? I nearly cast up my lunch."

Sweat pooled beneath his arms. It was too hot, too bright. The warm breeze carried the scent of fresh grass. A bird swooped in and perched on the tip of a marsh weed. Brown feathers? Red chest? A robin? His heart banged in his chest. These were summer smells. Summer sights. Where was the snow? Was he hallucinating? Had he died in that fucking pond?

"Are you . . . ?" He shielded his eyes from the sun, trying to keep his hand steady. "Some sort of angel?" She was beautiful enough with those wide eyes, long lashes, and soft skin.

"That line will never work on ladies. If you aspire to be a poet, I recommend trying harder." Her low, husky voice tinged with amusement even as she kept looking at him strangely.

Okay, so he wasn't dead. He mentally crossed that option off the shortening list of possibilities.

"So, what the hell is going on?" His frustration hit critical mass. He needed to make sense of this. Of the weather. Of *her*. An idea flashed and he clung to it as though it might carry him back to sanity. "Wait." He snapped his fingers. "Is this one of those historical reenactment things? You know, where you act like you are old-fashioned or whatever and run a black-smith shop?"

"A blacksmith . . ." Her brows knit as her voice trailed off. "Exactly just how hard did I hit you with that apple?"

He clenched his jaw. She was messing with him. "Look. You're good at your job. A perfect ten performance. But can you drop the act? Where's the car? I have to find my sister."

"Car." She frowned. "You mean a cart, sir?"

He released a frustrated sigh. "C-A-R. Car."

She stared blankly.

"It can't be summer." His head throbbed like he'd gotten a slapshot between the eyes.

"It's Midsummer's Day."

"Not December?"

She clicked her tongue. "Perhaps if I fetch a doctor and—"

"No!" He threw up a hand, trying to think, trying to make this make sense. "Wait! Okay. Let's say you aren't an actor, and it's actually summer. Where are we?"

"This is Hallow's Gate, England, sir. Midway between the towns of Ropley and Bentworth."

The place was the same. He felt like an idiot asking the next question. He swallowed it back twice. But he had to. "W-What year is it?"

Silence.

"Are you trying to amuse yourself at my expense?" she snapped.

He made a sound between a growl and a snort. "If I was, I could think of a dozen better ways to do it that wouldn't involve me getting my ass wet and asking stupid questions."

"Fair point." She turned over his words before giving a small shrug. "It's 1812."

The strange electric buzzing noise vanished entirely. The world was nothing but wind, birdsong, and waves lapping against the shore. If this was a dream, he better wake up real soon.

"You don't appear happy with the news," she said.

"No, I—" He released a bark of laughter, no humor, but better than exploding. "I can't say that I am."

"I need to think." She ripped out her bun, long waves of dark brown hair tumbling over her shoulders as she paced.

"You've voided your stomach, and don't know the year. However, you don't appear mad or in your cups."

"My cups?"

"Pickled. Drunk as a lord. Three sheets to the wind." She tapped her chin. "If you are indeed sober as a church mouse, it appears something very strange has happened to you."

"Understatement." A humorless smile twisted his mouth. "But yeah."

She continued to digest his words, but seemed to believe him. "What year did you think it was . . . 1912?" A hundred-year jump.

He snorted, scratching the back of his head. "Add another hundred years and then toss in some change."

"Ah." The color drained from her face before she stiffened her spine. "Well, you can't very well remain in Farmer Pennycook's pond. This doesn't make sense. Not even Jane Austen could come up with a plot like this."

"Jane? Jane Austen?" The name swam through his mind, bringing him back to his sister and Pip at the bar. "Does every woman know Jane Austen?"

But this woman wasn't listening. She was halfway up the hill, still talking to herself. "Best I take you straight to my cousin. Georgie will know what to do. She always has ideas."

The woman had a point. He couldn't stay here.

"Wait!" She lifted a finger in warning as he stirred. "Stop. I'll need to find a disguise, won't I? And where will I locate that? Does he have to be quite so large?" Her tone was annoyed, like his height was a personal affront. "Never mind." She pushed on, and he wasn't sure if she spoke to him or herself. "But he can't be seen in those clothes."

He glanced down at his down jacket, blue jeans, and lace-up hiking boots. So, yeah. He'd be out of place. "They don't, uh, stone people for witchcraft in 1812 . . . do they?"

"Witch what?" She gaped with utter confusion. "This isn't the sixteen hundreds. Now if you don't mind, I'm trying to come up with a plan. But if you keep interrupting me, I might be tempted to source an axe instead and be very Henry the Eighth."

The heated look she shot him packed pure spice. Damn, this woman was human hot sauce.

"There's nothing for it." Her words had a tone of finality. "You'll need to wait here until I get back."

"Are you serious?" He was just supposed to wait here and do what? Watch the minnows? No fucking way.

"You can't be seen like this." She waved a hand, gesturing to his clothing. "The village would never speak of anything else again. No, you must wait and not make a sound, Mr. . . ." She trailed off. "Pardon. I didn't catch your name."

"Taylor. Tucker Taylor. But you can call me Tuck. Most people do."

"Tucker Taylor." She spoke his name with a slight frown, like trying a bite of strange new food. "How very . . . American."

It took all his will not to roll his eyes. "And you are?"

She straightened. "Miss Elizabeth Rose Dashwood. My friends call me Lizzy, but I believe Miss Dashwood will do fine for now, Mr. Taylor." She dusted her hands on her skirts and turned to leave. "I'll return within the hour. If anyone comes close just pretend to be a frog and croak."

Chapter Four

*L*izzy pressed the back of her hands to her cheeks as she rushed toward the village road, in truth scarcely more than a narrow lane lined by moss-covered stones. A tapestry of wildflowers blanketed the field as oak and birch stood sentinel in the nearby wood, and yet she barely registered the charms, so at odds with London's bedlam. The heat weighed down on her, the humid air clinging to her skin like a blanket while the sun sought to challenge the efficacy of her precious soap. Her heart pounded fiercely in her chest, the rhythmic thud echoing in her ears. She half-expected someone from the nearby cottages to emerge, curious about the thunderous noise, as if a regiment were marching through the vicinity. She tugged impatiently at her damp bodice. Honestly, her corset had a single duty, to lift and separate her bust, but presently, it was more occupied with gathering the perspiration from beneath her arms.

She wriggled in discomfort. What if she ended up stinking like a stable while in the company of one of the most handsome gentlemen she had ever encountered?

Tuck's cropped, nearly black hair might be an unusual style, but it befit the resolute contours of his face, those narrow-set eyes, the slash of brows, and such straight, bright teeth. And then there was the matter of his size—the bulk of the shoulders, those massive hands with the thick scar banding one knuckle, the ridge of collarbone that revealed itself when he absently tugged at his shirt. A strange sensation coiled in her belly. Really though, how were anyone's teeth so white, so perfect?

She pinched her lips together. Could she be more ridiculous? Just this morning, her biggest concern had been the dwindling state of her soap bar, wrapped in a scrap of silk, infused with lavender and thyme. She hadn't been sure if she should ask for more to be sent from town or if that would incite Mama to pen a letter on the need for an unmarried woman to demonstrate frugality so as not to burden others. The idea of enduring that particular lecture felt as enjoyable as dozing off atop a wasp's nest.

Slathered in honey.

Naked.

Who gave a fig about exorbitant soap prices when a man from the future had crawled from the old cow pond? Her life rearranged itself in the span of minutes. And she couldn't put it back the way it had been before. A subtle shift filled the air, a crackling energy teeming with uncharted possibilities. It whispered of magic within reach, an unfolding adventure. The hair on her arms rose. For the first time in her life, she could truly say she didn't have the faintest idea what tomorrow would bring. And wasn't sure if the notion was exhilarating or terrifying.

And just what sort of name was Tucker Taylor? Perhaps common enough in America. But here? A soft, nervous laugh escaped as she reached the road. He might as well call himself Beasley Weaselwood.

Wind feathered her face as she licked her parched lips, trying to concentrate on the gravel poking into her thin soles. She needed to feel the ground, let it steady the dizziness threatening to spin her heart into her stomach.

Wait.

A new idea took hold. She hadn't gone stark raving mad and invented the whole thing, right? *Impossible.* She slid her hand beneath the thick coil of hair and kneaded her tight neck muscles. For starters, mad people don't worry about being mad. They'd simply accept a time traveler with a shrug and be off making daisy chains.

No need to risk a bruise by pinching herself. She seldom dreamed, and on the rare occasion she succumbed to reverie while asleep, her dreams involved her teeth falling out or flying around Westminster. Never hitting a time adventurer in the face with an apple.

The only viable choice was to entertain the truth of his wild claim and provide assistance in resolving the matter. Georgie's estate lay just shy of a mile away. Successfully getting Tuck there without incident depended on her ability to conjure appropriate male garb. How was that supposed to happen? A snap of the fingers? Luck?

A movement caught her eye, and she instinctively turned, silently thanking whichever guardian angel was watching over her. Beyond the yellow gate sat a farm—a humble brick abode half-covered in ivy and bordered by vibrant flower and vegetable gardens. On a hedgerow near the barn hung linen smocks, a few pairs of darned wool stockings, a neatly patched brown coat, a few plain shirts, and two pairs of breeches. How fortunate it was that the farmer had chosen today as his washing day—these were precisely what she needed.

Except she couldn't approach the front door and say, "Greetings, sir, delightful summer weather we're presently enjoying, don't you think? Now, if you would be so kind, I have an urgent need of your breeches."

But if she dared to snatch any clothes in broad daylight, and was apprehended in the act, she'd end up in the local gaol before she could hum Greensleeves. Then mother would lock her in their Mayfair attic out of sheer embarrassment, and Tuck would remain stuck in that stinking swamp until he really did turn into a frog.

What to do? What to do?

Turn over to read the grumpy/sunshine hockey romance

VIRGIN TERRITORY,

where Hellions goalie Patrick "Patch" Donnelly
meets his match!

Turn over to read the enemies-to-lovers hockey romance

HEAD COACH,

where Hellions coach Tor Gunnar meets his match!

DISCOVER MORE BY
LIA RILEY

HELLIONS HOCKEY

BRIGHTWATER

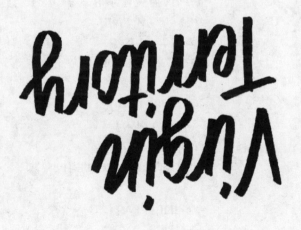

By Lia Riley

HELLIONS HOCKEY ROMANCES
Mister Hockey
Head Coach
Virgin Territory

BRIGHTWATER SERIES
Last First Kiss
Right Wrong Guy
Best Worst Mistake

EVERLAND, GEORGIA SERIES
It Happened on Love Street
The Corner of Forever and Always

OFF THE MAP SERIES
Upside Down
Sideswiped
Inside Out

ANTHOLOGIES
Snowbound at Christmas

Virgin Territory

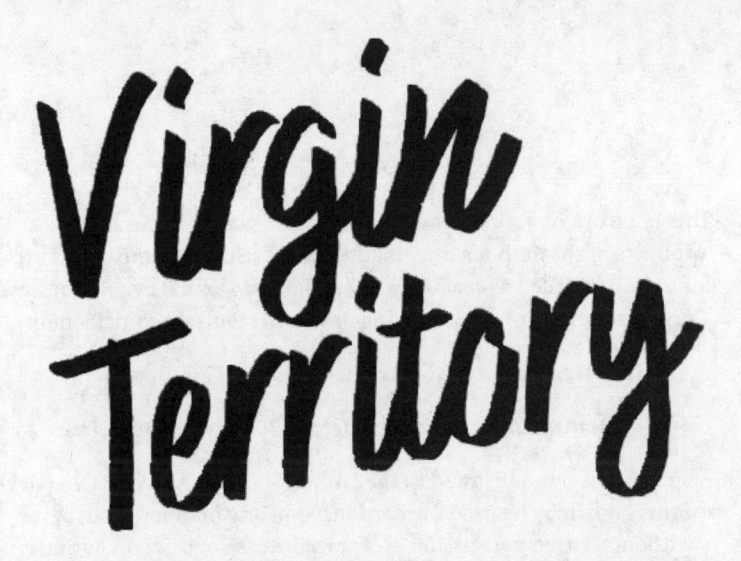

A HELLIONS HOCKEY ROMANCE

LIA RILEY

AVON

An Imprint of HarperCollinsPublishers

HarperCollins books may be purchased for educational, business, or sales promotional use. For information, please email the Special Markets Department at SPsales@harpercollins.com.

Originally published separately as *Head Coach* and *Virgin Territory* in the United States by Avon Impulse in 2017 and 2018.

Interior text design by Diahann Sturge-Campbell

Library of Congress Cataloging-in-Publication Data has been applied for.

ISBN 978-0-06-338344-9

24 25 26 27 28 LBC 5 4 3 2 1

To All You Nasty Women Who Are Persisting

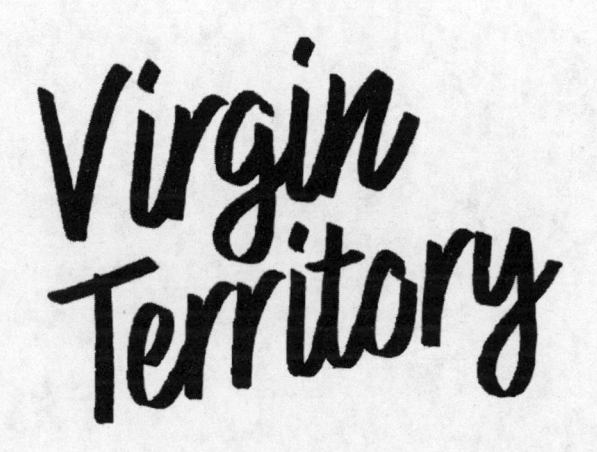

Chapter One

$\mathcal{P}$atch Donnelly ignored the stranger in the gray suit slouching behind the player bench. He had more important things to focus on, like the disc of frozen rubber racing toward his head. Inhaling the scent of freshly resurfaced ice, he blocked the backhand, and bent his lips into a faint grin.

Damn—it was good to be back.

The NHL season had been delayed for four months after breakdowns with collective bargaining negotiations. To celebrate the end of the lockout, Coach had agreed to make the first practice back a public event, and Hellions fans came flocking, bursting the stadium at the seams.

Patch dropped into a crouch, swaying from side to side. Out here on the line there was a palpable sense of being up against the world, and he wouldn't have it any other way. He knew he was a different breed. It took someone with a few screws loose to face down a puck traveling at a hundred miles an hour and love every second. But as he worked through the drills, his gaze returned to the bench. The suit's dead-eyed stare prickled his sixth sense, and if there was one thing he trusted in this shitty world, it was his intuition.

When something didn't feel right, it probably wasn't.

That inbuilt radar had helped him survive childhood, and left him with more than his fair share of paranoia.

The guy could be another NHL exec making the rounds. But tell that to the vise grip in Patch's gut.

At the end of practice, the suit made a beeline in his direction.

"Patrick Donnelly?" he said coolly as Patch stepped off the ice.

"Who's asking?"

Time dropped into slow motion as the suit smacked a manila envelope against the front of his jersey.

"You've been served." And with that he turned and stalked away.

The ever-vigilant media went nuts. Cameras flashed as journalists' questions hit him with rapid-fire intensity.

"What's up with getting served your first day back?"

"Is this going to affect the rest of your season?"

"Patch! Who's suing you?"

He strode to the locker room, head down, jaw rigid. No point opening the summons. He knew who was after him. He'd been expecting it.

The bad guys always come for you in the end.

Chapter Two

$\mathcal{M}$argot Kowalski hunched in the corner of the Cozy Clove Chai Shoppe frowning at her workbook. Her butt was numb. She'd been sitting here since midafternoon and *How to Write a Kick-Ass Business Plan in Under Two Hours* hadn't delivered on its ambitious promise. Although, in fairness to the authors, Margot's attention span mimicked a caffeinated squirrel inside a nut factory.

It didn't help matters that the college-aged girls at the closest table had forgotten how to use their indoor voices. And had a talent for ignoring Margot's pointed looks.

"Make sure to be honest." The one with the blunt-cut bangs had a laugh that could put screech owls in heat. "It says here that failure to do so will render the results inaccurate."

"Aye, aye, Sergeant!" Her friend in the Nordic knit poncho gave a mock salute, nearly upending her teacup.

Cue more screeching.

Margot gritted her teeth, eyes narrowing. She was a nice enough person—that is, until someone pressed her bitch button.

These two were inching toward the danger zone.

"Okay, okay. Question one." Bangs smirked at her iPhone. "Have you ever gotten a hickey?"

Margot rolled her eyes so hard that they threatened to pop out of her head.

The hand-calligraphed sign by the register read: THIS IS A SCREEN-FREE SPACE: NO LAPTOPS, CELL PHONES, OR IPADS. CONVERSATION, READING, AND DAYDREAMING ARE ENCOURAGED.

She'd selected the Cozy Clove specifically for this "No Screen Time" policy—insurance that she wouldn't waste the evening procrastinating on dating apps, sucked into an endless barrage of dudes flexing in sweaty postworkout bathroom selfies or posing with trout.

What was the psyche behind that particular phenomenon? Margot nibbled on the side of her pencil. A metaphor for being a "good catch"?

"Have you ever orgasmed more than once in a single session?"

For the past half hour, Margot had unwillingly eavesdropped on everything from Bangs's and Poncho's predictions for the next *Game of Thrones* season to the pros and cons of going Paleo. Now it appeared she'd been granted a front-row seat for an online sex quiz.

Whoop-de-doo.

She glared back at her workbook, and the sentence that she'd read at least four times: *Research the market thoroughly.*

The girls ignored her heavy sigh.

Margot didn't take pleasure in being a killjoy. After all, it wasn't like she didn't have opinions about their topics of interest. If playing the Westeros version of Fuck, Marry, Kill, her choices would be Jon Snow, Tyrion, and the Kingslayer in that

order (she'd never forgive Jaime Lannister for shoving Bran out that tower window). As for going Paleo, she refused to entertain any diet that banned her beloved IPA, a beer that was bitter and bold. Not unlike herself.

But this tea shop time was too important to squander. She'd called in a favor at work to get it, begging her fellow yoga teacher, Dusk, to cover her Intermediate Vinyasa class at Nirvana Yoga Studio. Her big plan had been to sip fancy tea while fleshing out her meditation business idea, a "treat yo self" Valentine's Day present.

This didn't have to be National Single Awareness Day. She could flip the narrative and celebrate it as an empowering reminder to focus on herself after ending her last disastrous relationship three months ago. And hey, even better, tomorrow chocolate would be fifty percent off!

"Next question," Bangs chirped. "Do you prefer to be the chased or do the chasing?"

"Chased, without a doubt."

Margot cast a beseeching glance toward the red-haired, dreadlocked barista nodding off on a stool behind the counter. Looked like no rescue was forthcoming from that quarter. She still took the time to check him out, an old habit. *Hmmmm.* Normally dreadlocks elevated sexy to a whole new level, but not in this case. He wasn't bad-looking, but she had a long-standing aversion to gingers.

She flicked back to the chapter on market need, stuffing her fingers in her ears to drown out the girls' chatter.

Her idea was to create a gym, but instead of working out your body, Sanctuary would be a place to work out the mind—with calm, thoughtfully designed spaces designated for group meditation classes, individual practice, art therapy, sand play,

and even flower arranging. She'd sell monthly memberships and daily drop-in passes. Given the hectic—often worrying—state of the world, people craved places to re-center and recharge, especially in her target market of Boulder—

"These questions are frigging naughty!"

Looked like her fingers couldn't cancel out Poncho's ability to state the obvious.

On and on they went:

No to sexting.

Yes to owning a thong.

No to oral—both giving and receiving.

Margot choked on her Matcha green tea. Wait a second. Poncho was sexually active and yet didn't get oral? What kind of national tragedy did she endure between the sheets? Good lord, even Stefan, Margot's douche-mcgouche ex, hadn't been *that* bad. And he was a two-pump chump.

"How many vibrators do you own?" Bangs purred in a husky stage whisper.

"Ew! None!"

"You paddle your own canoe?"

A sound escaped Margot's lips, not unlike a whale singing its death song. Paddle. Your. Own. Canoe? Get outta here. *Masturbation. Clit. Vagina.* These were not difficult words to master.

"Keep your voice down, bitch." Poncho cracked up. "Derek keeps me satisfied."

Margot doodled a stick figure impersonating Edvard Munch's *The Scream* in the margins. It took every last shred of her willpower not to grab Poncho by the shoulders and order her to ovary-up, and take responsibility for her own sexual pleasure. Of course Derek needed to work at being a good

lover. But at the end of the day, all women needed the ability to give themselves toe-curling, stutter-inducing, off-the-Richter-scale, orgasmic ecstasy.

"This is going off-script, but out of curiosity . . . what's your number?" Bangs queried.

Poncho's thin lips flattened further. "Number?"

"You know . . . how many people you've gotten with."

"Like made out at a frat party?"

"That's cute." Her friend shook her head, every strand of hair falling perfectly back into place. "Fine, I'll go first. Six."

"Six?" Poncho's eyes widened as a startled laugh burst from her lips. "You've slept with six guys?"

Bangs shrugged.

"Wow."

It was a skill to slip so much passive-aggressiveness into such a small word.

"Take several seats, Miss Purity," Bangs snapped. "It's not like I'm a sausage jockey."

"Well, my number is two. And it's staying that way."

"For real?" Bangs cocked her head. "You don't want to play the field before committing to Derek's dick for the rest of your life?"

Poncho sniffed. "And be some slut?"

Slut. The ugly word slugged Margot like a fist to the jaw. "Excuse me." Her lips were moving before her brain could register the fact.

The girls jerked, glancing over with identical "And what the hell do *you* want?" expressions.

"So . . . I've got a question. Did you know the correct term for a woman who's slept with six guys?" Margot slipped off her reading glasses and polished the lenses with the bottom of

her tunic. "Or what the hell, let's round up and make it sixty guys."

The bottom dropped out of Poncho's and Bangs's mouths.

"The correct word is *woman*." Margot stood stuffing her notes and workbook into her Nevertheless, She Persisted canvas tote. "Not a slut. Not a hooker. Not a skank. Not a whore. Wo-man. Say it with me."

"I've got a better question," Bangs retorted. "Why don't you keep your big nose out of other people's business?"

"If it doesn't involve you, then it doesn't concern you," Poncho piped in.

"All I'm saying is that if you have to slut-shame to make yourself feel better, then you're doing life wrong." Margot shoved her pink-knit pussycat beanie over her long, wavy hair and shot them a peace sign before beelining toward the exit.

Outside the tea shop, Denver's infamous winter wind stung her cheeks. The streetlight lit dull flakes of snow settling on the sidewalk. She cursed under her breath as she picked up her pace. Great. Thanks to her big ears—and even bigger mouth— she wasn't any closer to having her business plan done. All she had to show for jumping on the slut soapbox was a night of missed pay.

She hugged her arms to her chest in a failing attempt to retain body heat. Once upon a time, seventeen-year-old Margot had remained quiet in the face of that ugly-ass word. It had been a hard-learned lesson that getting attention for the wrong things can be worse than being ignored.

Seventeen was also the year that her bonehead professor father had cheated on her stepmom, Annie, who in response had fled not only Portland, but the entire state of Oregon. She'd packed up Margot's half brother, Atticus, and returned

to her hometown, the little mountain haven of Brightwater, set high in California's Eastern Sierra Nevadas.

Good for Annie.

Shitty for Margot.

Seventeen had been day after day of torture. Isolated. Confused. Lonely. Finally she'd graduated, moved out to Colorado, and started on a journey to figure out who she was and what she wanted out of life.

And here she was, nine years later, still a work in progress.

She ducked her chin and marched toward her place, swinging her arms to keep them from freezing.

At least she wasn't a scared, insecure teenager anymore. Thank God for small mercies. She'd learned that if she kept her face turned toward the light, the shadows would fall behind her. Better to try to have a sunny disposition than float through life like a pessimistic rain cloud.

Her phone rang, and she rummaged for it inside her tote. Her bestie's number flashed on the screen.

"What's up?" Margot batted back a lock of hair whipping her face.

"Are you in a wind tunnel?" Breezy yelled back.

"Just walking home from that new chai shop. It's blowing a gale."

"Ugh, I know. Wake me when it's summer. Anyway, do you have plans? I'm at the Watering Hole." Their favorite dive bar.

"On Valentine's Day?" Margot frowned. "Why? Don't tell me that Jed fell asleep on the job?"

Breezy's fiancé was Jed West, former captain of the Denver Hellions hockey team and all-around sex symbol. And happily, her best friend hadn't just scored a guy who was nothing but dreamboat eyes, cut abs, and delicious scruff, he also hap-

pened to be just as gorgeous on the inside. Jed treated Breezy like a queen, which is why it was so out of character that she'd be at the Watering Hole tonight of all nights.

"He has an away game in Washington State." These days he coached hockey for Denver University.

"Ah, got it. That sucks." It wasn't as if Breezy could jump on a plane and travel on a whim. She'd opened a children's bookshop, Itsy Bitsy Books, which was enjoying a fabulous grand opening, and keeping her as busy as a hamster on a wheel.

"He sent me Godiva truffles, but we're going to do our celebrating later." Breezy unleashed an evil giggle.

"Atta girl." Despite Margot's mood, and the lousy weather, a genuine grin took root. It was a beautiful thing, seeing her best friend so happy.

"But I had an epiphany in the shower today. It's half crazy, and half genius. And it happens to involve you."

"Okay." Margot giggled. "Color me scared, but curious."

"I need to explain in person, otherwise you might say no."

"Gotta say, for a successful small business owner, you aren't making the world's greatest sales pitch."

"Just hustle over here. Byeeeeee. Okay, awesome! She's coming—" Breezy sounded like she was talking to someone else as she hung up.

"Wait. Breeze?" Margot knit her brows. "Who else is there?"

But the line was already dead.

Two more texts followed with quick succession. First, a message from Annie: Atticus made you a valentine!

Her ex-stepmom attached a picture of Margot's kid half brother holding an origami heart pasted to construction paper that read: *Roses are red, violets are blue, my sister should visit and take me to San Diego Zoo (hint, hint).*

Margot's chuckle faded as she clicked on the next message. Ew, her ex. What did the douche-mcgouche want?

Hey, Hot Pants :) My place or yours?

"Neither," she muttered, hitting Delete.

She'd dated Stefan until right after Halloween. He was a tatted-up owner of an MMA gym across the street from her yoga studio. His lickable biceps had made her stupid. Because what had started off as sexy alpha attitude had turned controlling and unpredictable. She didn't have time for a jealous lover who hated the fact that she'd happened to have a sexual history that predated him. Then he started dirty talking about wanting to plant a baby in her. More than once. Kind of a lot.

Just say no to possessive womb-coating fantasies.

After she broke off the relationship, she hadn't mustered a single regret except for the fact that she'd wasted all of autumn on such a jerk. Then a few weeks ago, she'd had to get stern after catching him lurking near her car after an evening gentle flow class. It had been maximum creepy and she'd ordered him to leave her alone in no uncertain terms. After the ensuing radio silence she'd thought—at long last—that he'd gotten the memo.

Apparently not.

A chill zinged down her spine as she increased her stride. She normally felt confident walking alone after dark, and hated that he'd stolen that from her.

But at least the neighborhood was busy. Every restaurant she passed was brightly lit and bustling. The cozy bistro tables were filled with couples, leaning in close as they laughed at private jokes between shared bites of dessert.

Whatever. She was fine being single. The wind increased in tempo, whipping thin purple clouds across the cold moon. Better than fine. Yep. She was happy on her own, and it would have to take someone pretty unbelievable to change that. Bad boys had been her weakness, but it seemed impossible to find one who'd be good for her.

She shook her head, dropping her chin to her chest and hurrying on. Guys like that didn't exist; they were the male equivalent of unicorns.

Chapter Three

*M*argot stumbled into the Watering Hole moments before freezing into a human popsicle.

"Over here!" Breezy waved from the back booth that served as their unofficial meeting spot. She wasn't alone. Her big sister, Neve, and Neve's boyfriend, Tor Gunnar, head coach for the Hellions hockey team, were there as well.

"I didn't know this was going to be a party." Margot slid into the booth and removed her beanie. "What gives? First Breezy's spending Valentine's Day here, and now you two lovebirds?" She gave Neve a double take, taking in the bold slash of red lipstick and daring kohl-black eyeliner.

"I had a thing tonight." Neve shrugged under the scrutiny.

"Oh my God!" Margot clasped a hand over her mouth, realizing the date. "The burlesque show?" They'd done a four-lesson burlesque dancing class together back in November. It had been fun, but Margot had too many conflicts teaching night classes. Neve had stuck with it and the recital had been set for Valentine's Day.

"Why didn't you remind us?" Margot pressed. "We'd have gone and cheered you on."

"Save your breath." Breezy snorted. "I've already given her a stern lecture."

"Sorry, not sorry. Tonight wasn't for you guys," Neve stated in her crisp matter-of-fact manner. "It wasn't for anyone. Just me."

"Although *I* happened to enjoy it," Tor deadpanned before taking a sip from his pint.

"Mmm-hmm. I noticed that you kept the program open on your lap." Neve winked at her boyfriend.

"Guys! Guys! Come on. Let me pig out on these bar peanuts without gagging," Margot said with mock severity.

"What can I say?" Neve responded. "I love getting a rise out of my guy. Pun very much intended."

"All right, ladies," Tor cut through the giggling. "Not to rain on this parade, but Neve and I have dinner reservations at Julia's in—" He checked his watch. "T-minus thirty minutes."

"Julia's? Look at you, Tor-nado. Pulling out the big gourmet guns. You must have moved heaven and earth to get a reservation tonight." Margot teased. "But then, why not? There's so much for you two to celebrate, what with the end of the lockout and everything."

For the past four months, a lockout had halted the NHL's regular season. A Titanic-sized tragedy for the city.

Neve and Tor exchanged a long look.

"Indeed. Among other things." Neve coyly placed her hand on the table. A sapphire winked in the dim light as Breezy and Margot screamed.

"See?" Neve continued. "We aren't alllll work and no play."

"How? When? What! Oh my God!" Breezy blustered while Margot demanded, "Tell us everything. Leave no stone unturned. Sakes alive, I need smelling salts."

"Today, before the recital," Neve responded. "With the lockout over and my new position as head of Hellions Public Relations off to a great start, Tor thought we should kick off the rest of the season on the same team . . . in more ways than one."

"I'm freaking out. When will you have the wedding?" Breezy squealed, clapping. Her own big day was in two months in Aspen. "I have ideas. So. Many. Ideas. You could go vintage. Or rustic. Or Jazz Age. Wait, what about *The Wizard of Oz*? You could wear red ruby slippers and—"

"Stop right there." Tor held up a hand while giving his new fiancée an adoring look. "Angel. I'm happy to let you handle every last detail and spare no expense. Have a yellow brick road and flying monkeys. Invite fifty bridesmaids. Hire a petting zoo. Get a skywriter. But we're down to twenty-five minutes. I've booked your favorite table and have a bottle of Dom Pérignon on ice. Breezy begged us to come so let's wrap this up and then hit the road."

"Okay, okay. I'll be quick. I've . . . had an idea." Breezy drummed her fingers on the table for dramatic effect. "A breakthrough idea for dealing with the Patch Donnelly situation."

"Eeesh." Margot wrinkled her nose. "There's a guy whose issues have issues. I heard how he got served at his first practice back over that crazy bar brawl."

Back in October, the Hellions goalie had almost torn off the arm of a notorious personal injury lawyer who was locally famous for his cringe-worthy commercials. No one knew what went down; simply that Patch had issued an epic beatdown.

This suit was just the latest blight in a long string of altercations that had culminated in Patch getting thrown out of the

last game he'd played against the San Francisco Renegades, right before the lockout began.

Margot racked her brain but couldn't think of a single reason why anything about Patch Donnelly could relate to her. She loved hockey—ahem, hockey players—as much as the next red-blooded woman, but she wasn't exactly an expert on the finer points of the game. Certainly not enough to weigh in on player strategy.

Breezy shot Tor a pointed look. "He is going to be part of the starting lineup again, right?"

"I'm not prepared to comment on that." But an uncharacteristic look of uncertainty flickered over Tor's chiseled Scandinavian features.

"Why don't you ask Margot to help you out?" Breezy clapped her hands. "See if she'd be willing to do you a favor, and volunteer to treat Patch to a few yoga sessions."

"Margot?" Tor said, right as Margot cried, "Me?"

She gaped at her friend. What was Breezy smoking?

"She could teach him some basic techniques and see if yoga's for him. Think about it, Marg. Imagine if you could take the credit for screwing Patch Donnelly's head on right. Tor could put out the word about who helped, and maybe at some point the Hellions could do a plug at your yoga studio. It could be a great way to build your rep as you move forward with your Sanctuary idea. Plus," she arched a single brow. "You aren't into gingers so won't be tempted to mix business with pleasure, you little man-eater you."

"I don't know. Has Patch ever expressed even the faintest interest in yoga?" Margot asked, ignoring the taunt.

"No." Tor leveled the full force of his icy blue stare. "Never."

"Who cares? Show him what he's been missing," Breezy

said emphatically. "Patch's got anger issues, but sweet baby Jesus, he's talented. We all know he isn't playing to his potential, and you could be his secret weapon. What do you say, Tor? Because I'm telling you, if that guy can keep his cool, you'll have the best goalie in the league. Margot might be the answer to your prayers."

Margot stared at her friend, speechless and her heart swelling. No matter what happened, it was lovely to hear how much her bestie believed in her abilities.

"All I've got is one question," Tor said after a considered moment. "Why the hell haven't I thought of this before?"

Chapter Four

𝒫atrick dipped his fingertips into the brass holy water font and made an absent-minded sign of the cross. Morning confession hour at Our Lady of Perpetual Help was hopping. Two elderly women in black cardigans prayed the rosary in the front pew while a third padded her walker in the direction of the votive candle stand. If it got any more exciting, someone might break out their knitting.

But he'd bet twenty bucks that Father O'Sullivan wasn't bored by the peace and quiet. If he knew his old college roommate, Sully was kicked back in that walnut-paneled confessional perusing the *Denver Post*'s sports pages, which happened to be riddled with speculation about his lawsuit.

Patch's jaw flexed. Leave it to Guy Footscray, that slimeball ambulance chaser, to know how to make a scene.

Patch couldn't have messed with a worse guy. He pinched the bridge of his nose. Not that he'd had much of a choice in the matter. Not when he saw what Footscray was capable of.

Still, now he was in one hell of a shit burger. A shit burger that he didn't know how to escape.

Which is why he was here.

Patch had once heard it said that if a guy had one person

they could count on in life they should consider themselves lucky. Sully filled that description. He'd accepted a parish posting to Denver a year after Patch was drafted, and gained a reputation as an activist priest, supporting immigrant communities and advocating on behalf of the poor.

Only God himself knew why he made the time for Patch.

But whatever the reason, he was grateful that his buddy had the loyalty of a golden retriever. Sully was a good listener, and today Patch needed a trustworthy ear.

He slid into a pew. He could go receive the sacrament of reconciliation, but didn't feel like owning up to all the quality time he'd been spending with his right hand.

A frosty winter sun shone through a stained-glass window depicting Saint Anthony of Padua, a friar in a brown robe wearing a belt with three knots tied at the end, symbolizing the holy vows of poverty, chastity, and obedience. He held a bundle of lilies in his arms, a symbol of purity and a reminder to pray for grace during trying times of temptations.

Patch fingered the chain around his neck, the one that held his own Saint Anthony medal—a gift from Ma, the only thing of value that she'd ever given him. He glanced at the confessional again.

His head coach, Tor Gunnar, had called first thing this morning. With regular games resuming, Patch had braced himself for the news that he was being downgraded to second-string. The season needed to get back on track with no distractions. And getting served by Footscray hadn't done him any favors. It was another reminder that Patch was unreliable. A liability. A loose cannon.

The last thing he'd expected was for Coach to give him an address to a yoga practitioner along with the order to attend a

private class. "She's expecting you at noon. If you don't want me giving Reed your spot on the lineup, don't be late," he'd growled before hanging up.

Yoga? He bounced his knee, trying to ignore the churning in the pit of his stomach. What the hell was that going to fix? Did Coach seriously think going downward dog with some spacey chick would make everything copacetic?

He gazed back to Saint Anthony, air compressing in his lungs. He'd never spent time with a yoga instructor. Would she wear those skintight leggings? Would he have to sit and watch as she bent her limber body into all sorts of positions?

Sweat broke out at his temples. He needed that situation like he needed a third nut.

Screw yoga.

Since he'd been a teen, he'd kept the opposite sex at a distance. It had been easier than anyone might imagine. Sure, girls had always been around, and yeah, there were always chances. But he stuck with other guys at parties, hanging on back porches talking shit about hockey. No one ever noticed that he didn't go home with anyone. And if anyone ever gave him a hard time about his single status, all he had to say was that he was too busy with his game to have time for a girlfriend. People would just shrug and nod.

His rep might be notorious, but imagine if the real story got out.

A muscle ticked in his temple.

He was a twenty-five-year-old virgin . . . a virgin's virgin. He'd never gotten to first base, let alone scored a home run. No kissing. No nothing.

Once or twice he'd gotten drunk and had a chance with a pretty, willing girl. But both times he'd halted things, plead-

ing a headache or an early start to the next day. It wasn't that he believed sex—and other stuff—was for marriage. But if he did it . . . he wanted it to mean something. And for it to mean something, it meant caring. And the problem with caring was that it meant feeling.

And feelings were dangerous.

He gnawed the inside of his lower lip while twisting the championship ring around his finger. No one knew his secret. Not even Sully. Shit. Even *he'd* had a girlfriend before joining the seminary.

Patch tore his gaze from Saint Anthony. While the Church might value celibacy, out in the real world, male virginity wasn't any prize. If word leaked out, late-night comedians would have material for days. He'd be a punch line. A laughing stock.

The confessional door swung open and Sully lumbered out, suppressing a yawn. Patch rose from the pew and strode toward his friend, hoping his smirk hid his unease.

"Forgive me, Father, am I interrupting nap time?"

The priest wasn't holding a paper, but that didn't mean he hadn't heard the news.

"I'd tell you to kiss my donkey, but I'm afraid you'd like it," Sully muttered, stretching out his back muscles.

"Tsk. Tsk. You give the sacraments with that mouth?"

"Morning, Father."

Sully nodded at the passing parishioner before slinging his arm around Patch's shoulders and giving him a noogie. "I'm heading back to the rectory for a cup of coffee. Join me?"

Like Patch, Sully was Boston-raised, a gap-toothed Dorchester kid who'd attended Heaven's Gate—the rival to his own Southie parochial high school Holy Cross. At first,

they'd kicked each other's asses in game brawls until both were granted hockey scholarships from Boston College. There they'd flipped the switch, becoming best friends, although still never missing a chance to bust each other's balls.

"That depends on if you're still chugging that instant shit?" He jerked away, rubbing a hand over the top of his head. "I don't drink coffee unless it's Dunkies."

"Remind me why we are friends again?"

"You pity me." Patch spoke the words lightly, but meant every word.

And Sully, with his priest Spidey-senses, knew it.

"Mrs. Giaccomo brought over cannoli yesterday. I'm telling you, it's as good as anything in the North End. Come on."

Patch managed a chuckle. "This I got to see to believe."

Ten minutes later, Patch pushed back an empty plate in Sully's kitchen. "God bless Mrs. Giaccomo."

"Amen." Sully patted his growing gut. "This parish is making me fat. The flan. The pupusas. Oh man. The El Salvadorians make magic with their pupusas."

"Hit the ice with me sometime, I'll whip you back in shape in no time."

"Hmph. I hear you've got problems playing nice with others."

The smile melted off Patch's face.

"Read that you got served your first day back at practice? That's cold."

"That lawsuit is closed to discussion."

"If you say so," Sully replied mildly. "But you're here to talk about something. So what is it?"

Patch kicked out his legs and crossed his arms. "Coach says I can start on one condition. I gotta see this chick who teaches yoga and shit."

Sully nodded. "Go on."

"That's it."

"Yoga?" The priest cocked his head. "That's your existential crisis?"

"It's a load of crap." Patch got to his feet and paced the kitchen perimeter. "Coach should trust me or cut me. But I don't see how doing some doggy-style feel-good bullshit is going to make a difference."

"Studies show that meditation and yoga can do wonders for anger management."

"Why aren't you giving me some big lecture about how yoga leads straight to the devil? That's half the reason why I came out here."

Sully snorted. "Look, way I see it, as Catholics, we bend our knees in prayer. Body postures have a psychological effect. Does the church criticize yoga? Meditation? Probably in this case it would. But do I?"

"You're not exactly Mr. Orthodox."

"No. I'm not. Never have been. But the God that I believe in wants to see us happy. Peaceful. And you, my friend, are neither."

"I am when playing hockey."

"Three or four years ago, I'd have agreed. The game helped clear your head. But now, it is starting to feel like you can't get through three periods without knocking someone out. It's become part of the opposing team strategy—take an otherwise formidable goalie with the thinnest skin in the league. Poke a few times and he'll break apart. Something is eating at you from the inside out. It's Self-Destructive Tendencies 101. It's like you feel the need to be punished for what happened to your mom—"

"Don't want to discuss Ma either."

Sully went quiet a moment. "Do you mind if I ask what you're really afraid of with this situation? I don't feel like I'm getting the full story."

Patch didn't have to answer. But if you couldn't tell the truth to your best friend slash priest then what was the point of having either?

He mumbled the answer, half drowning it in a slug of coffee.

Sully arched an eyebrow and rubbed the bald spot appearing near the back of his head. "Gonna need you to swallow and repeat yourself."

"Don't talk to girls much." Patch grimaced as his throat muscles constricted. "Or women. Guess they're women at our age."

Sully grunted, his gaze softening. "I hate to break it to you, buddy, but you never did. And between you and me, it always seemed a waste, God giving you that face and then tying your tongue in knots."

"It didn't used to matter. Thought I'd be joining you, remember? Wearing a white collar. Ministering to my own parish. One that had a school with a decent hockey team."

"Well, that plan lasted a hot minute. Seminary dropout," Sully crooned using the same general tune as the song "Beauty School Dropout." "Remind me how long you were in? A month? Two? Before you went back to hockey. Let's face it. You'd have hated being a priest. Swearing is frowned upon. And blasphemy is out. You also need to be comfortable talking about feelings."

"Ballbuster," Patch growled.

"This was never your path." Sully didn't look the least bit intimidated. "You're too much in your head, my friend."

"Hey, it's good in here."

"Liar." The smile slid off Sully's face as his expression turned serious. "You came to see me because you wanted advice, so here it is. Tell your coach yes, you'll give this yoga instructor woman a try. Because what's the worst that could happen?"

"I don't know. It blows up in my face?"

"Seems like you're the one blowing up things lately, mostly opportunities."

Patch didn't respond. He didn't have to. Sully was right.

He didn't want to do anything differently, but if he didn't start making better choices then his life was soon going to be nothing but ashes. And he'd worked too damn hard, traveled too damn far from that skinny, scared kid in Boston, to go back now.

As he left Sully's rectory, he dug out the number he'd scratched down on a piece of scrap paper and looked at the name.

"Well, shit," he muttered under his breath before sending a short text. "Here goes nothing, Margot Kowalski."

Chapter Five

$\mathcal{M}$argot stared at her front door, pulse racing like a thoroughbred. Two minutes ago, after the unmistakable *thunk* of a slamming car door, she'd scurried to her living room window, peeking from behind a drape long enough to catch a flash of a Red Sox ball cap and a ginger beard.

Patch Donnelly should have knocked by now.

She wiped her hands on her favorite cat-faced LulaRoe leggings and chanted her favorite mantra. "Say no to stress and yes to ease." Simple and effective. She repeated it again, and then a third time for good measure.

This was silly. There was no reason to go palm sweaty over a hockey player. After all, her two best friends were marrying the former Hellions captain and the Hellions head coach, respectively. Jed and Tor were just men. More attractive than the average bears, yes. But men just the same.

And even if Patch was a freakishly delicious genetic merging of Chris Hemsworth, Channing Tatum, and Tom Hardy, it didn't matter, because she was a professional. There was to be no mixing business and pleasure. Her lady parts had gone on furlough for this assignment—one hundred percent out of commission.

Plus he was a ginger.

Red hair returned her to seventeen, and to her senior homecoming dance and the backseat of Chad Taylor's Toyota Tundra.

She raised her chin and swallowed back a surge of bile. Right now was not the time to skip down memory lane. She had to get her head in the game.

She had one job. Help Patch find his way around a yoga mat. Give him a few skills so that the next time an opponent lit his fuse, he'd calm his tits rather than blow his stack.

She was going to help him discover his best self, and there was a privilege in that, from the point of being a fan. Because Patch Donnelly played hockey the same way Mozart must have worked over the ivories. Every movement was fluid, instinctive. Lightning-quick perfection. Undeniable genius. When at the top of his game, he was a force of nature.

Unstoppable. Unbreakable. Unbeatable.

She wandered to the kitchen counter, picked up a water glass, and rubbed her thumb over a trickling drop before setting it back down again.

She braced her hands on the kitchen counter and sucked in a shaky breath. Tor was counting on her to help get his goalie's head screwed on. And if she succeeded, Breezy was right. This could well be the boost she needed to get on the path to launch her own business.

Squeezing her eyes shut she visualized the SANCTUARY: GRAND OPENING banner hanging over a front door.

She opened one eye and peered at the front door.

Still no knock.

She'd texted Patch her address, but he could have misread it. What if he was at her neighbor's place, that ob-gyn who

worked long hours. What if he thought she wasn't home, and left, and . . .

"Shit!" She scurried to the front door. Flinging it open, she rushed out to hunt him down.

White light exploded behind her eyes as the cartilage in her nose pulverized against a sternum.

"*Ooof.*" She reeled backward, clutching her nose, the sickening crunch ringing in her ears. She loved a rock-hard man chest as much as the next gal, but this was ridiculous. She screwed her eyes shut and dropped her hands. "Is it broken?" she squeaked.

The ions in the air did a subtle shift, ushering in a sensual hint of sun-warm wood, leather, and cinnamon chewing gum. Behind the throbbing pain came the unsettling sense of male physical proximity.

A *big* male.

Later, she'd blame the goose bumps peppering the sensitive skin between her shoulder blades as a physiological reaction to the wintry wind gusting through the open door.

"No blood. No bruising." The low answer was considered and grave, the voice containing more gravel than a backcountry road. "Does it hurt to breathe?"

She took a tentative sniff. "Not really. No." All seemed well in that department. "I don't look like a bulldog with a squished-up face?" Her sense of humor returned as the pain began to ebb.

"Bulldog?" That earned her a snort. "Nah, you don't have the jowls. But just in case, let's slap something cold on it."

She opened her eyes just in time to see the backside of the most infamous goalie in the NHL making a beeline for her shoebox kitchen. His straight-cut jeans fit nicely in the seat.

Provided the perfect amount of room for a set of seriously well-developed quads.

She trailed in his wake. Common courtesy demanded that she look away, but it took more willpower than she possessed to refocus her attention on her Let That Shit Go framed poster above her floor cushions, or Nibbles, her bubble-eyed goldfish.

He glanced over one shoulder. "Do you mind?"

"I'm so sorry," she blurted. "I didn't mean to stare but . . ." Her voice faded because a) there was no good way to end that sentence and b) his brow furrowed into a genuinely puzzled expression.

"I mean . . . do you mind if I grab a frozen veggie bag out of your freezer? I don't want to go busting in like I own the joint."

"Of course . . ." She folded herself onto a high bar stool and smoothed a hand over the top of her head. Face-plant notwithstanding, at least her topknot was still on point. No doubt she looked a whole lot less frazzled than she felt. "My fridge is your fridge. There's an acai pouch in there that'll do the job."

"Was that even English?" He opened the freezer and peered in as if expecting a boa constrictor curled up in wait. "A-sigh-what?"

"Acai. It's like a berry. They are from the Amazon. Lots of antioxidants."

"Like a berry, huh?" He reached in, grabbed the frozen bag, and wrapped it in the dish towel hanging off the oven with a quick, efficient movement before passing it over. "Where I come from we'd slap a raw steak on our face and call it good, but hey, I'm sure fancy berries work."

"I was told to expect a surly hockey player, not a comedian," Margot said archly, applying the cold compress.

"Surly? Coach said that?" Patch's face was unreadable.

He had peculiar features, each one strong almost to the point of being overpowering. His deep-set blue eyes made the sky seem colorless, while his close-trimmed beard held hues of wildfire and buckwheat honey. His cheekbones were sharp, and his long nose came to a point on the end. A moody face, brutish, but not cruel.

"Okay, that wasn't an exact quote. He might have used a phrase more like 'pain in my ass.'"

Patch's chuckle came and went so fast she almost wondered if she'd hallucinated it. "That sounds like the coach I know."

"Why were you lurking outside my door? Are you opposed to knocking?"

"Figured if I hung around long enough I'd be used for battering ram practice."

His deadpan delivery took her a second to process even as he evaded the question. "More jokes?"

"Should have aimed for *SNL* rather than the NHL."

"Ba-dum-dum-tish." She rolled her eyes, pretending to hit an imaginary cymbal.

"Ladies and gentlemen," he addressed an invisible crowd. "I'll be here all night."

She removed the acai pouch. "Let's have a do-over. Can I make you a cup of tea?"

He stared. "You think I look like a tea drinker?"

"I'm not in the habit of making assumptions."

"I am. For example, you don't have a single can of Coke in your fridge, do you?"

"I never drink soda."

"Shocker." His gaze ping-ponged around the kitchen. He wasn't blinking. Was he scouting for the nearest exit? "Forget the tea. We gonna start or what?"

"That depends." She leaned forward, tilting her head to one side. "Do you really want to be here?"

"Who doesn't want to twist themselves into a pretzel?" His sheepskin collar nearly brushed his ears. Tension poured off him in waves.

"How about we start slow, focus on breathing."

His brow arched. "I hate to break it to you, but I do that fine."

"Well, actually, you aren't inhaling deep enough." She rose and stepped forward. "May I touch you?"

He gave a curt nod.

She reached into his open leather jacket and brushed her fingertips against his stomach, quick as static shock. *Good lord.* There wasn't so much as a millimeter of give on this man. His abs were as solid as his chest.

Not that she cared one way or another. This was merely an impassive, factual observation.

"Feel this, right here?" She tried to ignore the tightening sensation in her chest. "This is the spot where you should be pulling from. It's called diaphragmatic breathing. Right now your ribs hardly move. It's too shallow. Why don't you come into the living room, lie down on the rug, and get more comfortable? Then I'll show you what I mean."

He didn't budge. "Thought I was doing just fine sucking air. After all, I've been doing it for twenty-five years."

She planted her hands on her hips. "I'm inching toward twenty-five. So try respecting an elder and get on the floor."

His features were an expressionless mixture of ice and

stone, as cold and inscrutable as a glacier. "You aren't what I expected, Margot Kowalski."

"Oh yeah?" She hooked a strand of loose hair behind one ear, feeling scoured by his stare. "Is that good or bad?"

"I dunno." He laughed hoarsely.

"Quite the endorsement," she quipped.

He didn't answer.

"Tough crowd." She pointed to the wool carpet on her bamboo floor. "That's where I want you."

"How long is this going to take?" he asked gruffly, shrugging out of his jacket.

"You believe in hockey practice, right?"

He arched a brow.

"Yoga is practice too." Patch looked so . . . big . . . kneeling down beside her pretty floral floor cushions. And overtly masculine. Like a piece of avant-garde art. Not pretty. Not conventional. But riveting in his own way.

"You're not what I expected either," she said carefully.

"Oh yeah?" He pressed his arms to his sides, stiff as a mummy. "Yeah?"

"I imagined you more of a bully." The admission burst from her. "I'm sorry. That came out wrong."

"No. It didn't." His gaze pinned hers. "Honesty is a lost art. If we're stuck working together, that's what I'm going to ask for."

"Deal." Her neck was hot, like sitting out by the pool and getting a slow sunburn. "I think that I expected someone meaner. Instead you're . . ."

He waited, his chest not rising.

"Different," she concluded.

Not nice. But . . . interesting.

There was perfect silence for two seconds . . . three . . . four.

She broke it with a shuddering inhalation, blinking fast as if coming out of a daze.

"So . . ." She nodded to his cap beside him on the floor, desperate to say something—anything—to fill the empty air. "Red Sox, huh?"

His brows knit. "What about it?"

So much for small talk. Looked like he preferred this strange, heavy silence.

"Never mind. Let's return the focus to the breath." She sat cross-legged beside him. "I want you to put all of your attention right here."

A tremor rippled through his abdomen at her touch. The motion vibrated through her skin, jarring her bones. Last summer, she'd been knocked around in the surf while boogie boarding in Mexico. The ocean spun her like a sock in a washer. Her insides now experienced a similar sensation.

"See, there goes your chest again, rising first." She swallowed thickly. "If you don't breathe correctly, it can leave you at a deficit during a game. Healthy breathing patterns are how your body maintains a fast metabolism and delivers oxygen to vital organs. If you breathe fast or don't inhale deep enough, the pH in your blood spikes. This decreases the amount of blood getting into your brain and muscles and as a result, less oxygen is released."

She put a hand over the spot she'd collided into and allowed a tight smile as she felt the pounding within. "Well, well, well, looks like you have a beating heart beneath all that brooding." She winked. "But don't worry, your secret is safe with me."

His hand gripped her wrist, moving so fast that she didn't have time to gasp.

He was bigger, broader than most of the skinny-hipster-

techy guys she encountered around the Denver singles scene. Just all around . . . more.

"What are you doing?" she asked. Not afraid. Despite his size, he didn't seem violent. Or angry. Just unsettled.

"No idea." He closed his eyes. "Don't know what I'm doing about anything anymore."

"You know, I feel like that way sometimes too. I think everyone does. They just don't admit it." When he released her hand, she reached up and pressed on his lats, where his shoulders met his neck. "You're carrying so much tension in your body."

"I get headaches." He stared at the ceiling.

"Often?"

"I guess . . ." His eyes darkened. "For a long time. Since I was a little kid." His gaze roamed the walls behind her as she began to knead the rigid muscles. It was like trying to soften frozen blocks of dough. "You have a lot of photographs."

She smiled at the frames. There was her half brother, Atticus, standing between her stepmom, Annie, and her husband, Sawyer, the mountains of the Eastern Sierras rising behind them. And Breezy their freshman year of college. Margot had come to Colorado lonely, adrift, and heartsick. She hadn't told anyone in her family about the incessant bullying, the slut-shaming. Her mom would have blamed her. Her dad was too busy trying to get it on with women that were barely older than her. Annie could have helped, but at the time she'd been reeling from Margot's dad's infidelity and Margot hadn't wanted to drop that on her lap.

There were other pictures. A photo of her doing tree pose in the Denver Botanical Gardens. Another of the beach in Punta Mita, Mexico, last summer. That place had been heaven on

earth. Warm clear water. Golden beaches. Sunsets that threatened to break a heart with all the beauty.

"You like photography?" he asked.

"Of course, don't you?"

"Don't have many happy memories to keep around."

The bitterness in his voice spoke volumes.

"Patrick."

Using his real name had the intended effect.

His penetrating gaze traced her face, light and soft, almost a physical touch. "Why'd you call me that?"

"It's your name, isn't it?" She spoke the words carefully, the slower cadence the only way to ward off a tremble. The way he stared . . . the intensity was unbearable. A painful pleasure.

How would he look when inside a woman?

There was a hiss and crackle in her clit, a delicious burn as if a flame had burst to life.

"Yes." He seemed to shudder. "But no one has called me that since . . ." His Adam's apple—covered by a thick scruff—bobbed. "For a long time."

"Since you were that little kid with the headaches?" Her own next breath was shallow, barely drawing oxygen into her lungs.

The vein in his neck pounded. God help her, she wanted to lick it, to taste the faint flavor of his sweat on her tongue.

She swayed a little, drunk with this unexpected desire, the cocktail of hormones.

Time to slow her roll. This was nothing. Just a normal, healthy physiological response.

There was no point to make a big deal over her body's reaction, or read anything into the mechanics of basic biology.

Right now she was simply reacting to the proximity of a big, brawny male. It had been a while since she'd gotten any action. This meant nothing.

She swallowed. Hard. "Our pasts can wield a hell of a lot of influence over our present. Our bodies are remarkably good at holding on to old trauma."

"I'm fine."

His sharp tone didn't win any convincing awards.

"Patrick." Her tongue slid over the roof of her mouth as she pronounced the *t*. "Take off your shirt."

Chapter Six

𝒫atch didn't move. He couldn't. A hot jolt had zapped him in place.

"I know that you heard me." Margot's fine brows drew closer together. "But I'll ask again nicely." Her throat clearing was loud and purposeful.

His gaze flicked to her throat, the soft delicate hollow where she made the noise. She might be joking around, but the last thing he felt like doing was laughing.

"Would you pretty please with maraschino cherries on top remove your shirt?"

He didn't respond—couldn't. Shed his clothes? Have the most gorgeous woman he'd ever seen put her hands on his bare skin?

Christ. He'd never be ready.

If God had tailor-made a woman designed to be his type, Margot Kowalski would be it. The moment she'd leapt back from her doorway—while he stood out there trying to psyche himself up to knock—and yelped about breaking her nose . . . he'd been on the fast train to Gonesville.

And now she waited. Patiently. Knowingly.

The question was why? What was it that drew him in? Was

it her disquieting gray eyes, the same color of a secret pearl? Those perfect-ten breasts filling out her black leotard? Or her long legs stretching somewhere into tomorrow?

But despite the dancer-type clothes and elegant bun, she didn't give off an air of untouchable yogi beauty. Her nose was too snub for starters, and her smile too warm. Then there were those freckles smattering her cheeks in two faint constellations. They slew him one by one.

He'd been prepared to endure an hour with a yoga teacher that he didn't take seriously, someone who wore healing crystals and was named Sunbeam Calmspring.

In truth, her apartment had more than its fair share of hippie knickknacks—macramé wall hangings, houseplants, star-shaped paper lanterns, and baskets . . . who needed this many baskets? But the curveball to the whole situation was how much he liked it, being here in her apartment with its lavender-painted walls and feminine energy. The faint trace of spicy incense was homey. It returned him to his childhood, of being an altar boy—a role that had brought order to an otherwise chaotic existence.

A life where Ma spent most of the day passed out on the couch bed, stinking in her own filth, her arms riddled with bruises while her boyfriend-of-the-week sipped malt liquor from a brown paper bag and watched Springer.

That dark, depressing world faded every Sunday under the soft light of the church. The cursing, the desperation, and the drug-fueled fights felt like a bad dream as he'd kneel on the altar, losing himself in the rituals. The Penitential Rite chanted in unison. The Liturgy of the Word. The unshakable belief that Father Kevin changed bread and wine into the flesh

and blood of Jesus Christ. *Lamb of God, you take away the sins of the world, grant us mercy. Lamb of God, you take away the sins of the world, grant us peace.*

Mercy.

Peace.

The church had been an anchor in the storm. A reminder that life didn't have to be a hustle for shoot-up money. Or scarfing down discounted hot dogs at the corner convenience store for dinner. Or—

"In case you're worried about protecting my virtue—" Margot broke into his thoughts. "Let me put your mind at ease. I can vouch that I've seen a few shirtless men in my day." Margot sat back on her heels. "More than that actually."

"Okay . . ." What was she telling him? That she'd been with men . . .

Many men?

"You're blushing." She pulled her knees up to her chest and locked her arms around her knees. "I'm sorry. I didn't expect you to be shy. Don't you and your teammates strip down together in the locker room? The way Neve talks, it's like naked man city after games. I guess I picture the players walking around with their junk waving—"

"This isn't a locker room," he blurted. And Margot Kowalski sure as shit wasn't just one of the guys.

"Whoa, Tiger." She blinked, registering his stricken expression. "Are you wound tight or what? Let's loosen you up before something snaps."

"I'm not big on getting touched." His tone was clipped—the verbal equivalent to yellow caution tape. "Not big on anything touchy-feely, period."

"Okay. I respect that," she said. "But I'm not asking you to hug it out. You need to relax if you want to start improving your breathing."

"Not big on loosening up either." The way he grew up, if he relaxed anything he'd fall apart. Better to be stiff and solid, shore up defenses.

She did a good job muffling her exasperated sigh . . . but not good enough. The exhale roared through his ears.

This wasn't going to work. It was a bad idea. He'd been a dumbass agreeing to come, even if Coach had him by the short and curlies.

He'd convinced himself that he could drive here, suck it up, and be a dancing monkey. Anything to keep his starting position. But Margot wasn't going to be a person that he could humor. A strange fact because he dismissed most people. Not hard to do when there were so many phonies and hangers-on floating around the NHL.

Most of the other players accepted attention as their due—the endorsement side hustles, and the blow jobs on demand, the trappings of celebrity. But Patch never bought into his own hype. And it wasn't that he was a pious stick-in-the-mud, no matter how many think pieces were written about his stint at the seminary. It's that he didn't play hockey to be worshipped.

He played because the ice was the one place on earth where he could escape, tune out his thoughts, for at least three periods and the occasional overtime.

"Earth to Patrick, come in please." Margot was so close that he could see a fallen eyelash on her cheek. "How about filling me in on what you are into then? What do you enjoy?"

"Hockey."

"Guess I walked into that." She gave a short laugh. "But

shouldn't that be a motivating factor if you want to start as goalie next week, or any week after that? If you want to play, it seems that you need to make a good-faith effort to work through your issues."

"What issues?"

"Uh-huh." Her gaze swung to the ceiling. "De Nile isn't just a river in Egypt."

"So what, taking off my shirt and letting you rub your hands over me will fix everything?" An invisible band tightened around his temples. The first sign of a rising temper.

"I'm saying it's a start," she said, not backing down.

Goddamn it. If he wanted a pig's chance in frozen hell to do the one thing in life he loved, he was going to have to let this maddening woman have her way. "Fine." He reached back and fisted the gray cotton of his T-shirt, yanking it over his head with one fluid gesture. He balled the fabric up and tossed it over her pretty floral pillow. The gray cotton served as a sullen rain cloud against an otherwise bright and serene palette. "Happy?"

"Ecstatic," she deadpanned.

Sully would like her smart mouth.

"Go on." He followed her gaze to the Saint Anthony's medal resting in the center of his chest. "Do your worst."

"Does that medal mean something important?"

He shrugged.

"Want to tell me about it?"

"Nope."

"All right, Big Talker, have it your way. You might not know to look at me, but I happen to have magic hands. And I'm about to use them to change your life."

"Bold promise, Magical Margot."

She giggled and grabbed a dark glass bottle off the coffee table, pouring a dollop of oil into her hands as he lay stomach-side down on her rug. The air filled with a lavender scent. Before he could form another thought, she swung her leg over his hips and sat on his ass.

"What the hell are you doing now?"

She huffed an annoyed sigh. "What I just spent the better part of five minutes explaining." She kneaded a tender spot beneath his right shoulder blade. "Quite an impressive knot you've got." She slid her hand down his ribs and paused. "Ouch, that's a mean-looking scar." She leaned in for a closer inspection. "Wait. Is that—"

"Nothing." What the hell? No one had ever looked at him this close.

"Are those cigarette burns?"

He bit the inside of his cheek hard enough to taste the faint copper flavor of blood. "Newports."

"Who did that?" Her voice was hushed.

"A hustler named Marco." Ma's pimp and a small-fry felon. Just one of the many men that circled through their home like it was a revolving door. So many men. Some smacked him around. All used his mom—sometimes in plain sight depending on how stoned they were—before leaving a wad of bills on the table.

None ever looked back.

Patch had made a pledge never to be the same, never be a man who used a woman. When he hit puberty, he'd become too uncomfortable to look at the girls his own age, let alone ask one out. They were so pretty, bright, and alive. And he'd seen too damn much horror. The idea of touching one felt like pressing dirty fingers against a clean piece of glass.

He'd never gotten a chance to be a kid. And he knew on some psychobabble level that he self-sabotaged relationships. That he pushed away everyone who ever tried to get close.

Ma was dead. The horror over. But still she haunted him.

He was so fucking sick of ghosts.

"It was a long time ago. Doesn't matter anymore," he muttered, almost to himself.

"I think it does." Margot's hands barely touched him and yet the sensation burned.

"Could have been worse." Shame gnawed through his gut. He hated that she saw this crack in him, the weakness. "What's done is done. End of story."

She pressed another part of his back and he grunted in barely contained annoyance.

"You are going to want to drink a lot of water tonight," she said softly. "The massage might make you sore."

"I can tough it out."

"Why do I get the feeling that you do that too much?"

Too much was this strange intimacy. Too much was this gorgeous woman on him, her nimble hands roaming over his body as she unearthed uncomfortable truth after uncomfortable truth. All that he had thought was safely buried was being exposed, the roots bared. Even though he was lying down, he felt ready to topple over.

Too much was the fact that she'd been right about her magic hands; the problem now was what would happen if she discovered that his erection was drilling a hole through her bamboo floor.

He had to get out.

Now.

His sanity depended on it.

"That's enough." He rolled out from beneath her, scrambled for his hat, and threw his jacket in front of his hard on. "I forgot I have to do something."

Before she could answer, he stepped toward the door, tripping over one of her floor pillows. His jacket flew one direction. He flew another, landing on his back.

Legs splayed.

And there was no way in hell that Margot Kowalski was going to miss his full salute.

Chapter Seven

"Oh my God. Are you okay?" Margot stifled a peal of horrified laughter. The struggle was real: half of her felt terrible that Patch Donnelly clearly wished the earth would crack open and swallow him whole, but the other half was curious about the rather large elephant in the room. That is, the elephant-sized hard-on straining the crotch of his pants like it was about to stampede through the African savannah.

These things happened. Erections were natural. She had professional masseuse friends who admitted men often got hard on the massage table. Some clients were perverts about it, but most were mortified.

Patch fell into the second category. He sucked in a great gulp of air, his broad chest rising and falling, a fine dusting of tawny hair spreading over his pecs, darkening as it etched the hard slabs of his abs.

"Let me give you a hand." She stepped forward, scanning his face for a clue of what to do next, trying her best not to glance back at that prominent ridge beneath his denim.

"Don't touch me!" He stood in one quick movement, unfolding to his full height, a good eight inches above her. His

cheeks were hot, the red stain spreading down his neck. "I'm not a joke."

The air left her chest in a sharp gasp as reality took hold. "I don't think that." He was hurt. And she'd done that.

His lips twisted. "You just laughed at me."

"No! Not at you. I mean, I did laugh, but it's just what I do when I get nervous. I wasn't doing it to be mean or make you feel—"

"Coming here was a mistake." He walked to the door, his gait stiff, his posture as rigid as his features. "Like I said . . . I've got to go."

She wanted to tell him that what just happened was fine, to provide reassurances. But the fact was that her knees trembled, and her own body flushed. If she looked in a mirror, no doubt her cheeks would reflect a similar hue.

"Patrick. Please. Stay and have a cup of tea and—"

"Don't drink tea. Or eat acai. Or do yoga. Or get massages." He addressed a point past her left shoulder before slinging on his shirt. "Look. You seem like a nice enough person. I'm sure you meant no harm. It's just . . . this isn't for me."

And without further ado, he slammed out of her apartment.

Her trembling migrated from her knees to her thighs. She slid to the rug before noticing that his Red Sox hat was still on the floor. She picked up the worn brim and ran her finger over the logo as a furtive movement caught the corner of her eye.

Nibbles stared from his fish bowl. His meditative, albeit bug-eyed, expression appeared all-knowing, as if he were a miniature aquatic sensei.

"I didn't mean to laugh," she snapped.

Nibbles glared.

"Come on, I'm not an asshole." Her voice raised a pitch. "You see me. You know me better than anyone."

Sadly, this might be true. With her two best friends in loving, stable, supportive relationships, Margot spent more and more time alone.

"Whatever." She wrinkled her nose and plopped Patch's hat on her head. Maybe it was her imagination, but she swore she could feel residual body heat in the cap's cotton.

She willed her heart to quit pounding. What an idiot she was being. It was good he bolted. Great even. She didn't need to invite more drama into her life.

There was a knock at the door, soft but definite. And her answering stomach flip proved her last thoughts to be a big fat lie.

Because she was glad that he had returned. For here was a chance for redemption, to put this right. She'd be honest. Physical responses happen. It wasn't personal. She wouldn't make fun of him. She needed this gig to work.

She walked to the door, turning the baseball cap backward for good measure. Maybe a little comedy would diffuse what would be a tense situation.

"Hey." She flung open the door.

"Hey yourself, Hot Pants."

The smile slid off her face as she regarded Stefan. Her ex leaned in the doorway, his left dimple putting in an appearance. He knew it was a selling point and made sure to use it to maximum effect.

"What are you doing here?"

He raked his fingers through his tight, black curls. "I was in the neighborhood."

"You live in Littleton." Not exactly her hood.

"I had a special delivery to make." He pulled a bouquet of roses from behind his back. "Happy late Valentine's Day."

"Pretty." She bit the corner of her lip, fighting the urge to recoil in disgust. "But I can't accept them."

"Can't? Or won't?" A hard edge crept into his smile. "You never hit me back last night. What's up, you had plans?"

"As a matter of fact, I had a date." She'd just leave out the part where it was with herself.

"Not cool." Stefan dropped the roses to his side. "This hot-and-cold shit sucks. I'm getting sick of your games."

"Games?" Her laugh was genuine. "Give me a break! You and I aren't a thing. It's over. Dead and buried. Never going to happen." She swallowed back the last part of the phrase, the automatic "I'm sorry" part that she normally tacked onto rejections.

She wasn't going to apologize for not being interested anymore.

"Red Sox." His caramel-colored eyes flew to the top of her head, his gaze shuttering. "Whose hat is that?"

"None of your business." She didn't like the way he was watching her. Or the fact he could switch on a dime from fun and flirty to cold and calculating. He was bigger than her, and meaner. Plus he knew how to hurt people for a living.

She had a gut feeling about this guy. Something was off and she didn't want to find out what. All she knew was that she didn't feel safe. His muscle and masculine intensity weren't sexy anymore.

They were scary.

A chill snaked down her spine. She'd experienced this sudden fear a few times lately, while walking alone, the sense of

danger, an unsettling sensation of being watched. But she had never had that feeling in her own cozy home. Not once.

Not until right now.

"I asked you a question." He took a step forward, just one, but it was enough.

"It's mine, asshole."

Patch loomed behind Stefan. Her ex was almost six feet, but Patch looked down on him.

Stefan turned, and she could see where she'd gone wrong. When they'd first met, she'd thought he had a boyishly cute charm, like Slater from the *Saved by the Bell* reruns. Conceited but cute.

The cute part turned out to be an act, while the conceited bit was genuine. Stefan thought he was God's gift, especially in the bedroom. His ego was the size of West Texas. But that cockiness hid some serious flaws. He once stopped sex mid-doggy-style to mention that she'd missed a spot shaving on the back of her thigh. Then there was the whole thing where he treated her vagina like a chew toy. Oh and don't forget how he had a habit of high-fiving himself in the bathroom mirror postsex.

Plus he hated—*hated*—the idea she'd ever been with anyone else.

He tried to make her feel dirty for it. Acted like it was something to be forgiven for.

Then he started talking about getting the baby in her and . . .
Yeah. No.

And yet here he was, puffing himself up like a rooster in a cockfight.

Patch didn't do anything. He didn't even look at him.

Instead, his gaze locked on her face.

"This fool bothering you?"

"Yes." Margot folded her arms. "He is."

"Come on, pal." Patch stepped to one side. "Exit's this way." His voice was quiet, almost mild, but the intensity held the real power. A controlled fury. A subdued thunder.

"Do I know you?" Stefan seemed to shrink, even though he didn't move. A rat caught ferreting around the kitchen when a light came on.

"No." Patch's voice was a husky rasp, flint grinding down a steel bar. "Now get the hell out."

Stefan opened his mouth to say something, but quickly thought the better of it. He scuttled out of the apartment without a backward glance.

"Good riddance," Margot said with a lightness she didn't feel.

"That guy try and fuck with you?"

"*Try* is the right word. But he didn't get very far. You were pretty tough back there."

"Yeah, that's me. Wicked tough." Patch kicked at the door-jamb, hesitating. "So . . . mind if I come back in?"

Margot smothered a smile at his deferential tone. Thirty seconds ago this guy had been primed and ready to crack skulls. Now he waited on her word.

"You don't have to ask," she said lightly.

"Yes I do." His tone was grave. "This is your home, and I respect that. You don't have to let me in, especially after the way I went out."

"What made you change your mind?"

"Forgot my hat."

The expectation that had been slowly expanding in the pit of her belly released with a slow *woosh*.

"Oh. Right. Of course. I just had it." She glanced around, careful to avoid glancing anywhere in the vicinity of his package.

"It's right here." He plucked it off the top of her head in a deft gesture.

Derp.

"I know you saw what happened to me." His voice deepened. "Earlier."

Her throat tightened, the walls closing in fast like a booby-trapped cave in *Indiana Jones and the Awkward but Necessary Air-Clearing.*

"Come in," she said, gesturing at the door.

"You're sure?"

"I'd like to keep out cold air and creeps."

He rocked on his heels. "When you rubbed on me—"

She reached out and pressed her fingers to his lips. They were warm. Of course. He was a living, breathing man. Why would they ever be otherwise?

But still, she hadn't expected them to be quite this warm. And with an intriguing softness to boot.

"I wasn't rubbing on you. That was a massage. That was professional."

"You were. I wasn't." When he opened his mouth to speak, his inner lower lips grazed her fingertip, the faintest trace of wet.

She fought against the instinct to flutter her eyes.

"It's no big deal. I promise. Bodies are bodies. They do all sorts of stuff."

"Do you find me attractive?"

Out of all the possible things to come out of his mouth, this one made her choke.

He bowed his head. "That a no?"

"No!" she gasped.

"Never mind." He moved to step away but she grabbed his wrist.

"Wait. I meant no as in yes, and—"

If someone had told her that Patch Donnelly was going to cup her chin, search her face like she had the secrets from the Mayan calendar tattooed between her eyes, mutter "fuck it," and then crush his lips to hers, she'd have said they were likely indulging in Colorado's recreational marijuana dispensaries.

She didn't even have time to close her eyes.

Worse, he didn't either.

They gaped at each other like two Nibbleses in opposing goldfish bowls. His breath hot on her skin.

It wasn't that he was a bad kisser. There was no tongue-shove down the throat. No slobber. He wasn't twisting his palms over her boobs as if waxing his car.

The problem was that he wasn't doing much of anything. His lips were whisper-light and not even fully covering hers. They dipped to the side. He'd frozen as if unable to believe he'd done it.

Well he had. And since he was here . . .

She had to admit to being a little curious.

She leaned into him, twining one hand up the back of his neck, clutching his hair, and in doing so felt herself tiptoe to the edge of a thing she didn't understand, gripped by a vague sensation that she was in danger of falling a very long way. The shock was disconcerting, but thrilling in its way. Like standing at a window at the top of a skyscraper watching the world crawl by below and wondering what it would feel like to let go and fall.

She wanted to do this. To kiss him.

An angel popped up on her shoulder giving her a stern wag of the finger. What about her resolve not to mix business and pleasure? What about her long-standing aversion to gingers?

But then her devil put in an appearance, wearing fishnet stockings and a crimson bustier. Of course her personal devil was a *sexy devil*. "Who has to know?" it whispered. "And as for red hair, you used to like it. A lot."

And the devil was right. She spent the four years of high school crushing on Chad Taylor, wide receiver for the football team. But after she lost her virginity in the back of his Tundra, word had spread faster than a speeding ticket. It didn't take long before the entire gang in Jock Hall taunted her every passing period. Even Chad.

Scratch that. Especially Chad.

Chad, who'd told her she was "beautiful," "such a cool chick," then went and made up the nickname "Eager Beaver," bragging about how she loved to gnaw his wood.

Chad with the red hair that put her off from gingers forever and ever amen.

Screw Chad. Screw the past.

She'd made it a point never to feel guilty about pleasure. And she wasn't going to start now.

"Come on," she said, tugging his hand as her invisible angel did a face-palm.

"Where?" His question was barely a whisper.

The hammering in her chest grew. "My bedroom."

"I can't," he said, just once but it was enough. He meant it. He withdrew his hands.

"What's wrong?" She stepped back as a growing horror took hold. "Wait. Oh God, you have a girlfriend, don't you?"

Shit. She'd just kissed a guy as the other woman. Her worst nightmare. After her dad's cheating antics, infidelity was an unforgivable sin in her book.

"Girlfriend?" His face darkened. "No."

Now she was lost. "Then what's the problem? You were the one who just kissed *me*. Or at least half kissed me."

"I don't do this," he said in a flat tone. "You got to understand something. I never do this."

"What? Kiss?"

"Yeah."

She frowned. "I don't understand."

He paused. "I don't kiss women."

She peered into his midnight blue eyes. The shadows beneath them were pronounced. His harsh features seemed to be even more severe, more brutal. "So you're . . . gay?"

"No." He made a frustrated sound in the back of his throat. "I'm—"

"Bi? Aro? Ace?"

"A virgin." Patch snapped his lips shut, swallowing hard. "I'm a fucking virgin, all right?"

"Oh." Her body stilled, her heart maintaining an even, steady thump. "I see." Later she would marvel at the fact. The fact she kept her cool, didn't betray even a slight hint of surprise.

He could have announced that he slept in a tinfoil hat and believed the president was an alien lizard disguised in human form and she would have been less dazed.

"No one knows either. No one but you." His look turned defiant, proud even as his fingers drummed against the side of his thigh in agitation.

"Why?"

"Long story."

"I have time." She narrowed her eyes. "I mean why me? We just met. Why trust me with this kind of a secret?"

"Don't know." Again his eyes searched her face with that peculiar intensity. "Guess I'm self-destructive. Isn't that why I'm here? Because I'm out of control? Making bad decision after bad decision. Here's yet another example."

She involuntarily licked her lips. His gaze honed in on her tongue.

"Yeah? Are you sure it's not that you wanted me to take you in my room and make you a man?"

"I'm man enough already."

Her stomach gave a quick, giddy shiver.

He wasn't bragging. She'd seen the size of his big bulge, and her nose remembered his chest's crushing strength. The image of that chest sheened with sweat as she dug her nails into his pecs and threw her ass into the grind . . . her breath quickened. Good lord, she needed smelling salts.

She'd had her fair share of one-night stands. That cute bartender at the Watering Hole. Gael—the hottest surfer in Baja. A guy she picked up at a concert. The rock climber in Colorado Springs. The idea wasn't to be denied on principle.

"Now that you know, you aren't interested." He didn't ask a question. It was a statement of fact.

"Look," she hesitated. "I've never taken a guy's virginity. It feels like a responsibility, as if I need to prepare you for a lifetime of emotionally rewarding and physically satisfying sexual experiences."

"I got an idea." He rubbed his hand over his chin. "Reserve the urge to punch me until after hearing me out."

Chapter Eight

$\mathcal{M}$argot listened to Patch stumble through his idea without getting her knuckles bloody. In fact . . . far from it. After he quit talking and waited for her answer, lungs threatening to explode, she'd said okay.

Shit.

Talk about being careful what you wish for.

But wasn't this the same way that he'd gotten out of Southie? By wishing? Wanting? Having faith?

Faith.

There's a feeling he hadn't had in a long time. Then today of all days, dangling at the end of a rapidly fraying rope—out of luck and out of options, he'd come across this woman, and was gripped by this unshakable sense that he was meant to meet her. That there was some mysterious plan and promise to their paths crossing.

This was the first time in his life that he'd ever felt the passion everyone else seemed to think was normal. The second that he set eyes on her, he had a moment of cellular recognition, like his atoms went, "Ah. It's you. You're the one."

He couldn't explain the phenomenon, but that didn't make it any less real.

All he knew was that he was going to stand here on the side of Margot Kowalski's pretty bed, covered with a blue quilt and light green pillows, and give thanks for this unexpected miracle.

"Can I try and pleasure you?" is all he had said. He'd never been with a woman. Anywhere. Any way. And if he was going to start, this seemed like the smartest way.

He'd never believed in the idea of "the one." The concept had seemed about as cliché as finding a needle in a haystack. And yet here he was, with his needle, and she pierced his defenses with a single look.

She raised her brows a fraction, enough to wrinkle her brow. "Are you going to stand there all day?"

"I like looking at you."

"Do you now?" A pleased smile tugged the corner of her mouth.

"Never seen anything like you before."

"Flattery gets you everywhere." Her chest shook with a shaky breath. "Especially when you stare at me with those eyes. Those are some baby blues. My compliments to your genetics."

He inclined his head. "I'll pass along the memo."

Their banter faded.

"You sure you want to do this?" she asked.

He nodded. "I want to start by giving. Not taking."

"With that mindset, I think you'll do just fine." She lifted herself up on her elbows. "A few tips. One. Start by teasing the lips. Two. A little thigh play is always in order. Light touch, but not too ticklish. Then clit to tongue and—"

"I might not have done this, but I have an idea how it works."

She looked amused. "Oh really?"

He didn't back down from a challenge. "Hey, I might be a virgin, but I'm sure as shit not a monk."

"So you've been with women, just not all the way."

"Nope." He crawled onto the bed. The mattress creaked under his weight. "I have one hell of an imagination."

The air in here smelled warm and sweet, like brown sugar and vanilla, and the fragrance only intensified the closer he got to her.

She still wore her black leotard and the leggings with the cats.

"I didn't dress for the occasion this morning," she whispered, glancing down. "No easy access."

"Take everything off," he ordered, a slow, insidious heat making its way over his sac. His cock felt warm and heavy.

She pushed down the right shoulder of her leotard and bared one creamy shoulder and the strap of a dusky pink bra.

Then the left side.

Then the whole damn thing came off, cat leggings too.

She was a vision in her satin bra and matching thong. Her thighs were slightly parted and the dark wet spot in the center of her whisper-thin pink panties hinted she wasn't unaffected by this encounter either.

His throat constricted as he slid his big hands up her thighs, the calluses on his palms rough against her soft skin.

She was like an exotic flower petal, all satin and silk. He couldn't stop rubbing, testing, and everywhere he explored she was the same. Smooth. Perfect.

His heart did its best jackhammer impression.

"Kiss me." She laced her hands with his, giving her bottom lip a little lick. "Don't worry. I'll show you how."

"I want to," he said. "I want to kiss you everywhere. Map your skin with my mouth. Memorize every last part."

"That's the spirit." She grabbed a fistful of his hair and tugged him close. It hurt but in a good way. The best kind of way.

And there they were again. Her lips. But this time they weren't mashed against his mouth in stunned surprise. They were opening, sweet and hot and there was the slick slide of her tongue, pressing against his, the rhythm slow and lazy, a pace he could follow. She trembled, her hands dipping down to clutch at his shoulders, urging him closer.

He was making her feel good, and the knowledge made him greedy. He wanted to make her feel better.

Whatever he did must have been right because the sound of her moan radiated to the root of his cock.

He closed his eyes. During the best times in his life, it was as if he'd watched a movie of himself. When he'd gotten a full scholarship to Boston College. When the Hellions had won the championship once and then again.

Now this.

It was like the part of his brain that should be able to comprehend happiness, or feel a moment deeply, was defective. Or worse, broken.

He'd mentioned this fact to Sully before, and his friend said it was a defense mechanism, that on some level he felt that if he dropped his guard to feel the good in life, he'd also more acutely feel the bad.

But maybe it was a good thing, keeping mental distance. Because this right here was him at his most self-destructive. He wasn't throwing his fist into some mouthy asshole's face.

No. Worse. He'd gone and admitted his Achilles' heel to an absolute stranger and put himself at her mercy.

She broke off the kiss and lifted her hips, not much—a few inches. But it was a quiet demand to get on with it.

In for a penny . . .

Her vanilla scent clouded his senses like a sweet drug. He moved before he could overthink any more of his actions. Her thong slid down by her knees and there was . . .

Everything.

She kicked the silk scrap off her ankles and her stomach went concave, the delineations of her ribs visible for a moment.

He knelt and studied. She had hair. He liked that. It was a rich chestnut and he trailed his fingers over the sleek curls. When he traced his index finger up the pale pink inner seam, a slippery polish slicked his skin.

He drank in the sight, how wet she was. How wet she was for *him.*

She gulped for air, her nipples stiff. A fierce flame of pride sparked in his belly, a burn that razed back the first line of his mental defenses.

He slid his finger back and stuck it into his mouth, sucking hard. He wasn't sure why she gasped at that. Maybe that wasn't what guys normally did? But fuck it, he needed a taste. And as her honey hit his tongue, his defense was eviscerated as he drew his finger clean, not willing to waste a drop.

He only knew one truth. If he didn't have his whole mouth on her sweetness by his next heartbeat, he would die.

He crawled forward and dropped low, spreading her open with his thumbs. She looked so feminine and delicate in contrast to his big hands, knuckles scarred from years of abuse on the ice.

He felt her stare and glanced up. She watched him, riveted. "I've never had anyone want to spend so much time seeing me."

What was wrong with other men? He'd never be able to look his fill. "I see you all right," he growled. "I see heaven on earth." He lunged forward, ready to devour, to feast, but paused an inch from his goal.

She sucked in a frustrated breath. "The biggest thing to remember is just to relax. Don't force anything. If you get uptight it won't happen."

"How do you want it?" he asked gravely.

She made a soft small sound, almost a purr. "Think of licking an ice cream cone." Her laugh was more a hitched gasp than anything. "Go slower than you might think, and don't be afraid to use your tongue. After a while go for the clit, but no flicking around. Move with intention. And add fingers. I like two or three."

Before he could move she squeezed his shoulder, halting any advance. "Wait. One more thing. While this isn't normally my recommendation for a beginner, if the feeling moves you, consider adding teeth. I mean, don't be a beaver building a dam, but—"

"A few soft nips wouldn't suck."

Her pupils eclipsed her irises as her thighs trembled. "Exactly."

He swept the flat of his tongue over all that flushed pretty pinkness, taking his time, not willing to cut a single corner. He hadn't waited twenty-five years to do a rush job. He was going to damn well taste every silken inch.

She whimpered. But it didn't sound like she wanted to stop. Especially not when she fisted a tight handful of his hair, slammed him closer, groaning, "Holy shit."

This was holy all right. It was some kind of communion.

He latched his lips around her clit and sucked hard, grazing the hood with the edge of his front teeth while plunging a finger into her heat.

This time he groaned along with her. How could anything be so soft? So wet? So fucking perfect?

His finger sank deeper, past the knuckle. Imagine pushing his cock in there.

Into her. Into Margot.

"Yes. God yes. You're amazing." Her toes curled as she draped her thighs over his shoulders.

And just like that, he slammed into the present, existed fully in the moment. The force of the realization that he was here, drinking the pussy of the most gorgeous woman he'd ever seen, stripped away every lingering defense.

He might as well be the one naked.

He didn't realize what was happening at first, when her body bore down, the walls of her slick sweetness milking his fingers in pulsing compressions. He was taking her there. Giving it to her and she wanted more. He knew it because that's what she kept whimpering. "Yes," "More," and "Oh God."

And damn if he didn't feel like a god in this moment. Invincible. Powerful. Capable of anything. Because he'd done this incredible thing, given this gift to a beautiful woman.

Afterward she lay still a moment before unleashing a throaty chuckle. "There is no humanly possible way that was your first time going down on a girl."

He shrugged. Easier than trying to talk when his throat felt like a desert.

She tossed her head back and gave a wide stretch. "If that's

true, you aren't just gifted, you're a frigging prodigy. Now get over here and let me get you pants-less."

"Why?"

"You don't think I'm going to leave you unfulfilled now, do you? Especially after that virtuoso performance. Now I'm the one with performance anxiety."

She reached for his buckle and he caught her hand. "You're talking about . . ."

"We're going to have sex, right?"

His walls were up in a flash. Not a full fortress this time, but a solid defensive structure. "I can't. Not yet."

Not if he wanted a prayer of mental sanity.

He'd gone mad with Margot Kowalski's pussy against his mouth. Imagine how he'd feel with his cock buried in her, that same wetness slick on his sac.

Shit. He'd never recover. And maybe that was okay. But he wasn't ready to commit to that. This was already swimming in the deep end of the pool. No point taking a swan dive.

"No. Don't you do that," she said, sensing the tension in his body, his need to run. "Bolting once from my house in a day is bad enough. Twice is unforgivable. Especially after what we just did. Rather, what you did."

"I . . . I'm not running to be a dick. I'm the kind of guy who has to think things through. And there's no chance of thinking when I'm close to you."

She regarded his face a long moment. "You're a difficult guy, aren't you?"

"I don't want to be. But what I just did . . ." He threw up his hands. His head was spinning.

"You ate me out."

He frowned.

"You can say it. I was there, remember? You ate my pussy. Went down on me. Made me come harder than any time in my memory. And for the record, none of those words are dirty, Patrick. What you just did, it wasn't dirty."

"Never said it was."

"Then why are you backing away?"

"Because you want more and I . . ." All he could do was leave her with the truth. "I don't know what I have to give."

Chapter Nine

*S*o, how'd it go with Patch?" Breezy greeted Margot without preamble, stepping aside to let her into the spacious condo she shared with her fiancé.

"It was . . . er . . . complicated." Margot sat down on the edge of one leather sofa, bracing her elbows on her knees. "Actually, scratch that. It's frigging complicated."

"Hoo boy." Breezy gathered a stack of financial documents off the coffee table and slid them into a folder. "Let's hear it."

"Sorry to barge in unannounced," Margot said. "You're busy, aren't you?"

"Don't worry. I was about to take a break. My eyes are burning from staring at spreadsheets. I'm doing a big Judy Blume push next month. Everything from *Tales of a Fourth Grade Nothing* to *Tiger Eyes*."

"Don't forget *Are You There God?* That book was very important to young Margot."

"*Forever* was my fave." Breezy grinned. "*Gah!* It'll be so fun. I can't wait to do the display."

"Aw, I'm so glad you're loving your work." They shared a quick hug.

"Speaking of work, let's get to it," Breezy said. "How did

your afternoon with Patch go? I've been waiting for an update."

"He left an hour ago."

"Wow. Okay. Long day on your end too. You guys must have gotten into it."

There wasn't a hint of innuendo in Breezy's statement. That was the worst part. Margot felt the heat spreading its tendrils up her neck, burning a path over her cheeks all the way to her ears.

"Margot." A spark of realization flicked in Breezy's eyes. "What happened?"

"I don't know?" Margot buried her face in her hands.

Breezy blew out a breath. "You slept with him?"

"No!" Margot got up and began pacing the room.

"Wow. You freaked me out. I thought you were trying to say that you hooked up with him."

"That *is* what I'm saying."

"Damn it, honey." Breezy fell back against her chair, covered her face with an outsized groan. "You were supposed to help him, not *hump* him."

"There was no p-in-v sex. Just the longest and most insane oral of my entire life."

Her friend peeked through her fingers. "You gave him a blow job as part of his mindfulness practice? Can't say I'm familiar with that particular technique."

"I didn't blow him. He blew me."

Breezy pretended to go boneless, sliding out of her chair and hitting the floor with a faint thud.

"You had Patch Donnelly come to your house for his first day as your personal client and you had him give you lady head?"

"Don't make fun of me!" Margot leapt to her feet.

"I'm not making fun. But this was a good professional opportunity."

"I see." Margot blinked. "I can read your mind. There goes Margot thinking with her lady head again. Can't bring her anywhere without her acting like a skank. Typical Margot wrecking everything by being some sort of low-key slut."

"What?" Tears welled in Breezy's eyes. "That's not at all what I meant."

The front door creaked and Margot swiveled her head. Jed stood frozen at the front door, clutching his black overnight duffel, looking as if he desperately wished his flight had been delayed by an hour.

"Sorry to interrupt." Jed eased in, taking the temperature of the room. "Everything okay?"

"Peachy!" Margot beelined toward the door.

"Don't go!" Breezy recovered her power of speech and was climbing back to her feet.

"No. I don't want to talk this out. There is too much I can't say anyway. I'm sorry to come in here and disrupt your night with my drama."

"You aren't drama. You're my best friend."

Margot stood by the door and balled her hands into two fists. "How I just behaved was inexcusable. To you . . . and to me. I'm going to go home, eat my weight in peanut butter ice cream, and rewatch the first season of *This Is Us* until I'm dehydrated. Once my head's screwed on, we can reconvene. Jed." She gave him a short nod. "Sorry for the not-so-warm welcome home."

"Margot, wait!" Breezy cried.

But she was already out.

When she left the building, the February air was a blessing for once. Her skin felt like living fire and she welcomed the light sleet. She stood still, jaw loose, belly soft, and took three deep breaths.

It had been a mistake to come here. Margot was a big girl now. And she had all the tools she needed to solve her own problems. She nibbled her nails. What happened today was intense and unexpected. Adrenaline and intoxication were still short-circuiting her system. Her laugh was short. Flustered. Slightly unhinged. And why wouldn't it be? Because Patch Donnelly had just given her the single most amazing sexual experience of her life.

And he was a freaking virgin.

She exhaled slowly and trudged to her car.

It was impossible to understand what made it so good. She'd had her fair share of attentive lovers. Of broody bad boys.

But she couldn't think about Patch anymore. What happened today could never be allowed to happen again.

No mixing business and pleasure.

She climbed into the car and slotted the key into the ignition. The silence was too deafening so she turned on the radio. Celine Dion was singing about how she didn't want to be all by herself.

A lone tear escaped, dripping off the side of her chin with a sullen plop.

She raised her fingers and rubbed away the remaining wetness. Where had that little sucker come from? She wasn't a crier. She certainly wasn't a "sit in the car alone and sob" type.

She didn't need to mourn something that would never happen. She needed to smile because it had happened. And move on.

Which meant that she also needed a plan.

And so help her, she'd drive up and down residential Denver streets until she'd concocted one.

The reality was that she ended up near Capitol Hill typing "Patrick Donnelly" into her phone's internet search engine.

The guy she encountered today wasn't the same guy who broke a man's arm in a fight. He'd run Stefan off, but he hadn't been violent. If anything, he'd been the opposite, cool and contained. The definition of self-control.

The first hit was a tabloid story of the fight. It had been back around Thanksgiving and the details were sketchy. The unconfirmed eyewitness reports were that Patrick and the lawyer got into a verbal altercation over a woman.

One thing led to another and both found themselves outside.

Patrick beat up the man. The rest they say was history. The lawyer's shoulder was dislocated.

No information about the woman was shared. Who she was. What she saw.

She tried searching different variations of the same question and all came out the same way. No name. No quote. No picture.

All the evidence pointed to the fact that Patch and this lawyer got themselves into some sort of cockfight. Not shocking behavior for two men at a bar. She'd seen it all before. Heck, she'd had two guys fight over her before. Neither had a chance, but they'd been too hyped on testosterone to realize that.

But the guy at her house today wasn't a player who thought he was God's gift to women. For as much as he was a stranger, she trusted her intuition.

The sleet turned to snow. The world outside vanished as the

windshield was covered in a blanket of white. Her breath crystallized in the cold air, an ephemeral cloud of white.

She typed his name into Wikipedia. It was jarring to have the page load and his picture stare back. Her stomach dipped as if she'd driven too fast down a steep hill. His gaze was so bright, it was as if he looked right at her. As if he knew she was here, parked on the side of the road, still warm between the legs, reading more about him.

She wasn't being a stalker. It was Wikipedia, available for any member of the public. But no one else had felt his tongue in their pussy today.

She confirmed his age. Twenty-five. He was a Virgo. Nothing much listed under family life. Just a mention he'd gotten a scholarship to Boston College. He'd spent time in a seminary before being drafted.

A jolt struck her core. She'd known this, but it had slipped her mind, the way hundreds of facts about strangers filtered through her mind on a regular basis. Was that why he'd been a virgin? Because he'd wanted to be a priest?

She tried to imagine him without the scruff, in the black, a white collar at his neck.

Whoa, mama.

The clench between her legs was most unholy. She'd never in a million years expected to have a priest fetish, or be interested in deflowering a man, but it appeared that Patch Donnelly was challenging all her preconceptions.

She skimmed the rest of his page. Everything else was hockey related. References to career highs, winning the Stanley Cup; and lows, the fights, the penalties, the notorious temper. She searched pictures. Losing herself in the images. Never was he photographed with a woman. Rarely did he smile.

A snow plow went by, snapping her out of her reverie. Her butt was frozen and her nose was numb. Great. She had officially lost her mind.

She drove home, trying to keep her mind empty. A cup of hot tea and a good night's sleep would go a long way to settling her frazzled nerves. When she pulled into her parking spot, a large delivery truck pulled up beside her. She gave the man a distracted wave as she trotted toward her apartment.

She was hanging up her jacket in the foyer when there was a knock on the front door.

The flower delivery man stood outside holding a bouquet of red roses.

"Margot Ko . . . walski?" he said carefully, double-checking a clipboard.

"Yes. Wait. Are those all for me? Oh my God! I've never gotten flowers before."

The older man chuckled, although not unkindly.

"Well don't go far, hun."

"What do you mean?"

"I'm coming back up." He jogged away and returned again with tulips. Then pink roses. Then orchids. Then . . . *huh*. She didn't know the more obscure flower species. And still more bouquets kept coming.

"Here's the last one." The delivery man was eclipsed by a profusion of long tropical fronds.

"This is too much. What do you think? Should I start selling tickets for my very own botanical garden?" Nibbles pressed against the glass, curious to discover that he now lived in a jungle. "Is there a card from the sender?"

The man shook his head.

It didn't matter. She knew who it was.

"What did your man do to mess up this bad? I've seen grovels in my day. But never anything like this. Did he run off with your sister or somethin'? Take your savings and blow it on the track?"

"I don't have a man," Margot replied softly. "But the guy who did this didn't mess up. Just the opposite."

"Well lady, looks like you found yourself some kind of keeper. Although gotta say, he makes the rest of us look pretty bad." And with that, the man tipped his hat and walked out.

"Oh wow," Margot murmured, looking around at the vibrant colors. The room was filled with intoxicating perfumes. In one fell swoop, the dreariness of winter had vanished before this bountiful, insistent profusion of life.

Had a guy ever done anything close to this level of over-the-top romantic?

The answer was simple: hell and no.

She reached out and plucked off a petal from the closest rose, smoothed her thumb over the velvet softness. Her shiver didn't come from the cold.

"I'm in real trouble here, aren't I," she said to Nibbles, to herself.

The heater came on, humming its assent.

Patrick Donnelly was leading her down an uncharted path. A guy who paid attention to her pleasure and made romantic gestures? This was new terrain.

Total virgin territory.

Chapter Ten

*P*atch played his heart out at practice. He wasn't a fan of drills. Yet another sore spot between him and Coach. Practice sharpened the rest of the team, but he feared it could have the opposite effect on him. A goalie was only as good as his instincts. The team lived and died on his snap-judgment decisions. Practice for a goalie could dull those instincts. Because guys took a few seconds to set up the perfect shot. There wasn't that sort of luxury in a game. It was all act, react. Act, react. Rinse, repeat.

But he was determined to turn over a new leaf. To get along. Go with the flow.

Besides, he had Nate Reed breathing down his neck. The backup goalie was across the rink serving as little better than target practice for a few of the shooters who needed extra work.

"Donnelly," Tor called him over. "You're looking sharp."

"Thanks, Coach."

"Now get off the ice."

"What?" He jerked. "Have I fucked up?"

"The opposite." Tor swung his gaze to his face, gave him a

cool, assessing look. "I've been thinking about what you said before the lockout. About how you hate practice."

Shit. "I know I've run my mouth. But I'm here. Putting in the work."

"You are. I see it. But I'm also not in this business to blow smoke up my own ass. What you said, it stuck with me. And I've spent the past couple months watching tapes and thinking, and . . . you were right."

"I was?"

Tor crooked his lips in a tight smile. "You're out there making saves, but you're also always aware that I'm watching, and playing to what you think I want. Not for who you are." He clasped Patch's shoulder and squeezed. "And if you're going to be starting, we need to trust each other."

Patch's throat swelled. He wasn't a guy who got emotional, but he respected Coach more than any other man besides Sully. His words? They meant something.

"We understand each other?" Tor asked.

Patch nodded. "Yeah. Yeah, Coach."

"And how was being with Margot? Man, she's something else, huh?"

Patch dropped his stick at the sound of her name. He bent, hoping that by the time he stood back up his face would have returned to its normal color.

"Yeah, something."

"Glad it's working out. With any luck, it's going to be life-changing."

"I'm not sure she's going to want to put up with me." He cleared his throat. "I'm not the easiest to get on with."

"I'd be willing to bet she likes you fine."

"No disrespect, sir, but why?"

"Because she's standing right over there."

"What?" Patch whirled around and there was Margot, standing on the stairs next to Neve Angel, the new head of Hellions Public Relations.

He jutted his chin in a half nod. He'd never read the playbook about the right way to greet a woman after burying your face between her thighs.

It seemed to work well enough as she wiggled her fingers in return.

Neve clipped down the stairs, swinging her arms briskly.

"Hey, lover," she said to Tor. "Good practice?"

"Not bad."

Patch looked at the two of them. They didn't leap into each other's arms. They weren't tearing each other's clothes off. Nothing exchanged except for the most basic of greetings. And yet, despite the rink's cool temperature, he'd have sworn it just increased a few degrees.

It wasn't in what they said. Or what they did. It was the look they exchanged, one heavy with unspoken language and clear affection.

That's love.

And he felt a pang in his own heart. Because it looked good—simple, honest, and true.

"I had lunch with Neve and she said practice was wrapping up," Margot said by way of explanation. "Thought I'd drop by and see if you were busy."

"For a session?"

She didn't blush outright, but the skin at her throat turned a delicate pink. "Yeah."

He heard the rest of her sentence in his brain. *Session. If that's what we're calling it these days.*

"We through here, Coach?" he asked.

Tor glanced over. "I'm going to keep the rest of the guys another hour. But you go. Like I said earlier. I want you to trust your gut. Be instinctive. I'd rather you go off and work on that than stand here fielding slap shots."

"On it." And there it was, the little gnaw of guilt, a familiar feeling because after all, he was a Catholic boy. He'd focus on his game. That's what he was meant to be doing with Margot. And if he wanted something more, well, he'd waited twenty-five years. He could set that aside while he focused on showing his team his commitment.

Because there was a date on his calendar coming up at the end of next week. Settlement negotiations. His lawyer said it was great they were moving fast. The statute of limitations could be years on such a case.

Soon he was going to face the music and maybe it wouldn't matter what he was doing, what leaf he was trying to turn over, because his name would be mud if he agreed to settle. But what hope did he have in getting Guy to drop his case? Patch knew it wasn't all about the money.

He'd hurt Guy Footscray right in the pride and that's where he'd strike back.

Margot's smile lit up her whole face. A lump lodged in his throat. She looked so pure. So perfect. And she deserved someone the same. Not someone who would drag her down in his shit.

"I guess you'll want to hit the showers," she said. "How about I wait down by the locker room?"

"Yeah. Sure. See you in a sec." And he skated away. Once they were alone, he'd tell her that all he could focus on was

hockey, getting his head on straight. That what had happened between them, what he'd done to her, had been a mistake.

"Holy shit. Donnelly's got a lady out there," Petrov announced a few minutes later, sauntering into the locker room. "Cute one too. I asked if she was lost and she said she was waiting for him."

"No shit?" Munro glanced in his direction and waggled his brows. "You holding out on us?"

"I bet you're right," Nicholson added. "She is lost. Lost . . . in your eyes." He crooned into an invisible microphone.

"You guys are idiots." Patch slid on his long-sleeved gray T-shirt and tightened his belt. "It's not like that."

"She's got legs for days," Petrov continued.

"Aw, damn," Nate Reed piped up. "This I gotta see."

"No." Patch stepped forward. "Not if you like living."

"That a fact?" The second-string goalie, Nate Reed, had a smart mouth and was chomping at the bit to replace his ass. "Or what? You going to break my arm too? How's that working out for ya?"

The room fell silent. Patch's fingers twitched reflexively and he balled them into a fist.

Then he heard Margot's voice in his head, as clear as if she was whispering into his ear.

Breathe. Just breathe.

He did and shit, she was right. It was too shallow. He tried again. From his diaphragm. Counted to ten and did it again.

The rage faded. His pulse returned to normal.

Not today, Satan.

He smirked at Nate. "Hey man, have yourself a good afternoon. I know I will."

And then he walked away, whistling for good measure.

And as he opened the locker-room door, his grin stretched from ear to ear. He'd gotten it back, the power. His rage was put in its place and he'd done it.

And the person who helped him get to that place was leaning against the wall.

"I came to thank you in person for the flowers," Margot said. "My house looks like a summer garden."

"I'm the one that should be thanking you," he said, deflecting. "I tried that breathing shit you talked about. It worked."

She bit her lower lip, trying and failing to hold back a smile. "I'm so glad 'that breathing shit' is working out. But I'm serious, what you did last night, with the flowers, I haven't had a guy be good like that to me before. It meant a lot."

"I can't decide if that's a damn shame or working in my favor," he rumbled. This was flirting. Nothing big. Not dangerous. But not strictly professional.

The problem was when he stood in front of her, face-to-face, he didn't feel professional. Or like the Hellions' fuckup goalie. Or the kid from Southie with another sad story. He felt like Patrick, the man he'd always wanted to be.

"I wanted to return the favor," she said.

"You sending me flowers to the locker room? Because I'll tell you right now, that happens and the guys will never let me live it down."

"No," she laughed. "This is just a nice gesture. A . . . token of my affection." She held out a hand. "You in?"

"Yeah." He closed his fingers around hers. "All in."

Chapter Eleven

For real? You're not telling me where we're going?" Patch said, amusement threading his tone. Outside the window, the University of Colorado campus flew by. "I never come up to Boulder."

"Good things come to those who wait," Margot replied enigmatically as she turned on the off ramp. They rode in comfortable silence for another two minutes, until she parked her car outside of a funky brick warehouse between a craft brewery and an acupuncture clinic.

"See that over there?" She pointed at the building across the street with a For Sale sign, the one that housed Stefan's MMA gym and two empty shops. It had foot traffic and amazing natural light.

"Yeah."

"It just came on the market. It's my dream to own that space and start a business." She explained the concept of Sanctuary as they walked into the Nirvana Yoga Studio.

"That all sounds great," he said, even as he hesitated outside the front door.

"You okay?"

"You're taking me to yoga class? No offense, but—"

"Do you trust me?"

He nodded.

"Good. Because I'm going to have to trust *you* an awful lot for the next hour."

Couples were already pairing off on mats around the studio. From the front, Dusk, her fellow instructor, waved.

"Hey, glad you made it," she called. "I've been trying to get you into Acrobatic Yoga for forever."

"Acro-what?" Patch murmured in Margot's ear.

She shivered as his hot breath skimmed her skin. "Acro-Yoga. It's like if acrobatics and yoga had a baby. And it's going to be fun."

He snorted. "This is a real thing?"

"It is indeed. And before you go rolling those baby blues, hear me out. Acro is for fun. No one can take themselves all that seriously while doing it. So I think it's going to be good for you. But it's not all ridiculousness. You're going to be the base. I'm the flyer."

"Base? Flyer?"

"All right everybody," Dusk called in a strong but calm voice. "First move of the night is going to be a warm-up, get you connected to your partner, and your hearts activated. Plank on Plank."

Patch stared around as couples—men and women, women and women, and men and men—dropped to the mats. The bigger partners got down into plank pose, arms shoulder-width apart.

"The key here is keeping your core engaged," Margot said. "So that you are strong and stable. Then, I get on you."

"I don't know about this."

"You promised." She took his hand and gave it a soft squeeze. "Trust me to let you have some fun."

"Fine." He got down into plank.

"Nice form," she said.

"If you wanted an excuse to check out my butt, there are easier ways."

She laughed. "Okay, I have to get on top while you do a plank. I'll face your feet and place my hands on your ankles. My toes will balance at your shoulders while I do a plank in reverse. That's why it's Plank on Plank, get it?"

"Got it."

"Good." She got into position then and felt his muscles hard beneath her. "Are you okay?" she asked.

"Could do it all day," he fired back. "Want to challenge the other teams? I think we got 'em all beat."

"Yoga isn't a competitive sport," she teased.

They went on from there. Next was the Base Test pose, almost like doing the famous *Dirty Dancing* lift while he was on the ground. She reached back and grabbed her ankles to finish the pose.

"Remember to lock eyes," Dusk called. "This is a great way to build trust between the base and the flyer. Remember that fear is just trapped joy. Soft gazes, soft breath."

Margot looked down and Patch was staring back, his face expressionless.

Self-doubt rose within her. Maybe this was a terrible idea. It had felt right on paper, when she was in bed tossing and turning last night. A way to continue establishing a working relationship, but still let her touch him. And for him to touch her.

But maybe this was all a little too airy-fairy and touchy-feely for him. Just because this was her thing didn't mean it would be his.

"What's going through your head?" he murmured.

"Wondering what's going through yours," she admitted.

"Not much."

"You hate this."

"No. I mean . . ." He looked around at the other couples, currently engaged in silent nonverbal communication, the atmosphere intense.

"It's not what I'm used to," he whispered. "But I can think of a million things I hate more than watching you above me."

A bubble of hope floated through her belly. "So you are having fun."

He screwed up his face. "You know what? I think I am."

She burst out laughing and he joined her, his legs wobbling. She went lopsided. "Oh no!"

But before she could tumble from her perch, he caught her with a firm grip, lowering her down to his lap.

"That was close."

"Not even. I'll never let you fall."

"And you're a man of your word?"

His face got serious. "I am."

As they finished class, Dusk came up to give her a hug. She glanced at Patch. "Do I know you from somewhere?"

"Maybe."

"Oh!" Her eyes brightened. "You work at that new vegan pizzeria. I love the pesto with artichoke hearts and pine nuts. Keep up the good work. Namaste."

Margot held it in until she got back into her little Honda; then she let it out.

"You finished?" Patch said wryly as she paused to gasp a breath.

"Your f-f-face. When Dusk said namaste."

That set her off all over again.

He watched her, bemused. "The vegan part is what got me. Vegan pizza. How is that a thing?"

"I know what you mean, but that pizza place is legit."

"Let me get this straight, you eat vegan pizza. What about the cheese?"

"It's actually quite delicious. I'll take you there sometime."

"Please don't." He buckled his seat belt. "Actually, sure. What the hell? Vegan pizza. Can't be all bad."

"Well I don't know about you, but I'm absolutely starving after getting flown around for an hour. Dinner date?"

"When I'm with you I'm doing stuff I never thought about in a million years."

"You say that like it's a good thing, Mr. Donnelly."

He grinned. "That's because it is."

The restaurant, Flatiron Pizza, wasn't far or too busy. No surprise given that it was a Tuesday night. They were seated quickly and Patch deferred to Margot for ordering.

"As long as it doesn't have any of those acai berries on it, I'll eat it."

She ordered them an Indian-style pizza and two iced teas.

"Indian-style?" he quizzed after the waitress walked away.

"It's the best one they do. There is this coconut curry sauce, and the sausage is—"

"Sausage?" He brightened. "Vegans eat sausage?"

"Sorry," she chuckled. "It's more like tofu chorizo. Did you just go pale?"

"I might pass out. I'm eating a pizza with curry and tofu? If

anyone in Boston saw me right now, let's just say it would not be a good situation."

"You're so brave."

It didn't take long for the pizza to arrive. Margot pushed it to the center of the table. "Do you want to say grace?"

He gave her a sharp look. "Why do you say that?"

She hesitated a second. "Look. I did some more reading about you. I knew you were Catholic, but I didn't realize you were quite so enrolled-in-a-seminary-for-a-few-months Catholic."

"Can you see me being a priest?"

She took him in—his size, the restless brutal energy that marked his face, the beard, the magnetic eyes. "Organized religion's not my thing, but if you led mass, I'd be in your front pew every Sunday, rain or shine."

"What do you mean?"

"Do you want me to spell it out for you? You are *H-O-T*." She ducked her head, suddenly embarrassed. "And speaking of hot, here, let's serve you some hot pizza because trust me you don't want this cold." She undercut her awkward joke with an equally awkward forced chuckle.

"I enrolled in seminary after Ma died," he said suddenly. "And even though we weren't close, she was still my ma. And the way she went . . ." His throat worked hard, his Adam's apple bobbing. "It wasn't good."

"Did she get sick?"

"Yeah, the disease was called heroin." His smile was bitter. "As you can imagine, she ran around with some pretty shady characters. One of 'em must have killed her. No one knows who. An old lady found her body dumped in a parking ga-

rage in Rhode Island. Ma was on the concrete. Gunshot to the head."

"That's terrible." Margot's stomach heaved.

"Police never got a lead, never found who did it. I'd majored in theology at Boston College. Growing up, there was this guy, Father Kevin, and he saw me through a lot. He was a parent for me when no one else was. When my pal Sully decided to enter the priesthood, I decided why not. 'Relieve the troubles of my heart and free me from my anguish.' Psalm 25:17."

Margot felt trapped in a confusing confluence. On one side, there was her honest admiration of a man who'd faced extraordinarily difficult circumstances and tried to find an outlet for healing. On the other side was the fact she was turned on close to a ten out of ten. What was it about hearing this big lug of a man quoting Scripture that got her motor running?

She didn't know, but she was willing to find out.

As the thought hit her, it was like a record scratched.

Bad motor! Turn off. Go back in the garage and think about what you've done.

She glanced at the kitchen and pointed, grateful for a distraction. "Look. I think that must be the doppelgänger that Dusk mentioned."

Behind a food counter a tall, bearded, ginger-haired guy was tossing a pizza.

"Is he wearing hemp necklaces?" Patch said in a strangled tone.

"At least four or five. And that looks like a genuine vintage Grateful Dead T-shirt."

"I got mistaken for *that* guy?"

"Hey, he's pretty handsome."

Patch turned around and cocked a brow. "Your type."

She shrugged. "I'm what you call an omnivore. Geeky. Bad boy. Mountain man. Sporty."

"Sporty, eh?"

"I mean, my last boyfriend owned an MMA studio."

"That asshole who was at your house."

"An apt description."

"I don't like him."

"Something we have in common. But I don't want to talk about Stefan. I want to hear your verdict on the pizza. Go on, you haven't taken a bite. Don't think that I haven't noticed."

He glanced down with a sigh.

"Don't be a baby. You face down slap shots traveling a hundred miles an hour. Enjoy the cheez."

"That's the problem," he said glumly. "There is no cheese here."

"*C-h-e-e-z*," she spelled out.

"Fuck." He shoved a piece in his mouth and chewed. His features remained inscrutable as ever, even as a vein rose on his neck.

"Don't keep me in suspense, what's the verdict?"

He took a deep swallow of his iced tea. "My taste buds are never going to forgive me."

"Not your thing."

"Not even a little."

His unexpected grin revealed slight imperfections in his white teeth; the two top incisors were crooked. Little lines grooved the skin on either side of his eyes. The humor transformed him, and the muscles between her legs clenched painfully tight. "Well, you know what? It doesn't have to be. But

I'm proud of you for trying. Just like I'm proud of you for giving Acrobatic Yoga a chance."

"Now that was fun."

"Really? You enjoyed it?"

"Hell yeah. Tofu sausage can suck a nut. But watching you above me? I could do that all day."

"Could you now?" she said softly.

He wiped his mouth. "Tell you what. We've been on your terms today. How about you come be on mine?"

"What do you have in mind?"

He pushed away his plate. "For starters, something that doesn't involve curry on pizza."

They were out in a flash. But in the parking lot her front wheel was flat.

"Oh crap," she groaned.

Patch crouched, pulling out his keychain. There was a penlight on the end. "Someone slashed it."

"Are you serious?" She glanced around as if she'd see a villain lurking in the shadows of the closest streetlight.

"Probably just some random punk hating on people who eat vegan pizza." But while his tone was joking, the smile didn't reach his eyes. "You got a spare? I can change this in no time, and you can get a new one tomorrow."

"Yeah, in the trunk." She gave a distracted hand wave to the back of her car. It was a bad feeling to be targeted, even at random. The night had felt warm, happy. And now a cold wind blew through it.

But that unsettled sensation quickly faded as she watched Patch efficiently remove the damaged tire and install the spare.

"You're staring," he said, squatting and screwing in a bolt.

Her tongue grazed her top lip as she admired the view. "I like to see a guy who's good with his hands."

"Then I got news for you." He leapt to his feet with an effortless bound, not even using his hands. "You're going to love me."

And as unbelievably stupid as it sounded, she believed him.

Chapter Twelve

"What's the verdict on my culinary skills?" Patch knew he was hovering, but didn't care. His gaze didn't leave Margot's lips as she popped the second bite of his homemade Denver omelet into her mouth.

Her wide eyes went wider.

"Have I got skills or what?"

"It's good." She covered her mouth with her hand, chewing. "Damn, boy. That's really, really good."

"Hell yeah it's good." He demolished half of his own omelet in three more bites. "I know my way around an egg."

"If the way my ovaries exploded as you whisked was any indication, I'd have to agree."

They shared an easy laugh and continued to eat their omelets, and buttered sourdough toast, in companionable silence. This was new. He didn't usually have people over to his place. In fact, he'd been a little self-conscious to bring her in here. It was big, but barren. He'd wanted a place to invest his hard-earned salary, and his financial advisor pushed real estate, but more often than not he just bounced around the three stories. Five of the six bedrooms were empty.

"It's a little stark," he'd said sheepishly, when he'd unlocked the front door and turned off the security.

"Um . . ." She had taken in the bare white walls. The leather couch, coffee table, and flat screen with a PlayStation were the only furniture in the living room. A pool table held court in the dining room as he preferred to eat at the island in his kitchen. "You like the minimal look?" she teased. "Maybe you're more Zen then you let on."

He'd brought her into the kitchen, determined to impress. A bonus of cooking from the age of eight was that he could improvise.

She nibbled another piece of toast. "How long have you lived here?"

"Bought it last year." He shrugged. "At the time I was too busy with hockey to worry about figuring out furnishings. And besides, what does a guy like me know about interior decoration? During the lockout, I had more time . . . but was in a bad headspace."

"Because of the fight?" She leaned in closer, searching out the secrets of his face. "The Jury Room is a classy bar, the décor feels like a library in Oxford. You must have been one of their first fights."

His mouth flattened. "Lucky me."

"I hate Guy Footscray's commercials. He talks so loud I'm surprised spit doesn't fly out of the television screen."

"Out of all the gin joints in the metro area, and I cross paths with that prick."

"Well . . . prick or not, you didn't have to dislocate his shoulder. Even if he isn't that nice of a guy."

He remembered how it felt, having Footscray's arm between his hands, the blind rage he'd felt. The fucker was

lucky he didn't rip the appendage off and stuff it down his throat.

"You want to talk about what happened?" she asked lightly. "Because from where I sit, it looks like there is a lot going on between your ears."

Heat rose within him as memory washed over him. His temples pounded. His stomach clenched like he was trying to do a sit-up.

Fuck.

He didn't want to feel this way around Margot. She was all that was good, light, and happiness. Freckles. Flying in his arms. This thing between them was pure. The last thing he wanted to do was taint it with his anger.

"No." He screwed the lid off a bottle of Gatorade in front of him and took a swig. "Not really."

"I know I'm not a qualified therapist or anything," she said lightly. "But sometimes talking to a friend can help."

"Let's make one thing crystal clear." He set down his drink. "You're not my friend, Margot."

She blinked. Did she set a world record for the longest lashes?

"Margot, eh? You're using my name in a sentence. That makes this a serious conversation."

"I'm a serious guy."

"So I'm not a friend." She dabbed her pink lips with a napkin. "What's that all about? You don't like me?"

"I more than like you."

She went quiet a moment. "You didn't invite me to your house to eat an omelet, did you?"

"And you didn't come to my house to eat an omelet, did you?"

She huffed a small laugh. "No."

The air was thick with everything going unsaid. He tried drawing a full breath, just like she'd taught him, but his lungs might as well be encased in plaster.

At last she huffed a husky laugh. "This isn't easy."

"Be more specific."

"This." She waved her hand in the narrow space between them. "This. This. This. You. Me. I don't know what is happening. I'm not a poet. I don't have the best words. I just can't deny that when you look at me, I feel . . . more me. The most me. I don't just like you either. It's more than that."

"Those sound like pretty good words from where I sit."

"But can't you see? You've been waiting a long time for someone special. And I haven't." Her chin raised an inch. "And I won't apologize for having more experience."

"Don't see anyone asking you to."

"I don't have the best track record with relationships." Her words picked up speed. She spoke faster and faster. "I can teach yoga. I have friendships. But when it comes to guys, and dating, I'm no expert. Far from it."

"Stop. Stop right there."

"I'm sorry." She rose in a rush, knocking her bar stool over. "There is absolutely such a thing as too much honesty. You are dealing with your own baggage. You don't need me here adding to it."

On the rink, he might have lightning-fast reflexes. But here, with this woman, he was stuck in slow motion. He reached, but she'd already moved away, evading his grasp.

"I'm being stupid, and that's not my intention. I don't want to make this more dramatic than it has to be," she said, backing toward the kitchen exit. "I abso-frigging-lutely acknowledge that I am, in fact, wearing a drama queen crown. What

we need is headspace. Tomorrow you're traveling for your first game. I want you to focus on that."

"Here's a fun fact. I'm able to think of more than one thing at once. It's sort of my job."

"And you're good at your job." She pursed her lips, appearing to swallow a smile as she stuck on her pink pussycat hat and shrugged into her jacket. "Really good, Patrick. And you could be even better."

"Now you're the one saying my name in a sentence."

"Because I mean business."

She stood on tiptoe, clutching the front of his T-shirt, and kissed him full on the mouth. Their ragged breaths mingled a moment. He tasted the brown sugar in her lip gloss before she broke free, pressing a quick second kiss to the tip of his nose.

"Go to bed," she whispered, clearing her throat and stepping back. "And win tomorrow."

It took every last shred of Patch's willpower not to close the space again, to consume her. "There's something you should know."

"Shoot."

"I'm not going to get a lick of sleep if you leave."

"If I stay, you won't sleep either," she shot back.

"I'll take those odds."

She shook her head slowly as if with reluctance. "Good night."

He took her hand and held it between his own. Her skin was cooler than his. He didn't like that. He wanted to tuck her against him, warm her up. "Do me a favor and call when you get home. I want to know you got back safe, especially driving on that spare."

"It's been a long time since anyone has cared if I got home,"

she said with a smile. "Careful, you might be turning into a gentleman."

"The things that I want to do to you are far from gentlemanly," he said in a husky tone.

She rocked her head back and unleashed a frustrated moan. "Quit leading me into temptation. I'm trying to respect your virtue here."

"My virtue can take a long jump off a short fucking bridge."

"That might be. But . . . if we end up taking that jump, I want it to be special. That's important. I want *you* to feel special."

Blood rushed to his ears. "Funny, I feel the same way about you."

"Then we're in agreement and I'm leaving." A wicked gleam entered her gaze. "But while you wait for my call, slip into something more comfortable."

"Like?"

"Nothing at all." She blew a kiss, pirouetted, and was gone.

After the door snicked shut behind her, it was as if all the gravity had exited too. He floated to the living room, watched a couple minutes of news, nothing sticking, the words running over him. He ended up in the master bathroom, where he brushed his teeth and splashed water on his face, and because he couldn't think of any good reason not to, stripped down to skin.

He stared at his familiar reflection in the wall-to-wall mirror as if trying to see himself for the first time. Discover what he was working with. He had a good body. It wasn't arrogance, just a statement of fact. He used it for his job and it looked it. The muscles in his stomach weren't perfectly cut and defined like a bodybuilder, but he was carved around the V-line and

his pecs and arms were large. The hair on his lower belly ran in a thick mahogany line down to his cock, which also didn't seem to give cause for any complaints.

He didn't know a ton about dick but his seemed good.

He grimaced, rolling his eyes. What the hell was he doing? Here he was . . . twenty-five years old, and he still didn't have a definitive idea of how a woman would view his junk.

His phone started ringing. He glanced down, a flicker of relief lighting inside him.

Margot.

Except the call was coming in on FaceTime.

No way was he going to answer the phone buck-ass naked so he hauled ass to his king-sized bed, sliding beneath the down comforter, ensuring the blanket was tucked in around his waist before clicking.

"Surprise!" she sang out. "I made it home in one piece."

"Your cheeks are pink," he answered. And her hair was damp around her face as if she'd recently washed her face. Just seeing her twisted his heart.

"I took a shower."

"A cold one?" he teased.

"Ha! It's below zero tonight. I probably used up all the hot water in the building, but it was glorious." She eyed him. "In bed, eh? And shirtless."

"I followed your instructions to the letter," he said in a raspy voice. "What can I say? I'm an eager student."

"Impressive." She cocked an eyebrow. "A-plus for effort."

"This is what happens when I'm hot for teacher."

The blush in her cheeks deepened. "I thought it would feel safer having you miles away. Instead it still feels dangerous."

"What are you wearing?" he asked, tilting his head back, determination rising within him.

"Not a lot," she admitted.

"Show me," he growled.

She cast the screen down to reveal a white bath towel wrapped around her gorgeous curves. And her long legs poked out the bottom. Legs he'd love wrapped around his neck again.

"Nice."

"Thanks." Her lips twisted wryly. "Are you planning to return the favor?"

He cast his own screen down and she made a murmur of approval.

"What's going on below that blanket?"

"If you were here, you could find out," he said in a teasing tone.

Her forehead creased in frustration. "Maybe . . . you could describe it for me?"

"Are you trying to seduce me, Miss Kowalski?"

She giggled, her tongue darting from between her lips, the tip stroking along the seam. "Apparently I can't help myself."

He leaned back against the headboard and slid his big hand beneath the sheet. He was already hard. "It's . . . full."

"Go on."

"Big," he rasped. "Ready."

"You're stroking yourself?"

He gave a short nod, his thighs throbbing.

"Are you cut or uncut?" There was only the slightest catch to her throat.

His cock twitched in his hand. "Cut."

"God, look at your face."

He lowered his chin. "What about it?"

"You're beautiful." Her pupils filled her irises.

"Shouldn't that be my line?"

"You're welcome to plagiarize."

A low groan ripped from his throat. "What about you? Going to join in or let me have all the fun?"

"Ooooh. Challenge accepted." Her camera slipped to one side before she got it righted. "There we go."

"By there you mean you've dipped your fingers in your pussy."

"That's one way of putting it."

"Your pussy is a good place." He stroked harder, imagining pushing into the hot, sweet ache between her thighs. "The best place."

"Glad you like it." A soft wave of hair fell across her cheek. He longed to smooth it back.

"It's all that I think about."

"We really do have a lot in common." Her laugh hitched. "Because having you there again is all that I think about too."

"What are you doing?" he asked. "How are you touching yourself?"

"Right now I'm just going slow, light, just a little circling."

"Over the clit."

She nodded. Her top teeth closed on her full bottom lip. "I'm imagining it's your cock, pressing against me."

His intensity rose, his sac constricting, pulling up tight beneath his shaft. "What about slipping a finger inside?"

"Usually I use both hands. But seeing as I'm holding a phone."

"Ah, right."

"I don't mind. Trust me, this works fine. How about you? What are you doing?"

"Slowing down," he said through a moan. "But increasing pressure."

"That's how you like it."

"Yeah," he barked.

"Then that's exactly what I'd do. I'd get my hand between your legs and I'd feel the weight of you in my palm." Her words sped up. "I might even be greedy and inch a few fingers lower. Graze your balls. Would you like that?"

How he managed to nod he'd never know.

"Then I'd pull back and lick my hand to make it wet," she purred.

Jesus Christ. He couldn't even regret the blasphemy.

"I'm using both hands. One cupping your sac, fondling, gentle squeezes, that sort of thing. The other hand? I'm taking it up and down with a little twist at the end."

His chest shuddered. He was a goner, seduced by her provocative words, the smolder in her clear gray eyes, the mouth-watering way her hair fell over her shoulders, a few strands flirting with the curve of her throat.

"That's good?"

"Yeah, babe." His voice was taut.

"If it's really that good, you're going to get a little wet on your slit. Precum."

Heat slid through his veins. His pleasure was drawn tight, a hard knot. She was going to kill him tonight.

"You have any of that?"

He ran his thumb over the bead of wetness at his tip, mas-

saging it into his sensitive skin. "Yeah." His belly was tight. The muscles rock hard. His whole body was revving. "I do."

Her eyes closed to slits. "Perfect, because I'm going to drop to my knees and lick it clean."

He couldn't hold back the grunt of pleasure. "I'm getting down beside you," he gasped. "I got my hand between your legs and you're riding my fingers while you suck me."

Now it was her turn to make a sound, the cutest exasperated whimper that he'd ever heard.

"You like sliding over my skin?"

She nodded. Another shallow moan of pleasure.

"Answer when I ask you a question."

From the look on her face, she loved that, him taking charge and being bossy, and that was good because he could get addicted to this sensation of power.

"You're fucking my fingers right now," he said, gruffly, luxuriating in his strokes. "They are deep in you."

He was rewarded with another of those cute-as-hell sounds.

"Whose fingers are they?"

"Yours." The word cracked.

His hips sped up and the pulsing sensations took root and spread. This was too good. Too much. He squeezed down on his slick crown. "Babe, I'm close." He couldn't choke back the rough sound of building desire.

"I think I'm passing you by." She rocked her head back and as he watched her fall apart, he became undone, the climax bursting forth from inside him, internal spasms of sensation like he'd never known.

It had never been that good. Not that he'd had a lot of experience, but he didn't even know his cock could feel that way.

"That was amazing," she said in a sleepy, satiated voice.

"All I want to do is suck your fingers clean."

She shuddered. "I'm an idiot."

"Why?"

"Because right now I could be with you and this could all be real."

He wanted nothing more than to kiss that pout off her face. "Babe, if you were here right now you'd have been fucking a lot more than my hand, that much I can tell you."

She swallowed. "When do you come back from the road?"

"Two nights."

"Am I going to see you?" she whispered, very softly.

"More than you might want to," he answered hoarsely. He ached to reach through the smartphone and touch her, lean in and press his forehead to hers, devour her vanilla scent.

"That's impossible. And I'll watch you play tomorrow night. You've got this."

He inhaled sharply. "As long as I've got you."

Chapter Thirteen

Margot watched the Denver/Kansas City game from a Watering Hole bar stool beside Breezy. When the game ended with a Hellions win, they'd broken into cheers, falling into each other's arms. The atmosphere of the room was electric, the fans stomping their feet and pumping their fists.

The long lockout had sucked for any self-respecting hockey fan, dragged out over the holidays and into the miserable cold of January. At last there was light. And a win.

And best of all . . .

"Patch kept his cool! Did you see it? Did you see?" Margot cried, nearly knocking Breezy off her kitten heels.

"I think the team's back on track," Breezy said. "Finally."

"Looks like Westie wasn't the only magic on the team." She nudged her friend's ribs.

"Ha." Breezy gave a good-natured grin before taking a gulp of water. "You know Jed doesn't believe all that hype, right?"

"Of course not. Because Jed West isn't just Mister Hockey, he's Mister Awesome. And humble. And let's face it, practically perfect in every way."

Breezy sighed. "He really is, isn't he?"

"Are you ready to be Mrs. West?"

She waved her hands. "It's crazy to think a year ago we were probably right here, and I was probably ogling him on the screen, never dreaming that he . . . that we . . ." She heaved her shoulders in a happy shrug, lost for words.

"Bet it was the night we stole that cardboard cutout of him from here."

Breezy groaned. "I still can't believe we did it."

Margot sipped her IPA. "Is it strange, having the fantasy come to life?"

"Sometimes, yes," Breezy said honestly. "But I can't explain it. As soon as we were around each other he stopped being this untouchable idea, and became a regular guy."

"I don't know if I'd say regular. I mean, he's got the heart of a Boy Scout and the body of a Greek god."

"I still don't know what I did right to deserve him," Breezy said with a smile.

Margot smiled back. "I do. You were your awesome self."

"Aw, you're the greatest friend." Breezy seized her and gave her a bear hug.

"I meant to apologize for freaking out the other day. I was a mess, but you weren't the place to put it."

"How are things with Patch?"

"Hard to say." Margot wrapped her arms around her waist, as if that could put a clamp down on the butterfly riot. "Not practically perfect. We're more a perfect mess."

They both had broken parts. But when he looked at her as if she was the last woman on earth, as if he couldn't believe that he was lucky enough to be in her airspace, it wasn't an ego stroke. It gave her a sense of home, of belonging.

"Do you like being with him?" Breezy asked, pulling out

a hand mirror from her purse and checking her half-beehive hairdo.

A pointless gesture because it was perfectly styled, as per usual.

"Yes." She loved being around him. He made her feel whole.

"Because I don't know anything about him. I don't think anyone really does. Jed once mentioned that he has a buddy who is a priest, but besides that he keeps to himself."

"He has a snarl that's for sure, and that glare. It keeps the world at bay."

"It's intimidating."

"But beneath it, I wouldn't say he's a cuddly teddy bear . . . but all the gruffness manages to hide some real, bona fide, and undeniable sweetness. I feel weird saying it, but as strong as he is, I am scared that I could break him." She ran her hands over her head, interlocking the fingers behind her neck.

"It sounds like he really opened up to you. And I don't think he's a guy who opens up to anyone."

Sitting back in her chair, she absorbed Breezy's words a moment before responding. "Here's the deal. I can't keep feelings professional where Patch is concerned. I know everyone thinks that I'll chase any hot man on two legs, but there's more here than just attraction."

Her friend reached over and squeezed her hand. "Then what's the harm to give in?"

Margot wanted to tell her friend how Patch was a virgin. How it felt like a responsibility that she wasn't sure she could live up to. She slid her hand into her purse, distracted a moment. "Hey. Crap. I don't have my phone. It must still be hooked to the charger in the car. I need to call him soon. I told him I'd be watching."

"Go on," Breezy said. "I'll get us one more drink. Unless you want me to come outside with you."

"Why?"

"It's dark!"

"I'm a big girl. Don't worry." Margot blew Breezy a kiss and tore to the door.

She couldn't wait to hear Patch's voice. To tell him how proud she was. Her heart had burst with every play. Every move he made. And when they won she swore that for half a second he looked straight at a camera, straight at her.

She jogged to her car. Cheeks blazing. Peering through the window, she saw her phone on the passenger seat, just like she'd suspected. It had been a long day. She'd had to teach two classes, get a new tire, and through it all she fretted over the game.

Fretted for nothing.

"Hot Pants."

Margot froze, hearing the slick drawl and hated nickname. Slowly she turned around, hugging her purse to her chest.

"Stefan." She darted her eyes left and right, cringing on the inside. No one was around. Here she was in a city of almost a million people and no one was frigging around.

"Watching the game?" He leaned against the side of her car like he owned it, his hands stuffed into his leather jacket.

"Watched," she answered flatly. "It's over. We won."

"Knew I'd find you here."

"That's some fantastic deductive reasoning seeing as the Watering Hole is an extension of my living room." She reviewed the contents inside her purse. Nail clippers. Lip gloss. Wallet. Parking change.

Great. Her options were pinching him or pelting his face with a handful of quarters.

"We met here, remember?" He spoke in a lazy tone, like he had all night. Like she hadn't asked him repeatedly to leave her alone. Like he didn't purposefully have the upper hand here in the dark, outweighing her by fifty pounds of muscle.

She swallowed hard. "I remember."

She'd been playing air hockey with Neve and Breezy when he'd sent her a beer. She'd glanced over and noticed black tribal tats on his biceps, that deep dimple and thick tousled black hair. He was the definition of sexy. She'd given a wave and he'd waved back.

"What we had was good."

"For a while."

He snorted, a mean, ugly sound.

But she meant it. The first couple months *had* been fun. He was a player, and so was she in her way. They flirted and had hot sex. Not a lot of emotional connection, but that wasn't the point. She'd liked visiting his MMA studio, watching the kickboxing and jujitsu. It was out of her wheelhouse and he'd loved showing her off to the guys.

But she hadn't loved the jokes he'd told them, about the benefits of dating a yoga teacher, the benefits of flexibility in the bedroom.

And when she tried to share her dreams about opening a business, perhaps someday even taking a lease on the great building his MMA studio was in, he'd made fun of her ideas.

It had gone downhill from there.

He narrowed his eyes. "I want you to come with me."

"Then you're going to be disappointed," she shot back, glancing at a streetlight. Were there security cameras in the parking lot? Regret swelled that she hadn't agreed to have Breezy come out with her, just as her anger grew. Because she should be able

to duck into a well-lit parking lot of a popular neighborhood bar without being afraid of being accosted by a giant creep.

"I'm serious." He stepped closer. "You've been hanging out with that hockey nut job. Donnelly is no good. I don't like it. I don't like it one bit."

"And the whole part of us breaking things off means that it doesn't matter what you like, or don't like," she snapped, faking a calm she in no way felt. "It's flat-out none of your business."

"You aren't listening." He grabbed her arm. "You have to hear the truth from a guy who knows a thing or two."

Annoyance turned to fear.

"Let me go! You're scaring me."

"Jesus," he snapped, a fleck of spittle flying from his lips. "Will you calm down? I'm not even hurting you."

"You don't get to decide that. Let me go."

"You make me crazy, you know that?"

"I don't make you anything. I've repeatedly asked you to delete yourself from my life."

"The idea of Donnelly putting his hands on you. It makes me sick. I watched you."

She went rigid as wood. "What do you mean watched?"

"At your studio. Him lifting you up. His hands all over your body."

"You've been following me?"

What a stupid question. Of course he had. For the past month she'd had a growing sense of unease, been denied the ability to feel safe in her own skin.

And now her worst fears were being confirmed.

"You work across the street from me. It ain't hard. But what if I did? Because I was good to you. I treated you nice. And

you didn't make no complaints when I was giving it to you. You liked it, you liked everything I did. Some of my friends tried to tell me I was a cuck. I know you've been with a lot of guys. But I went to the mat. I defended you. After all, some people like to eat a lot of donuts. You stuff your face with dick. It happens."

"Are you seriously comparing dicks to donuts?" Her jaw was about to drop on the pavement.

"Don't deny you went in Donnelly's house. That do it for you? That NHL money. All that power. Does he have a big dick? Is his dick bigger than mine?"

God save her from fragile male egos.

"What are you even asking?"

"I want to know. I don't care if it is. I'm confident." He shrugged. "So is his dick bigger than mine? Is that it?"

It took every ounce of strength not to roll her eyes. If she wasn't so scared, she'd laugh in his face.

"You need to get off 4chan or Reddit or wherever you are hanging out messing up your mind with ideas on women and realize that whatever this is . . . it's not working. It's not going to win me over."

"You turned slut after the breakup. But I've thought about it and I can forgive you."

"I'm going to ask you something, and I want you to tell me the truth."

"What?"

"You slashed my tire, didn't you?"

He averted his gaze, his swagger deflating some. "Our relationship wasn't even cold in the grave, and you spread your legs for someone else. That shit is cold."

"You don't get to decide what is or isn't okay."

"Look." He shook his head. "This is coming out all wrong. I know this dude, see. A lawyer who's got a hell of a lot to say about your hockey player. He works out in my gym. You've seen him in the news, the lawyer who nearly got his arm ripped off. We got to talking tonight and I'm telling you, he's got a lot to say, a lot to say. Interesting things about your goalie."

Margot jerked her wrist, trying to wrench free. "If you don't let go of my arm on the count of three then I am going to scream."

"Can't you see I'm looking out for you? Guy Footscray says Patch is a creep, that up close he has the eyes of a psychopath."

"One . . ."

"That he was going to put powder in a girl's drink at the Jury Room."

"Two . . ."

"I'm just saying you got to come with me and we'll call Guy. He can tell you. He tried to stop him and the fucker attacked. That's some crazy shit."

"Three."

"Margot." He stepped forward. "Be reasonable."

But she was not staying silent so he could be comfortable.

She screamed. She screamed bloody murder, and clocked him across the face with her handbag. He hadn't expected that and a leather tassel poked his eye. He dropped her arm, swearing.

"Goddamn it. What'd you do that for, you stupid slut?"

She turned and ran, didn't look back. She ran straight into the bar, and didn't stop until she was next to Breezy, shaking like a leaf.

Chapter Fourteen

The Hellions went into the third period against Kansas City with a score of one to one. That's when Petrov scored his second goal of the night for the Hellions with three seconds remaining, his incredible backhander giving the Hellions their first win of the season. The game wasn't a blowout, but a hard-fought scrabble, not without casualties. Munro had exited in the second period with an apparent shoulder injury and was joined by Nicholson a few minutes later.

Still, as Patch skated to the bench at the end of the game, he couldn't wipe the grin off his face. He hadn't bit the few times the offense had got in his crease. He'd been on the ice the whole time, and his playing had been aboveboard. It had been a tough night for the Hellions' defense, but he'd stopped twenty-six out of twenty-seven shots.

Everyone talked at once, slapping each other on the back. They'd been solid, played a great team game.

"That was a notch above," Tor said from near the center of the circle. "We've got some work ahead of us but tonight you men clicked in a way I haven't seen in months. This was a whole different level, and we're going to keep building on that hard work."

He glanced at Patch and gave him a nod. Hell, he even cracked a smile, which was rarer than a unicorn walking down Main Street.

Patch imagined Margot watching the screen, studying his breath, the way he tuned out the shit talk and cheap shots, how he refused to take out his frustration on the net when he let the one goal slip in. Instead of slamming his stick to the crossbar, he'd shaken it off. Breathed. And breathed some more.

Because somewhere across the high plains, Margot Kowalski was watching, and he didn't want to let her down.

When he got back to his hotel room, he was still riding the high. He dialed her number as soon as he dropped his bag, and she didn't answer. No big deal. They'd connect soon. He took a shower and came back. Still nothing. He turned on the TV and mindlessly clicked until he found a sports channel.

"Hellions showed some of their old fire tonight, didn't they, Bob?" a bald commentator in a suit was saying to another guy behind the desk.

"They sure did."

"Patch Donnelly was on point tonight. Did you see that behind-the-back save?"

"Snatched it out of thin air. That's the Donnelly who wins championships."

"Guess that's the questions for what's left of the season. Will the Hellions be getting that guy from tonight or the one who gets into bar fights?"

Patch clicked off the television.

He stared at the ceiling without blinking until his eyes burned, until his vision distorted and blurred.

It had been two hours since the end of the game. If Margot hadn't called him by now, she wasn't calling him period.

He turned off the phone and the light, rolled over, and punched the pillow twice. Sleep didn't come easily, but eventually the adrenaline of the night faded and sleep took hold.

He was back in the bar, the Jury Room, which wasn't far from the courthouse. It had been the anniversary of Ma's death, a night that he alone in the world remembered or mourned, a night when he thought about the fucking prick who still was out there sucking air, the one who'd put a bullet in her head. The one who'd never been apprehended no matter how much Patch had spent on private investigators.

Some shadows were too dark to penetrate.

He'd seen the girls right away. They were far too young to be there. No doubt the bouncer turned a blind eye to their fake IDs because they were beautiful. And he wasn't the only one who noticed.

He'd leaned against the bar, sipping his single malt as a man in a suit began to case them.

First it was a nod. A smile.

Neither looked a day over nineteen. But they were harmless, having fun, dancing, sipping a cocktail, not getting too stupid.

Patch decided to keep an eye on them from a safe distance. He wasn't interested, but the interest he saw on the other man disquieted him.

He'd seen the same looks on the men who'd come to see his mother. The hunger. The predatory gleam.

The blonde girl went to the bathroom, wobbling in heels she might have stolen from her mother's closet. While she was gone, the man in the navy pinstriped suit sidled closer to the redhead.

She smiled at whatever he said, but it was stiff, polite. She didn't want to talk to him and Patch didn't blame her.

Hell, the man was old enough to be her father.

That's when he saw it happen. It was fast. So fast he knew with sickening surety that this wasn't the first time it had happened.

As the man spoke, he removed a small paper envelope from his trouser pocket and sprinkled something in the blonde girl's drink.

For a moment Patch wanted to believe he'd made it up. After all, this was a night that lent itself to dark thoughts. But the churning in his gut was no lie. This had happened. Make no mistake. And the only question he could think as the world turned red was: How bad was this shithead going to pay?

He sauntered over, just as the blonde got back.

"Hey, I know you." She grinned, her smile sunshine bright.

Unlike the suit who was as old as their dad, he guessed he was in the demographic they'd come to seek. An older guy. Twenty-something. But not too old.

The redhead turned over one shoulder and let out a pleased gasp. "No way. Patch Donnelly?"

"Can we get your autograph?"

"Or a selfie?"

"Sorry to be the bearer of bad news," he said. "But you're going to want to take those drinks and flush 'em down the toilet and then get outta here."

"Excuse me?" The blonde started to cop an attitude.

"I'm serious," he said, clapping his hand on the asshole in the suit's shoulder, holding him in place. "Because this guy— who isn't going anywhere by the way—just slipped something in your drink."

"That's a lie," the man choked.

Around them people were starting to stare, to point.

"If you want we can get the girls to call the cops. It's not hard to test for Rohypnol."

"No cops," the blonde said.

"Shit. Let's get out of here." The redhead grabbed the drinks. "Creep," she snarled at the suit and then they were gone.

"Keep your eyes on your own lane," the suit snarled, stepping back, his eyes unfocused and his tie coming undone. The man was drunk. It didn't matter. It didn't excuse what he'd done. "Go find your own piece of ass."

"Can't do that. See, I got this thing. When I see a man who wants to hurt a woman, then it gives me pleasure to hurt him back." He reached and grabbed the guy's elbow, spinning him around so his back pressed to Patch's chest as he yelped.

"Hey!" another bar patron yelled. "Quit that."

"Quit? I've only started." The room felt far away. He put pressure on the arm. He did it slow. He wanted it to hurt. He wanted the fucker in his arms to feel a taste of the fear and horror he'd been about to inflict on that girl tonight.

The suit began to scream, back-kicking, struggling to get away.

Patch didn't yield. He was past caring. All he knew was the urge to hurt. To break. To destroy.

Yelling. So much yelling. Someone screamed.

The suit went limp.

That's when the arm dislocated. He felt it go, the pressure give out.

Patch dropped him to the floor and gave him a kick for good measure.

"Scumbag."

Patch sat up in the dark. His heart pounded. His mouth filled with the sickening taste of bile.

The dude was gutter scum, yes, not to mention one of the most litigious personal injury lawyers in the city.

And without evidence, Guy Footscray spun his story, that Patch Donnelly had tried to muscle in on him talking up a pretty young woman. Typical, arrogant hockey bastard.

He worked the press like a fiddle and within twenty-four hours, everyone was singing the same song.

Patch let it happen. What was he going to do, get into a pissing match? Compare dick sizes? No way were two underage girls going to show up and provide witness statements.

If the world wanted to think he was a monster, let 'em.

And so he'd brooded. And spiraled. And gave in to the anger.

But the lawyer bided his time. He'd been humiliated and wanted payback to be a bitch.

He brought the personal injury suit against Patch, saying he hadn't filed a police report because he hadn't wanted to see a local hero arrested, didn't want to do that to the kids. He was going to represent himself, wanted a million for pain and suffering.

Patch would give it to him too, if it meant he could stuff each dollar down the wannabe rapist's throat until he choked on it.

He and his lawyer were meeting Footscray after he left Kansas. And if he wasn't going to be able to stuff the asshole full of bills, he had the choice to fight back.

But what was the point? To clear his good name?

What a joke. His ma died alone, afraid, and was left like a

pile of yesterday's trash. He hadn't been able to save her. To inspire her to save herself.

He just hadn't been enough.

He hung his head, alone in the dark. As far as the world knew, his name was mud.

And he needed to pay for all of his crimes.

Chapter Fifteen

$\mathcal{M}$argot slipped as the chair she was standing on tipped forward. "Crap!" she cried, reaching out to brace her hand on her closet door. Sure, all men—and women—die. *Valar morghulis* and all that jazz. But when the day came for her to shuffle off her mortal coil, here's to hoping that it wasn't breaking her neck while digging her senior year yearbook from the top of her closet.

She grabbed the blue leather-bound book and jumped down to the floor, heart pounding.

Walking to the edge of her bed, she sat down and cracked open the cover, flipping through the faces. She'd been out of high school for how long? Nine years? Ten? For a time in her life that felt so intense, so all-consuming, now she couldn't even remember the names of all the faces she glanced over.

But there was one.

She'd never forget Chad Taylor.

In one picture a girl is walking down the hall; she's wearing a short skirt, part of the dance line school uniform on game days. That girl walking away while Chad crouched behind, baring his teeth like a mad rodent; that girl was her. All

around him were guys doubled over. The caption read: Football star considering enrolling in Oregon State. What an Eager Beaver!

Even the Yearbook Club had been in on the joke.

"Ea-ger Beav-er," the team would chant as she lined up for hot lunch.

"Ea-ger Beav-er," they'd holler as the bell rang and they filed out to the school buses and parking lot.

Her friends got sick of all their catcalling. Inexplicably, a few got jealous and acted as if Margot was lucky to get the attention of the hottest guy in school.

She resorted to eating PB&J in the library. At least she'd been able to raid her stepmom's novels and escape for forty minutes a day to worlds populated by devastating dukes, suave assassins, heroines who always had perfect comebacks, and no men who ever made a woman feel degraded after sex.

She'd come so far from those days, from being that bewildered girl. Worked her ass off to feel confident in her sexuality and choices.

Her senior year picture stared back at her. It had been taken a month before the homecoming game in a studio near her childhood home in Portland. A home that was sold when her stepmom and dad divorced. That girl in the photo had no idea what was ahead of her in life. The good, the bad, the ugly.

Margot was surprised to find tears welling in her eyes. It was so easy to be critical about herself. But when she looked at her earnest, seventeen-year-old face with that questionable haircut and shy smile, she could summon more empathy. If

she wouldn't blame the younger version of herself in the photo for her troubles with guys, then she shouldn't be annoyed at her present self for poor dating decisions. If a dude turned out to be a jerk, that was on him. Not her.

Picking up her phone from beside her legs, she didn't hesitate. She deleted all the dating apps one by one. For so long she'd been looking for a guy who seemed worth it to quit playing the field, to settle down and risk commitment.

She deserved good things in life, and a good guy, and for once she really felt like she'd found one.

As the last app vanished from her smartphone, there was a knock at her front door.

She stood, knowing who it was before taking a single step. *He* was out there.

She slid the yearbook under her bed. She hadn't spoken to him since their phone sex.

With a deep breath, she opened the door.

"Margot," he breathed, and his gaze didn't leave her face.

"I watched the game last night." She stepped aside so he could come in.

"We did good. Coach was happy."

"All of Denver felt the same way."

"I practiced some of what you said. I breathed. I said . . . mantras. Positive self-talk. Turns out you know a thing or two."

That made her smile.

"Tea?" She winced. "Sorry, no tea. It's a force of habit. When people come here I tend to force it down their throats."

"Why not? Maybe I'll like it. I like coffee."

"Two entirely different substances."

"Both are hot."

"Milk and orange juice are both cold, what's your point?"

She let her fingers brush over his arm as he walked past, needing the connection, however small.

"Touché. I thought you were going to call after the game last night," he mumbled, taking a seat. "I waited."

"I ended up leaving my phone in my car and catching a ride to Breezy's," she said quickly, a white lie, but she didn't want to give him the full story and risk setting him off. "Jed was gone so we had a sleepover."

He nodded, something like relief entering his expression. "I should have just called, you might not have had your phone, but looking back on it, it feels as if I was giving you a test. And that's stupid."

"A test of what?"

The pot on the stove began to whistle, drowning out his quiet words.

"Sorry, did you say something?" she said, snatching up the pot, pouring the hot water over two mugs of chamomile tea, and then drizzling in honey.

"Forget it."

She licked her finger. "No."

The baddest ass in the NHL glowered at her and she dished it right back.

He blinked first. "Fine." He sighed. "I said, a test about whether or not you cared about me."

"You weren't sure?"

"Being a needy asshole isn't really my style."

She touched her fingers to a faint bruise on his cheek. "It's needy to want reassurance of affection?"

"It is if you've got to ask for it."

"I disagree." She took a small sip of tea, let the herbal sweetness wash over her tongue. "I've been thinking today that if

I want something, I need to feel like I deserve it. Sounds like we're in a similar boat."

"I don't know if I deserve you, Margot." He made a small noise when he realized he'd spoken her name, a short laugh. "But I want to try."

She took a deep breath and spoke in a rush. "I'm sorry I didn't call after the game." He had to hear the truth about what happened with Stefan, but he wasn't exactly known for his levelheadedness. What would he do when he found out? How was he going to react?

He shrugged, glancing at the wall. "Whatever. It's fine."

It sounded like he was trying to convince himself more than her.

"I'm serious. I wanted to. In fact, I meant to. I went out to the car to get my phone, but . . ." She cleared her throat. "Well, I had an unexpected encounter."

He watched her now, stern, but calm.

"Remember my ex?" She toyed with a loose thread on her sleeve. "Honestly, it feels stupid to use that word. The term seems to lend too much weight to Stefan's position in my life."

"You're talking about the asshole who was bothering you the day we met."

"Yup. That's the one. Turns out he's not happy I've been spending so much time with you."

"Oh?" He squinted, a muscle clenching in his jaw like he was biting down. "And how would he know?"

"Because it looks as if he's gone stalker lite. Actually, full stalker. Remember my slashed tire? Yeah . . . that was him."

"You sound scared." His eyes heated, the blue going almost black. He managed to nod, and the effort looked like it cost him. His whole body radiated tension.

She paused, wondering if she should stop. Her shoulders sagged and she felt closer to one hundred than thirty.

"I'm not scared of Stefan." But her words sounded hollow, steeped in bravado.

Because the truth was, she'd been unsettled in the parking lot. No. Scratch that. She'd been freaked out.

Scared.

"His temper got the best of him."

"I want to hurt him for making you feel that way." He sounded *pissed.* Hulk-smash-pissed.

Her heart sank. "That's what I was afraid of."

"I didn't say I was going to. Just that I want to." He raked a hand through his hair and began to pace around the room.

"What are you doing?"

"Breathing," he said, before dropping to his knees in front of her. "I am calming myself down, the way you taught me. Because this isn't about me, and my reaction. It's about you, and what you need right now."

God, she could kiss him for that.

But there was something else.

She put her hand on the side of his cheek. "He said something else too, something I think you need to hear."

"What's that?"

It was work to finish what she needed to say. "He said the lawyer you had the fight with works out at his gym." She could barely get out the next words. Her stomach threatened to come out of her throat. "And he's telling people that you tried to roofie a girl at the bar."

Patch closed his eyes, just for a second, and Margot had the sense that he was retreating somewhere deep within himself. A place she couldn't reach.

"I don't believe it," she rushed out. And that was the truth. "But I want to hear the truth. From you."

The silence was as loud as a gunshot.

"Does it matter what I say?"

She'd never heard him use that voice before. He'd gone still. So still. She wasn't even sure if he was breathing.

"Of course it does."

She tried to grab his hand, but he moved then, picking up the teacup and taking a swig, grimacing. "That tastes like grass."

"You've consumed a lot of grass in your time?"

"You always such a smart ass?"

"I am just curious where you became a lawn epicure."

"A lawn epi—*pffft*." He snorted. "You're really something."

"Why thank you. A compliment that warms the heart. And you're not answering."

His expression turned deadly serious. "I didn't do that. Put a drug like that in a girl's drink. But here's the thing, if I had, I wouldn't tell you, would I?"

"You wanted to be a priest once, didn't you?"

"Yeah. For a hot minute. You think I have Catholic guilt."

"Or morals."

He heaved one shoulder in a half shrug. "I wanted something bigger than myself." He reached up and idly pulled out the chain he wore around his neck, clasped his fist over the Saint Anthony medal. "But I'm not cut out for that life."

"Why?"

"Because how could I help people if I couldn't help the one person that I loved more than anybody?" The words were ragged, the pain so raw that she felt them as a visceral pain.

"Your mother."

"I was her son. All she had. She gave me this medal and said Saint Anthony was the patron saint for lost things. And yet, I lost her. Got into enough trouble that eventually the state moved me to a foster home. And without me there . . . she had no reason to try at all. And then she was lost for good. And no medal was ever going to bring her back."

"So you joined the seminary."

"I'd have made a terrible priest, just like I made a terrible son."

"I'm not going to pretend to be religious with you. I don't know what I believe. But I do know this. To live in this world . . . we need to have a little faith. And when I look at you, I see a guy that I can trust. That I can believe in. I don't think you tried to drug a drink. I think that lawyer is lying."

"Shit." Patch covered his face and from behind his hands, Margot listened to his truth. To what he saw in the Jury Room, the two vulnerable young women, and how he felt a desperate desire to help. How his anger flared at the man who wanted to hurt them.

When he was done, they sat in silence.

"I have just one more thing to say," she said.

"Shoot." His voice was still husky with emotion.

"When I look at you, all I see is a good man. A great man. The best man."

He feigned staring around the room as if looking for someone else.

"Yeah, I'm talking about you." She knocked his foot with hers. "And actually I have a question too. But if you aren't ready to answer, there's absolutely no pressure."

"Got it."

She took a deep breath. "Patrick Donnelly, would you mind if I took you to my bed? I'm not going to say I'm going to make

a man out of you, though. Because honestly, you've done a great job of that all on your own."

He glanced down at the teacup. It looked almost like a toy in his big hand. "And here I was hoping I'd get to hang out and sip hot grass juice."

She should have expected his speed, his agility, his complete control of his body. After all, she'd watched him play countless times. But it felt like a heartbeat and he was standing, and she was in his arms, cradled to his broad chest.

"Is that a yes?"

"Where do you want me to take you?"

She waggled her eyebrows. "I like that you're open. But for this first time . . . I think we'll both feel more comfortable on my bed."

Her room was dim in the winter light. He settled her down on the mattress and walked to the window, drawing the curtains.

"What are you thinking about?" she asked.

"The last time I was in here with you."

"A good memory."

He turned around, facing her fully. "The best. I wasn't sure I'd be able to top it. But it looks like I've gotten lucky."

She rose to her knees and slid off her top. "You're certainly about to."

Chapter Sixteen

*H*e'd be tempted to stop time, except for his intense impatience. It was as if he was crawling in the desert, but the oasis was right there, so close to bliss, just a few more inches.

"Get over here," Margot ordered. "Hurry."

"That's what I'm afraid of."

Her face softened. "It's going to be quick the first time."

"I'm sorry."

"Don't. This is basically the honor of my life. Besides, after the first time there's going to be a second time." She reached down and unsnapped the clasp in the front of her bra. Her breasts hung pale and perfect. His mouth watered at the sight of her light pink nipples.

"And a third." He shed his shirt. "You got a condom."

She reached out, flipping open his belt buckle with expert skill. "I do, but you have a choice. I'm on birth control and had a clear STD screening after my last partner. So I defer to you. Your choice."

She popped his button and ground down the zipper. His cock threatened to explode from his black boxers.

He reached out and stroked the side of one of her breasts. The velvet-soft skin riveted him. He wanted to bend down and

suck the tip of her nipple into his mouth, lick her until she bucked into his mouth, but he couldn't move. If he budged so much as an inch, he would shatter. The pressure of the cotton on his shaft was too much. The idea of the hot, slick tunnel he'd once licked—

He swallowed, sucking a breath, fighting for focus, for self-control.

This might be quick, but so help him, it wasn't going to be *that* quick.

She arched like a kitten, sinking her claws into his V-line of muscle, grazing his skin with such soft, but precise, pressure that he clenched his ass, fighting to hang on.

He focused his gaze on her shoulders. If presented with a stack of Bibles, he'd swear up and down that he'd never seen anything as beautiful and delicate as the slope of her shoulders rising up to her neck.

"Are you sorry," she whispered, "that this isn't my first time too?"

"But it is," he rasped. "Your first time with me."

He bent, tangling his fingers in her long hair, memorizing the delicate texture between his fingertips, tugging it ever so slightly so that her head dipped back. She let him slide his tongue over hers, tasting her sweetness, coaxing her to deepen, not to hold back. He'd never kissed a woman before Margot, never experienced this raw essence, taking the opportunity to taste her until she trembled in his arms. He wanted to consume and be consumed in turn.

It went quickly after that. Relentless. He'd covered his mouth on hers and moved his body down. She was tall, lank, and lean, but he was bigger. Broader. Her hair spread around

her face like an open fan and her eyes were hazy, but she wasn't
far away. When their gazes locked, he knew she was close, as
close as it was possible to get.

Except that was a lie. Incredibly, soon, they were going to
be even closer.

"Hey." She smiled.

"Hi."

She reached out and held the Saint Anthony medal dangling from his chest between her thumb and forefinger.

"Patron saint of lost things, huh? Well, I've found you.
You're not lost anymore."

"Margot" was all he could manage to reply. It was impossible to say more. His emotions were running too high. There
was a low hum emanating through his skull. It was as if he'd
turned into pure electricity.

"You still have your boxers on."

"Not for long." He started to tug down the sides, but she
got there first. And then he was freed, long, thick, and bared,
and she was right there.

The edge of him brushed up against the edge of her, and
in that place, that space where they pressed, came a rising, of
thick pleasure, concentrated and extraordinary. Every muscle
was taut. He was so hard. So hard and she was all lush softness. And he fell. Sliding. Slipping into the heat.

A gasp.

His or hers. Both. He didn't know. The world was reduced
to these sweet inches, the tumble into absolute pleasure. She
locked her legs around him, driving him in farther until he
was at the hilt, his sac nestled against her ass.

"This is it," she gasped, her features seemingly torn be-

tween pleasure and pain. And he understood, because he was gripped by the same sensation. The goodness of this feeling and the sense that it was almost unbearably too much.

"This is what all the fuss is about," she finished.

"I'm falling in love with you." He hadn't planned to say it. But as the words left his mouth he realized he meant them.

"That's just the sex talking," she said, putting a hand on his cheek.

"Don't humor me." He hiked a hand under one of her thighs, spreading her a little wider; holding himself with one hand he began to move, a slow grinding rock.

"I fucking love fucking you. But I'm also falling in love with you. They're two separate things, but better when they're together."

She arched up at his words, the small of her back leaving the mattress, getting just that little bit closer.

He glanced down and saw a hint of her clit, pink and pretty in the slit. He remembered what she'd done the last time he'd been there. His mouth there, feasting, exploring, demanding. God, it had been glorious.

Now he wanted to see what would happen with his finger.

He circled once, twice and she called out his name and clenched down. When those hot wet muscles bore down on his shaft he didn't have a chance. Not a prayer. His orgasm arrived like a force of nature; to resist would be like standing on a porch in Florida and trying to blow away a hurricane.

Pure sensation tore through him and he was lost. This time for good.

And when the quiet returned it was as if he was looking at the world made new.

"How did you know to do all that?" she whispered.

"I just moved how it felt like I should."

"You're a natural."

"Did you . . . come too?"

"No, but I was close." She giggled to herself. "Crazy close."

"Shit."

"Stop! Are you kidding me? I've never been that close so fast ever. Never ever."

"That was fast?"

She wrinkled her nose. "It was fast."

"So you're saying it's going to get longer."

"With your skills? Uh yeah. It's going to get longer. Better. Everythinger."

He pulled out with a sharp stab of regret. Not ready to have lost what he'd so recently gained.

"Let me just go clean up. I'll be right back."

He realized as she got up what that meant. He'd marked her. Claimed her. And there was something so primally right about that fact that it made it hard to breathe.

She appeared a minute later, pausing in the door, backlit by the room behind. Her body was curvier than the Himalayas and he wanted to spend the rest of his life discovering its hidden secrets.

"I meant what I said. I'm falling in love with you." The more he said it, the better it sounded.

She drew closer and he took her hand, pulling her down on him. "And right now, since my dick's not inside you, maybe you'll hear me. I'm telling you plain. I know what I know. And what I got in my heart for you is the best of me. And I'm going to give it a name, and call it *love*, and I'm going to give it to you, because you are the best person I've ever known. I was lost and you found me."

"And I was lost and *you* found *me*." Her lips trembled. "But this is fast."

"So? Do you care?"

She laughed, breath catching. "Not as much as I should."

"When it's right, who cares . . . it's allowed to be right. It's okay to find each other. I don't want to be lost anymore."

"Me neither." She bent to kiss him, her hair following around him this time, no longer a fan but a curtain, blocking out the world, until only two people existed.

Him. Her. Him. Her. Two beats of a heart. Two bodies made one.

Chapter Seventeen

*P*atch was beneath her, six feet and who knew how many inches of big hard man. He claimed that he was falling in love with her. Had a man ever told her that? Yes, a few times. But she'd never felt the truth like she did tonight, a truth that resonated all the way down to her soul.

He stirred against her, hardening again.

Oh yeah. She grinned. She hadn't been doling out false flattery when she said he was a natural.

"Ready to go again?"

His eyes drifted closed. "I don't know how I'm ever supposed to stop."

She raised her hips and took him inch by slow inch, savoring the slide, sinking to the hilt. Her pussy was already primed from their first attempt, her delicate folds slick, flushed with expectation.

"You feel so good," she murmured, smoothing back her hair from her face, riding him in a lazy rhythm.

His hands found their way to her ass and he squeezed, kneading her muscle, deepening their rhythm.

Her breath went weird, all hitchy and raspy. Need coiled deep within her, clenching every tender secret place.

"I love doing this." He sat up and her breasts pressed into the hard muscle of his chest, her nipples hard against his sweaty skin.

She bit the damp, corded column of his thick neck and he let out a roar.

Her arms and legs encircled him, holding on tight as he took over, hearing him growl how good she felt, how wet, how tight.

She'd imagined she'd be the one setting the rhythm, acting as the teacher, but he was making all new rules and all she could do was hold on and let it happen. Her hands slid down his ribs, bracing either side of his chiseled obliques. Her back hit the headboard, her spine pressing into the wood, not enough to hurt but pinning her in place so that all she could do was go mindless, and give herself over to his relentless grind and her own driving need. Her sex was swollen, aching. He moved in ways she'd never known. Had never thought of. What they were building here was bigger. Bigger than anything.

"I love doing this," he growled, staring down at her with heavy-lidded eyes.

"What a coincidence, because I love you." There it was. And strangely enough, admitting the truth was the easiest thing in the world.

Her words put him into high gear, dropped his guard. Nothing about what he did was restrained or gentle. She couldn't begin to describe the feeling.

"Thought we didn't know each other well enough," he snarled, rolling his hips, going deeper. It was impossible how deep he went. And still, there he was.

"I know enough." She bucked as he angled the length of his shaft over her clit. "Oh. God. I know."

His expression heated to the point she thought she could come from that alone.

"Margot."

She'd never get tired of the way he said her name.

He dropped his forehead to hers, his thrusts faster. Harder. An inexorable erotic pressure took her almost to breaking, and there it was, her orgasm right there, ripe for the taking, and for the first time in her life she didn't rush to meet it head-on. Take it and run. She wanted to wait. To savor.

"Come," he growled as if reading her thoughts. "I got to give that to you."

"Not. Alone," she managed to gasp.

He pumped and rutted, until her clit pulsed. Until she could hear her own wetness, the syrup-like damp coating her inner thighs.

"I told you to come," he ordered.

"With you." She dug her fingers into his hair and pulled.

There was a smack, a bite of flesh.

She yelped. "You're an ass-slapper, now?"

"Give it to me," he ordered, and the bossy man had her number.

She gave in and gave up, biting down on his shoulder, tasting the salt, the sharp sweet tang of desire as pure sensation washed over her. And as it kept going she felt him unravel. His movements jerkier.

Once, last year in Mexico, she'd been caught in a riptide and dragged out, the shore retreating. She knew not to fight, that to fight the current was to drown. So she let the rip carry

her farther and farther and that's how it was now. Except she never wanted it to run out, the feeling to ebb; she wanted him to keep taking her on this wave until they found a new shore, a place that was them and no one else.

"Margot." Her name was a prayer.

And he reached down, pulled her closer, pulled her mouth to his.

"I've waited my whole life for you." He squeezed her fingers gently.

"Tor is going to shit a brick when he finds out what we've done. And I'm not sure my friends are going to understand."

"It doesn't matter what Coach thinks. Or anyone. If you are for me, who can be against me?"

"That sounds almost religious."

"Romans 8:31. With a few key modifications."

"Patrick." She wiggled in closer. "You can't quote the Bible while you're still inside me."

"Don't be a hypocrite, babe." He tweaked her nipple, soothing the slight sting with a long, slow suck. "'Cause you were screaming for God the whole time."

"Jesus take the wheel!" She buried her face in his chest. "What will the neighbors think?"

"Anybody asks, say 'prayer circle' while looking 'em dead in the eye."

She dissolved into giggles, glad when he anchored his arms around her because it felt as if she could just float away. "You're terrible."

He shifted against her, still inside, the hardest part of him in her softest place. "I don't want to leave you."

She glanced up. His eyes were closed. The individual hairs

of his beard were a fascinating mix. Honey. Tawny gold. Cinnamon. Amber.

"Then don't."

She let her own eyes drift closed, and as sleep tugged her down, she could swear that she spied a glimpse of that far-fabled shore.

Chapter Eighteen

*P*atch pressed a kiss to the back of her neck. "Wake up, sleepyhead."

"Mmmmm." She burrowed into the pillows with a disoriented smile. "You smell like coffee."

"The best coffee." He set a cup on her nightstand. "I made a Dunkin' Donuts run."

"You're kidding." Her eyes flew open as she sprang up to sit, glancing around in confusion. "When?"

"While you were sleeping." He smoothed back her hair. It did little to settle down the wild waves. She looked freshly fucked and he loved that he gave her that particular style.

"How long have I been sleeping?" She yawned. "It's like I've been in a time warp."

"You were out a solid couple hours. Snoring and everything."

"You're joking."

He wasn't. "It was cute."

Her brows smashed together. "Snoring is never cute."

He shrugged. "Is when you do it."

"I'm going to need a gallon of this stuff." She turned and resolutely grabbed the paper cup, taking a long sip. "Yum. Cream and sugar."

"And a couple of maple cream donuts." He set down the Dunkin' box on the bed, opened the lid, and peered inside. "Plus crumb cakes. Two Boston Crèmes, because of course. And the double-chocolate. My personal favorite."

She leaned down, staring at the glut with amazement. "You can't think we'll eat all that."

He scoffed. "What's this about *we*? That's my order."

This time it looked like her brows might just lift straight off her face.

He burst out laughing. "Kidding, babe. Obviously you can have one."

"A regular comedian," she muttered, reaching for a Boston Crème.

They cuddled beneath the covers, feeding each other sweet dough. In the end, they indeed cleaned the box, famished from their exertions.

"See this grin?" he said, glancing over. "I can't kick it. 'Cause as good as it was to fuck you . . . this is even better, me, you, just hanging out—demolishing a dozen donuts in bed."

"I'd offer to let you eat a donut while riding you," she joked. "But on second thought, that might be a fetish that's too weird, even for me."

"I won't tell if you don't." He took his time licking the frosting off her fingers. And it didn't take long until he was licking her other places.

Everywhere.

The next week passed in a blur of hockey and Margot. Patch played a game at the home rink against Vegas. Luck ran out for Sin City's season-long winning streak as the High Rollers were forced to give up three power play goals. Petrov scored two, one a chip shot from the side of the crease and another

from the point. The defense worked together but Patch made the saves when they mattered, comfortable and well prepared.

As a team, they gelled again. The Hellions played clean, worked hard and smart, a lethal combo. But the real test was going to be the next game on Saturday night, when they went up against their biggest rivals, the San Francisco Renegades, a team who took no prisoners. The fans expected fights, and rarely went home disappointed.

Tomorrow Patch had negotiations with Guy Footscray, who wasn't going to just be contented with money. He wanted to turn the tables, blame Patch for what he had done.

But for tonight, this moment, Patch wasn't going to let that fucker bring him down. He'd done good. And had a hunch why.

"Hey, Coach. Can I talk to you?" he said as they were going to the locker room. "In your office. After I'm cleaned up."

"Sure, kid. See you there."

Thirty minutes later, he knocked on the door to Tor Gunnar's office. Coach was his height, but not as broad. Still, something about Coach's stony stare could put even the baddest badass down for the count. He called Patch kid, but wasn't that old. Maybe forty.

But for once, no frustrated frowns came at him from Coach's direction. In fact, he reached out and clapped Patch on the back in greeting.

"You're making progress faster than I could have hoped."

Patch cleared his throat. "Thanks to Margot Kowalski."

"How's that working? From where I'm standing it seems as if she might be your secret weapon."

Patch studied the photograph of Neve on Coach's desk. "I'm in love with her."

A hush fell over the office. "What?"

"I'm in love with Margot Kowalski. The yoga teacher."

"Shit. Thought that's what you said. You've only known each other for what? Not long enough."

"Really, Tor?" Neve Angel pushed through the door that had been opened a crack. She clicked her heeled boots briskly across the floor. "I hope you're not mansplaining how long it takes for people to fall in love. Because I have it on good account that there was once a couple who fell in love over the course of a single weekend."

She braced her hands on the back of his big leather chair, and bent over to give him an affectionate kiss on the top of his head.

"A couple that knew each other for years prior," Tor grumbled.

"And had their heads shoved so far up their own asses that their assholes had assholes."

Tor looked bemused, but when he glanced up to lock eyes on his fierce-eyed fiancée, it was clear that nothing but affection was in his tone. "Can I help you, Angel?"

"With so many things. Like can you order takeout tonight? I'm feeling like orange chicken from that new Chinese joint on the corner."

"That's why you're here?"

"That and I saw Patch walking into your office. And the door didn't shut all the way. So I just so happened to have lurked outside to listen to what you two men were talking about. And I heard a little about love feelings and how they applied to one of my best friends."

Tor snorted. "You can be head of Public Relations for a thousand years and you'll still be a nosy reporter."

"I can't help what's in my blood," she said without apology. "And those who want to be off the record should close their doors, just saying. Now." She clapped her hands and pointed at Patch. "You."

"What about me?"

"You said you have feelings for Margot? Real feelings?"

He shoved his hands in his pockets. "Realest ones I know."

"Did she tell you about her ex-boyfriend who tracked her down in the parking lot? Grabbed her arm. Scared her half to death."

"Yeah." His world tinged red.

"My sister filled me in. I was just on my way to go have a word with good ol' Stefan. You want to ride shotgun while I track him down?"

"I know where he works."

"Jesus, Angel." Now Tor was on his feet. "The kid is already ass-to-eyeballs with the ramifications from his last fight. Don't go dragging him into another."

"He accosted my friend. That can't stand."

"No." Tor raked a hand through his hair. "No, it can't. But there's got to be a better way than issuing justice through a back-alley beatdown."

"God, when you talk like that it sort of turns me on," Neve breathed.

Tor glared daggers. "Angel." Warning laced his tone.

"Gunnar." She met his glare with a nuclear scowl.

Patch unleashed a low whistle. This woman was tiny but scary. "Remind me never to get on the wrong side of you."

"This guy." Neve glanced over with a wry smile. "I'm liking you more and more."

"Both of you quit arguing before World War III breaks out."

Patch stepped between them before wondering if that was wise.

"Argue?" Neve looked honestly confused. "This is how we always talk."

He glanced at Tor for confirmation.

"She's not lying," he said with a shrug. "We're not normal, but we seem to work."

"What can I say, fighting is our foreplay." Neve shrugged.

"TMI," Tor said with an exasperated chuckle.

"I'll pretend I never heard that. And don't worry. I've already got a plan. And—"

"Neve?" An executive assistant appeared in the coach's doorway, holding a tablet with a concerned face. "Thank goodness. Jason thought you were here. I've been looking everywhere."

"Everywhere?" Neve wrinkled her brow. "I was at my desk fifteen minutes ago."

"A lot can change in fifteen minutes."

That's when Patch realized the assistant was casting him short, furtive stares. And not of interest either. More like disgust. And fear.

And her stares weren't lost on Neve or Coach.

"What's going on?" Tor said, holding out his hand for the tablet.

"This interview just went live." The assistant placed it in his hands.

Patch didn't move as Neve and Tor hunched together. He had ears. He could hear what they were saying.

Looked like Guy Footscray was going on the offense. With the settlement tomorrow, he was trying to turn the crank, attack. He'd gone to a tabloid and said Patch tried to drug a girl at the bar.

"'I saw him put a powder in the drink. I hate trashing a hero, but from where I stand that doesn't look heroic to me,'" Tor read, before lowering the tablet.

Patch felt the intensity in his gaze. He looked as though if he glared hard enough, he would be able to see the truth.

Patch squared his shoulders. He had a reputation for fighting. For being gruff. For not always having command of his emotions. In this moment, he had a choice. Was he going to pay the jerk off and make this whole situation go away like his lawyers advised? He wouldn't have to admit to guilt. But the world would think settling meant he did it. Until recently, he hadn't given a shit what the world thought. He'd even welcomed their hate, like Sully had said.

But he could quit blaming himself for not saving his mom, being enough to make her get clean and live, for carrying the guilt of his failure like a yoke, plowing a barren field for the rest of his life.

He could fight for the truth.

He didn't deserve to be punished.

"I didn't do it," he said.

"Can you prove it?" Neve asked, crossing her arms.

"Nope." He shook his head. "My word against his, I guess."

"Where's the girl involved?"

Patch shrugged and explained the real story in curt sentences.

"What a damn mess," Tor said.

"A public relations nightmare," Neve chimed in.

"I'm sorry," Patch said.

"No." If Neve was nuclear before over Stefan, two hydrogen bombs exploded in her eyes now.

Patch half expected that if he glanced up, a mushroom cloud would be towering overhead.

"You aren't giving that lying liar a single cent," she said. "I believe you. And for what it's worth, you have the full weight of the Hellions behind you for support."

"For real?" Patch glanced at Coach.

"If that guy did what you said? I want you to fight," Tor said.

"Thank you. For believing me."

"You're a pain in the ass," Neve said. "But you're not the predator; *he* is. I'm going to issue a statement." She leaned down and planted a kiss on Tor's cheek before walking away.

"I came to tell you about Margot because I didn't want you to think I wasn't taking the opportunity to work with her seriously," Patch said. "You've given me chances. More than anyone. And if you want Reed to start for a few games while this goes down . . . I want you to know . . . I understand."

"What's your job on the team?"

"Is this one of your rhetorical questions?"

A ghost of a smile. "Sure is."

"Fine. I'll bite. I'm the goalie."

"And I'm the coach. Are you responsible for the lineup?"

"No, I'm not. I was just saying—"

"I don't care who you love or don't love, as long as when you show up on the rink, you are playing with your head. And if you can have your head in the game on Saturday night, you're starting. Can you have your head in the game?"

"Yeah." He cleared his throat. "Yes. Yes, I can."

"Good. Then we're on the same page. Now get outta here. Get some rest. You're going to need it for tomorrow."

Patch moved to walk out. "Oh and one more thing," Tor called right as he reached the door. "Tell me, have I ever said that I'm glad you're here? That it's a goddamn privilege watching you play?"

Stunned, Patch shook his head. "Can't say you have."

"Ah. I see." Tor picked up a pair of black-frame glasses and shoved them on his face. "Then that's an oversight on my part."

Coach didn't say more. That wasn't his way. And Patch was glad because shit, he could handle only so much. But as he walked out, knowing his team was behind him, that Coach believed in him, was proud of him, then combined with the presence of Margot in his life, he had courage.

His walk turned into a jog and into a run.

He wasn't going to back down. And he wasn't going to accept the bad stuff life threw his way as his deserved punishment.

He didn't have to live haunted by ghosts.

Not anymore.

Chapter Nineteen

𝒫atch asked Margot not to come with him to the law office. "It's going to be a three-ring circus, babe," he'd said, kissing her on the nose as she finished her morning sun salutations.

"I don't want you to face it alone." Margot frowned, wiping a gym towel over her damp brow.

"And I appreciate it. I do." He slid on his shirt, his hair still wet from the shower. "But the world doesn't get to drag you into my shit. I'm a big boy. I'll take care of business. Let me get in my head and do what I gotta do."

"I'm a big girl. And if you hurt, I hurt. That's how it works."

"I won't let anyone hurt me."

"I'm into peace and love, but I swear to God, if Guy Footscray opens his fat mouth and tries to blame his predatory behavior on you, then I'm going to stick him in a vegan pizza oven myself."

"Note to self. Never piss off a hippie."

"Damn straight. Namaste, motherfuckers."

He burst out laughing, grabbing her off the yoga mat and hauling her against the wall.

"I'm having déjà vu," she said, tapping her chin.

"Pretty sure you were in this position an hour ago."

"Ah yes, sorry. All this monkey sex really blurs together."

He growled low in his throat, a mock glower on his features. "I blur for you."

"Sadly, no. I can picture us all too clearly." She heaved an exaggerated sigh. "All the time. I can be at the grocery store, picking up my kombucha before class, and suddenly, I'm back in my bedroom, worshipping your cock. These fantasies are getting to be a problem."

"Then I wish you nothing but a life riddled with this problem."

She wiggled, wanting to get loose, and he let her go. That's how Patch was. He never hung on or forced her to do a single thing she didn't want to do. And because of that, they worked well together.

She opened his suit pants.

"Babe," he groaned as she slid to her knees. "I'm going to be late."

"Hang on, your cock is trying to tell me something. What's that, boy?" She tilted her head, pretending to listen intently. "You want to slide down my throat? Have me do that thing with my tongue?"

"Shit, the tongue thing? Fine. I'll pencil you in."

"Don't worry. I have it on good authority that I can work fast."

She slid her mouth over his head, wrapping her fingers around the root. He twitched in her mouth, and she loved it. She loved that she blew his mind with everything she did. And she didn't take his lack of experience for granted. She wouldn't just phone it in, assuming he'd be impressed with anything.

Nope. She was playing her all-star game.

Which got tricky when a guy was as thick as he was. Relax-

ing her throat, she took him down, down, gagging a little at the halfway point.

"Shit, you don't have—"

She pulled off. "I don't have to. I *want* to. You're gorgeous. And trust me, I don't mind a challenge." She got him all in this time and began to work his shaft in a bobbing rhythm, flicking her tongue at the base of his head to drive him wild.

And true to her word, she got him there fast, especially when she used her other hand to brush his sac, kneading the sensitive skin with tender pressure.

"Babe. Shit. Babe." His hands buried in her hair, pulling as he began to lose control, come apart, buck in her mouth. "Careful. I'm close, I'm going to . . ."

She grabbed his hard ass and urged him harder, not to hold back, to let go and she could handle.

"How am I supposed to function?" he rasped once he was spent. "I think you just sucked my brains out."

She licked her lips with a Cheshire grin. "While you are brainless, this is a good time to mention that while I won't walk in with you . . . I'm absolutely planning on being at the law offices. Neve is going to drive me. Breezy's coming too. You're our people now. And we don't mess."

They both cleaned up and she got dressed. Patch left first and Margot waited until she heard the front door close before picking up her phone.

She had some unfinished business of her own to attend to.

Stefan answered on the first ring.

"Hot Pants. I thought I might be hearing from you."

"Oh?"

"If you want me to forgive you, you'll have to make it worth my while."

She made a face at the phone. Oh this sad little man. It almost hurt to destroy him.

"I'm not calling to apologize for anything."

"Then why are you wasting my time?" he shouted over the background sounds of a noisy gym.

"You lost."

"What?" The sounds faded as if he stepped outside.

"You wanted to take something from me. My peace of mind. My security. My right to say no. And I just wanted you to know that none of it worked. I'm happy, do you hear that? More than happy, I'm in love."

"With a freak?" Stefan spat. "Congrats."

"No. A good man. A guy who is better than you in every way. I'm too strong to be around fragile masculinity. You could never handle me or my past. You wanted me to be small. To be some plaything just for you. But I'm too big to be shoved into some guy's box. Where I've been has made me who I am now. And I like this woman. I'm proud of her. So take this last opportunity and enjoy it. Savor it up."

Stefan cleared his throat. "Savor what?" The cockiness had drained from his voice. He sounded like what he was, unconfident and small.

"The sound of my voice, because if you ever, and I mean *ever*, contact me again, I'll hit you with a restraining order so hard that your head will land in the next county."

And with that she hung up and blocked his number. Good God . . . she felt like Wonder Woman.

And the feeling only increased once Neve and Breezy picked her up and drove her to the offices of Barker, Barker & Barker.

"It seems like they could have just gone for Barker," Breezy quipped as they got out.

A few members of the press milled by the front steps.

"Ugh," Neve groaned. "Look. Todd's here. From the AP. He's an idiot. Why don't I try and diffuse the situation?"

"You do what you have to do," Margot said. "I'm going around the side entrance."

"How do you know there's a side entrance?" Breezy asked.

She held up her phone. "There's this thing called Google Earth. It's pretty magical. Especially the zoom feature."

"Stealth." Breezy high-fived her. "Look at you go."

"I won't barge in the offices. But I hate having him in there alone."

"Is he face-to-face with the jerk?"

Margot shook her head. "He said they'll be kept in separate offices. Lawyers will go between them trying to work out a deal."

Neve frowned. "And there's not going to be a deal."

"Nope." Margot exaggerated the *p*. "If this goes to trial, it could screw over the rest of Patch's season. And worse, there's just no proof. Only his word. And he's not the type to try and use the biggest microphone."

Another car pulled up, a nondescript brown sedan. A priest climbed out, young, kind-faced, a little round, with close-clipped hair and a thinning patch in the back.

"Morning, Father," Breezy greeted him.

"Are these the law offices of Barker and Barker?" he asked, polishing his glasses on a cloth handkerchief as they fogged in the winter air.

"And Barker," Margot added.

He looked confused.

"It's the law offices of Barker, Barker & Barker."

"Why don't they just say Barker?" the priest asked.

"Thank you!" Breezy said, throwing up her hands.

"Wait a second, are you . . . Sully?" Margot asked. Patch had told her about his best friend, a priest who worked in Sun Valley, one of Denver's poorest neighborhoods.

"Father Sullivan, my child," he chided, exuding an air of pious formality.

"Oh right, sorry," she fumbled.

"I'm just messing with you," he said, cracking a wide smile. "Let me guess. You are Magical Margot."

She raised her brows. "Magical?"

"I've never seen Patch like this, and I've known him for over ten years."

"And how is that?"

"At peace." The priest put his hands on her shoulders and gave a gentle squeeze. "You brought him peace."

Margot swallowed thickly before tossing her head. "Did you come to offer thoughts and prayers?"

"Actually, I used to play hockey myself."

"Patch told me. He said you were good."

"I was. He was better, the asshole. But I thought about bringing my old stick."

"To the law offices."

"I want to see Guy Footscray."

"Are you threatening violence, Father?"

"Lead me from temptation." He pressed his hands together and looked up at the sky.

Another press van pulled up to the front.

"I've got to get over there," Neve said. "See if I can throw some water on the fire."

"I'm coming too." Breezy trotted over.

"And you?" Sully asked.

"I was going to slip in at the side door. I won't barge up to the office. But I want to be close."

"Want company?" He offered his arm.

She took it. "I'd love some."

Chapter Twenty

*P*atch broke the news of his decision upon arriving in the law office. "I'm gonna fight this tooth and nail. No settlement." As expected Guy put up a fight. They'd gone three rounds of negotiations, lawyers shuffling between the two rooms as go-betweens. Guy wanted the money to make a point. That was his official line. But now that Patch was being difficult he also wanted an apology thrown in, a public one.

That's when Patch set down his mug of stale office coffee and snapped, "Fuck this, I'm taking a piss."

As he walked back out of the bathroom, he nearly plowed into the man himself.

And from how Footscray was standing, positioned next to a potted plant, arms crossed, it didn't seem like a chance encounter.

"This isn't going to end well for you. I'm going to win. It's what I do." Guy had slicked-back Don Draper hair, but without the husky build. He was thin, his skin a pasty gray from too much time spent indoors. But his eyes were what chilled Patch's blood. They reminded him of the men that used to come to Ma's apartment. Blank. Devoid of emotion.

"You want an apology? How's this. I'm sorry I didn't re-move your creepy arm from your body."

"What a temper." Guy's cold smile vanished. "Don't jerk my dick, Donnelly. I ain't wearing skates. When I attack, I hit hard."

"I heard you like to fight for fun," Patch said evenly. "And get trained by a creep named Stefan. Didn't know Denver had an Asshole Club. I could build you a treehouse if you promise never to come down."

"You think you're such hot shit. That night . . . you liked hurting me, I saw it."

"I did. You know what? It feels good to bring pain to a sick prick who wants to prey on young girls. You do that a lot? Drug women? Shit. What a prize you are."

"I was getting somewhere before you moved in. I got money. I drive a nice car. Have a place in Breckenridge. But does any of that matter to women these days? I tell you, nothing is enough anymore. You can't even tell one to smile without her getting her thong in a wad. Feminazis won't be satisfied until the entire male sex is nothing but a bunch of nutless cucks. And you know who's the worst?" He was spitting bullets now. "Little bitches like those two chicks that night. They flaunt their honey, but if you try to move in for a taste, they act like you're the one in the wrong. What I did was level the playing field. Take back some of the power. But I don't expect you to understand. You're a cuck too, and it's my word against yours. And even if I don't get the money. Even if you fight this. I still win. Because no one will ever know for sure about you. You'll be under suspicion forever. And every day when you wake up under that little gray rain cloud, you're going to feel it."

A warning growl rumbled through his chest. "What?"

"Me. Fucking you." Guy grabbed his cock and shook his hips in a vile gesture.

"Sorry." A familiar voice rang out. "Looks like somebody just got neutered."

Patch walked around the corner and there was Margot kneeling on one leg in a waiting room chair, holding out her smartphone. "Check it out! I managed to get almost the whole convo on my record app."

Sully stood beside her. "And I was able to get a clear visual ID on the speakers."

Guy backed up.

"Not so fast," Margot said. "You have a big mouth, Mr. Footscray."

"And made a big mistake," Sully answered. "Actually a series of big mistakes, ranging from attempted drugging of a minor to trying to frame an innocent man. You a Catholic?"

"No," Guy spit.

"Pity, because I'd love to select your penance."

"Shit." Guy fled and Patch stared at them.

"We were reading magazines, waiting for you to finish," Margot said, holding up a copy of *Popular Mechanics*. "And heard everything. He had no idea we were here."

"I didn't either."

"Guess we're your lucky charms."

Sully gestured the opposite direction from where Guy had just fled. A door slammed. "Shall we go put an end to this circus? What I just witnessed will no doubt influence the outcome of the suit."

"A bad man did more bad things. Shocking, I know, but

they tend to do that," Margot said. "You two go in and talk to the lawyers. I'm going out front."

"What? Why?" Patch reached for her waist.

She leaned into him, her hand rubbing small circles on the low part of his back. "Because there's press out there ready to act as your public judge and jury. I'm merely setting the record straight with this." She held up her phone. "My guess is that Guy Footscray is going to be persona non grata in this city for a long time to come. And I want his face shown far and wide so people can remember him."

"No one better mess with you," he said, impressed.

"Or my man."

He pressed a kiss on her upturned lips. It was meant to be quick. A wordless thank you. But his tongue had other ideas.

Finally, Sully cleared his throat.

"Go," Margot said, running a hand over his hair. "I'll be waiting."

THE TIDE OF public opinion turned so fast that Patch was left breathless. The next night the Hellions stadium rumbled with the anticipation of a sold-out crowd. Signs were in the audience, supporting Patch. Overnight the news headlines had flipped in his favor.

Now it was time for business. The Hellions and the Renegades had come up against each other six of the past eight playoffs, and an intense rivalry burned bright between them. As the players listened to the national anthem, the tension was nearly palpable.

At opening faceoff, Patch crouched in front of the net, shifting his weight from side to side. Watching. Waiting. Ready.

Puck drop. The stadium exploded.

Patch's mind emptied like a sieve, just like he'd practiced with Margot. Gone was the stress of the past few months. There was no room during the next three periods for thought. Only breath. He had to live moment to moment.

Hellions went on the offense early. Petrov got a back-shot that the Renegade goalie blocked with a core move. He dropped low on the ice, knees drawn in close with his legs splayed out.

It was like Patch had told Coach before the game. The Renegade goalie was good, with a solid well-deserved rep. His moves were honed to textbook perfection. But he was a slave to his habits.

"That's how to beat 'em," Patch had said. "Let me color outside of the lines. Feel each play and react in the moment."

Tor had agreed. And that trust meant everything.

Patch stayed on his feet, agile and reactive, moving around the crease, defending the puck. He could drop low when he needed to; the important thing was to optimize all of his reflexes to be prepared for whatever was coming at him. Time went by and he barely registered the plays, fully in the zone, "giving over to the unconscious mind," as Margot put it.

Whatever it was called. It worked.

By third period the score was still zero to zero.

"Enjoy your night with the big boys," Ryker Fury grunted, skating in close after Patch blocked one of his famous snap-shots. "You'll be back in the minors before you know it."

Donnelly didn't budge. Hell, he didn't even blink. He took a deep breath, pulling the air right to where Margot had taught him. He was the base, holding the team. And they would be able to fly only if he stayed steady.

"Come on," Fury taunted, getting in his crease. "Give it to me. I'd like to see you try."

Patch forced his shoulders to relax. If he locked up, he'd lock out. Coach was right. Baiting him was part of the opposition's strategy. They wanted to trigger him and rack up the penalties.

But rather than giving himself over to the rage, he pictured Margot's face. The adorable way she looked eating donuts in bed, the curve to her wrist as she poured a cup of tea. The thoughts provided him with a safe anchor, allowed the storm inside to retreat.

"Not today, Satan," he muttered.

"You say something?" Fury pressed, eager to get into the shit.

Yeah. He did. He wanted to go home tonight, head high. He wanted Margot, who was watching somewhere in the screaming chaos, to be proud of him. He wanted to go all three periods without letting a single puck get by.

"Actually I'm good," he called out in an easy tone. Letting go of his ego. Of fear. Of shame. "And why wouldn't I be, seeing as we're gonna win?"

Fury moved on in frustration as Petrov landed a one-time slap shot, edging them into the advantage.

Tor punched a fist from the sidelines. Patch dropped back into an active crouch and let the world go silent. He tuned out and tuned in, reminding himself why he was here. Why he was *really* here.

Love.

He did what he did for love. Fear had gotten in the way, but no more. The clock ran down . . . five . . . four . . . three . . . two . . . one.

Whistle!

He saw her face in an instant, impossible to believe in a crowd of this size. But the moment the game ended, he glanced up and locked in on a familiar freckled face. On some level, he must have known she was there the whole time.

She blew him a kiss, and although she wouldn't be able to see behind his mask, he knew she'd know that he was grinning ear to ear. Because for one night, in one city, in one stadium, on a block of ice . . . love won. And of course it did. He chuckled as he skated in, toward victory, toward his team, toward his coach, and the arms of the woman who gave him the courage to risk everything.

Love always wins.

Chapter Twenty-One

Two months later

"Come on, come on, don't be a stick in the mud!" Margot tugged Patch's wrist with a playful jerk. "How can you resist this opportunity of a lifetime? We're in a mountain meadow. There are wildflowers. The sun is shining. It's Aspen. Now take my hand and let's frolic."

He grinned down at her as she cavorted beneath him. "With what? A hundred people watching?"

"They don't care about us. They're focused on the bride and groom."

She turned over her shoulder and grinned. Breezy looked radiant in a strapless white dress that hugged her curves, her thick blonde hair drawn up into an elegant chignon. Jed was unable to take his eyes off her, much to the annoyance of the photographer who was trying to get a few shots as the guests milled around them, holding champagne flutes.

"Lucky for me, I'm more interested in the bridesmaid," Patch drawled. "And I'm not going to skip, but I *will* walk with you." He bent and plucked a small, violet-colored blossom and

handed it to her. "Besides I want to ask you something and this seems like the right time."

"This sounds serious," she said lightly.

"I've been waiting for the right moment. Hard when I haven't seen you much the past couple of weeks. Our schedules have been crazy. Me on the road, you at work."

She'd been taking a night class in small business management, in addition to teaching her yoga classes. She had the business plan developed for Sanctuary and Dusk had agreed to join forces, merging the Nirvana studio with her once they located a space.

"Yeah, time is flying. The season is going to be over soon. How are you feeling about it, O Captain! My Captain?"

Tor had made it official last week. Patch Donnelly was now the Hellions' captain. It was a highly unusual choice picking a goalie, but the Hellions were shaping up to be an unusual team. Scrappy. Unpredictable. Playing more from their hearts than their heads.

"So far, so good. It's going to help having Petrov as the on-ice captain. We're figuring out our path forward, and adjusting to the new reality of life without Mister Hockey up there." He nodded toward Jed West. "We won't make the playoffs, but next year, it's going to be a whole new level."

"You had to go through growing pains."

He grimaced. "I feel like my life is one big growing pain."

"Hey!" She swatted his chest. "I'm part of that growth."

"I'm not saying it's not good." He drew her in, and did the thing she loved, where he pressed his forehead to hers, held still, and they just breathed together. "It's just not easy."

"I'm so proud of you," she said. "Those words don't even come close to cutting it actually."

"This morning I tried imagining what would've happened if I hadn't gone to you for help."

"And?"

"I felt like screaming."

"You'll never be lost again." She reached up and fingered his Saint Anthony chain. "I've found you."

He clasped his hand on hers. "So I did a thing," he said. "And I don't want you to be mad. Because I know this, you, me, is still early days, and I don't want to scare you."

"Do I look scared?"

"Never." He kissed her nose. "Remember how your ex's martial arts studio closed down last month?"

"Do I remember when the bank repossessed Stefan's gym because he'd been committing tax fraud? Yeah that rings a bell, and a warm happy feeling. But why are you bringing him up on this perfect day?"

"Because my financial advisor is up my ass to make more investments. He's a believer in real estate. Says Denver is booming."

"Okay?" She furrowed her brows, unsure where this was going.

"I want what they have," he murmured, turning her around, holding her at the waist as they watched Breezy and Jed kiss. Tor and Neve stood beside them for the picture. Tor's face was serious until Neve sneaked out her fingers to tickle his ribs.

He rested his jaw on the top of her head and she leaned into the solid strength of him. "I want to put a ring on your finger."

"I'm not in opposition," she said slowly, her cheeks flushing.

"But first I want to give you something else. Something that's just for you. No strings attached."

He stepped away and she turned as he got down on one knee, removing an envelope from his pocket.

"What is this?" she asked with a startled laugh.

"I bought the building," he said. "Your dream building. It seemed a fair trade given that you've made so many of my dreams come true."

"You . . ." Her brain flatlined. "You are giving me a space to start Sanctuary?"

"Seems fitting, considering you're mine."

"Patrick, I don't know what to say."

"You sign that and your name is on the deed. Co-owner."

"Co-owner." Her lips moved soundlessly. "I don't know what to say except that I love you so much. It's one thing to believe in my dreams. It's another thing to back it up with a building."

"I'm the base. You're the flyer. That's how we work. Right?"

"Does this mean you're going to keep doing Acro-Yoga with me?"

He stood up and grinned down at her. "If it means I get to keep touching that sweet ass, I'm willing to do anything."

"You're bad," she said, looping her arms around his shoulders. "But you are so good for me."

"Would you settle for me sweeping you off your feet in a meadow?" He pulled her up, cradled her against him, and spun around.

"You think this will really work? Us as business partners."

"Forget all the reasons why it won't," he murmured. "And think of the one that will."

And then he kissed her, the way he did everything these days, with focus, with purpose, and with love.

About the Author

LIA RILEY is a contemporary romance author. She loves wandering redwood forests, beach fog, procrastinating, and a perfect pour-over coffee. She is 25 percent sarcastic, 54 percent optimistic, and 122 percent bad at math (good thing she writes happy endings for a living). She and her family live mostly in Northern California.

You can also find her co-hosting the weekly *AfterNoona Delight* podcast, exploring the wonderful (and trope-filled) world of Korean dramas through a writer's lens.